TANGLED DREAMS

A DREAM WEAVERS & TRUTH SEEKERS NOVEL

CECILIA DOMINIC

ABOUT TANGLED DREAMS

When nightmares break free...

...Sleeping with the lights on won't save anyone.

Restaurant reviewer Audrey Aurora Sonoma's life is like a steakhouse meal: utterly predictable, comfortable, and just exciting enough to satisfy her independent streak.

But when odd characters from her dreams show up during daylight hours, the menu goes from familiar to fusion.

Policeman Damien Lewis works the night shift so he doesn't have to bother with real life. And forget dating. But after encountering three naked, delirious Jane Does on consecutive nights, a terrifying new world pulls him in over his head.

The boundaries that keep nightmares in the Collective Unconscious are crumbling. Can Audrey and Damien face their biggest fears and work together to stop the waking world from being overrun by creatures that no human has dared to dream of? Or will their nightmares become real – and permanent – when the pathways open for good?

Tangled Dreams

Copyright © 2018 by Cecilia Dominic

ISBN: 978-1-945074-37-0

Edited by Holly Atkinson

Line edited by Angel Durham

Cover art by Best Page Forward

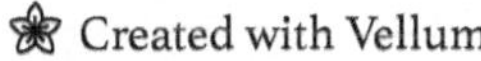 Created with Vellum

ACKNOWLEDGMENTS

This book required quite a bit of real-life research to get certain details right. Luckily I like research, and I had access to some great resources who were generous with their time and information. I may have tweaked a few things for the sake of the story, so please know that any mistakes, either of commission or omission, are mine alone.

First, I'd like to thank Dustin Hadley for his invaluable advice on emergency medical procedures. He's my EMT on call for questions of what to do when _____ happens to someone, in this case, a broken collarbone.

Second, I can't express enough gratitude to Lieutenant Jennifer Ross of the Decatur, Georgia Police Department. First, she agreed to meet with me and spent two hours answering my questions about her department before taking me on a tour. Then she invited me to join the Decatur Citizens Police Academy, where I spent ten Thursday evenings learning about both the department my heroes work for and police work in general. I'd also like to thank Officer Josh Speed (yes, that's really his name) for his kindness, explanations, and making sure I didn't get hungry on the ride-along I got to do with him as part of the citizens police academy. He may get a cameo in the next book.

Thank you, as always, to my husband Jason and to my parents for your support, and to my critique group, Kimberly, Susan, and Denise for your feedback. All of you make me a better writer in different ways.

Finally, I couldn't do this without the support of my readers and fans. Thank you so much!

1

————

"My baby! Someone stole my baby!"

The cry jolted through Audrey, and she dropped her sausage and egg biscuit. It landed with a splat on the plate and fell apart, but she didn't notice, having half-risen to search for the flurry of activity that should accompany that kind of cry. But the only curious glances she saw were directed her way. She sank back to her seat, trembling with unspent adrenaline.

"Did the sandwich try to escape?" J.J. wiped a bit of mustard from his close-cropped beard. "Or did you just see that cop you've been coffee-stalking?"

"No." Audrey glared at him and attempted to suck in a couple of belly breaths. "Didn't you hear that? Someone just got kidnapped."

"The only thing I heard was your breakfast hitting the paper and falling apart." He gestured to the table between them.

Audrey looked down. He was right. The sausage hung over the open bottom half like a panting tongue, and the scrambled egg pieces had scattered in a half-hearted bid for freedom. She retrieved the top half of the biscuit from its precarious position at the edge of her plate, but she had to clench her hands in her lap to stop their shaking. She snuck glances to either side. How had he not heard the panic-stricken call for help? Or anyone else?

"That's what I get for asking them to hold the cheese," she attempted to joke.

J.J. raised an eyebrow. "Told you it'd be better with it all melted together. You should listen to your brother."

She only half-listened to him, her attention on the nearby moms with small kids, but no one indicated they'd heard or made the cry.

"I know I heard it." With mostly steady hands, she did her best to reassemble her breakfast, but her fingers still felt weak. Was this the first step to madness?

"You're edgy today. Did you get enough sleep?"

She snapped her gaze back to him. Something tickled the back of her mind in response to his question before it was swallowed up by the tension that always overtook her when he tried to "brother" her. He was her editor, not her brother, for Pete's sake! Okay, he was her brother, but they were here to discuss her next day's assignment, so she tried to keep things professional. But she had to answer.

"Yes, Kyle gave me a sample of something last night. Some drug that's been getting a lot of press." She cringed, anticipating his reaction.

As expected, J.J. rolled his eyes. He was nice and predictable like that. "Just because the media likes it, doesn't mean it's good for you."

Instead of getting into the same old argument, Audrey took a bite of her biscuit, but her heart still beat in her throat, and a piece of sausage stuck. She coughed, and J.J. reached across the table and thumped her back.

"Maybe you should take the rest of that home," he

suggested. "You're not doing so hot with thinking and eating at the same time."

"You're probably right." With a sigh, she wrapped up the rest of the breakfast sandwich and stuck it in the paper bag with the apple she hadn't touched. She hated it when he was right, but there was no point in choking on a bite due to her imagination, which had been going strong since the night before with vivid dreams she could only remember in flashes. She'd woken feeling like she'd hardly slept.

J.J. stood, as did she, and another glance revealed her favorite cop, who walked into the coffee shop. His uniform hugged his broad shoulders, and she knew from previous sidelong glances that he had a nice, tight ass to go with them. The best part for her was his gray eyes—bedroom eyes, her mother would have called them—that stood out against his olive skin and wavy dark hair. Somehow his appearance calmed the deep inside part of her that still trembled with the sense that something was very wrong.

"What are you smiling at?" J.J. turned around. "Oh. Is that him?" he asked in a stage whisper.

"Shut up before I punch you," Audrey said through clenched teeth behind her smile.

The policeman must have heard them because he turned toward them and cocked his head when he saw J.J. like he thought he looked familiar. Then his gaze met Audrey's, and he smiled.

Audrey returned the grin and waved before following J.J., who'd suddenly become eager to go out into the bright autumn sunshine.

"Do you know him?" Audrey asked once the door closed behind them. "He looked like he recognized you."

"Nah, you know I've got one of those familiar-looking faces." But J.J. didn't slow his pace. "You could talk to him, you know. Actually say hi, give him your number."

Although the idea thrilled her, Audrey shook her head. "And what? Ruin the fantasy?" She practically trotted to keep up with him. She'd forgotten how long his legs were. "Besides, haven't you forgotten something important?" She poked him on the biceps with each word. "I. Have. A. Boyfriend."

"I wouldn't know," J.J. told her. "Considering I never see you with him or hear of you hanging out with him."

She couldn't argue with that. Instead, she reminded him, her smile gone, "You know my rule: no dating cops. Too much of a chance they won't come home."

Finally J.J. slowed and looked at her. She guessed they both had the same sadness in their green eyes. "Like Dad."

Why did thinking about that horrible night still make her throat swell with tears that should have run out by now? "Right, like him."

J.J. gave her that mixed sympathy with a look that said, "Your reasoning is a flimsy excuse," but he only asked, "Do you want a ride home?"

The cry came from Audrey's right. "My baby!" She turned so quickly she almost lost her balance. Two women sat on a restaurant patio with brightly-colored tables and chairs. Between them, they had five children, all young, a laughing, squirming, tumbling mess. One of the moms held out her arms to a blonde cherub, who toddled around in a diaper and pink T-shirt.

"There's my baby," she cooed. "What a big girl you are, walking all by yourself."

Audrey blinked to clear the buzzing sound from her ears, and the sense of wrongness returned. "Yeah, a ride would be good so I'd get home faster. I need to lie down before Kyle gets off. I'm hearing things."

J.J.'s cupid's bow lips curled. "It's probably your biological clock."

She punched J.J. in the arm. "Just because you don't want

kids doesn't mean I'm going to pick up the slack for you."

He smiled, and the corners of his eyes crinkled. "But really, how are things going with Kyle? Do you actually have a date with him this afternoon, or does he just hook you up with sleep drugs? That's a dealer, not a boyfriend."

"No." She sighed. "I'm hoping he'll have time for coffee. Since he's on his sleep rotation, he's got to be back tonight to observe study hookup, but he said he might stop by after they're done rounding at the hospital."

J.J. used the keychain remote to unlock the car, then opened her door for her. "I don't like how he treats you."

Audrey slid on to the soft leather and waited until he got into the driver's seat before saying, "Not everyone was raised a gentleman like you. Besides, he's a medical resident. Things will get better once he goes on fellowship."

"Uh huh." J.J. pulled the car out of the square and turned right. Audrey wondered how to continue the conversation, but decided not to. J.J. liked to be overprotective.

But what if he's right?

Audrey rolled down the window to let the air in to cool her cheeks and distract her from her doubts. The Bartlett pear trees, red at the top, yellow in the middle, and green on the bottom, ruffled in the breeze, which carried hints of chilly nights to come. She took a deep breath, savoring the autumn smells: dried leaves, wood smoke...

Wood smoke? It's warm to be running a fireplace.

The aroma disappeared.

The car carried her through the neighborhood and past a small park, where someone had dug up the bed in the middle to plant a flat of pansies. The flowers sat by an abandoned set of tools, and the red clay stood out against the still-green grass, a gash in the earth.

Audrey's vision tilted, and dizziness made her grab the door handle to anchor herself. She'd seen something like that recently. The memory tickled at the back of her mind. *That's where I heard the cry the first time.* But it had all been a dream...

"My baby!" A distraught woman in tan robes screamed and looked into a pit of fire. Hands held her back from jumping in.

Audrey blinked, and the scene faded. It had only been a dream, a vivid dream. So why had her stomach knotted just thinking about it?

"Audrey? Audrey!" J.J. shook her shoulder, and she realized they'd pulled up in front of her duplex.

"Sorry, daydreaming." *Or day-nightmaring.*

He didn't release her. "You look like you're coming down with something. Maybe you should just take the night off from everything, even Kyle."

"I'll think about it." She hoped he didn't see how she had to clutch at the door to keep her balance when she got out of the car. He didn't say anything, so perhaps not. She waved as he drove away.

"Someone took my baby! My baby girl!"

The cry reverberated through Audrey's head and faded into throbbing pain. She'd managed to distract herself after her weird morning. But now that she had time to take a nap, she couldn't get the sound of sobbing out of her head. Listening to music hadn't blocked it. Talk radio only made it worse—no surprise there. She rolled over and clutched her pillow to her face, willing away the sensation that someone stood just out of view and watched her attempts to sleep.

Why won't this dream go away? She hit the pillow in frustration and opened her eyes. The clock said three fifty-four. Kyle would arrive soon for coffee, which she had brewed. Maybe. If the afternoon didactics hadn't run long. If he didn't get caught up in conversation with his fellow medical students. And if the sleep lab wasn't totally booked.

"If, if, if. And I have a major headache, so I'm totally justified in eating all the cake. Right, Athena?"

Athena the calico cat meowed, and Audrey scratched her behind the ears. After deciding a change of scenery might help, she and the cat both curled up on the sofa, and the cat's purring had almost lulled Audrey to sleep when she got a text from J.J.

"Have a bad feeling about tomorrow's article research. Don't go to Bistro Moderne."

"Now you're just being weird," Audrey texted back. *"No one's blown my cover yet."*

"Trust me on this one. There are more secrets than just yours."

"Huh, I wonder if this has anything to do with the cop at Java Lemur." She once again wracked her brain for any connection her decade-older stepbrother could have with a cop, but came up with nothing but the vague sense she didn't know J.J. as well as she thought.

Athena pushed her head under Audrey's hand.

"I'm talking to you a lot these days, huh, Athena? I need a normal man in my life, not a paranoid, overprotective stepbrother or a distant boyfriend."

As if on cue, her phone buzzed with a text from Kyle. *"Can't make it. Too much work. C U tomorrow?"*

Audrey hesitated before replying. Two could play at this game. But she hated to be the jealous girlfriend. Medical residency was intense, but there was a major payoff at the end of all the training. She'd get through it with him, not make it more difficult.

With a sigh, she replied, *"Don't work too hard. Tomorrow's tight."*

"Will call u." Then a kissy-face emoji.

Would he? Or would it be another day of excuses? She silenced her phone and flopped on her back. *And that's why I need sleeping pills, even if they do cause weird dreams.*

Maybe I'll dream up a solution for what to do with my screwed-up life.

LIEUTENANT DAMIEN LEWIS looked around and, not noticing anyone paying attention to him, leaned against the desk in the emergency room. He'd just dropped off another live but disoriented Jane Doe. Exhaustion made his arm heavy, but he checked his watch so he'd have the correct time for the report. Yep, three in the morning, just like the last one. This girl had given him a scare, too. At first glance, she'd looked like his coffee shop girl with her slight build, brown hair and big eyes, but Jane's eyes were dark brown rather than bright green, and she didn't have a point to her ears.

"Got another one for us, Damien?" asked Arthur Rizzo, the E.R. doc in charge that night and Damien's sometimes poker buddy. He'd also been the one to recommend the coffee at Java Lemur.

"Yes," Damien straightened and told Rizzo. "Just like the last two."

"So that would be what? Disoriented, not sure of where they are or who they are, but with no sign of trauma or drug intoxication? But coherent enough to say yes when you asked if they wanted help?"

Damien wondered if Rizzo put everything in categories. "Pretty much. But this one was naked, too."

Rizzo's eyebrows crawled up his forehead like two furry caterpillars. "Naked?"

Damien hid his smile. He didn't think much could surprise his old friend at this point. Rizzo looked more like a mad scientist than a medical provider with his round lenses over alert green-gray eyes, gray beard that needed to be trimmed, and sunken cheeks from too many missed meals on busy nights. In other words, like someone who had seen everything and who might have done much of it himself.

"Naked." He blinked to clear the image of her athletic frame from his mind. "And seemingly fine with it, too. So you might want to run a full drug screen."

"Will do, Doctor Lewis. Actually, already have. The lab was backed up, but I should have the results from the first two in a few hours."

Damien hadn't heard any indication he'd offended his friend, but he held up his hands palm-out. "No offense. I'll leave all the doctoring to you guys in the white coats."

Rizzo didn't laugh. Instead, he stroked his beard and leaned against the counter at the triage station.

Oh, god, I did insult him? Damien forced a grin. "Think of something, Doc?"

"That depends. I'm always thinking of something, but since we have a lull right now while they triage your nymph, let's go back to my office."

Damien hesitated—he'd done his part, after all, and he needed to get back to his patrol. But he respected Rizzo as a doctor, especially after he had patched Damien up after a firefight one night. Damien had been caught without decent cover and still had the scars on his legs, one dangerously near his groin. It would make for a great story if he ever had women over, but then they'd get all concerned about his ability to have kids. Not that he wanted any. Not right now, probably not ever. No one needed his crazy genes.

Deciding if he could trust Rizzo with those parts of him, he could also trust the doctor with his time, Damien followed him out of the E.R. Rizzo's caterpillar brows now met over his nose, and Damien bit back the questions he wanted to ask. They went through a couple of white tiled hallways, up two floors on the elevator, and to Rizzo's office, which overlooked the ambulance docking bay. Damien had expected something more hectic, but everything on Rizzo's desk sat in neat piles, his bookshelves full but uncluttered. Small statues of bizarre human-animal forms, each made of stone or wood, stood among the books.

"Nice office." And then, because he couldn't help it, "Why are we here?"

"Thanks. Being the department head has perks." Rizzo perused his bookshelves. "What do you know of Greek mythology?"

Damien tried to remember back to high school English class, but he couldn't recall much through the confusion. "Twelve gods and goddesses, fought a lot, screwed with humans for fun."

Rizzo chuckled. "Yeah, something like that. Do you know anything of the lesser beings?"

When he had been a child, Damien had loved to read about the escapades of Hercules and Prometheus, and the memories dribbled into his mind. "When I was a kid, I soaked the stuff up. But that was a long time ago."

"Not so long." Rizzo pulled a large, brightly colored volume from the shelves and handed it to Damien. "Read that for a review."

"A review of what?" Damien tried to hide his reaction, but his hands shook, and he was transported to the first time he'd seen that particular volume in the tiny library in his home town. His grandmother had suggested it to him and had talked about the Greek gods like they'd been real people to her. He remembered the almost psychedelic colors and the picture of Apollo on the front of it, in his sun chariot with the white stallions. "This is the one I had as a kid." He looked up. "But what does it have to do with the Jane Does?"

"If you've read it before, you should get through it quickly. We'll discuss its relevance later. Now, if you'll excuse me, I need to stitch up the hands of the young woman you brought in. They should have her cleaned up soon."

"Is she ready?" Damien shook his head to bring him back into the present.

A harsh beeping filled the room: Rizzo's pager. "She is now."

THE NEXT MORNING, Audrey sat at her kitchen table, a mug of coffee cooling in her hands, and had the argument with herself again. She knew she must seem crazy because the cat sat a good six feet away and looked at her quizzically.

It was real, her journalistic instincts told her.

Her logical self replied, *It was only a dream.*

But it seemed so real!

You always have vivid dreams.

But this one was different. Who dreams up a vegetarian dragon?

It was your subconscious saying you should've had salad last night instead of pizza. Way to go with the comfort eating.

This isn't working. She stood. *I shouldn't have stress-eaten after Kyle ditched me. I'll take a walk and grab breakfast at Java Lemur. That'll clear my head.*

Athena licked her paw as if to say, *Is that the* only *reason you're going?*

"Fine. I'll see that cute cop if I time it right." The shadow on his cheeks and the fatigue in his eyes told her the cute policeman stopped by at the end of his shift. Then it would be time to get to work on the assignment she and J.J. had discussed the day before —the *Decatur Dish* wanted an article on a restaurant that had just opened, and she had applied for a serving job to get the behind-the-scenes scoop on the place. Her interview was at ten-thirty.

Audrey left her duplex on Sycamore, a quiet, residential street with smaller houses that had been built during the transition from bungalow to ranch styles. Hers had been split into two parts, the other half inhabited by Lucy, professionally known by the name Madame Lucia, who had a little palm-reading shop on Lawrenceville Highway. Audrey paused and almost knocked on her neighbor's door to see if she might have any answers—in a purely hypothetical sense, of course—but shook her head and went on her way. What would she do if the psychic said she was crazy? Then she'd really be screwed.

Instead, she headed to downtown Decatur, where she knew a good cup of coffee and breakfast awaited her. Or a caffeine and carb escape. Whatever worked. The sign out front with the wide-eyed lemur clutching a little ceramic cup like a furry caffeine fiend always made her smile.

When she got there, she noticed that the store beside it, which had always sold international, mostly far Eastern, knick-knacks, jewelry, and saris, had been replaced by a magic and crystal store. Her heart skipped a beat when she saw the name: The Crystal Cave. It wasn't open yet, but prominently displayed in the front window was a little purple dragon with gold wings and emerald eyes that seemed to wink at her.

"Zin?" she thought, then shook her head. *There's no way...* But the beginning of the dream, which had eluded her memory, came back with clarity.

A CLOUDY GRAY sky seemed moments away from erupting in an almighty thunderstorm. Her heart beat in her throat, and her skin tingled with the electricity in the air. She stood in a field of wheat, which glowed bright yellow-gold against the gloom. The sobbing and wailing resumed, and Audrey walked toward the sound.

A small group of people gathered at the edge of the wheat field. Toppled stalks revealed a jagged gash in the ground, two feet wide and about ten feet long. It pulsed with scarlet light like a window to Hell.

"My baby! He took my baby." A woman in the center of the gathering wailed, and the wind swirled her long robes the colors of autumn leaves. A man and another woman, both in business attire, tried to comfort her.

"Of course he didn't—he's standing right over there." The tall man with salt and pepper hair and a clean-shaven square jaw gestured to a younger man with long blond hair and beard. The older man's pinstripe suit contrasted with the younger one's casual black attire.

"Demeter, we don't know what happened, but we'll figure it out." The petite woman sounded like she'd softened her tone in an attempt to be soothing, but Audrey heard distress, too. She struggled to remember why the name Demeter was familiar. A Greek goddess, perhaps?

"Come with me," a voice whispered in her ear. "There are many things not right in this world, and we need your help."

A dragon with shimmering purple scales, big green eyes, and golden wings stood behind Audrey. She stepped back and jumped when a wheat stalk snapped under her foot.

"You're not part of Greek mythology." She crossed her arms and cocked her head, challenging him to justify his presence in her dream.

"Honey, what I'm about to tell you is gonna rock your mythology." With a wink, the dragon turned away from the group and the mourning Demeter.

Oh, what the hell? Audrey followed him and found herself in a cave. The inside resembled the core of a geode, but on a massive scale. Amethyst crystals lined every inch of the perfect dome and sparkled with light from candles in wrought-iron sconces. A plush, dark green layer of vegetation covered the floor. An old-fashioned open hearth in the middle of the cave held a smoldering fire, and the smoke curled up through a hidden ventilation shaft in the top, but it still had a pleasant wood fire smell.

The dragon cocked his head. "My associate is on her way. I think I hear her now."

"Knock knock." A young woman about Audrey's age entered and ducked to keep from hitting her head on a protruding crystal. She wore a long, light blue satin gown embroidered with silver, and a matching ribbon tied her strawberry blonde hair back.

AUDREY BLINKED herself back into the waking world, which seemed to blur into her dreams. The smoke from Zin's fire had the same odor she'd smelled yesterday when J.J. had driven her home.

"Coincidence, that's all," she muttered, like hearing her own voice say it would make it more believable, never mind that talking to herself wouldn't help her appearance of sanity. "I obviously haven't been eating enough vegetables, and I must have seen something like this statuette before."

She tried to push the dream out of her mind as she walked into the coffee shop and found herself in the middle of the kind of weirdness that made her wonder if she was, indeed, awake.

2

A udrey stopped just inside the door and stared. Two girls in diaphanous green dresses and glittery wings stood in front of the pastry case and debated over which treats would make them too heavy to fly. The barista didn't seem to think it was odd, but then, he had horns growing out of his head and wore strange, furry pants under a tailored hipster shirt. Meanwhile, a couple of short, stocky, bearded men in rough work clothes sat and sipped at large coffee mugs that looked more like beer steins. In addition to the barista, there seemed to be another presence behind the counter, a patch of fog that moved as though preparing drinks.

Audrey almost backed out of the café, but she took a deep breath and joined the line. *Maybe they're in costume. Is the Decatur Halloween parade today? Is this a side effect of the sleeping pills Kyle gave me? Another thing to ask if he ever comes over again.*

Her stomach again twisted with the feeling something was terribly wrong, but ten times stronger than the day before. *I've been too much in my head lately. Maybe I need a vacation.* She hadn't even noticed the store next door moving, and she'd been here every day except when she'd gone to a Halloween parade in Little 5 Points. She preferred to blend into the background, to watch rather than be observed.

She ordered and paid for a coffee and muffin, and she was so busy gawking at the strange costumes on the way down to the seating area that she almost ran into the one human-looking guy who stood in line—her coffee shop cop. She stepped back to avoid sloshing her coffee, but one of the fairy-looking girls turned, and Audrey lost her balance trying to avoid being poked by a wing. A pair of strong hands reached out and steadied her. She looked up and found herself inches from his gray eyes. Something like electricity jolted through her, and she had to drop her gaze to his metal nametag, which said, "Lewis."

"Thank you," she said and looked back at his face. He had a dimple in one cheek, and the stubble on his face gave him an almost dangerous look. But she had to say something. "I'm such a klutz first thing without my coffee."

"You're welcome," he replied with a smile, and the dimple deepened. "It's last thing for me, and I'm the same way without that final pickup." The pressure of his hands eased, but he didn't release her completely. "You steady now?"

"Yes," she said. She wished she hadn't when he let go of her arms, leaving cold spots where his fingers had been. Her heart beat in her throat, and she couldn't help but notice the dark circles under his eyes, which were striking with his coloring. Damn, even tired looked good on him.

She didn't want their encounter to end, so she offered, "Please let me get you a cup of coffee for saving me from falling down the stairs."

"That's quite all right." He had reached the front of the line, and the horned barista handed him a coffee.

"No charge, sir," the creature said in a squeaky voice. "Thanks for stopping by and for your service."

"Thanks," the police officer said.

"Can I get you a muffin or something?" Audrey persisted. "The chocolate chip ones are quite good."

"I appreciate it, but it's not necessary."

Audrey followed him to the side bar, where he put cream in his coffee. *Keep talking, keep talking...* "Do you get free pastries, too?"

He shook his head, and Audrey noticed the flush in his cheeks.

"Oh, no, I didn't mean to imply you shouldn't." Her face heated. "I'm sorry, I should let you go protect and serve or whatever it is you do." She bit her tongue. "And that sounded even worse."

He turned back to her, his expression bemused—thank goodness—rather than insulted. "Maybe you should drink some more coffee," he said. "And try to have a nice day."

She watched him leave through the back door to the patio and couldn't help but notice his butt still looked pretty amazing in his uniform pants.

What the hell was that? I don't usually get flustered, and him being a hot guy shouldn't matter since I have a boyfriend.

But I was a lot closer to having breakfast with him than with Kyle. Not that I could ever date a cop.

She pushed the old, sad thoughts away and avoided looking at the other patrons. She held her head high as she left, but one of the winged girls snickered, probably at her.

The crystal and magic store was open when she came out. Needing something to distract her from her self-bashing thoughts—*Officer Lewis must think I'm an idiot*—she checked her watch: eight-thirty. Early for retail, but maybe they were trying for pre-Halloween business. *Maybe they've got something that can calm my dreams. What are those net-looking things with the dangly pieces called? Dream catchers.* She took another look at the dragon and pushed through the door.

"Man, some guys have all the luck." Lieutenant Charles Allen MacKenzie caught up to Damien later that morning. He'd had to return to the station after leaving his house keys in his locker. Sleep deprivation was a bitch, and coffee could only do so much.

Jolted out of his haze—why couldn't he just be left alone?—Damien rubbed his eyes. He tipped the coffee cup to dislodge that last drop before replying, "Yeah, Charlie, my body doesn't like being on nights, and I managed to not talk too long to a pretty girl at Java Lemur when I stopped by earlier. Some lucky bastard I am."

"C'mon, dude, forget about the coffee shop chick."

"She was kinda cute when she got flustered," Damien murmured. "Really pretty green eyes. She offered to buy me breakfast." *I should've been nicer. She must think I'm an idiot or a jerk.* But he'd never been good with women. Had never bothered to learn how.

Of course Charlie pounced on the information. "But she was wearing clothes, right? You get to haul three beautiful women to the E.R., one of them buck naked, and then some hot girl wants to buy you food, and you don't consider yourself fortunate?"

"Not really." Damien laced his fingers behind his head and stretched. "But you're jealous, aren't you? You haven't gotten that close to a naked woman since Academy, when you tried to seduce Cindy Lawson for her forensic notes."

"It would've worked, too, if she'd taken any."

Damien snorted at his friend's rueful expression. He couldn't be jealous of Charlie even if they'd graduated from Police Academy in the same class. Charlie had quickly risen through the ranks and been made a detective and a special lieutenant with an office. Damien, on the other hand, was still a uniformed officer who rotated on and off night shift and took whatever computer was available if he had to correct a report.

Yeah, yeah, that's my choice. It keeps me from having to date.

"Your three Jane Does' cases have been given to my team to investigate," Charlie said, "so I've got some questions for you before we try to talk to them."

Damien just wanted to go home and sleep, but he knew he'd feel better with his friend managing their cases, so he said, "There's not much to tell, but go ahead. Everything should be in my reports."

Charlie rubbed his temple with his pen. "That's the problem."

"What is?"

"The reports. All they have filled out are the times they were filed and your name. Nothing else."

"What?" Damien swallowed against the rush of adrenaline. "They were complete when I uploaded them."

"That's what Cherie said. Even saw the sergeant's signature on them. But now they're blank."

"Damn computers." Damien's heart thudded and his face heated. Had he been so tired he'd fallen asleep in his car and only dreamed he saved them? But the clerk had seen the reports. "I don't know what to tell you, Charlie. I'll redo them before I go."

"Nah, don't bother right now, just give me the scoop."

Damien fished the memories from his fatigue-fogged brain. "The first call came in October seventeenth. Some chick in a weird outfit wandering down College Avenue."

Charlie scribbled in his notepad. "Okay. What'd you do?"

"Picked her up. Good thing, too, since she looked like she might try to climb the fence to the tracks. Might have already tried. Her hands were scratched, so I ended up taking her to the DeKalb E.R. after she said she needed help."

"Did she say anything else?"

"Nah, she was mostly incoherent after that. I just got her in the car and to the E.R. and handed her off to Rizzo, the attending."

"And the other two?"

"Same story. October eighteenth and then this morning, the second without the bloody hands, but the third looked like she'd been in a fight with a barbed wire fence. I ended up taking them to DeKalb, and with them being confused, I followed the substance abuse protocol. The only difference was that the one last night was naked. At first people thought it was a convincing Halloween costume, but the poor girl was as out of it as the other two."

"Did Rizzo do drug screens? Are they back yet? And are the girls still there?"

"Yes, and he said they'd be in this morning. I can introduce you on my way home if you like." He looked at the now empty coffee cup, his poor judgment hitting him along with the jitteriness that occurs when too much caffeine meets too little sleep. But if he didn't go to Java Lemur, he wouldn't get to see the cute girl. "It'll be a while before I can sleep, anyway."

"Good morning." The store proprietor called out from behind the counter and smiled when she saw Audrey. "Oh, good, you found me." She smoothed the red apron over her black jeans and a black silk blouse—not the blue satin dress from Audrey's dream. "You wouldn't believe the favors I had to call in to get this place set up."

A wave of dizziness washed over Audrey, and she plopped back on a chair carved to look like a throne. "Margaret?" she whispered. Whereas the dragon statue in the window could have been a coincidence, the woman standing in front of her assuredly was not. Her eyes sparkled behind lightly tinted green lenses, and her straight red hair fell around her shoulders in stylish layers. "Where's your dress?"

"Maggie here, actually. Just don't call me Mags. It really pisses me off. As for the dress, it was a dream world manifestation." She walked around the counter and approached Audrey.

Audrey massaged her temples, not sure if she wanted to run or stay and get her questions answered. Curiosity won. "So all that I dreamed last night... It was real?"

"Yes. Did you suspect it might be?"

"Well, no. Yes. Maybe?"

Maggie patted her shoulder. "Don't worry, the dizziness will pass. It's a natural reaction to your paradigm shifting."

Audrey looked at her with a frown. "What happened to the store that was here?"

"The owner was going to take an extended vacation to India anyway to care for her sick mother, and then she was told by a spirit in a dream to close the store and sub-lease the space out in case the mother's illness turned out to be more than she expected. Don't worry—we'll have everything back to normal when she comes back."

"Oh, gods, did you make the mother sick?" Maybe she should bolt if these beings, whatever they were, would do such a thing to an innocent old woman.

"No, don't worry, she was already ill."

Audrey exhaled and then asked. "So all those interesting people next door...?"

Maggie folded her arms. "Which interesting people?"

"There were some little guys who looked like garden gnomes, but bigger. Some chicks with wings who were worried about their weight. And some cloud of something that was fixing coffee drinks. But none of the regulars reacted like anything was strange."

"You saw them?" Maggie clapped her hands. "That's incredible. You do have the gift!"

Excitement flared in Audrey's chest, then was replaced by trepidation. "What gift?"

"The gift of seeing, and going to, different planes. To the non-gifted customers, the creatures look like regular people. They get temporary access to this plane of reality today in exchange for setting this place up for me."

"Lovely." Audrey leaned back, put her feet up on a plush purple velvet footstool, and covered her face with her hands. "Does this gift come with a return receipt? This is too much."

Maggie sat on the red stool next to hers and put a hand on Audrey's shoulder.

"Don't worry, you'll get used to it. Have you found your guide yet?"

Audrey dropped her hands. "My what? This gets more complicated?"

"Your guide to the Collective Unconscious. It's law 5HT-324, that every human novice shall have a spirit guide to help them navigate the unfamiliar territory of the dream and spirit worlds."

Audrey shook her head, but her mood lightened at the thought she wouldn't be in this alone. "Nope it's just me so far."

"It's not supposed to be me or the dragon Zin. That much I know. It's strange though." Maggie bit her bottom lip. "Has anything else tried to make contact with you?"

"Nope, and I haven't seen the ghosts of past, present, or future, either. But I do have new sympathy for Ebenezer Scrooge."

Maggie laughed. "That's a delightful tale. And Charlie was such a doll."

"Charlie?"

"Dickens. He could see us, you know. That's how he came up with the whole thing. It happened to his great uncle. The gift runs in families."

"Right." Audrey stood. She wanted to thank Maggie for her

time and get the hell out, but managed a polite, "I should go. I have to prepare for an interview."

"Where?" Maggie pushed the glasses up on her head, took a feather duster from behind the stool, and flicked it over the window display shelves.

"A new restaurant. I'm doing a behind-the-scenes review, and I'm applying for a serving job. I have to make this one good because everyone in the hospitality industry seems to know each other here, and it's only a matter of time before they figure me out."

Audrey put a hand over her mouth. She didn't usually talk about her assignments or her secret identity, especially not to strangers.

Maggie shrugged. "Sorry, I didn't mean to make you spill your guts. It's part of my job as a Truth Seeker. It doesn't happen when I wear my glasses, but the tint on the lenses makes it difficult for me to fine-tune the displays."

"Right, no problem." Audrey paused. She was already here, so she might as well get her questions answered. She was a journalist, after all. "Wait. Can you help me remember the rest of the dream? I feel like it's important, like I'm supposed to do something."

"Yes, I can, and yes, it was. No wonder you're so confused." Maggie turned the sign to *Closed* and brought Audrey behind the counter and into a small office. "Just sit and relax, and I'll have you remembering in no time. Then you can ask me any questions you may have. I imagine there will be a lot."

Audrey sat but couldn't relax, her desire for knowledge again warring with a sense that if she walked out now, she could forget the whole thing. Again, curiosity won. She only hoped that the proverb about the curious cat didn't apply to her.

~

THE E.R. still bustled when Charlie and Damien arrived.

"I don't know what's in the water, Officer Lewis, but we got another crazy in here," said the triage manager at the front desk. "Doctor Rizzo's talking to him now."

"We'll wait for him," Damien said. He glanced at the clock, which said nine-thirty. The jitters had worn off to be replaced by a crash, and he wanted nothing more than to go home and sleep.

He and Charlie leaned against the wall across from the triage station, and Damien's eyelids grew heavy. He'd almost fallen asleep standing up when he heard gunshots. Without thinking, he snapped his gun out of its holster, and with Charlie behind him, ran into the chaotic ward.

"Police! Is anyone hurt?" Charlie yelled at the mass of people that rushed past them. Damien couldn't tell if their injuries were new or what had brought them to the E.R. They shoved past the couple of nurses who tried to restore order and went down the hall, looking into rooms. Damien went left, Charlie to the right. The individual examination rooms stood empty except for one, in which all he could see was a pair of feet. He crept around the corner into the room and came upon Arthur Rizzo bleeding from wounds in his chest and abdomen.

"Man down," he said into his radio, his voice thick. His training kicked in even though he was already in a hospital. "Medic!"

"I.D.?" came Charlie's voice.

"It's Rizzo."

3

Maggie's golden eyes put Audrey right back into the dream where her memory left off.

S HE STOOD in the cave with the dragon and folded her arms over her thudding heart. "Are you going to eat me?" She eyed the dragon's fangs.

"Look, baby girl, the fact that you're here means you gotta help. There's something rotten in the state of the C.U."

"The C.U.?"

"Collective Unconscious. That's where you are, where dreams come from."

Audrey looked around. She'd never dreamed anything like this, not as far as she could remember. "Since when is the Collective Unconscious a place? None of this makes any sense."

The dragon rolled its emerald eyes. Audrey didn't know dragons could roll their eyes. *This is turning into some strange dream.*

"Look, Audrey." The dragon lightly placed one clawed paw

on Audrey's arm, its weight light but significant. Instead of a reptilian set of claws, it looked like a human hand covered in scales. "I know this all sounds weird, but trust me, I'm a vegetarian. Plus, you'd be able to smell it a mile off if I had any foul intentions. You have the potential to be a great Dream Weaver."

She ignored the latter part, dismissing it as her dream ego. "You're...a vegetarian?"

"Yep. So damsels and the like are safe. Eggplants aren't."

"What do you do, grill them with your flame?" She imagined the purple dragon holding a stick with charred vegetables on it.

"Something like that."

She smiled. "Ah, what the hell? It's only a dream, after all."

"There ya go, throw caution to the wind, live a little. Now make yourself comfortable. I'm afraid I don't have much for humans to sit on." The dragon sighed and gestured to the ground.

"The floor looks fine."

Audrey sat cross-legged by the hearth and put her hands on her knees. Her clothes had changed at some point. She now wore a skirt of rough-hewn brown fabric and a cream-colored blouse to match.

"Guess I'm a peasant, huh?" She fingered the rough material. So much for dream ego. "But the Greeks were in modern clothes."

"As you journey through the C.U., your aspect takes on different appearances unless you're powerful enough to assert your desired one. They are that powerful." The dragon sat on its haunches, its tail curled around its feet. "I do apologize, darling, I never introduced myself properly."

"No worries. I'm used to my dreams starting in the middle of stuff and not worrying about social niceties."

"Oh, this is more than a dream. Much, much more." He bowed with a flourish of one scaly hand. "I'm Zin."

"Zen? Like the Eastern religion?"

"Oh, no, honey, I'm not cut out for all that philosophy stuff. We reptiles don't have that much in the way of frontal lobes, you know." He tapped his head with an index claw. "No, it's Zin, as in Zinfandel."

"As in the wine?"

"The elixir of life, you mean! And you are...?"

"Audrey Aurora Sonoma." She shook Zin's paw. "It's nice to meet you. You're named after my favorite wine."

"Or maybe it was named after me." He winked. "Well, Miz Sonoma, you've walked here before, although you may not remember it, and your presence is strong. We need your help."

"'We?'"

Margaret entered as Audrey remembered.

"Audrey Aurora Sonoma, meet Margaret of Cornwall, also known as a Truth Seeker and the missing aunt of King Arthur."

"Really?" Audrey shook hands with the woman, who must have been centuries older than she looked. Dream weaver, truth seeker... These dream folks like their weird titles.

"Really. When the others went back to Avalon, I stayed in the world and got recruited."

"Recruited by whom?"

"The Truth Seekers, an organization dedicated to law enforcement among supernatural beings."

Audrey accepted a cup of tea from Zinfandel. "I didn't realize supernatural beings have laws."

Zinfandel proffered a tray with delicate bone-colored porcelain pots and tiny teaspoons. "Sometimes they don't, either. But they do, otherwise human kind would be in a lot more trouble than they already are. Sugar or honey?"

"What?" Audrey didn't follow the subject change. He lifted the tray higher, catching her attention, and she said, "Oh, honey, please."

"Yes, dear?"

Audrey laughed. This was the most interesting dream she'd had in a long time.

"So, anyway," Margaret said, "something is allowing too much commerce between here and the waking world."

"Really? How do you know?"

Margaret accepted a cup of tea from Zin. "Well, the C.U. has been in flux for a while. First, it almost became a ghost town, well, more than the normal ghosts. People are getting less REM sleep. You do know what that is, right?"

Audrey thought back to the psych class she took years ago. "It's Rapid Eye Movement sleep, when people have vivid dreams."

"And when they come here if they're able. If they can, the archetypes play their roles, and it keeps them busy. It's kind of like the difference between being in a situation and watching it on television. Those who have the talent, dream weavers, are the ones who have the lucid dreams, and they take an active role. Others feel like they are, but it's only because of archetypal images overlaid on their everyday experiences." Margaret's eyes took on a far-away look, and she sipped her tea. "So a movement was planned for the inhabitants of the C.U. to escape, but it was quelled. A mortal like you made a grand sacrifice."

A chill slid down Audrey's spine. "Someone got killed?"

"Banished, actually. It was her choice. But now something is opening the doors that keep the C.U. residents out of the real world. They step through the trap door and don't realize they're stuck until it's too late."

Audrey remembered Demeter's distress. "Like Persephone?"

"Exactly," Margaret said with a nod. "I can pass between the two worlds because of who I am, but I need help finding her in yours."

Audrey lowered her teacup. "My world is a big place. She could be anywhere."

"But you heard Demeter's cries, which means you're a key to finding her daughter. Just keep an eye out for her."

It seems like a long shot, but Audrey asked, "What does she look like?"

"A real pretty girl," Zin said. "Tall and slender with long legs, flowing brown hair, and beautiful big brown eyes."

"Also, if a goddess is in the C.W., or Conscious World, strange things are likely to happen around her."

The hearth crackled and popped, and Audrey scooted backward from a shower of sparks.

"Margaret, I should have known you would be here," a black shadow in the midst of the flames intoned.

Margaret frowned. "Hades, for gods' sake, stop trying to make an entrance and just walk into the room like a normal being. This is no time for games."

"That's what Demeter said," the shadow replied. The flames lengthened, and the handsome blond man from the wheat field stepped into the room. He again wore all black. "The woman has no sense of humor."

"At least not where you're concerned," Zin muttered.

"Lay off, dragon," Hades said. He stood tall enough to look the dragon eye-to-eye.

Zin slapped Hades' rear end with his tail. "I just love it when you play hard to get."

"Zin, down," Margaret snapped. "Hades, do you know what happened?"

He shook his head. "It was just another interminable visit with Demeter, the last before we were to get in my chariot and ride to our winter home."

Zin leaned toward Audrey and stage-whispered, "That's what he calls the underworld."

Hades ignored the aside. "So Persephone noticed that the fall mums were in bloom, and she went out to gather some. I wanted to go with her, but Demeter wanted me to fix her computer. Again." He rolled his ice blue eyes under bushy blond brows. "All I can tell you is that I heard 'Sephone scream and saw the fissure open up and swallow her."

"Where did she go?" Audrey asked.

Hades shrugged. "I immediately took my chariot into the underworld to look for her." He spoke quietly. "But she was nowhere."

"So let me get this straight," Audrey said. "You're missing a goddess, she's nowhere to be found here, and so you think she's in my world?"

"It's the next logical guess." Margaret blew on her tea before taking a sip. "And that's where all the signs are pointing."

"What signs?" Audrey pictured street signs—*Caution-Goddess This Way.*

"Divination signs, oracles, that lot." Hades waved a hand. "Bunch of rubbish if you ask me. Everyone wants to know when they'll come see me..." He grinned, and the image of a skull flashed over his face. "But I'll never tell."

Audrey tried to look nonchalant but suspected she didn't hide her racing heart very well. *Does the C.U. have cardiologists?* "I'll look for her. Do you have any idea where she'd go if she was dropped in my world by mistake?"

"Honey, she'd be so dazed and confused, she wouldn't know what to do," Zin told her.

"But she's got a good head on her shoulders," Hades put in. "She's extremely practical, so if she was stuck somewhere she couldn't leave, she'd put her skills to work."

"So she'd get a job. What kind?"

Zin tapped his lips with one long nail. "Something where she gets to take care of others in a practical way."

"That doesn't narrow it down much." Audrey thought about all the service industries in the waking world.

"Well, girlfriend." Zin handed a mug of coffee—black, of course—to Hades. "Like I said, you're tied into this, so it's likely to be somewhere close to you, maybe even one of your regular haunts."

"All right, I'll help. Is there anything else?"

"Not for now." Margaret stood, and Audrey took her cue that it was time to leave. "I'll keep in touch. Look for me in your world."

"Thanks for the tea, Zin."

"My pleasure, Audrey."

Audrey fumbled for proper Greek god etiquette and came up with, "Hades, I'm not sure it's appropriate to say that it's been nice to meet you."

The dour man laughed. "Most people don't, but I appreciate it anyway."

Audrey stopped in the doorway and asked, "What do I do with Persephone once I find her?"

Maggie responded, "I'll know when you do, and I can get her back here. Above all, be careful! You don't know what pulled her into your world, and there's no way to know what they'll do to keep her there."

"Now you tell me," Audrey mumbled. Evening shadows covered the hills with dark patches that grew until they clouded her vision.

THE DOCTOR's pulse fluttered under Damien's fingertips.

"C'mon old friend, hang in there," he muttered. "You can't leave like this. Not now."

"Is it Arthur?" said a woman in scrubs.

Damien waved her off. "Ma'am, be careful. We haven't secured the area."

Obviously ignoring him, staff pushed past him and began emergency procedures. He was relieved to see that a couple of men wore Kevlar vests over their scrubs. Damien ushered everyone else out, then checked under the bed. There was no other place for anyone to hide, and the mattress bowed in as though not just one, but two people had sat on it, one of them very heavy.

What the hell happened in here? Adrenaline had chased the sleep fog from his mind, but he couldn't shake the sense he had missed something. But whenever he reached for what, fear for his friend clouded his brain. He stepped back so they could wheel Arthur to surgery.

Someone laid a hand on his shoulder, and he jumped. "Backup's almost here," Charlie said. "C'mon, Dame, pull it together. The gunman got out in the rush, and he could be hiding anywhere."

"Or he could be halfway to Marietta by now," Damien mumbled, but he followed Charlie into the hallway. They and the hospital security team confirmed the area as clear.

Then a thought hit him. "Oh, shit, Charlie. Rizzo's office!"

"What about it?"

Damien clutched at his hair in frustration. There was too much to describe, so he could only get out, "He had strange things in there. And books."

Instead of skepticism, Charlie's expression betrayed curiosity and...excitement? "Lead the way."

They sprinted up the stairs. Without breaking stride, Damien burst from the stairwell and ran to the doctor's office, which looked like a tornado had hit it. Medical journals mixed with books on mythology, shamanism, and alternative healing methods lay scattered and open on the floor.

"Damn," Charlie said when he arrived a moment later, puffing. "How'd you get in so much better shape than me?" He looked at the office and held Damien back from entering. "Never mind that. Does it always look like this?"

"Nope. It was neat when I was in here earlier."

"Shee-yit, look at that stuff." Charlie knelt at the door and poked at a book with a fingertip. "Astral projections and familiars? What the hell? Is he a medical doctor or a witch doctor?"

Damien wanted to defend Rizzo, but he couldn't lie. "I'm not sure. He had hobbies."

Sirens sounded outside. "Ah, the cavalry has arrived," Charlie said. "Stay here and keep the room secure. I'll send someone up to relieve you in a minute."

Damien stood in the door and replayed his last conversation with Rizzo. The doctor had said something about "lesser beings," but that was all he could remember. And then Rizzo had given him the book to read.

He blinked to clear the fuzziness from his vision and looked up. A hazy glow turned the fluorescent light into a soft, glowing rectangle. *So tired...* He yawned, checked his watch, and tried not to think about how much sleep he hadn't gotten the day before. His shift had run over due to having to fill out the now-blank report on Jane Doe Number Three. He struggled to keep his eyes open, but something heavy weighed on him.

Still, I should be pumped up, not falling asleep on my feet. Some bastard shot Rizzo!

"Wake up, Lewis." Charlie nudged him on the shoulder.

Damien shook his head. "I wasn't asleep." He squinted at the light, but it looked like a normal fluorescent fixture now.

"Do that again, and it's a reprimand, understood?"

Damien nodded. "Yes, sir. It won't happen again."

Charlie left another policeman at the door. "Actually, you confirmed something for me," he murmured as they walked down the hallway to the elevator.

"What do you mean?"

Charlie had a gleam in his eye that had never meant anything but trouble for Damien. "I'm going to tell the Chief that you've got detective potential. Plus, this night shift is killing you."

"Charlie, no. They'll think I'm going soft."

Charlie stopped walking, and Damien pulled up short beside him. "Look," Charlie said, pinning Damien with his blue gaze, "you're much better suited to be a detective, and the chief owes me a favor. Getting you off nights is going to free you up to help me. I need you for this investigation."

Yep, trouble. "Why?"

"Because there's something fishy going on, and you're involved somehow. Otherwise, how would you have known to come up here? Besides," Charlie said with a wink, "when was the last time you had a real meal? A date? It's time to rejoin the land of the living, my friend, and you deserve to be a detective."

"I eat all the time. And I'm not into dating." As for whether he deserved to be a detective, well, he'd never been asked. Charlie was the only person who seemed to notice that he made extra effort to help with ongoing investigations.

"That's what I thought. Your sergeant has to chase you out of the station in the mornings. You need to cut it back to forty hours, dude. Not fifty or sixty. Once we get this case closed, of course. Which is going to take a while."

"Why? I thought you had leads."

"I thought so, too. But the doc who treated your Janes is now in emergency surgery for gunshot wounds with his assailant still at large, and someone trashed his office, likely looking for something. This case has taken on a whole new level of complexity."

Damien hated complexity. "How do you know they're related?"

"That's the Damien I know." Charlie clapped him on the shoulder. "And I can't say too much, but let's just say I've had a hint that there are larger things afoot."

The back of Damien's neck prickled, and he looked over his shoulder but didn't see anything strange. "Maybe I don't want to help on this case. You have plenty of other detectives you can ask. Why me?"

"You and I have known each other for a long time, Dame. Seeing the stuff in that doc's office... We're dealing with some strange shit here, like I said. You're the only one I can trust to see it through with me."

A chill went down Damien's spine. "You think it's a cult?"

Charlie's mouth curled into a one-sided smile. "I wish that was all we were dealing with."

Charlie's radio squawked. "Sir, we need you down here. We found the shooter."

"Where?"

"In the E.R. exam room next to the victim's."

"How did we miss him?" Damien asked, wracking his brains. He'd searched thoroughly...hadn't he? "We checked all the rooms."

Charlie frowned. "That's what I mean. Expect things to get a lot stranger, my friend."

4

---

udrey opened her eyes to see Margaret's, which were golden, gazing at her.

Margaret's eyes faded to blue. "Remember now?"

Audrey nodded and attempted to swallow past her heartbeat, which had moved from her chest to her throat. Had her dream been real? Did she want it to be?

Nothing to be done for it now. She couldn't have made Margaret up. The woman stood in front of her.

"Part of me wishes I didn't remember. How am I supposed to find Persephone?"

"Remember, strange things will likely happen around her."

"I've got a whole new definition of strange." Dazed with one thought leading to another before finishing, Audrey stood and followed Maggie to the door. She looked at the dragon statuette in the window. "Is that Zinfandel?"

Maggie smiled and handed it to her. It barely fit in the palm of her hand, but it weighed as much as a small brick. "Isn't it cute? He doesn't like it—he says it makes him look fat—but I think it's adorable."

Audrey examined it and handed it back. "Is all the art in here of real creatures?"

"Most of them. The artists are dream weavers, too."

"Right. And what is that, again?"

"Someone who can travel to the Collective Unconscious and still be aware while there. Like lucid dreaming, but more powerful because if you can influence events there, what you do there can be reflected here."

"Um, right. That sounds cool and terrifying. Thanks, Maggie. I'll keep you posted about what I find." *But don't expect it to be much. I doubt I'm a dream weaver like you seem to think I am. Otherwise I'd make something happen to make Kyle spend more time with me.*

As soon as she stepped outside, her phone beeped with a news alert: *Shooting at Dekalb Hospital E.R. Extent of casualties unknown. At least one staff member confirmed injured.*

Her hands shook, and she almost dropped her phone. *Staff member? As in resident? Kyle's supposed to be home by now, but sometimes he stays late doing paperwork.* Trembling fingers made it difficult to call him. He finally answered on the sixth ring, and she sagged to a bench in relief.

"Hey, babe." Rock music played in the background, and he sounded oddly cheerful. "How did that sleeping pill sample work for you the other night?"

She decided not to tell him about the headache and the odd dreams, at least not on the sidewalk where she would be overheard. "Fine, I guess. Where are you?"

"Still at the hospital. The day tech likes to listen to music while he scores the sleep studies."

"Are you okay?"

"Why wouldn't I be?"

It hit her with a sinking feeling. *He's not at the hospital. They would have alerted everyone who's there.* "There was a shooting at the E.R. Surely the place is on lockdown."

"Well, you know how it goes with the sleep lab. It's a little world unto itself over there, uh, here in the professional building."

"Uh huh." She clenched her shaking knees together and swallowed the tears that wanted to erupt. "There was at least one staff person hurt. Anyone you know?"

"They, uh, haven't released the name yet." His tone and apparent lack of concern told her he was making it up as he went.

She gave him one chance to redeem himself. "So, are you coming over this evening?"

"Can't, babe. I need to watch another sleep study hookup tonight, and I'm backing up the student in the E.R. so I'm just going to grab dinner at the caf and do some reading."

Her heart fell. "Oh, okay. I'll see you tomorrow, then. Be careful."

"I will."

"Okay. Call me if you get a break." The line went dead.

Hmm, he's not at the hospital. She sighed. *Forget it. I'll deal with him later—I need to get ready for my interview.* But it was harder than she thought to get her mind off him and the feeling that he wasn't telling her the truth. Was that why she thought about the coffee shop cop so much—who was more trustworthy than a policeman, after all?

Damien followed Charlie downstairs. *Could it be this easy?* But when they arrived back in the E.R. he discovered no, it wasn't.

Another policeman had found the young man hiding under one of the gurneys in the exam room next to the one where Rizzo had been shot. He lay curled in a fetal position, shaking, his black hair in a wild tangle of curls and his clothes matted with red clay, leaves, and what looked like ashes. His black eyes darted from face to face to things only he could see.

"Sir, we got this away from him." One of the deputies handed Charlie a gun nestled in a towel. Charlie waved it off.

"Send it to the lab for fingerprint and ballistics analysis. And test this guy's hands for residue."

"We already got the swab, sir." The deputy gave Damien a small wave. "Burning it at both ends, eh, Lewis?"

The clock said ten oh-five. "Just another day on the job."

Charlie coughed, which sounded suspiciously like a laugh, and Damien wanted to elbow him. Instead, he said, "What can I say, DeMarco? Maybe I need to get me a fine woman like your wife so I have a reason to go home."

"In your dreams, Lewis."

Charlie coughed again. "That's enough, DeMarco, Lewis. Bring the suspect to the station for questioning."

"Detective?" The woman's voice was low, soothing.

"Yes? Oh, hello, Dr. Lee."

A willowy blonde woman in a lab coat stood behind them. A real looker even with her glasses, she held a clipboard with a patient chart on it. "Would you mind waiting to question this particular patient?"

Damien wanted to shout no, he needed answers, but he clamped his lips shut and let Charlie answer.

"Is he one of yours?"

"Yes, and I need to get him stabilized so he's coherent and can answer your questions. You won't get much from him when he's like this."

"Is that why he looks like that?" asked Damien.

"Yes, keeping these patients compliant with their medications is a challenge because even though the new ones have a much milder side effect profile, they can still be hard to deal with."

"How much time do you need?" Charlie flipped open his pocket calendar.

"Come back tomorrow."

"Will you be here?"

She looked over Charlie's shoulder to check the date. "Absolutely. I'm rounding in the morning and have office in the afternoon."

"It's a date, then."

She accompanied the young man, escorted by two orderlies, out of the room.

"You're incredible," Damien told Charlie as they walked out of the hospital.

"I've dealt with her before. She's a good psychiatrist."

"She's a psychiatrist, huh? Do you think she would have seen any of the Jane Does?"

Charlie smacked his forehead. "Damien, Damien, Damien... See? This is why I need you on the investigation. So I don't forget important things like that." He sighed. "Let's go back in."

Damien didn't mention he didn't want to leave until he'd gotten news about Rizzo. But as he'd found out, gunshot wound surgery could take a while.

~

"DREAM WEAVER," Audrey murmured to herself, but her mind was only half on the strange events of her dreams. The supernatural beings could have their crisis. She had her own to deal with.

"An about to be single dream weaver, I wager. I bet it's that blonde chick he's been hanging out with. Chastity? Huh, hardly."

She munched on the leftover portion of the muffin she'd bought earlier while she walked home. But she hardly tasted it or saw where she was going as her mind clicked all of Kyle's lies into place. By the time she turned on Sycamore, her eyes burned with tears, partially for the end of the relationship, but also for the end of how she'd imagined their life together would be. She pushed aside the little voice that whispered her disappointment came more from the loss of certainty than of Kyle himself. What could be more secure than being a doctor's wife?

Too bad I didn't get the cute cop's number. Oh, wait, I don't date guys who might not come home. A tear splashed on the last bite of muffin, creating a soggy spot. *But apparently that applies to more than law enforcement.*

By the time she arrived home, Audrey decided that of the two realities she'd been faced with—Kyle's betrayal or the existence of a place that holds mythical beings that people go to in their dreams—she'd rather deal with the dreams, after all.

It almost seemed foreordained when she found her neighbor Lucia sitting on the Adirondack chair on her side of the porch with a steaming cup of coffee.

Lucia had moved in a few years ago, just a few months after Audrey. Instead of the petite Romany lady that Audrey had expected when she'd heard who her new neighbor would be, Madame Lucia stood at a good six feet of solid mahogany-colored muscle. Her micro-braided hair started gold at the top of her head, darkened to orange, then red, then brown, then Lucia's natural black at the ends. And if Audrey believed in such things, she'd say the woman had amazingly positive energy.

"Good morning," she said in a lilting accent. "Are you all right, dear?"

"Morning, Lucia." She tried to force a smile but gave up. "I guess there's no keeping stuff from you, is there?" Audrey plopped in the other chair.

"Your energy is disturbed. You're feeling betrayed. And you

have the dream shadow in your aura, dear. It tells me you've been to the Collective Unconscious recently."

"What do you mean?" She sat up straight and bit her tongue so she wouldn't say too much like she had to Maggie. *Crap, does everyone know what happened to me?*

"It's nothing to be too concerned about, but not many can."

"So I hear." Her neighbor's words hit her as less threatening than Maggie's. But then again, it was easier to trust someone she'd spent many a late night on the porch drinking wine and talking about strange experiences with. Not that any of their previous conversations could compare to what she'd seen this morning.

"Come in. I have fresh coffee."

Audrey hesitated—she did have the interview to prepare for, after all—but, seduced by the thought of someone taking care of her for a change, she followed Lucia inside.

A fire in the fireplace dispelled the autumn chill, and a mug waited on the kitchen table.

Lucia waved Audrey into a chair at the table and poured coffee into the cup. "A little bit of sugar and cream, right?"

"That's exactly right."

Lucia fixed the coffee and sat across from Audrey. "I know it's a big adjustment, dear. You've been called for an important task, and whatever disappointment you've faced will no longer be relevant to your life soon."

"How do you know?" She recognized it was a stupid question to ask a psychic, but she no longer cared. And her disappointment felt very relevant. "And how did you not know before?"

Lucia shrugged. "I had a hunch. But it's not just your quest to find the missing goddess. You must also find the source of the proliferation of journey paths that is eroding the boundary between the C.U. and the waking world."

"I don't know where to start." Audrey looked into her coffee.

"She could be anywhere, and my mind isn't on the task right now."

Lucy seemed to ignore Audrey's hints that something else was wrong. "Did you meet Hades? And did he give you any ideas? He's notoriously difficult. Never shows up how or when you'd expect."

Audrey smiled. She suspected Lucia tried to distract her and make her laugh while getting information, but she trusted her. "Just that she might go somewhere that will allow her to be of service to others."

"That was my thought as well. And have you met Maggie?"

"She's set up shop next to Java Lemur."

"I shall have to visit her. That was a smart choice—there's a thinness in the walls between the realms of fantasy and the world of reality in that building. I imagine she got some extra help."

"Yep, they were hanging out at Java Lemur this morning."

Lucia smiled, her teeth large and white in her dark face. "They'll visit me if they want me to see them."

A thought tickled the back of Audrey's mind, and she closed her eyes to tease it to the surface through all the crap about Kyle. Something about creatures... "Maggie said that I should have a spirit guide. Do you know anything about that?"

Lucia frowned and tapped her finger against the ceramic of the cup with a series of clinks. The motion made her leaf-shaped silver and topaz ring sparkle. "It is highly unusual that you have not encountered your guide. Something may be keeping him or her from you."

"Like what?" Of course there would be a complication.

"Like whoever or whatever is causing the rifts. It makes your journeying much more perilous."

"Oh." Audrey didn't like the sound of that. "Is there some way I can find him or her?"

"I shall perform a ritual when I get to the office. I will let you know tonight."

"Thank you."

"It will be a long ritual, so I should start early."

Audrey didn't need to be psychic to take the hint. "I'll be on my way, then."

Since Lucia had been too distracted by the Collective Unconscious stuff, Audrey dialed J.J. as soon as she got inside her own apartment to tell him his suspicions about Kyle were likely true. His phone went to voicemail, which was strange because he always answered when she called at this time of the day.

You can't abandon me, too, stepbrother. She left a brief message and took a deep breath.

"Well, Athena," she said to her cat, "it looks like I'm going to have to be an independent woman and do what I need to do in spite of all this boy crap."

Athena just opened an eye and flicked her tail as if to say, "I didn't like him, anyway."

"Yeah, that's the problem," Audrey said with a sigh. "I did. A lot."

AMANDA LEE's psychiatry practice was in one of the professional buildings attached to the medical center. After Charlie and Damien waited for half an hour, she appeared.

"Couldn't wait 'til tomorrow, Detective MacKenzie?" she asked with a grin.

"What can I say, Amanda? You do that to me."

"And this is...? He was there earlier."

"Detective Damien Lewis."

She arched a golden eyebrow, which appeared above her glasses. "Yet he wears a uniform."

"You're very observant. He's helping me out on a trial basis."

"So now that we've established who everyone is, what can I do for you?" she asked. "I'm afraid that Mr. Smith isn't able to be questioned right now; he is heavily sedated."

Damien, tired of everything, but especially of being talked around, said, "We actually wanted to ask you about the three young women who were brought in over the past few evenings."

"Ah, yes, Jane One, Jane Two, and Jane Three. You policemen aren't very original with your names, are you?"

Charlie shrugged. "What can I say? We're just simple men."

"I doubt that. What would you like to know about them?"

Charlie gestured to Damien to ask the questions. Damien sensed it was some sort of test.

"Well, first, why they were so disoriented." He tried to adopt a confident tone without being insulting. "Did someone check them out? Were they on drugs?"

She shook her head, and the tightness at the corners of her mouth told him he'd been too harsh. "Urinalysis and blood tests came back negative for all substances, both legal and illegal."

"Where are they now?" asked Charlie. "Can we see them?"

"You could, but I don't know that it would do you much good."

"Why not?" Damien looked up from his notes.

She spread her hands as though she held the answer in her long fingers. "They're housed on a locked ward. Two of them share a room. The first one was unresponsive, just sat and rocked, until the second one was brought in. They seemed to recognize each other, so we kept them together to see if we could observe some communication that would allow us to identify them and find out where they came from."

"What happened when the third one came in?"

She smiled. "The other two were very happy to see her. They spoke with each other, but it was all gibberish."

"Gibberish?"

"I'll concede that it might be a language I'm not familiar with. I'll ask the nurses and see if any of them has overheard or understood them. But I don't see how letting you question them can help, and it may cause them to lose what little progress has been made."

"May we see the charts?" Damien asked.

"If you wish." She called the front desk and asked for a copy of the hospital records for the policemen to look at. "I can't release them, of course, but I'm willing to do you this favor to help the investigation." Her smile was all for Charlie.

"And what about the young man who was found in the E.R.?" Damien tried to keep the bitterness out of his voice. "The one who shot, *allegedly* shot, Rizzo?"

Dr. Lee shook her head. "Daniel Smith is a frequent flyer on the ward. He has paranoid schizophrenia, and he will not stay compliant with his medication. Unfortunately, his family will not consent for him to be institutionalized, and we can only involuntarily commit him for seventy-two hours at a time."

"But psychotic people don't usually become violent," Damien said. "Has he ever done anything like this before?"

"No, that's what is so perplexing. He has never had hallucinations or delusions with violent content. Usually his ideas are of reference."

"Of what?" Damien asked.

"Of reference. Meaning he feels that things like billboards and televisions are displaying messages specifically for him to see, but the worst he will do is run and hide in the woods until he is brought in." She paused and cocked her head at them. A nurse knocked on the door.

"Your next patient is ready."

"Excuse me, gentlemen, I must get back to work. You can look at the records at the desk. Just respect confidentiality."

"Thank you for your time," Charlie said and shook her

hand. "Please let us know when Mr. Smith is ready for questioning."

"MR. AMES IS ready for you now."

The mundane words Lyle Ames' secretary had said a thousand times before made his heart skip a beat, and adrenaline rushed through his system with a crackle like electricity. *Show time.*

"Calm down, Lye," he told himself, using the nickname from long ago when he had been just another kid struggling through college, working two jobs so he could afford to take the extra classes he needed to qualify for the MBA program. He'd succeeded and become one of Atlanta's top businessmen. But nothing he'd studied had prepared him for this.

Three men walked through the door. The one who immediately drew the eye had an air of confidence, like he could snap his fingers and make anything happen. This attitude wasn't a game—he could make many things happen, although his talents were attenuated in the conscious world. He wore a pinstriped navy suit, and no beard covered his square jaw or lent softness to his harsh profile. His hair showed gray at the temples, but only enough to give him a distinguished look and highlight his olive skin and black eyes. The other two men, venture capitalists, looked as nervous as Lyle felt, so he smiled to put them at ease. Yes, hanging around Zeus could do that.

"Please have a seat, gentlemen. I assume you met in the waiting room?"

The younger one nodded and swallowed before he spoke in a tremulous tone. "Yes, we met Mr. Zeus."

"Excellent, Mr. Feinstein. And what do you and Mr. Donnell think?"

"The business plan sounds fair enough," the older man

spoke up. He had the look of a hungry hawk with beaked nose, sparse gray hair, and sunken cheeks. His eyes, the color of a smoggy summer sky, missed nothing. "Mr. Zeus mentioned that you have done some pilot testing of the product and that since it is already FDA-approved, there will be no interference from that agency."

"It's more that the product is making the difference we need to implement the plan." Ames pushed the button on his desk that caused blinds to slide across the windows. A projection screen rolled out of the ceiling at the back side of the room, and everyone else turned their chairs to face it. Diagrams, abstract figures that didn't mean much but looked impressive, appeared on the screen. "As you can see, the, ah, personnel is arriving in the area, and we should be able to acquire a supervisor soon."

"Is this someone you're hiring?" Donnell asked.

"In a sense." Ames smiled at the venture capitalists. "This particular supervisor is an expert in her field, and we predict that once we get the business established, revenue should skyrocket."

Feinstein, the younger man, leaned forward. "You mentioned a unique method of discretion."

Lyle smiled at him with the look of mischievous understanding that men get when they give each other permission to bend the rules. "Yes, indeed. It has even fooled my wife, and she watches me closely, although I've never given her reason to." He avoided looking at Zeus, whose indiscretions were literally legendary.

Donnell, the older of the two, laughed, a dry coughing sound. "Really, Mr. Ames, we had no idea you would be tempted into such activities."

Lyle shrugged. "I had to see it for myself once Mr. Zeus told me about it. You may try it out if you like. Mr. Zeus will be your guide."

The god inclined his head. "I have some amusements picked out that I'm sure you two will enjoy."

Donnell and Feinstein looked at each other. "I think that before we make an investment of this magnitude, we should see what all the fuss is about," said Feinstein.

Lyle held his breath. He knew the younger man wouldn't do anything without the complicity of his mentor.

Finally Donnell said, "That seems like a wise choice."

Lyle grinned and reached into his desk drawer, where his hand closed around a small bottle. "I thought you gentlemen might want to see for yourselves. If you'll follow me, I'll show you how to enter the temple."

5

When Damien arrived at his apartment, an in-law suite at the bottom of the house in a quiet neighborhood, he let himself in and collapsed on the couch. He should have been tired, but the strange events of the night before and that morning replayed in his mind. Every time he felt his eyes drifting closed, another bizarre memory popped them open. Plus worry for Rizzo clawed at his chest.

While his grandmother—talk about strange memories—wouldn't have forced him to eat, he couldn't help but remember her admonishment that it was difficult to think clearly on an empty stomach. Of course she would pop into his brain at a time like this. He shoved himself off the couch and went into the small kitchen to heat up a can of soup. Then he remembered his microwave was broken and ended up having to make it the old-fashioned way—in a pot on the stove. While it warmed, he went into his bedroom to take a quick shower and change.

As he waited for the soup to finish heating, he flipped through his phone, mostly to distract himself, and nearly dropped it when it rang. The number was unfamiliar but showed a local area code, so he answered it.

"Hey, Lewis."

The voice sounded familiar, and Damien realized it was Paul DeMarco, the deputy that had been giving him shit earlier.

"Yes?"

"Hey, I know that sometimes I give you a hard time, but I wanted to warn you about something. Uniforms gotta stick together, right?"

"Right." Damien turned off the stove since his lunch, dinner, or whatever it was bubbled.

"So anyway," DeMarco continued, "I saw you hanging around with Lieutenant MacKenzie earlier. You know he was with the county for a while, but nobody was sure what he did, just that he took cases that nobody else wanted."

"And what's so bad about that?"

"Well, that's the weird thing. These cases never got solved, just closed. And for the strangest reasons."

Damien rubbed his eyes. "Look, do you have any real information for me? This is sounding like fairytales."

"I'm just trying to help you out. I don't know what Charles MacKenzie is up to, but it's not worth sacrificing your career over, no matter how interesting it might sound. Nobody takes a cop who goes off the deep end seriously."

Damien's stomach rumbled, and he knew with as much certainty that the soup wasn't going to satisfy it as he did that DeMarco was again full of shit. But there was no reason to be rude. He thanked DeMarco for the warning and hung up. He grabbed a soup spoon and had just dipped it into the small pot of chicken noodle when his phone buzzed with a text. It was Charlie inviting him to lunch.

$\sim$

THIS IS UNBELIEVABLE, thought Audrey for the twentieth time. She'd seen enough restaurants by now as a reviewer to categorize this one as "modern bistro", fitting because its name was Bistro Moderne, but the diners in this particular lunch crowd—at a restaurant that wasn't even supposed to be open yet—surprised her.

A couple of women in navy blue robes, their pointed hats on the table beside them, and their brooms bristle-side-up in the umbrella stand, expounded on the relative merits and hazards of modern witchcraft. Dwarves like the ones Audrey had seen that morning quaffed amber liquid out of large mugs, and from their inebriated state, she guessed it wasn't coffee. The most disturbing aspect of the whole crowd was that the woman interviewing her *didn't see or hear them.*

So this means either they're real but with some powerful enchantment, or I'm truly losing it.

"I don't really know what to tell you." The woman who had introduced herself as *Cece the manager, soon to be owner if things don't get better soon because by god, I'm not going to look for another gig,* sighed. "We've had a hard time keeping people, and I know reviewers are going to come in soon. We're desperate for help, so as long as you're minimally competent and not easily stressed, you'll do well."

One of the dwarves belched, and Audrey jumped as the rest of the little men giggled.

"Don't worry." Cece flipped through Audrey's application. "It's just the heating in this place. It makes funny noises all the time; it's ancient."

It's not the only thing, Audrey thought. She watched a couple of gargoyles exit through the glass front door—without opening it—and take wing.

"Let me show you around."

Cece walked by the dwarves' table and knocked one of the knives, which hung over the edge, to the ground with a clatter.

"How'd that get there?" she asked and picked it up. "Oh, look, it's filthy. I'm going to have to get the dishwasher checked again."

"Bitch," mumbled the dwarf. Audrey hid a smile and tried not to look at them for fear they'd discover she could see them.

They walked by the table with the two witches, and Audrey couldn't help but sneak a glance at them.

"I've been to Gallows and Things, but not to Life, Death, and Beyond," one of them said. "What do you think of the prices?"

"Oh, they're great if you have the immortal coupon. They never expire, you know."

Audrey turned away from the table before the witches caught her eavesdropping and...what? Turned her into something? *Unbelievable.*

Cece held the doors open, and Audrey looked around the kitchen. She watched, fascinated, as the chefs, a pair of tall elves in chefs' whites with their pointed ears sticking out the sides of their toques, whisked all evidence of their preparation out of sight. The smell of cooking food made Audrey's stomach grumble.

"Look a' that'un," one of them said, his voice low like the murmur of windblown autumn leaves. "She's got pointed ears."

"And the sight. But she doesna wan'ta give that away. Donna worry, honey, we won't let your secret out."

Audrey inclined her head to acknowledge and thank them.

Cece moved to the sink and paused when she saw it already filled with soapy water. "Hmm, must've left it from last night." With a deep breath, she asked, "So when can you start?"

"Any time. I'm between positions right now."

"Great!" She exhaled with relief, and Audrey felt sorry for her. "You can start tonight."

"Just out of curiosity," Audrey asked when they walked back into the dining room, "has anyone else interviewed for any positions here this week?"

Cece shook her head, her lips pursed in a pout. "Once it got out that the restaurant is haunted, the interviewees dried up. We're lucky to have the staff we do. I do have one more interview this afternoon, and if she works out, we'll at least have the minimum necessary for dinner business."

"I see."

"Great, we'll see you at four, then, for some quick training and so you can try the specials." Cece steered Audrey out of the restaurant and locked the door behind them. "Gotta run!"

"Wow, I don't know if I'm ready for this." Audrey walked back to Java Lemur to grab a salad for lunch and tell Maggie what she'd seen. This would be an interesting assignment, but the feeling that it wouldn't end well lingered. She checked her phone to see if J.J. had called her back yet, but still nothing. She texted him again with a plea to answer her as soon as he could.

The Crystal Cave was closed with an "Out to Lunch" sign in the window. *Damn, Maggie must've already made lunch plans.* She decided to grab a taco across the street instead.

DAMIEN FELT TOO wound up to sleep, so he agreed to meet Charlie and his associate for lunch at Java Lemur. He had to admit that part of it was to prove to himself that Charlie wasn't up to anything strange. And another part might have been to see if that cute girl came back. He might have strict rules about dating, but he did appreciate a good flirt every so often. After he and Charlie arrived at the coffee shop and ordered, he made sure to sit where he could see the door. The young woman didn't appear, but a striking redhead did and came directly to them.

"Ah, Margaret." Charlie stood and shook her hand. "It's so good to see you again. This is my associate, Detective Lewis."

"Pleased to meet you, Ma'am." Damien stood and held a

hand out, intrigued. Normally women buzzed around Charlie, and he took in all the attention with cool detachment. But this time the redhead regarded Charlie with professional politeness, and his friend had a decidedly smitten grin on his face. Had someone finally caught Charles MacKenzie's interest?

She shook it. "Margaret Cornwall, but Maggie works just fine. Please don't call me ma'am. It makes me feel dreadfully old."

Charlie stifled a laugh, and she shot him a dirty look. Damien sensed they had known each other for a while and guessed they had some sort of inside joke.

"All right," she said after returning from placing her order at the counter. "What have you got for me?"

Charlie signaled to Damien to tell his story and started eating his sandwich. Damien recounted the tale of the three women and Rizzo's shooting. Maggie picked at her salad while she listened, but she soon put her fork down.

"And what about the shooter?"

Charlie dismissed him with a wave. "Floridly psychotic."

"And will probably say the creatures he hallucinated made him do it," Maggie finished for him. "It's the neatest way, really. Cover up with a mental health issue."

"Neatest way to do what?" asked Damien. He ate carefully to avoid getting anything on his shirt—he really needed to do laundry—and thought he caught an approving glance from Maggie.

She waited until he was done chewing and said, "Cover up a crime of a more, ah, supernatural nature."

Damien almost choked on the bite he was swallowing and had a coughing fit. "Of. A. What?"

"You didn't tell him," she said and sighed.

Charlie shrugged. "I tried, but you're better at it than I could ever be. More practiced."

"Okay, here's the deal, Damien Lewis." She leaned forward,

took her purple-lensed sunglasses off, and made full eye contact with him.

The force of her gaze felt like a punch to the solar plexus and took his breath away. Her formerly blue eyes now looked gold.

"What's your full name?"

The words tripped off his tongue without any effort on his part. "Damien Armand Lewis."

"Date of birth?"

"July twenty-sixth, nineteen ninety."

"Worst thing you ever did to a younger sibling?"

His face heated. "Tricked my little brother out of all his Halloween candy when I was five. I told him it had bugs in it." He stopped, mouth agape. "Why did I just tell you that?"

Charlie laughed so hard he almost knocked his water off the table. "That's low, man."

"Shut up."

"It's because I'm a Truth Seeker," Maggie explained and put her lenses back on. "It's an ancient organization whose sole purpose is to keep supernatural events from interfering with the flow of the living world. I'm a police officer of the other side, if you will."

Damien shook his head to appear nonchalant and kept his hands under the table so she wouldn't see them shaking. "And you're expecting me to believe this?"

"I can truth-spell anything with a conscience. And it sounds like you've gotten yourself mixed up with some interesting company, like it or not. I'm actually looking for one of the girls you found, probably the one you brought in last."

"The naked one? Yeah, she was the prettiest by far."

"Show some respect, man," Charlie said. "She was a goddess."

Damien frowned. "How would you know? You didn't see her."

"No, he didn't," Maggie told him. "But that was the goddess Persephone."

Damien couldn't have heard that correctly. "The who?"

"Really?" asked Charlie with a grin. "I was just kidding, but Dame had a goddess in his squad car? You lucky dog, you."

Maggie looked at the ceiling as though praying to something for strength.

Dear God, she's serious. Damien checked to make sure he could protect anyone who was sitting nearby if she snapped. He knew most crazy people weren't violent, but also that you never could tell; just look at what had happened that morning, which made his gut clench every time he thought about Rizzo's wounds. Was he out of surgery yet?

As for Maggie, she had the same expression on her face that his grandmother had when she'd told him with absolute certainty that she could talk to spirits, and the voices she heard were saints and deceased family members.

"There's something eroding the barrier between the two worlds, and we don't know what it is yet," Maggie said. "But the fact that the doctor who treated the girls was attacked shows that he may have stumbled on to it. Can you take me to his office?"

"Sure." *Let's get her away from all these people.* "Charlie, do you think forensics is done with it yet?"

"They should be. They'll probably want to break for lunch soon anyhow."

"Then finish eating, boys, we've got to get over there before someone—or something—else does."

⁓

WHEN THEY ARRIVED, Maggie paused in the doorway and surveyed the mess in the office. Damien watched her. She didn't *seem* crazy, but there was that thing she'd done to him that made him tell her his secrets. Weren't some mentally ill people really charming?

Yeah, that's it. I'm exhausted and fell for the charm of a pretty woman.

She nudged one of the books with her toe and said, "Doctor Rizzo has some interesting hobbies."

"When you're living so close to life and death, you get curious about the other side," Damien told her.

"Do you know him well?"

"Sort of. He fixed me up when I got shot about a year ago. We'd chat when I brought people into the E.R."

"Does he have any family?"

"I'm not sure. The hospital should have an emergency contact on file."

"Hold off on notifying anyone for now, at least until I can figure out who did this and if anyone else could be in any danger, too."

"You make some big demands, redhead," Charlie put in. "It's going to be hard to keep the hospital from notifying next of kin. They probably already have."

"Telling someone could put them and Rizzo in further danger. I wonder if he's out of surgery yet."

"Maybe. It's been a few hours, but bullet wounds at close range take time to patch up." Damien crossed his arms, a defensive posture. "Trust me, I know."

With one last look around the office, she said, "Well, I've got to get back to my cover job. Charlie, keep me posted."

"Will do, Ma'am."

"Don't start."

After she left, Damien grabbed Charlie's arm. "You just let her go? Can't you tell she's mad?"

"Why? I didn't do anything."

"Not like that. She's one slip away from landing at Peachview."

"The mental hospital? Oh, Damien," Charlie said and rubbed his temples. "Go home and get some sleep. This will all make much more sense to you later."

Damien watched Charlie walk away, his mouth agape. *Is everyone crazy but me? Shit, maybe DeMarco was right.*

∾

AUDREY WANDERED around Decatur and kept her eye out for any signs of a goddess-type on the loose. Her interview experience had convinced her that yes, her Collective Unconscious wandering had been real, and there were beings coming into the waking world.

She walked by Bistro Moderne a few times to see if the new hire would turn out to be Persephone, but every time, it was locked up and dark inside. Her one possible lead gone, she wandered back to Maggie's shop. The door chimes tinkled when she entered.

"Ah, there you are," Maggie said. "Any luck?"

Audrey picked up the Zinfandel figurine. "No. My interview went well, and I got the job. There was another supposed interviewee this afternoon."

Maggie tapped her lips with the pencil in her hand. "That's a promising lead. I may have to stop by there tonight. You say they're desperate for help?"

Audrey thought back to what she'd said. "No, I didn't."

"Whoops, sorry. Your mind is very open."

The thought of someone poking around in her thoughts made Audrey cringe. "What do I do to close it?"

"Just try not to think so loud. Imagine your words occurring behind a screen."

Audrey imagined a black screen surrounding her thoughts. "Is that better?"

"Is what better?"

"I guess so, then."

"Right. So," Maggie said and tore a piece of paper off the pad in front of her, "here are some places for you to check out."

"What are they?"

"The locations where three mysterious young women were picked up over the past few nights. The one with the star is Persephone, I think."

"What happened to them?"

"The cop brought them to the E.R. They're at the hospital now, but I don't want to go barging in there until I determine that they are, indeed, from the C.U."

"I see. They're all on College Avenue."

"And that's likely where you'll find signs of the crack they fell through."

Audrey looked up from the paper, her brows furrowed. "And what, exactly, am I looking for?"

"Remember the scene you witnessed in the C.U.? Look for something similar."

"So I'm looking for a grassy area...? Oh, I know a possibility near these places."

6

———————

Cold rain drops stung Audrey's cheeks, and she kicked an old, dirt-encrusted bottle. So far her search of the empty lot's overgrown surface had turned up nothing to indicate where the goddess and others had appeared. Yet she didn't want to return empty-handed. Or minded. Or something.

Why should I care?

Chilled and feeling like the only person for miles in spite of the whoosh of traffic over the wet pavement outside the construction fence, Audrey told herself she should go before the low-hanging gray clouds completely opened up. She shouldn't care what Maggie thought of her, but she'd been through enough therapy to know she liked the idea of being special. The concept of being a dream weaver appealed to her. And she never let anyone down. Well, except maybe herself. But back to the task at hand...

She took one last look around. The lot, like many others in the area, had recently been sold to developers for condos or some other form of ridiculously expensive in-town living, and it sported a sign—*Coming Soon! Another Ames Development*. The house itself had probably been run-down, condemned, and then burned by vandals, and it still emanated an air of stagnant sadness in its almost-gone state. The old stones of the foundation poked through the weeds and litter like a monument gone bad. The lot itself seemed to have male-pattern baldness with blank patches in the front and in the middle. Broken bricks and charred bits of something lay interspersed with decaying beer cans and other filth that Audrey didn't try to identify.

"Remember what you saw in the Collective Unconscious," Maggie had told her. "That's going to be your biggest clue."

The distress Audrey had witnessed and Demeter's pitiful cries had almost blotted out the rest of the initial scene Audrey had walked into. She tried to remember the visual details, but the images had faded as most dreams do. She recalled a field with grass, and the gash in the ground had not closed completely. Rather, it glowed like lava smoldered at the bottom. She turned her attention to the middle of the lot again, the charred area in the middle of the foundation. She could see that grass had grown there, but something had recently burned it. Which would make the rift down the center of the house. She knelt on a stone to get a closer look.

"They used to say it was haunted," a male voice said from behind her, startling her to her feet. She looked up to see—*oh, shit!*—the coffee shop cop. But he wore jeans and a black leather jacket, making him look more bad boy than cop. And twice as appealing. She combed her fingers through her curls, sure they were frizzed and must be writhing Medusa-style.

"Um, I'm not trespassing, am I?" she asked, then mentally slapped herself for such a dumb question.

"The answer is yes. I saw you over here and thought I should tell you that this is private property. Have you lost something? Your coffee, perhaps?"

She grinned at his attempt at a joke, but she could only hold the expression briefly before reality set in. "If I told you, you probably wouldn't believe me."

"Try me. I've had a very strange day."

His voice shocked her with its edge of old hurt. Earlier that day, he'd been friendly but firm. Now he just looked exhausted, his tone impatient.

Not sure, what to say, she blurted, "Aren't you on a patrol or something?"

He glanced down at his attire but didn't state the obvious. "I was just on my way home."

"Oh. Well, if I told you what I was looking for, you'd probably try to take me in for being crazy."

"You wouldn't be the first." An almost-smile played around his lips. "There must be something in the water."

"Or the trash? Wait a second..." She brushed her hands on her jeans. "Were you the policeman who brought the three women to the E.R.? The ones who randomly appeared?"

He scratched the back of his head. "I'm not really supposed to talk about it."

"You're the one. Maggie talked to you today. Redhead with wacky eyes?"

This time the color faded from his face. "Okay, you should be moving along now."

"No, really, this is incredible. Please tell me you're an ordinary mortal. You know—a normal guy." She bit her lip to keep the tears from starting. *Please be normal, please be normal.*

"I'm about as normal as they come." His grin spread slowly, enveloping her in warmth and relief, and she couldn't help but smile with him. He held out his hand. "I'm Damien Lewis. I apologize. I should have introduced myself this morning after you so kindly offered to buy breakfast for me."

She accepted the handshake and enjoyed the excuse to look into his eyes. "Audrey Sonoma."

"Nice to meet you. Do you go to Java Lemur often?" He sounded like he wasn't used to making small talk, but there was something significant about this moment of mundane happening in the middle of the waking weirdness they'd both encountered. She pushed away the thought of how she felt more connected to him than she had to Kyle in a while.

"I'm a freelance writer, so I like to haunt coffee shops." She cringed—maybe haunt wasn't the right word.

"I read a fair bit to keep up with what's going on, but I'm sure I would have remembered an Audrey Sonoma byline. Do you write under a different name?"

"Yes." She decided to take the plunge since she sensed they'd be tied together by their circumstances. Or maybe she just hoped they would. "I write as Annie Smith."

"Oh, you're the exposé restaurant writer."

"Right. For now. The hospitality industry is a small world, so I'm just hanging on 'til I get found out. Please don't tell anyone."

"Your secret is safe with me." Now he teased, "Do you also cover things of the, ah, paranormal sort?"

"Oh, hell, no." She shook her head to emphasize each word of her denial. "For me, it's usually restaurants and club openings with a few pet shows and festivals thrown in for fun." Something in his face made her reach out and touch his arm. "This is all new and weird for me, too."

He jerked away. "So what exactly are you looking for?"

She tried to ignore her stung feelings but crossed her arms. "Would you believe signs of a rift between this world and the dream world?"

"At this point, I'm not sure what to believe." He glanced at the slightly open fence, but he didn't move toward it. "What have you found so far?"

She crouched to look more closely at the charred grass. "It's burned, but the fire that destroyed this house was a long time ago."

He knelt beside her and touched a singed blade. It disintegrated and left a sooty mark on his finger. "You may be right. This makes no sense. There haven't been any fires around here, at least none that were called in. Or that I saw when I was on patrol the past few nights."

"So no bonfires or anything like that?"

"No. I was here last night. Well, right down there." He pointed to a corner about a block away. "That's where I found the last one wandering. Buck naked."

"Are you kidding me?"

"No, and she didn't care at all, either. She just asked if it would be good enough for the king, whatever that meant. Do you know?"

"I haven't a clue. But this seems to be the spot."

"And the point in finding it was...?" He stood and offered her a hand.

She allowed him to help her to her feet. In spite of the cold, his hand was warm. "I really don't know that, either. I'm a beginner at this. Oh, crap!" A MARTA bus drove by, and Audrey checked her watch. "That was my bus. The next one's not for another twenty minutes, and I was already cutting it close. I'm going to be late for work." She huffed, annoyed with herself. "And it's my first night."

"Let me give you a lift."

"But not in your squad car?" The only car she could see parked nearby was a sensible dark blue sedan.

He arched an eyebrow, which gave him an adorable, rakish look. "Not this time, but maybe later. Are you feeling naughty?"

Audrey blushed again. "I just might be. Are you going to make me ride in the back like you would a criminal?"

She couldn't get enough of his smile and his eyes. It was hard to remember he was a cop—and therefore not for her—when he kidded her.

"This time I'll let you ride in front."

❧

DAMIEN COULDN'T BELIEVE he'd offered the girl a ride home. Not that it took him that far out of his way, but she seemed to be tied up with that Maggie woman, whose sanity he still wasn't convinced of. But the things they'd talked about made some sort of sick sense. Plus, he didn't feel comfortable with her walking all that way by herself in the rain.

When she got in the car, the ease he'd felt with her vanished, and he glanced at the rosary his grandmother had given him, its black wooden beads worn in the centers with the thousands of prayers she'd said. Not that it had done her any good. But it was a reminder of what he risked with this seemingly small act of kindness.

"It's not too far," Audrey said, and he nodded.

"Just tell me where to go." He started the car, and a faint moldy odor came from the vents with the initial blast of air. He hadn't noticed until then how she smelled of fresh air and rain.

She lived not too far, but across the tracks, making a straight route impossible. He tried to come up with something to say once she'd given him her address, but his mind remained stubbornly blank, and she seemed lost in her own thoughts. Or maybe she had the same problem? The thought made the corner of his mouth twitch, but he refused to smile at the ridiculous thought of this poised, accomplished young woman —a professional writer—at a loss for words.

She directed him to a small driveway by a squat ranch style house with two front doors and matching Adirondack chairs.

"Duplex?" he asked.

"Yes, it's just me and my cat, so I don't need much room." She leaned over and touched him on the arm. This time he didn't flinch away. He didn't know how to tell her that her first touch had shocked him. Not literally, but more in a not-used-to-human-touch way.

Had he become that isolated? Damn, maybe Charlie was right.

"All right, be safe tonight. Weather looks nasty." There, at least he could talk about the weather.

"Thanks for the ride. I really appreciate it." She tilted her face up to his, her cheeks pink, and a small smile playing around her lips.

Was that a kiss request? It had been so long. She couldn't possibly want to kiss him, could she?

He automatically said, "You're welcome," and leaned toward her but didn't close the distance, testing. The sway of the rosary's cross caught his peripheral vision, and he closed his eyes so he wouldn't see it, let it pull him away from the moment. The thought that he shouldn't be doing this tickled the back of his consciousness, but the cold rain smell of her contrasted with the warmth of the breath on his face and short-circuited his normal caution.

Before his brain caught up with his body, he touched his lips to hers. It was his first kiss in years, and when she leaned into it, he couldn't help but respond. He quivered with the need to be gentle, to not give into the urge of a man who's starved for so long he forgot how to be hungry until faced with a feast. Her mouth opened to his, and he explored it with his tongue. He'd just lifted his hand to cup her head when her phone rang. She pulled away with a curse, and he slumped back like she'd sucked the willpower from him.

She fumbled with her phone, her hands shaking. The tinkling ringtone filled the car with its sporadic bursts of melody.

"I'm sorry, it's someone I need to talk to," she said, her cheeks pink.

"That's fine."

But she still didn't answer it. Nor did she meet his eyes. "I'm working tonight at Bistro Moderne if you want to meet later for a drink."

"I'll think about it," he said. He might be out of practice, but he could tell when a girl was uncomfortable. Had he done something wrong? "I should get some sleep. I've been awake for almost twenty-four hours."

"Right, it's probably for the best," was her cryptic reply. She hopped out of the car, her phone to her ear. "Lucia?"

Damien rested his forehead on the steering wheel. *Stupid, stupid, stupid. Just because Charlie is trying to drag you into the real world, it doesn't mean you need to go.*

The internal argument continued as he put the car into gear and turned right on Ponce de Leon Avenue toward home and hopefully sleep.

Like he would be able to sleep after that. *Or that you need to be so happy that she lives alone and that whoever called her wasn't a boyfriend.*

Rest, he needed rest. It would straighten his brain out and give him the discipline he needed to resist the pull of a certain pair of green eyes and lips that tasted like coffee.

He couldn't help but shake his head at everything Audrey had told him, especially the "rift between dimensions" stuff. He caressed one of the smooth beads on the rosary and hoped that she wouldn't end up—what had his grandmother used to say? —"touched." People who were "touched" were never quite the same, and he suspected Maggie was one of them and was drawing others into her web of crazy.

Still, of all the women he'd picked up on Dekalb Avenue that week, Audrey was by far his favorite, even beyond her apparent skepticism, and she hadn't even been naked. Something stirred in his chest, and a smile escaped before he forced his expression into its usual neutral frown.

In spite of his internal battle between regret and a softer emotion he dared not try to name, he crashed into sleep as soon as his head met his pillow. But he didn't even get the chance to dream about what she might look like naked because it seemed that just as he dozed off, his cell phone rang. He rolled over and looked at the clock: had he really been asleep for two hours?

"Lewis," he said automatically when he answered it.

"God, Dame, I'm sorry to wake you up, but I need you back here." Charlie's voice was panicked.

"What's going on?"

"Our girls have gone missing."

"So it turns out someone saw one of our Janes leave," Charlie told Damien when he arrived at the station.

"Which one?"

Charlie's grin answered before he did. "The naked one."

A dull ache bloomed in Damien's left temple. "Was she naked when she left the hospital?"

"No, one of the nurses gave her clothes from their Take Back the Night stash, so she's running around in baby blue sweats."

"When was she last seen?"

"This morning at around eleven."

Damien plopped on the couch in Charlie's office and ran his hands through his hair. "Why weren't we notified?"

"They thought they'd find her wandering around the hospital."

"How'd she get out?"

"Just walked off a locked psych ward, apparently."

"What? How?"

"I don't know, but I bet Maggie will."

Damien glanced over his shoulder to check that no one hovered near Charlie's office door. Then he closed it and turned to his former friend, now—something. "Okay, look, now that we're alone, do you really believe in this stuff, about the goddesses tumbling down from the dream world and getting lost?"

Charlie sat back at his desk and steepled his fingers. Damien's cheeks heated. *Am I about to be reprimanded?*

"I don't know." Charlie sighed. "I know your bias against all things supernatural—you're the only one in the station who doesn't mind working Halloween so you can avoid celebrating it. All I know is that this Maggie chick has helped me crack some really tough cases, and she always turns up just before a bizarre one comes along. Like this morning, I came in and found this." He flicked a business card at Damien: The Crystal Cave Magic and Novelty Shop, Proprietor: Margaret Cornwall. "That's when I knew it was going to be a crap day."

"I know better than to believe that."

Charlie didn't argue. "Not that I don't love a challenge. Speaking of which, did you see anything on your drive down College Avenue?"

"Just another young woman, but not one of supernatural origins."

"Oh, really?" Charlie raised his eyebrows. "Do tell."

Damien didn't mention he'd kissed her. "It was the coffee shop girl. She was in that lot that's just been sold for condos, you know, the one with the house that burned down years ago."

"Yeah, people used to say it was haunted. What was she doing there?"

Damien hesitated, then said, "She said she was looking for signs of a rift between dimensions."

"And did you find anything?" Out came the notebook, but Charlie didn't seem surprised.

"Just some charred grass that shouldn't've been, nothing more."

"No more naked nymphs?"

Damien couldn't help but smile. "Just the real girl."

"And she's still hot, right?"

"Very. Slender, tall, light brown hair, green eyes..." Something that had been bothering him popped into his head.

"And...?"

"Ears with pointed tips. But not freakish, just cute. I never thought much of them before all this." He could picture himself kissing them and stopped that line of thought before it led to another blush and more teasing. And more bad decisions later.

The phone rang, and Charlie answered it. While Charlie talked, Damien half-listened, but the gray clouds drifting across the sky mesmerized him with their shifting patterns. It had been a crisp autumn day, but now that evening fell, the air temperature dropped, a change noticeable even from inside. This weather was made for sleep. He yawned and rubbed his eyes, willing his eyelids to stay open.

"We've got one," Charlie said and hung up the phone. "Taylor found her."

"Which one?"

"Do you remember a blonde?"

The image of a slender girl with hair the color of ripe wheat and blue eyes that reminded him of a perfectly clear fall day came to Damien's mind. "She was the first one."

"Well, she's been hit by a car. Killed instantly."

"Son of a..." Damien recalled her innocent face, and anger stabbed through him for whoever had ended her young life. "Where?"

"Down Clairmont near Emory Commons. Let's go."

They took a patrol car so that they'd be able to use the lights and the siren to cut through traffic. When they got to the tangle of police cars, paramedics, a Dekalb County CSI truck, and yellow tape that blocked the major artery between Decatur and I-85, they found the coroner had already arrived and was examining the partially tarp-covered victim.

"What've you got, Leo?"

The tall man with a shock of red hair, square jaw, and black-framed glasses sat back on his heels and took off his blood-stained rubber gloves. "Looks like a pretty simple hit and run to me. Classic bumper marks. She died of a ruptured spleen and fractured neck, as far as I can tell."

Charlie turned to the patrolman who had called it in. "Any witnesses, Taylor?"

With a nod to Damien, the policeman said, "No, sir. Looked like she was trying to cross right over there, and that's when she was hit."

Charlie took his flashlight and examined the road, already wet from the cold, stinging rain. "Did you get any pictures?"

"Yes, sir. Not that they'll tell us anything."

Damien knelt on the pavement where the impact had happened and aimed his flashlight at it. "There aren't any skid marks. They didn't even try to stop."

"Then when we find the bastard who did this, it will be a pleasure to feed them to the lawyers. You know what else I'm thinking?" Charlie asked.

"Yeah." Damien tried to blink away the image of what must have happened from his overtired and therefore over-imaginative brain. "We've got to find the other two before something worse happens to them."

"Exactly. But I can tell that you need some sleep, so how about this? I'll get some guys on locating the others, and I'll call you the instant we find something."

"That works." Damien released the breath he'd been holding. "But call me if you need help."

"Will do. Oh, and come in streets. The Chief gave you temporary permission to join me on the case as an investigator-in-training, and we may need to go places that the uniform wouldn't be welcome."

"Thanks, Charlie, I really appreciate this." *I think.* He wiped his hands on his pants before opening the door to the squad car.

"The problem with you, Dame," Charlie told him after he

got in the passenger seat, "is that you're too self-effacing. You need to put yourself out there."

"Yeah, I know." He'd heard variations of that his entire life. But there was something to be said for being invisible.

"So this is your big break, man. If we can crack this one, then the Powers That Be may promote you to investigator."

"That would be incredible." He brushed something wet and very cold off his sleeve and tried to do the same with the doubts planted by DeMarco. "Is that sleet?"

Something ticked against the window, and the wipers swept little chunks of ice away.

"Looks like it."

"Since when do we get sleet in October?" He looked out the window and up at the dark sky. "The more we get into this, the more I'm convinced that there might just be something to your supernatural theory."

"Then you'd better get home and sleep while you can. It's gonna be a long night."

7

———

Audrey sighed and tried not to touch her lips, which she swore still tingled from the kiss Damien had given her. How else could she explain the desire to smile every time she thought about it? She wished she'd not tried to answer Lucia's call—she had missed her anyway, but when she finished trying to call right back and leaving a voice mail, Damien had already left.

Not that she had much to smile about otherwise. It was going to be a long night. Even if Audrey had wanted to ponder how Damien kissed so much better than Kyle—he seemed to actually pay attention, for instance—or keep an eye out for the missing goddess, she didn't have the time or mental space.

Bistro Moderne was busy for an evening with crappy weather, and apparently two more of the wait staff had quit that day, so it was just her, a guy named Tim with a self-proclaimed "high weirdness tolerance," and a new girl named Stephanie, who had obviously been hired out of desperation. She had no idea about waiting tables and followed Tim around for the first hour. So, between one waiter, one new to the restaurant, and one green trainee, they were lucky none of the customers had walked out on them yet. Even with the hostess and Cece pitching in, all three ran around like mad people.

Then there was the kitchen. The elves had rearranged things to their liking, so it had been everything that Cece could do to keep the chef from leaving in a huff. Audrey made a mental note to mention that blatant interference in human affairs to Maggie. Even with Cece's coddling, the chef sulked through the evening, and they all heard about it every time a favorite pot or utensil was not in its correct place.

Audrey had followed Tim around the first half hour or so until she learned the specials and figured out the serving order and table numbers. Water, bread, salads... It was pretty standard stuff. Plus, she got the chance to take a good look at the food, to taste the specials, and to observe the flow in the kitchen.

So, all in all, the night progressed pretty well until a flood of people came in at six-forty.

"What the heck is all this about?" she asked Tim. She hurried to fill a water pitcher from the filtered tap and ended up with a stream of ice-cold water down her forearm to her elbow. "It's still early."

He looked at her with raised eyebrows and a smug grin. "You're obviously not Catholic."

She refrained from asking if he always looked like a demented clown when he was being condescending. "No."

"There's a big Catholic church down the road, and the evening service just let out."

"Ah, so they figured it was too late to cook and came out?"

He patted her on the shoulder, and she flinched away from him. He didn't seem to notice. "Exactly. You see, Audrey, you have to know your area as well as your restaurant."

She was relieved when he ran to take another order before she could smack him for being such an ass. *He's likely working a weekend night because he has no friends.*

Shaking off her mean thoughts, Audrey checked on Stephanie, who filled water glasses. There was something strange about the girl, but she couldn't put her finger on it. She learned too quickly, for one thing. After her observation hour, Stephanie had taken to waiting tables like a veteran, and she'd had the most incredible luck. Audrey had to fight for fresh rolls for her customers, but she noticed that Stephanie seemed to instinctively know when to grab them so they'd be warm, but not hot enough to burn fingers.

"So," Audrey asked her once the evening rush wound down, and more customers left than came. "What do you think?"

Stephanie smiled but wouldn't meet her eyes. She spoke with a slight accent. "It wasn't as bad as I thought it would be."

"Have you ever done anything like this before?"

"Just some private party stuff. Nothing on this scale." Stephanie looked up like she'd heard something call to her. "Excuse me."

Audrey watched her walk into the kitchen. She started to follow, but when she turned around, she saw a familiar face at the bar.

Dressed in plain clothes, khaki pants and a white Oxford shirt, Officer Damien Lewis leaned on one elbow and smiled when her gaze met his. He had washed his wavy dark hair, and it curled slightly. Even better, he watched her with laughter in his eyes, and a smile played on his lips. Lips that she'd kissed when she really shouldn't have, but thinking about it made her own curl upward with the memory.

"You have a boyfriend. You have a boyfriend. You're not officially broken up yet although it's headed that way," she chanted under her breath, but she could never discuss the day's happenings with Kyle, who wouldn't talk to Madame Lucia because he believed she was a charlatan. Plus, she wasn't entirely sure of his whereabouts, only that he was likely playing doctor with one of his fellow medical students. She walked over to Damien.

"Howdy, Officer. What are you doing here?"

"Call me Damien." His dimple showed, but the laughter faded from his eyes. His very tired-looking eyes.

"Did you go home and nap?"

The dimple vanished. "For long enough. I couldn't sleep this evening, so I came to fill you in."

Audrey looked over the restaurant. "I have one table that's on dessert, but then I should have a moment before I have to help Stephanie, the new girl, out. It will probably be about twenty minutes."

He shrugged. "No problem. It'll take me that long to get through half of this beer. I'd actually like to talk to her, too."

"Good." But her heart sank. This seemed like more of an official visit. *You really shouldn't have kissed him. You have a boyfriend... Who doesn't seem to care much for you right now,* that little doubtful voice reminded her.

Audrey walked back to the kitchen and found Stephanie waiting for the decaf coffee to brew.

"These things take forever," complained Stephanie. "I thought it was ready."

"Here, watch this." Audrey grabbed a cup with her left hand, snatched the pot from the coffee maker, and without spilling a drop, substituted the cup under the stream. She reversed the process after it filled. "Now you try."

"Isn't that cheating?"

"Not if you have customers waiting."

Stephanie grabbed the coffee pot, and with a deep inhalation, pulled it out and put the cup under the stream, but she misjudged the angle, and hot coffee spilled over the rim.

"I'll get you a towel..." But the coffee hovered in the air and splashed to the counter without touching Stephanie's arm or her white shirt sleeve. The stream froze until she repositioned the cup.

Stephanie appeared not to notice, her tongue stuck out in concentration. Of all the strange things Audrey had seen that day, that had to be the weirdest. She looked again at the girl, really seeing for the first time the slight aura of gold around her, barely visible under the glare of the kitchen lighting. She fit the description of the goddess, too, with her long dark brown hair and big brown eyes. Was her accent Greek? A slightly pointed chin and high cheekbones made her a delicate beauty and gave her a definite resemblance to Demeter from Audrey's dream.

How did I not notice before? And how do I get her to Maggie?

"So, ah, how long have you been in town?" Audrey asked.

"Not long."

Audrey opened her mouth to ask another question, but something sizzled and popped outside, and darkness fell over the restaurant. Behind them, the chef cursed. The slam of the door and blast of cold air told Audrey that had been the last straw.

So much for that review. This place'll be closed by morning.

Cece burst into the kitchen. "The transformer down the street just blew. The tables all have candles, so you girls should be okay. Just watch your step when carrying hot coffee and use the manual credit card slips in the drawer under the register. Luckily we're done cooking for the night, and try not to open the refrigerated dessert case for too long." Then she rushed out.

Stephanie's laugh eased the thickness of the tense silence. "She reminds me of someone."

"Who?"

"My mother, I think." She frowned. "I'm not sure. Ah, there we go." The coffee finished brewing, and she poured the last two cups, balancing them on a tray as she walked out to the dining room.

Audrey knew she should follow with her own guests' coffee, but she stood and watched the light on the coffee pot. The light that blinked without electricity. Then it went dark.

DAMIEN SAT at the darkened bar and watched the shadows of the wait staff as they moved through the flickering pools of candlelight. He wished he could clearly see the waitress who wasn't Audrey—she looked like the young woman he'd picked up that morning, but she'd never managed to turn fully so he could get a good look. *It's funny how long ago that seems now.*

"You need to put yourself out there," Charlie had told him. So here he was, at a new restaurant, waiting for a girl whom he didn't even know was available for pursuit. Sure, he had an excuse: he wanted to keep her up to date about the situation and tell her about the hit and run. But he had to be honest with himself, and he didn't want Maggie the True-Speller or whatever she was to figure it out before he could sort through his own feelings. Feelings he shouldn't be having considering he'd sworn off dating.

Something felt right about being near Audrey. Sure, the restaurant got spooky with the lights off, but it had a cozy, romantic feel. Or it would have if he could shake the spiderweb across the back of the neck sensation that something was wrong.

He kept looking out of the nearby windows, but only the sleet sparkling in the glow of the street lamps looked out of place. Luckily the ground was still warm from the previous day, and the temperature wasn't supposed to get too low. Otherwise it would be a nightmare for traffic the next day if the stuff stuck.

He turned his seat back toward the bar. Maybe he could get Audrey to join him for a drink after the shift was done, if not here, then at one of the bars or coffee shops nearby. *Just to talk, of course.*

"Another drink, sir?"

Damien shook his head. "Not right now."

"Waiting for the young lady?" the tall, gaunt man asked. Damien looked at him, surprised. That wasn't the bartender who had given him the first beer. This one had no hair, sharp eyes, and a narrow beak for a nose.

"I might be. Where'd the other guy go?"

"His shift has ended," the man intoned and lit a candle. The flash from the match highlighted the contours of his skeletal hands, and his pronouncement took on a sinister air.

The hair on the back of Damien's neck and arms stood to attention. Did more than four servers move among the tables? There were only four, right? He blinked, sure it was the lack of sleep and looked back at the bartender, that he'd made a mistake with his estimation of him as threatening. But the strange man gazed over the room, his lips parted in a slight smile. The smile vanished when their eyes met, but not before Damien saw the hint of something pointed.

A fang? What the hell? Halloween isn't for a few days yet. Maybe it's part of a costume, but who would go to work with vampire teeth?

He shook his head and watched the last customers, a couple in their early thirties, leave the restaurant. The wind had picked up, and the woman snuggled against her boyfriend. Damien sighed. *Not for you, my friend,* he told himself, but his mental words lacked conviction. Here he was in theoretical pursuit of a woman whom he didn't know anything about because of some wild case that Charlie had dragged him into. A case that might wreck his career. He wished for the thirtieth time that he had gotten tangled up in a normal case, not one involving goddesses, nymphs, and a young woman he couldn't stay away from.

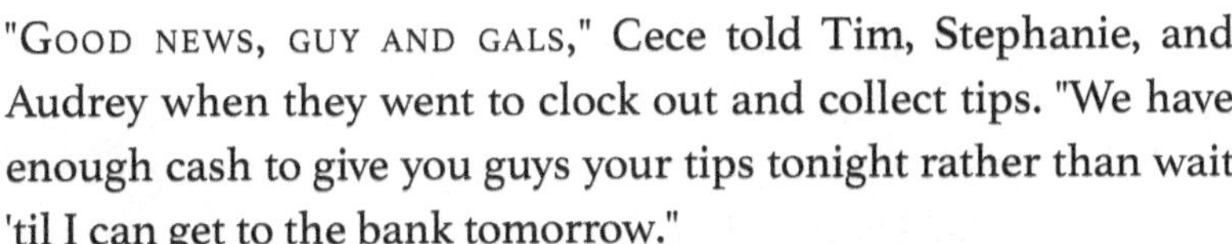

"GOOD NEWS, GUY AND GALS," Cece told Tim, Stephanie, and Audrey when they went to clock out and collect tips. "We have enough cash to give you guys your tips tonight rather than wait 'til I can get to the bank tomorrow."

Audrey debated telling Cece that she quit—the restaurant wasn't going to last long enough to make a review worthwhile, and she felt bad about the deception—but she didn't want to cause a scene even though the only people in the restaurant were the four of them, Damien, and the bartender, who counted out the cash in that register. She'd told Cece that Damien was waiting for her, so with a wink, Cece had let him stay.

Audrey watched Cece count out Tim's tips. Her cell phone vibrated in her pocket, and she pulled it out to check the caller in case it was Kyle. She simultaneously anticipated and dreaded the conversation. Nope. Madame Lucia.

"Excuse me," she murmured and walked to the far corner of the restaurant.

"I'm sorry I missed you," Lucia said. "A client came in earlier than expected, which makes me a horrible psychic, I know. How was your day, dear?"

Audrey didn't know whether to laugh or cry—*when was the last time Kyle had started a conversation asking about her? Never.* She sighed. "Weirder and weirder, but I met a nice guy."

"I'm sure Kyle will like him if you do, although I wouldn't be too worried about him."

"Yeah, yeah, I haven't figured that part out yet. I may have to consult you about that. But the new guy is tied in with all this, too."

"I would tell you my premonitions, but I don't want to concern you."

Audrey leaned against the wall by the kitchen doors. She bit her tongue over the flood of questions she wanted to ask, ones that would make her seem crazy to her coworkers who didn't know what was going on. "Did you find anything out about the spirit guide?"

"All I could find out is she wasn't ready for you. You arrived before you were supposed to."

"What does that mean?"

"You were destined to be a dream weaver, but you went through before your designated time. The rift seems to be working both ways. That may be how you ended up so close to one of the portals."

Audrey took a deep breath. "What should I do?" *About everything.*

"I don't know. I have some books that I can look through when I get back home, and I'll tell you tomorrow."

"Thanks. That would be great."

"Just please be careful, Dream Weaver. We are in a powerful time right now for those who would cause mischief."

"I will be very careful, I promise." Audrey looked at Damien and smiled. "I'll have good protection tonight."

She hung up and pushed herself off the wall to walk back toward the register.

Something reached out of the kitchen and grabbed her wrist in a cold, steely grasp. She looked down to see a very white hand with black fingernails. It was attached to a long arm in a dark sleeve, but in the gloom, she couldn't see who it belonged to. Not that she cared—she pulled back as hard as she could, but it may as well have been made of metal.

"Hey, let go!"

It pulled her so hard through the swinging metal doors that she banged her head on one of them. The pain faded into blackness.

8

———————

Audrey's cry drove Damien to his feet. The barstool crashed to the floor behind him, but when he got to the kitchen, he only saw one candle flickering on the metal counter top by the sink.

"Audrey?" he called.

He tried to dash around the center station but tripped on something. He rolled over to find himself looking into the glazed eyes of a corpse. The man's dress said it was one of the line cooks. Poor guy—yet another casualty of the strangeness they'd gotten caught up in.

"Don't come in," he shouted to the rest of the restaurant wait staff, who crowded the door. "Someone call 911."

He pulled out his flashlight and darted around the kitchen, both hoping he'd find her and fearing he'd find her body. Satisfied she couldn't be in there, he ran to the back door, but the alley was empty.

"Do you see anything?" the other female server called.

"No..." He turned around and saw her face clearly for the first time all evening in the flickering glow of the candlelight, and recognition jolted through him. "You stay inside."

Damien sprinted through the alley past dumpsters and piles of garbage bags, which took on monstrous shapes in the gloom. When he looked out on the street, he didn't even see the tail-lights of a car. Whoever had taken Audrey was long gone.

"Looking for something? Or should I say someone?"

He turned around to see the spooky bartender standing behind him. "You had something to do with this, didn't you?"

An eloquent shrug, hands with tapered fingers and black fingernails palm-up. "I was inside the whole time, my friend. You saw me. You were sitting right there."

"That doesn't eliminate you as an accomplice."

Another shrug, this time with a full smile...and a full set of fangs.

What the hell?

"If you want to see her again, stay out of this," the—whatever *it* was—continued. "There are powers at work with which no mortal should interfere." With that, he melted into the shadows.

I did not just see that. Damien's training kicked in and prevented him from being paralyzed with shock and fear. *Make sure the other civilians are safe, then...* He kept himself from running into the street after whoever had taken her—again, it was too late. He did run out of the alley and back to the front of the restaurant, and as expected, there was nothing overtly suspicious. When he entered, he sighed with relief to see the others still waiting inside.

"Did you find her?" asked the female server who looked so familiar. She and the G.M. huddled by the dessert case, both out of reach of the kitchen and away from the windows.

"No, she's gone." He looked at the young waitress. "But I have some questions for you."

"Wait, are you sure?" the G.M. asked him. "Maybe she went out for a smoke break?"

"She doesn't smoke," Damien snapped. "And time is of the

essence. I need to talk to your servers. Both of them, but her first."

"Fine, but not for too long. I can't lose any more wait staff, but..." She shook her head. "I'm sorry. I just don't know what to think. I guess now we have to call the police."

Damien held up his badge, and he didn't care if she saw he held it so tightly his grip turned his knuckles white with frustration. "Didn't you call 911?"

"We thought you might be able to catch them. I'm telling you, Officer, people around here listen to their police scanners, and this place doesn't need any more bad press."

"Give me a second." Damien turned so she wouldn't see the fury on his face. He flipped his phone out and made a short call to Charlie, who didn't manage to say hello before Damien told him, "I'm at that new restaurant near the tracks, Bistro Moderne. Audrey's been kidnapped. I found Persephone. Call Maggie. And we need an ambulance, probably someone from the medical examiner office."

He closed the phone. "There. They've been called. They'll be here soon." He gestured for Persephone to follow him away from the kitchen to the now-empty bar. "Don't look back there," he told her. "You won't like what you see."

He guessed he wouldn't, either. He hadn't seen the original bartender leave, which meant there may be another body like the one in the kitchen. If the cause of death was what he suspected, he knew the medical examiner would have fun trying to figure that one out. Or maybe he'd worked with Charlie before. But vampires? Every neuron in the skeptical part of his brain told him that this was all impossible, that he must be dreaming or Charlie was playing the most elaborate Halloween prank ever. But he knew what he had seen, who he had talked, to and—most importantly—he had to focus on his one lead to finding Audrey.

Persephone sat on a stool and stuck her lower lip out. "You don't know anything about me."

He took a deep breath to keep from snapping at her. She seemed strangely unconcerned for having witnessed a kidnapping and possibly two murders. "You're right. I know nothing of your kind. But I do know there are lots of people looking for you right now. And maybe some non-people, too." The flashing lights from outside illuminated her in alternating red and blue, and she looked like the ethereal being she claimed to be.

A tear rolled down her cheek. "I was lost. You left me in that awful place with all those people, and I wanted to leave. So I did."

"How did you get out of a locked ward?"

She shrugged. "The machines here run on energy. It doesn't take much to figure them out. A little zap in the right place, and they open right up."

It figured. And her explanation was annoyingly logical. "That's a nice trick. And where did you get the clothes for work tonight?"

"I didn't have any. Cece was so desperate for help, she loaned me some of hers. That sweat suit was hideous."

Before he could say anything else, Maggie's and Charlie's simultaneous cries interrupted him.

"Persephone!"

"Is that her?"

Maggie shoved him out of the way to get to the girl. She cupped Persephone's cheek and looked into her eyes.

"Are you okay? What happened?"

The young goddess moved from tears to sobs, and Damien turned away. He rubbed his arm. Maggie was stronger than she looked.

"Crocodile tears," he muttered.

"Not too impressed with her, are you?" asked Charlie.

"I'm not concerned about her at all, if that's what you mean." He choked out the words, "They got Audrey."

"The coffee shop girl?"

"She worked here as a waitress." Damien loosened his fists, which he didn't remember clenching. Why was Charlie being so obtuse? Probably because he was near Maggie.

"And look at you all dressed up, you dog." Charlie playfully punched him on the arm.

Damien winced. "It didn't matter. They took her."

"Who's *they*?"

Damien looked at his friend, willing him to clue back in. "Would you believe vampires?"

Charlie's concerned expression didn't change. "I'll keep an open mind."

"Then look behind the bar."

Charlie walked to the swinging door on the side of the bar and peered over it. His face went white, and he disappeared briefly from view when he went through and knelt to get a closer look.

"I might believe vampires after all," he conceded after he joined Damien at a table. "One bartender, dead, seemingly drained of blood with two classic puncture wounds at the left carotid artery." He flipped his notebook open and made notes. "They're not even trying to be subtle."

"I'm going to take Persephone back to my place," Maggie told them.

Charlie shook his head. "Not until we question her. She was a witness to all of it." He held up a hand to forestall Maggie's protest. "I don't care if she's a goddess, she might have seen something, and I'm very interested in her perspective if what Damien and I suspect is true."

Maggie waved Persephone over and gestured for her to take the fourth seat at the table. Charlie flipped to a blank sheet in his notebook and started the questioning.

"Name?"

"P. Stephanie Smith," she replied with a smirk.

"Okay, residence?"

"In the eternal summer from March through October. In the underworld for the winter months."

"Use my address," Maggie said and reeled off the street address of a condo in one of the nicer Decatur complexes.

Charlie raised his eyebrows but didn't comment. "Did you notice anything out of the ordinary tonight?"

Persephone shrugged. "I don't know. It was my first night, so everything was new and strange. The only weird thing was that the power went out."

"Did you notice any non-human creatures in the restaurant?"

"That's gonna look interesting in your report," Damien muttered. Why wasn't he getting to the good stuff?

The goddess shook her head. "But I wasn't paying that much attention. We were really busy."

"Can you think of anything that might help us find Audrey or figure out what happened to her?"

Damien watched Persephone to see if she was lying.

Her eyes filled with tears again. "No. I'm not here by choice, remember? I don't know who brought me here or why. I just want to go home." She looked at Maggie. "Can we go now?"

"I see what you mean," Charlie told Damien. They watched the two women walk away. "She may know something, but we're not getting it out of her. She's also scared stiff."

"I bet they were after her, not Audrey." That at least made logical sense. As for the rest of it... He remembered his grandmother telling him that there were things he couldn't even imagine in the supernatural world.

His grandmother... Crap. She'd believed all that airy fairy shit, and look where it had gotten her. Damien punched Charlie on the arm. He heard the desperation in his own voice but had to make damn sure all this crazy stuff was real before he jumped down the rabbit hole, too. "Okay really, you can stop playing these games now."

"What games?"

"The 'it's almost Halloween, so something creepy is happening' game. C'mon, it's over. Where's Audrey? Is she in on it?"

He counted the two heartbeats before Charlie replied.

"Seriously, dude, it's not a game. There really is something creepy going on, and I don't know where your girlfriend is."

"She's not my girlfriend." And now a pang of guilt stabbed him in the gut and almost chased out the simmering terror that he'd gotten mixed up in something beyond what he could handle. He should have been watching more closely after he'd seen the fangs on the bartender.

"Okay, potential girlfriend. Where was she when she disappeared?"

"Right over there by the kitchen. She had gotten a cell phone call. They were getting their tips, so she was able to take the call."

They walked over to that part of the restaurant. The candles still flickered on the tables and sulked in their pools of wax.

"Wait a second..." Damien pulled out his flashlight again. He knelt and saw what he was looking for—a dark rectangle beneath one of the tables.

"What is it?"

"Audrey's cell phone." It was locked, but her fingerprints guided him to decipher the swipe pattern to unlock it. His hands were shaking, so he handed it to Charlie.

His friend scrolled through the call log. "Let's see... Most recent call: Lucy. Who's that?"

"You've got me there." Then Damien recalled Audrey answering her phone when she'd hopped out of his car. "A friend, maybe? Audrey was talking to her earlier."

"Hmm, let's look further. Most received and dialed calls. Uh oh..."

"What?" Damien's breath caught in his throat, and he knew what Charlie would say before the words came out of the detective's mouth.

"The top one is a local number, and she's got it listed under 'Kyle."

"Of course." He expected to feel relief—of course she was seeing someone, so he could let go of his feelings for her—but disappointment overtook it. "Let's call that other number first."

A QUICK CHECK on the number led them to Madame Lucia's cell phone and her business and home addresses. They went to her home after questioning the other wait staff to see if they'd noticed anything unusual. Of course it had been so hectic they hadn't. Satisfied they'd exhausted all leads at the restaurant, they headed to Madame Lucia's house.

"Nice place, very Decatur bohemian." Charlie used the brass knocker on the door.

Damien's stomach flipped. When he'd dropped Audrey off here earlier, it had seemed like a friendly little neighborhood made for families with kids. Now the white siding of the house glowed in the moonlight, and the street lamps cast skeletal shadows through trees that had been whipped bare of their leaves by the wind.

The lady herself answered the door and only took a cursory glance at their proffered badges. "You're just in time for tea, gentlemen."

She led the way back to the kitchen, where three cups sat on the table.

"So, you're a psychic?" asked Charlie. "I haven't worked with you before."

The look she gave Charlie would've withered Damien's balls had he been on the receiving end.

"No," she said, "I always make tea for three at half past ten at night." She gestured for them to sit.

Damien complied and stifled a laugh, which turned into a yawn. "Sorry," he mumbled.

"You've had a long day, dear. And to answer your question, Detective, yes, I'm a psychic, but I don't involve myself with forensics. Such violent images stay with me for too long." She shook her head like she wanted to clear the unpleasant thoughts, and the beads at the end of her braids clinked.

"We're here regarding your neighbor, Audrey." Charlie said. "You called her earlier this evening?"

"Yes, she consulted me on a spiritual matter."

"Do you mind telling us what that was?"

"Yes, I mind." A firm nod with more clacks. "I have my professional ethics, boys. I'll just say it had something to do with a project that got dropped in her lap today."

"Meaning the kidnapping of Persephone?" Charlie leaned forward.

Lucia inclined her head and eyed him over the rim of her mug. "You know about that."

"I sometimes work with Margaret the Truth Seeker."

Damien watched the exchange, fascinated and half-horrified with himself for beginning to believe it all.

"Ah, so that *was* Maggie I saw in town earlier today."

"Yeah, she's around." Charlie's nonchalance sounded forced. "But while Persephone is now in her capable hands, we have a new problem."

"Which is...?"

"Audrey has gone missing. We think she was kidnapped from her job earlier."

Lucia's hands trembled, and she put the chipped blue ceramic mug down. "I didn't see any signs of her being in danger specifically," she said. "But Persephone was surrounded by chaotic energy. Perhaps Audrey was not the intended target, and she will be returned once the mistake is discovered. They would bear a resemblance to one another, especially in dim light."

"The power was out, it was all candlelight." Damien struggled to keep his voice even and pushed away the memories of the two corpses. "But even if they did grab the wrong girl, that's not really how it works, ma'am. She's more likely to be killed. The beings, whatever they are, don't hesitate to take innocent lives."

"She needs protection, then." Lucia sighed. "Or needed. I should have seen this coming. I warned her to be careful."

"Can you tell us any more about what she asked you to work on?" Charlie asked. "It could be connected."

"She has lost her spirit guide. The guide exists and is trying to find her. I only pray she won't be too late."

"Do you have any idea where she might be?" asked Damien. He tried to maintain a professional, not panicked, tone, but Lucia's sympathetic look told him she could hear it.

"If I knew, I would tell you. I'll try to help you find her sooner."

Damien started to protest that soon may not be soon enough, but Charlie interrupted, "Any help you can give us is greatly appreciated."

She looked into her teacup and blew across the surface of the liquid. Damien opened his mouth to ask what she was doing, but Charlie put a hand on his arm.

Finally Lucia looked up. "Wherever she is, she is close by. Keep your mental eyes and ears open." And she added with a sly smile, "Especially you with your silver eyes. She may try to contact you however she can."

"I don't have any kind of special abilities like that," Damien told her. He hoped she didn't hear the trembling in his voice.

"But someone you loved did."

That was enough. They could talk about their crazy super-natural stuff, but they needed to leave him out of it. Damien stood. "Thank you for your help. We should be going."

To Damien's surprise, Charlie rose, and after the typical pleasantries, they left. Leaves scraped and crunched under Damien's feet like the snickering of old bad memories.

"Psychics pray?" asked Damien once they were back in the car. "Is that what she was doing?"

Charlie glanced at him as he started the car. "I guess you can't predict everything. And trust me, you don't ever refuse free help from a psychic."

The next stop was Kyle's apartment, located in a gated community near Emory University.

"You think he's still up?" asked Damien. They waited at the call box for one, two, three, four rings.

"Probably not." The call went to voicemail. Charlie took out a remote and opened the gate with a click of a button.

"How'd you score one of those? I thought we couldn't use them without a search warrant."

"Sometimes I get to skirt the rules. It's one of the perks of this job. Hence how we're not bringing in the Dekalb PD on this."

DeMarco's warning played back in Damien's head. Was that how Charlie resolved his cases—he didn't follow proper proce-dures? But then how did anyone get convicted in court?

Damien didn't have time to think too much. These apart-ments were several steps up from many of the ones Damien had visited in the course of duty. Small trees lined the side-walks, and the paint on the wooden balconies of the brick and white siding buildings was fresh and un-chipped.

"Thirty-four C..." Damien matched the building number, then the apartment number. "That one."

"Would you like to do it, or shall I?" asked Charlie once they stood in front of the door.

"Be my guest."

Charlie pounded on the door. The knocks echoed through the apartment. "Mr. Creely?" he called. "Dekalb police."

Damien heard cursing and smirked. Not that he had anything personal against this guy. He was sure he was a perfectly nice man worthy of Audrey's affections.

The perfectly nice man himself answered the door in nothing but a pair of boxers. A little on the scrawny side, Damien decided. A blond surfer boy. He resisted the impulse to shift his position to show his brawn.

Kyle blinked at the light and squinted at their badges. "Can I help you, Officers?"

A woman's voice called from the back of the apartment, "Kyle, what's going on?"

He ran his hand through his hair and shouted over his shoulder. "Police. Just stay there."

"You have company, Mr. Creely?" Damien was glad Charlie had spoken. Flames burned his face from the inside, and he suppressed the urge to wrap his hand around surfer boy's neck and choke that sheepish grin off his face.

"Yeah, my girlfriend."

"Now that's interesting, sir," Charlie kept on, the image of polite inquiry, "considering that she was abducted in front of witnesses this evening."

Kyle's jaw dropped. "Who was?"

"Audrey Sonoma, or were we mistaken?"

A young woman about his age and dressed in an oversized t-shirt came out of the gloom. "Audrey?" She swept tousled blonde curls out of her face and squinted at the bright porch light. "I thought you broke up with her."

Kyle ran his hand through his hair again. Damien wanted to grab his wrist and make him hold still. "I, ah, didn't get the chance to talk to her about that."

"What?"

Damien tried to hide a smirk and hoped it came out as a polite smile. "Sir, we appear to have caught you at an awkward time."

Charlie elbowed him so fast he didn't have time to react, just take a quick breath and process the hint to shut up.

"Can you tell me when you last spoke to her?" Charlie asked.

Kyle shrugged. "This morning, I guess, on the phone." Now it was his turn to grimace from an elbow to the ribs.

"You talked to her today? And you didn't break up with her after you'd asked me over yesterday afternoon? That's it, I'm leaving." She spun on her heel to stalk back into the dark apartment.

"Ma'am?" Charlie called after her.

"Chastity, wait."

"What?"

"Ma'am, have you been with Mr. Creely all evening?"

"Since about ten. This morning." She glared at all three of them. "Apparently I've been wasting my time."

"Well, we appreciate it," Charlie said. "We'll be in touch if we have any more questions."

"Yeah, you do that. Just call first next time," Kyle muttered and slammed the door.

"We did," Damien said through clenched teeth. His upper arm throbbed from the third hit that evening. "What the hell was that for?"

"I could tell you were simmering and wanted to hit the guy. Hey, you should be happy."

"For what? That her heart's gonna be broken?"

"No, for the chance to be the dude to comfort her in her time of emotional travail."

Damien didn't feel like lecturing him on how he wasn't the type of guy to take advantage of a girl's feelings. Or how his head spun between relief at her unattached state and regret at how hurt she'd be when she found out about it. Regardless of that emotional tangle, they still had one big problem.

"We have to find her first."

9

———————

Something roared in Audrey's ears, and her hard, cold sleeping surface rocked. She opened her eyes to a blue sky through a clear pane. She lay on her side on another one, beneath which she could see sand, but when she tried to roll over, she couldn't move. A glass box about four feet long and three feet tall and wide encased her and kept her from being able to straighten in any direction. She couldn't break it, no matter how hard she kicked or pounded the sides with her fists. Water splashed against and over it, and with each wave, it sank further into the sand, and she grew more panicked.

"Help," she screamed, but there was no one on the deserted beach to hear her. Gray, rocky cliffs rose from the white sand to her right. To her left, the cliffs jutted to the sea in a formation that resembled a large donut. Water splashed through the hole and sprayed a rainbow mist.

She tried kicking again and only succeeded in hitting her head. She looked for seams or cracks, anything that might keep it from being solid, but found nothing. Singing caught her attention, and she paused to listen.

"He came to the sea,

My dark-haired lover.
He came to meet me
Where the water comes over
He came to be free
From his land-worn lover
He came to heed my call."

A YOUNG WOMAN with dark brown hair walked on the sand toward Audrey, who banged on the walls of her crystal box, but the woman stared straight ahead. She walked slowly along and hummed the melody to the song, the wind whipping her hair around her face, her sea-green eyes focused on the donut rock. Rather than a cloth garment, she wore swirling mist anchored to her by seaweed strands. Small seashells woven into her hair gave her a tropical look.

"*He came to the sea,*" she sang again. Water foamed around her ankles, and she held her arms out. When her hands passed through the hole, she disappeared, and the song ended with a scream of terror.

Audrey shrank back in her box, and her heart beat a staccato counterpoint to the waves. *What the hell was that?* She fought her rising terror and heard the song again, and the woman came walking along the beach a second time.

"Don't go to the rock," Audrey screamed, but the woman still didn't hear her. The scene played out again, and the woman repeated her actions and disappeared.

Okay, what am I seeing? It's obviously a rewind and replay of some moment in time. But who is she?

"Nimue," the waves whispered.

"What?" she asked out loud.

But nothing answered. The box shook with the fury of the water, which roared its frustration at her lack of understanding.

"Who is she?" Audrey asked again, the haunting melody in

her ears, her throat raw—why couldn't she be heard? What had the waves said? The woman appeared again.

"Nimue," Audrey whispered, and this time, the woman turned her head.

"Wake up," the woman said. "Please wake up."

Audrey woke, once again on a hard surface, but concrete this time. Her hands and feet were bound, and her heart pounded somewhere in the middle of her head.

"Are you okay?" The voice sounded at first like the wind on the seashore, but the question ended on a frightened tone that was all too human.

"I think so." Relieved to be out of the box, Audrey took a few shaky breaths and did a quick mental scan of her body. "I don't feel like anything is broken. Who are you?" She squinted into the dim light and could barely make out the features of the speaker, the woman from the seashore. This was no radiant nymph, but a frightened girl with a smudged face and tangled hair. She, too, was bound, but sat propped up against some sort of crate. She wore tattered jeans and a T-shirt that proclaimed, "Destin is for lovers."

"I don't know."

Audrey tested her bonds. "Does the name Nimue mean anything to you?"

The woman's eyes widened. "Yes, that is my name. Wait. It's coming back to me now."

An aquamarine aura surrounded the woman, and Audrey had to ask, "What are you?"

"I am a water nymph, and I am a servant of Her Radiance, the goddess Aphrodite." She wrinkled her forehead with a frown. "Or at least I was."

"Was what?"

"Aphrodite's servant." She looked down and shook her head. "I slipped away to meet a lover and found myself here."

"Here?" They were in a warehouse. Boxes barely illuminated

by a glow that could have been from outside or minimal security lighting cast deep shadows. The acrid, oaky smell of fresh
wood mingled with the scents of mildew and rain.

"Not here, mortal." The woman leaned forward. "On a street
in this realm. And a man brought me to a place that smelled..."
She wrinkled her nose. "I don't have words to describe it. The
bright lights hurt my eyes, and people in white coats poked and
prodded and asked so many questions."

Audrey's lips tingled, and she had to ask, "Describe the man
who brought you there." Thinking of Damien, how he'd have
the situation under control, gave her some measure of calm,
but it merely took the edge off her rising fear again. What the
hell had happened to her? She'd been in the restaurant, and...

Everything was fuzzy. The ropes burned at her wrists, and
she had to remind herself to stop straining at them or she'd
hurt herself further.

"He was very handsome, much like my lover, with dark hair
and silver eyes, a strong face, and dark clothes."

"Damien," Audrey murmured. She pictured him guiding the
nymph to his car, asking her questions, and trying to calm her
panic at having landed in this strange place. She wondered if
the nymphs and goddess had felt the same calm when they'd
been near him that she had.

A clap of thunder rattled the windows, startling her out of
the feeling she'd almost reached.

"Is it water?" asked the nymph, looking up with wide eyes.

"What does that have to do with—" Audrey took a deep
breath. She had to remember that the immortals had their own
agenda. "I don't know. It may be a storm, but it's cold for
thunder."

"Demeter is displeased her daughter is missing. If I could
get one drop of water, real water without all the things you put
in it, to touch me, I could be away from here."

"How long have you been here?"

"Since this afternoon. This morning, Her Loveliness, the goddess Persephone, got us out of that awful place, but then Germa—she's a wheat nymph and one of Persephone's servants—and I got separated from her in the confusion, and two men grabbed me and brought me here."

"Right." Those had to have been Damien's three Jane Does. A small bubble of humor rose through her racing thoughts. Boy, was he going to love that—two nymphs and a goddess. The poor guy had been so distressed by the idea of supernatural involvement. Now she was in over her head, too. Although perhaps she and Nimue could help each other.

"Can you untie me?"

"I cannot untie knots that were made by human hands, otherwise I would."

"Something makes me doubt that they were human." Audrey remembered the strange appearance of the hand that had grabbed her. "Did you see who or what brought me here?"

Nimue cocked her head. "They may have been vampires." She shuddered. "Awful things. But even so, there is one more thing."

Audrey cursed under her breath, her fear turning to anger at her suggestions being blocked. Didn't the stupid girl know what could happen to them? And vampires? *What the everliving hell? Just my luck, getting stuck with a useless nymph.* "What?"

"My fingers are numb and stiff."

"Oh." Anger deflating under hopelessness, Audrey flexed her fingers but could barely feel them. "Mine, too."

Her head throbbed in time with the thunder, and she wondered if she had a concussion. That meant she probably shouldn't sleep. But her fear and then anger had worn her out, and fighting her drowsiness seemed as easy as escaping from that damn clear box.

Maybe I can use this to dream-spin or whatever it's called to find some help for us.

"Well, while you wait for your water, I'm going to catch some sleep. Hopefully."

"Fair travels, Dream Weaver."

"What?"

But Nimue had gone back to staring at the ceiling and didn't respond.

Giving up, Audrey tried to get comfortable against a wooden packing crate and soon a floating feeling, her usual signal that she was about to fall asleep, took over.

Find help, find help, she chanted to herself, and the vivid dream of the Olympians that had started it all came to mind. Soon, bright sunlight stung her closed eyelids, and the rough concrete she laid on smoothed out to warm marble.

LYLE AMES LOOKED at the city lights that twinkled below his office window as the pill melted under his tongue. He thought about all the people in the condos and town homes he'd built and then sold at premium prices. Were they finished with dinner? Maybe reading their kids a story? How about cuddling with their spouses, partners, significant others, or whatever other "other" category Atlantans defined for themselves?

He loved this city and its veneer of Southern charm over a lustful pulse that never faded. *That's why Scarlett O'Hara had fit in so well here, fictional though she was. She had drive, ambition, and the beauty and talent to make the most of it. Too bad she had to fall in love. Calculated lust is so much more profitable.*

"We have problems."

He turned toward the speaker, a little toady from the Other Side. The squat man in an ill-fitting suit lifted his bulging eyes toward Lyle with an expression both nauseating and placating.

Lyle wondered if Zeus had assigned this creature as his liaison just to irritate him, or maybe because he'd annoyed Zeus.

"What kind of problems?" He pressed his fingertips to the window and took comfort in its cool hardness.

"The women at the hospital, they got out, and we chased down two of them like you said, and we thought we caught the other one."

"Thought?"

The man's head bobbed nervously. "It turns out it's not her," he said out of the corner of his mouth so quietly that Lyle almost didn't hear it.

"Then who is it?" Lyle didn't yell, but his tone left no doubt he was furious.

The toady shrugged. "Just some mortal who looks like her."

"What concern is this of mine?"

"Well." The little man coughed and spluttered like the words in his throat were being drowned with phlegm. "The boss wants her. He wants to arrange a trade."

Lyle turned back toward the window and the lights. Some poor mortal who should be at home in bed but had gotten snatched by gods-knew-what. He certainly didn't want to know. But his conscience pricked him at the thought of giving this girl to Zeus.

"Where is she?"

"At the warehouse with the water nymph."

"Then Zeus has probably already found her. I pray that she can keep her wits about her." He shivered as he remembered his first interview with the king of the gods. "You may leave. Bother me only if it's a true emergency."

The toady shuffled out the door, and Lyle tried to clear his mind of everything but the lights. In his head, they muted and softened until they were the glow of a thousand temple candles. He sat back in his office chair and waited for the journey to begin. It had been a rough day, and he deserved a little reward for all his hard work. His breathing slowed, and a slight smile played on his lips at the images that formed behind his eyelids: marble steps leading up to row of white columns. Diaphanous pastel-colored curtains fluttered in a door that stood open and inviting...

AUDREY WOKE TO A SMOOTH, hard surface like stone that had felt the heat of the sun. She opened her eyes and squinted against the bright sunbeams that poured through the columns, beyond which gardens, and farther off, mountains stretched. She still lay on her side, her hands and feet tied. This prison was a lot prettier than her last one. Purple, royal blue, and gold hangings stirred in a gentle breeze and cast dancing shadows over the white marble floors, columns, and ceiling.

Had she made it to the Collective Unconscious? Her heart quickened with hope. Maybe she could find Maggie or Zinfandel or—

"You may stand," said a woman's voice, hard like the marble and colder than the snow-capped mountains in the distance.

Her optimism dashed like the woman had poured cold water over it. Audrey squirmed into a kneeling position, but that was all she could manage with her tied feet. She scooted around to face the center of the room, where two people she recognized from the kidnapping scene sat on jewel-encrusted gold thrones. Now that she saw them in context, Audrey identified the man and woman who were comforting Demeter as Zeus and Hera, and she deduced she must be on Mount Olympus. Demeter, who looked like an older but very well-preserved version of Persephone, stood next to Zeus' throne in all black, her dark eyes red from weeping.

"Uh, Your Highnesses," said Audrey. She tried to bow from the waist and nearly toppled over.

"Human, do you know why you are here?" asked Zeus, his voice like the low growl of thunder.

"Not really. I think there's been some sort of mistake."

"There's no mistake," said Demeter. "I remember you from the day 'Sephone disappeared. You were there in the field with that useless dragon."

Hera crossed her legs and twitched her foot. "That does not necessarily mean she's involved, Demeter. We've had a lot of traffic recently."

"But she has been captured by the night creatures." Zeus raised a suspicious eyebrow at Audrey. "They must have caught her at something." He grinned as though he imagined what.

"Only if waiting tables badly is a crime, Your Majesty." Audrey bit her tongue. That probably hadn't been the right time to make a joke, but the thought they might let her go if she told them about Persephone made her want to giggle hysterically. Hera hid a smile behind her hand.

Zeus, on the other hand, glowered at her and hit the arm of his throne. "Silence!" A clap of thunder shook the building, and the light faded. "It should be, but that is not the issue here."

"If I may, Your Highnesses," Audrey told them. "I have seen Persephone."

"You have?" Demeter's eyes lit up. "Is she unharmed?"

"Yes, Lady, she is. She is currently in the care of Maggie, er, Margaret the Truth Seeker."

Instead of looking happy, Zeus brought his brows together. "Perhaps you should investigate the veracity of this claim, dear sister?"

"I shall do that, brother. Hera, would you like to accompany me?"

"Of course. I have something I need to check on, anyway."

The two women vanished, which left Audrey with the brooding king of the gods. Zeus pressed his fingertips together and frowned at her from under bushy eyebrows. He stared at her so long she struggled not to squirm, and the gleam in his eyes made her wish she could cross her arms over her breasts.

Finally, he spoke. "You have gotten yourself mixed up with a rather interesting crowd, young human."

"I guess so, sir."

"You have made the acquaintance of a dragon, a Truth Seeker, and gods only know what else. You are obviously a dream weaver, yet your talent is untrained, and you have no Spirit Guide."

Audrey ground her teeth so as not to defend herself. She sensed he wanted an argument. "Do you know where I may find it? Sir?"

Zeus dismissed her question with a wave of his hand. "That is beyond my control. I am curious to know how you insinuated yourself into the company of supernatural beings and ended up bound like a little hog on a warehouse floor."

"You know where I am?"

"I can see the reflection of what you've seen in your eyes."

Her mouth dried, and she hoped that he wouldn't zap her for her impertinence, but she was desperate. "Then can you release me or send help?"

He chuckled, but his answer didn't give her any hope. "That is your task, young Dreamer. I hope we are better matched when we meet again."

He vanished, and she woke with his unpleasant laughter ringing in her ears.

"Who were you talking to?" asked Nimue.

"No one. I'm surprised you're still here."

"I tried to crawl out the door, but the men are still out there."

"Which men?"

Nimue lowered her voice. "The ones who want to do terrible things to us."

Audrey scraped her tongue against her bottom teeth to get some moisture in her mouth, which had suddenly gone dry, and her heart echoed in her brain again. "What kinds of things?"

"I heard them talking about it. They want to torture us. For pleasure. They're arguing now with the vampires about who gets who first."

Audrey closed her eyes. Better matched, indeed. *What if I don't get out of this alive? But why am I here to begin with?*

She looked at Nimue, who had her head turned toward the door to hear the conversation outside. She took a deep breath.

"I'm going to try to reach someone. I don't know if this will work."

Nimue nodded, still not looking at her. "Hurry, there isn't much time."

Audrey found it difficult to fall asleep with her heart pounding in her throat. *Think about the fun parts of the day,* she told herself, and the kiss in the patrol car came to mind. She couldn't help it—her lips curled into a smile.

"At least one of us can smile," Nimue grumbled. "Aren't you supposed to be going for help?"

"Hush, I'm trying."

"You're pursing your lips like someone will kiss you," the nymph persisted. "I am not a follower of the cult of Lesbos."

"And I'm not thinking about you." Audrey returned her mind to the kiss and focused on Damien's gray eyes and how they'd lost some of their guarded expression with her. Again, she felt like she floated, but this time with no clear sensations.

"Damien... Maggie... Help!"

10

Damien sat at Charlie's desk and traced the kidnappers' possible routes of escape on a map of Decatur, Stone Mountain, and the various small areas between them and downtown Atlanta itself. The chances of finding Audrey alive dwindled with every ticking second, but Damien couldn't give up.

"Dude, take a break," Charlie said. His eyes also showed the strain from poring over the maps and trying to find hiding places where the vampires—were they really vampires? Charlie hadn't seemed surprised when Damien had proposed the idea—would be able to stay out of the sun during the day. There were just too many possibilities. They had to narrow it down somehow, or it would take a year to find her.

"I need to get some air." Damien rubbed his eyes, which he knew must be red.

"You need sleep. Lay down for a few minutes on the couch. I'll keep working on this."

"I can't afford to sleep." But his body told him he couldn't afford not to. The effort of raising his eyelids increased exponentially with each blink.

"Sometimes sleeping can help you solve sticky problems," Charlie pointed out. "And it will definitely keep you from face-planting on my maps. Seriously, dude, rest."

"You sound like Arthur," Damien grumbled, but that meant he couldn't argue. And they were both right—Damien often came up with creative solutions after sleeping on a tricky question. Giving up, Damien took his friend's suggestion and stretched out on the sofa in the corner of Charlie's office.

Before Damien had time to wonder how Charlie rated such a perk, sleep descended on him like a heavy blanket.

But not a warm one.

Cold raindrops pelted Damien's head and soaked through his shirt. He stood on the front steps of the station and gazed out into the deserted night. Shadows moved at the corners of his vision, and he knew they meant trouble.

Damien walked down the steps and leapt over the small stream of water that always flowed by the stairs when it rained. Instead of landing on the sidewalk in front of the police station, he faced a row of warehouses. The shadows were thicker here, and he ducked behind a tree and watched.

"Damien," the wind whispered.

"Who's there?" he replied.

"Damien," it said again, his own name a cold tongue that licked his ear. He shivered. *This is not a normal dream.*

"Damien, come inside."

He followed the voice and walked into the first warehouse. The shadows clustered especially thick in there, but they didn't move, and he inferred that they couldn't see him. A faint glow lured him toward the back of the building. On the way, he noted large crates with numbers and letters stenciled on them. He could barely make out two words in chipping white paint: Avondale Lumber.

The glow took him between two cartons, where Audrey lay bathed in light along with the first girl he'd rescued from the street. Both had bruises on their arms like they had been handled roughly, but they were both alive, just asleep.

"Damien," Audrey murmured. He knelt down and brushed a stray strand of hair from her forehead.

"I'm here, Audrey," he said. "I just need to know where *here* is." He pressed his lips to her cheek, and she smiled.

He hated to leave her, but he needed to know more about the warehouse than that it held Avondale Lumber crates. He walked back outside, careful to avoid the shadows, which stirred when he passed. He crept around the buildings and, across the street, spotted some sort of conveyor device and large piles of rocks.

Of course. The steel plant at Ponce and Clarendon. The women are stowed in a nearby warehouse.

He turned back toward Decatur, stretched out his hands, and imagined himself back on Charlie's couch at the police station. He woke when he landed on the floor.

"Are you okay? That wasn't much of a nap." Charlie ran to help him up. "You were twitching, moaning, and talking the whole time."

Damien almost shoved him out of the way to get to the map. "I know where they are."

THE VISE-LIKE GRIP of cold fingers on her arm jolted Audrey awake from a dream about Damien. She found herself in the clawed hands of a creature that made the gargoyles from Bistro Moderne look like teddy bears. It stared at her with wide round eyes the color of mucous, and its sharp teeth dripped with something slimy. Patches of dark gray fur clung to its pocked gray-brown skin.

"Where is he?" it asked.

The foul breath of the creature made her cough and splutter, bringing her into the reality of where she was. "Who?"

"The man who was just here."

"There was no man." She tried to twist away from creature's stench. "It was only a dream."

"You said a name."

"I don't remember." She gasped when it flung her back to the floor, and she landed on her left shoulder. She was able to avert her face so she didn't break her nose, but the impact jolted her collarbone, and waves of pain and nausea washed over her.

"We should just eat 'em," said another voice.

"Wait 'til day, when we turn back into men. Then we can have some fun with them."

"Awww, look, you broke it."

Audrey tried to ignore the laughter and focused on taking deep, soothing breaths. She stopped writhing in pain and pictured it as being separate from her, in its own envelope. Like she had with other pain, physical and emotional. The continued conversation of the creatures interrupted her efforts.

"The boss says we can do what we want with that one," said the first one. "I can break it if I wanna break it."

"I still think we should eat it."

A shadow covered Audrey. Nimue.

"Oh, not you, pet," the second being crooned. It not-so-gently nudged the nymph out of the way. "The boss wants you as you are. He's got a special thing for you to do."

"Don't hurt her," Audrey said, and the creature kicked her.

"And what about you?"

The pain seared her consciousness such that she was hardly aware of what she was saying. "Please untie me. It hurts so much."

"It hurts, does it?"

"Please untie my arms."

"What the hell? She's not going anywhere."

The ropes released, and Audrey gasped as the bones ground together. She tried to overcome the pain again, but it was too strong. All she could do was rock and cradle her arm while praying that the creatures would do what they wanted quickly so she wouldn't have to suffer much longer.

"Damien," she whispered through the white-hot pain, his name the one bit of hope she had. Had he seen her? Would he rescue her? Her cheek tingled where he'd kissed her in her dream.

Audrey's scream tore through the early morning silence and confirmed Damien's dream vision.

"In there," he called to Charlie. He lifted his binoculars, but they didn't show him anything useful. He shifted his weight from foot to foot, but he had to wait for Charlie's command. He was out of his jurisdiction, and they had teamed up with a Dekalb County S.W.A.T. team.

The sky lightened to the east; sunrise would be soon. Charlie glanced at the sky, and with the appearance of the first ray of sun gave the word. The S.W.A.T. guys busted the doors open. Damien followed them around the crates he remembered so well from his dream. He found Audrey crumpled against one of them holding her left arm, and the other young woman shielded her from two creatures that looked like giant, lightly furred bats. The creatures spread their leathery wings and took off with angry screeches, only to be felled by silver bullets from Charlie's gun.

"Are you okay?" Damien asked Audrey. He brushed her disheveled hair out of her eyes.

She turned her tear-streaked face up to him. "I'm hurt. I think my collarbone is broken."

He let his fingers linger on her cheek. *I did it. I found her!* Elation warred with confusion, and he pushed the realization of how he'd found her out of his head; he'd deal with that later.

With his knife, he cut the ropes holding her feet. Mindful of her injury and the fact her feet would be numb but soon prickling as the feeling returned to them, he picked her up as gently as he could and let her whimper against his shoulder. The sky, now a leaden gray, drizzled a fine mist on them. He handed her off to the paramedics.

"Don't leave me again," she said.

"I'll stay right here."

She bit her lip, her face pale, and he wished Charlie had left the creature who'd hurt her alive so Damien could punish it himself. The paramedics put her arm in a sling, then put a pillow against her chest and secured the sling against it with a band to keep it immobile.

"Your collarbone might be broken," one of them told her. "We'll take you to the hospital so you can get an x-ray to make sure." As he talked, the other one gave her an injection of something, and Damien relaxed along with her when he saw the relief on her face.

"Damien, is she questionable?" asked Charlie.

"I don't know." She'd had a horrible night, and she didn't even know that her boyfriend was cheating on her.

This morning is gonna get worse before it gets better.

"Take your time," Charlie told him with a hand on his shoulder. "Just remember we don't have much. Maggie's going to need a full report, and I have to notify her of those things in there before anyone else finds them." The E.M.T. stepped away, talking on his radio, and Charlie added in an almost whisper, "We found vampire coffins, too, so that will take care of them, at least."

"What about...?" Damien nodded to the three S.W.A.T. guys who'd gone in with them and had seen the whole thing.

"They're my special ops team for things like this. They won't talk."

"I'll go with her to the E.R."

"No," said Audrey, her speech slurred, "you won't. You have enough to worry about." She wrinkled her nose. "I can call... Kyle. I guess." She looked up at Damien, and he wanted to think she didn't like the idea any more than he did, but he couldn't assume.

Damien glanced at Charlie, who said, "Let Damien stay with you for now. Your boyfriend probably isn't up yet."

"Okay." Either the medicine and injury had mellowed her out, or she knew something was up. Damien suspected the latter.

"I have a lot of things to ask you," he told her. "I can stay with you until he comes. If you decide to call him."

"Fine."

The young blond E.M.T. who had explained things to her returned and helped her into the ambulance, and Damien hopped in beside her. He turned to see Charlie talking to the other young woman, who looked familiar.

"Who is she?" he asked, more to keep Audrey distracted from the pain, although it seemed that whatever they had given her was working. She lay on the stretcher, and her eyes fluttered open and closed.

"She's a water nymph," she mumbled. "Nimue."

He wanted to ask her more, but he noticed the strange looks from the E.M.T.s and remembered not everyone knew about their supernatural drama. It would probably sound strange to any sane, normal human being. Hell, it still sounded strange to him, and he'd seen the were-bats and spoken with vampires. He looked at Audrey, who seemed to be resting, her brows drawn together in a little frown. The thought popped in his head that he hadn't imagined she could be so vulnerable and that she looked pretty adorable lying there on the stretcher. The cynic in him told him he had better be careful for more than his usual reasons.

No one wants to be the rebound guy.

The sounds of an argument distracted him, and he saw Charlie in earnest conversation with the water nymph.

"You have to go. They need to make sure you're not hurt."

"I don't want to go back to that awful place."

Damien pulled himself away from Audrey's side and joined the conversation. "Look," he said, "I promise I won't let them lock you up again. Besides, they might not let me go into the exam room with her, and she might need you."

Nimue turned suspicious eyes to him. "And how do I know you'll keep your promise?"

Damien had no trouble answering honestly. "Because now that I know who your friends are, I'm too frightened not to."

"Go," urged Charlie. "If you wander off again, your mistress may not be able to come and get you."

"I can't return on my own, so I will go with the human." She crossed her arms. "Her dream-weaving got us rescued. This will allow me to pay my debt. But if you try to lock me up again..."

A cold drop of water plopped on to Damien's forehead.

Damien raised his hands. "I get it."

DAMIEN HELD Audrey's hand the entire ride to the E.R. She closed her eyes, her face pinched against the pain, and he wished he'd thought to make Charlie break the news to her that when they had talked to Kyle, he hadn't been alone.

He looked away, too tired to think about how to handle that sticky situation, and tried to remember where he had seen the blond E.M.T. before. He was so lost in his thoughts that he didn't notice they had reached the E.R. entrance until the doors opened and they wheeled her out.

"Officer Lewis?" The E.M.T.'s voice snapped him out of his pondering.

"Yes?"

"They need to see what happened to her collarbone and make sure there aren't other injuries. The other young lady can come back with us. You may want to stay close by in case they need to ask you about how Ms. Sonoma got hurt."

"I wish I knew," he said, more to himself. "Ms. Nimue can likely help you more with that. And this has been driving me nuts. Where do I know you from?"

"I was there when Doctor Rizzo was shot." The young man sighed. "I wish I could've gotten there sooner."

"I'm sure you did the best you could."

Now Damien added guilt to the stew of emotions that roiled just beneath the surface of his thoughts, guilt that he found Audrey so attractive in her vulnerability and that he hadn't been able to prevent what had happened to Rizzo. Or to her. He decided to wander out to the waiting room and watch television until the nurses called him back. He didn't have to wait long.

"Officer Lewis?" It was the dark-skinned nurse he'd talked to on the morning Rizzo was shot. So much for distraction.

"Yes?"

"Would you like to see Doctor Rizzo while you're waiting? He's in a coma, but he may know you're there. He'd probably like it, actually. He hasn't had any visitors outside of the hospital staff." She shook her head. "No family or anything."

"Sure, but—" His desire to see Rizzo warred with his need to stay close to Audrey.

"I'll let them know where to find you."

She led him to the I.C.U. where the patients each lay in a separate glassed-in room. Rizzo looked fragile and sunken, the I.V. tubes snaking out of his arms. Without his eyes twinkling behind his glasses, he looked more like an old man and less like the vibrant doctor Damien knew.

Damien sat on the chair by the bedside and forced himself to look at the man he'd considered to be a force of nature. He'd heard that people in comas knew if others were talking to them, so he decided to give it a try.

"Wow, old friend, you wouldn't believe the last couple of days. It seems like there's a whole world I had no idea existed, and between the two of us," he said and looked around to make sure no one heard him, "it scares the shit out of me. My grandmother knew about it, and we all thought she was hallucinating. But she, well, she couldn't handle it."

He looked down at his hands, not sure how to phrase things. The words stuck in his throat, but then he remembered the books in Rizzo's office.

"I don't know how much of this you can hear, but I think you'll believe it because of what I know about you..." He went on to tell him about Persephone, the nymphs, Maggie, Audrey, the cheating boyfriend, and Charlie being mixed up in it, too. Then about his dream and how it had led had them right to the captives.

"I know it sounds silly to say that my reality has been turned upside down when you're in a freaking coma, Arthur, but that's how I feel. It's like I've stepped out of the world I knew and can't go back. Maybe I don't want to be a detective, not if this is what I have to deal with."

He thought Rizzo's eyes moved beneath his eyelids, but he wasn't sure.

"And the weirdest thing is that I think you knew about it, and you were trying to ease me into it with that book you loaned me. I haven't even had time to read it with all the crap that's gone down. I don't need to read about the gods and goddesses anymore because I've met some of them. How crazy does that sound? They're not myths, they're real."

He put his face in his hands and hoped no one heard him. He recalled his grandmother saying something similar just before they'd locked her away in a nursing home for mentally unstable old people. She'd died within a month.

"I really need you to wake up, Arthur. I know you're hurt and hurting, but I really need you to help me make sense of all of this."

Rizzo's face didn't change. Damien watched him so intently he didn't realize he breathed along with the rhythm of the E.K.G. monitor, nor was he aware when he closed his eyes and succumbed to the adrenaline crash from the morning, the sleep deficit of the past two days, and the relief at being able to tell everything to a sympathetic listener.

He opened his eyes to a sidewalk swirling with mist.

"It's about time you found me," Rizzo grumbled.

11

————————

Lyle Ames woke, stretched, and watched the sun rise over the Atlanta skyline. Last night had been a particularly good one in the temple. He thought he'd recognized the two venture capitalists to whom he had given a tour earlier that week and who had left with samples. That was encouraging. Support was good, addiction even better.

He looked down to the street and saw a familiar brown sedan parked across from his building. So Amelia's private investigator was earning his keep. Not that he'd have anything interesting to report other than her husband had slept in his office again. Lyle didn't mind the man's presence or the insignificant toll the man's fees would put on his finances. On the contrary, it would be more material for the sales portfolio: "Guaranteed P.I.-proof."

After a quick shower and shave in his private full bathroom, which he'd stocked with work clothes for times like these, he was ready to face the day. The first buzz from his secretary after he'd sent her to fetch a cappuccino from the coffee place on the corner put him in a cautious mood.

"Mr. Zeus to see you, sir."

"Send him in."

Mr. Zeus, or just Zeus to his friends, strode into the room, and immediately the lights flickered out.

"I told you never to have that fluorescent crap on while I'm in here."

"I apologize, Zeus, but I didn't have much warning."

Lyle studied his business partner and once again tried to ascertain what gave the man such presence. Zeus had been straight with him and let him know that he was a Greek god—and he'd proven that fact many times in their acquaintance, leaving no room for skepticism—but there had to be something more, something that could be translated and used by mortals. If nothing else, maybe Lyle could get him into motivational speaking.

"And to what do I owe the honor of your visit? Things are going well with the investors, and didn't you say you weren't going to appear here too much? You don't want Hera to get suspicious."

"Hera is out of Olympus today, and things are not going as planned." Zeus took a seat in one of the overstuffed leather chairs and turned toward one bank of windows. "The goddess Persephone has been rescued and will be returned to Olympus shortly. One nymph has escaped, the other one killed and trapped in Hades, and there's a certain dream weaver who needs to be monitored. Also, we've come to the attention of the authorities."

"The police? But how?" Lyle frowned. "And what would they care? We're not breaking any laws."

"No." The way Zeus looked at him made him feel all of six inches tall. "The supernatural authorities, the Truth Seekers."

"Right." Lyle tried to appear like he knew what those were. *Think in two worlds,* he reminded himself. "So our risks have increased?"

"Luckily they have not found the temple, and I'll keep it

such that they won't until we have all the links in place, and it will be too hard to destroy it."

Lyle really needed that cappuccino. His brain chugged along, processing what Zeus had been telling him. "Wait a second. You said one nymph has escaped?"

The look on Zeus' face made Lyle wish he hadn't asked, and the tone of Zeus's voice reminded him of the ominous rumble of an approaching storm. "The nymph has been rescued by the human authorities."

The muscles in Lyle's face loosened, and his jaw dropped. "From the warehouse?"

"Yes, from the warehouse."

"But they could then trace it all back to us. To me." He got up and faced the window, pressing his fingers against the cold glass to ground himself. After a deep breath, he turned and asked, "Okay. What do you need me to do?"

"I'll make the paper trail disappear. The humans won't have much time for close investigation yet. My sources tell me that the dream weaver has been damaged and is in the hospital." Zeus' smile made Lyle shiver. "She has been accompanied by a nymph named Nimue."

"The one who *escaped*. I remember. Are the barriers still in place to keep her from returning to the C.U.?" Lyle sat behind his desk. He knew the large mahogany piece of furniture couldn't protect him from the god's wrath, but it helped him to feel secure and powerful.

"Yes. Which means that her mistress will be here to fetch her soon."

The smile on Lyle's face mirrored Zeus' own. "So we can take her then. Won't she be angry her other nymph was killed?"

"The other one belonged to Persephone, so she was expendable," Zeus said. "As for capturing Nimue's mistress, I don't want to use the vampires and were-bats. Any supernatural activity will be too obvious. I shall dismiss the vamps and keep a minimum number of were-bats to guard the transfer site."

Lyle pondered the logistics. "I'll get my men on it. Your description still applies, correct?"

"I'll have Toady give you the materials you need to trap her here. Let me know when you have succeeded."

"Will do."

"Oh, and Lyle?"

"Yes?"

"If you fail at this, all will be lost." Zeus stood and leaned forward on the desk, his fingertips touching the surface. He towered over Ames, and the angle of the light highlighted the harsh planes beneath the carefully groomed exterior. "More than the mortal investors will be unhappy if this falls through."

Lyle watched Zeus turn and walk out the door. He waited for his heart to stop pounding in his ears, picked up the phone, and dialed with trembling fingers.

"You're looking a lot better here than in the hospital," Damien said. He wore his police uniform and stood beside Arthur. *Even if this isn't real, I'll take it.*

"As are you. You look like you're not missing any sleep in spite of all your adventures." Arthur looked hale and well-rested. He wore a long white robe and was accompanied by an owl and a small silver dragon.

Damien laughed, but he suspected he still had dark circles under his eyes even in the dream world. "I was hoping you could tell me what's going on."

"I'm not sure, but I know I'm not supposed to be stuck here like I am." He huffed his frustration. "I got a summons, so I take it I'm supposed to find something. Maybe it's you."

Damien touched the weapon in the holster at his belt. "At least I'm armed this time. Lead the way, Doctor."

"That will likely not help you here, but if it helps you feel better..."

The wind picked up again, and Damien shivered even though he now wore his police windbreaker. Arthur's owl took wing and landed on a scrawny tree, the dragon following. The mist retreated to show a familiar area: an open rectangular concrete "square" with a bandstand surrounded by grass, on which picnic tables stood empty.

"Let's go that way," Arthur suggested and pointed toward the stairs to their right, which led to a long sidewalk with shops and restaurants, all closed and dark. "My spirit guide is telling me that's our direction."

"Your what? I've heard that somewhere before." Damien followed him. His instincts told him to be careful, but also that Arthur could protect him, although he didn't know how.

"It's a projection of your personality into the dream world, the unconscious part of you that's in touch with the deeper, more intuitive aspects of the spiritual realm."

"Do I have one?" He hoped it might be the dragon; the small creature was fascinating to watch as she darted about. She flew more smoothly than a bird, her flowing movements like an underwater creature.

"Everybody has one, but you must accept the reality of this realm and your experiences before it shows itself to you. The dragon is accompanying us temporarily until she finds her own human."

"Oh."

Damien's rational mind refused to let go of the desire for a logical, concrete explanation for everything, including the fact that it was morning, and they walked through a deserted city that was never quiet during the day. No cars lined the streets or competed for the few coveted parking spaces. Even the subway station stood empty. The only noises that came to his ears were their footsteps and the wind. And something else.

"Stop for a moment," Arthur said, and Damien halted. He turned his head and caught it, a whooshing sound. Arthur put a finger on his lips and motioned for Damien to follow with his other hand.

The sound stopped and started, but it soon became apparent that it came from the Java Lemur coffee shop. They walked in the door to find chaos.

"What the...?" Damien's jaw dropped. He'd seen the place during the morning rush, but it had never been as wild as this.

The steaming of dairy products for espresso drinks punctuated the various conversations of a multitude of beings. A giant spider stood behind the counter at the top of the short flight of steps and prepared beverages with two legs, served baked goods with two, counted out change with two more, and stood on the others. Dwarves, elves, sprites, fairies, nymphs, and any other creature that would come out in daylight sat in Java Lemur, drank coffee beverages, read the human books and magazines, and laughed and chatted with others of its kind.

Now I must be the one who's touched. Damien tasted acid at the back of his throat and backed through the door. "I'm out of here."

"I think the psychological literature classifies this as flooding," Rizzo said, "or hitting you with all your fears at once." He grabbed the back of the departing Damien's jacket and dragged him back through the door. Now Damien knew with certainty they were in another realm; in reality, Arthur would never be strong enough to manhandle a police officer, at least not from what he could tell. Or maybe he had underestimated how much strength the waking world Arthur hid in his spare frame. The doctor held Damien's wrist and brought him through the shop, up the short flight of stairs, and to the coffee bar.

"What would you like?" he asked.

Damien shot him a dirty look but said, "Coffee, black."

"I'll have a café mocha. I've wandered a long way to come here."

The spider served them and pointed them to the condiment area.

"Do we need to pay you now?" Arthur asked.

"No," the spider replied in a sibilant voice. "Her Graciousness invited you and will cover your bill."

"Her who?" asked Damien.

"That one." The spider pointed to a petite woman in a silk beige suit and dual-toned designer pumps who stood behind them. Diamonds flashed at her neck, wrists, and ears, and her honey-colored hair was pulled back loosely in a tortoiseshell clip. She regarded them with the even, steady gaze of a queen who is accustomed to dealing with uncooperative subjects and a husband who refused to be ruled.

"Milady." Arthur bowed, as did Damien, if a bit awkwardly.

"Come join me, gentlemen," she said. "Arachne, I'll have another soy latte."

"Yes, Majesty."

They followed her to the wine bar part of the café, which was quieter. Arthur pulled one of the high stools away from a tall table, and she accepted the seat. He and Damien joined her. She studied them with golden eyes, and Damien couldn't help but notice that she was one of the most beautiful women he'd ever seen. The look on Arthur's face said he felt the same.

"Your thoughts are loud, Doctor," she said to Arthur, "but I do appreciate the compliment. And who, pray tell, is your handsome companion?"

"This is Damien Lewis, a police officer here in Decatur, Milady. He has been involved in our, shall we say, interesting situation. More than I have, actually." He winced when Damien kicked him under the table.

Can she hear what I'm thinking? Oh crap, oh crap.

"I see. Yes, the situation is, indeed, interesting." She nodded to Arachne, who brought out her soy latte and another mocha for Arthur. She blew on her drink and sipped the foam.

Damien stuffed his urge to get the hell out of there and forced himself to simply wait for the goddess, as he had identified her, to continue the conversation. From her demeanor and command, he guessed she was high-ranking, possibly even Hera. He sipped his coffee and glanced out the window, where a group of fauns and nymphs cavorted on the patio and sloshed red wine from a cask into waiting glasses.

"I don't have much time to explain," the goddess told them. "Zeus is up to something. I spoke with Margaret earlier, but I just can't communicate with her. That's why I summoned you—you're involved in this, if reluctantly." She inclined her head toward Arthur. "And you, poor creature, are stuck and cannot change form. Something is definitely amiss."

Damien raised his eyebrows at Arthur. "What does she mean?"

"There's no time to explain now," Arthur said and patted Damien on the arm. "What do you think your husband is planning, Your Highness?" he asked the goddess, who must be Hera.

"I don't know, but I fear that some of our number may be in danger. Zeus is so focused on his goals sometimes that he fails to see how his wild schemes affect others." She sighed. "Not that that's ever concerned him."

Damien spoke directly to the goddess for the first time. "Did Persephone make it back?"

Hera inclined her head. "Yes, but with difficulty, and that whole situation is worrisome in itself. The barriers between our world and yours are crumbling, and something caused Persephone to tumble through and not be able to return. Others have disappeared since she did. You were probably too busy chasing her to notice."

Stung, Damien sat back. "I haven't recovered any more wandering women or heard of anyone else who did."

"Who else has disappeared?" Arthur asked and nudged Damien, who got the message: *don't be defensive.*

"Mostly nymphs, dryads, and other female immortals. I have lost count, but several of my number are missing. Hestia is up in arms about her bookkeeper being gone. The one who seems to be missing the highest number of attendants, or maybe she's complaining the most, is Aphrodite."

"The goddess of love?" Damien asked. At least he remembered that much.

"Precisely, although I would term it lust. She's quite perturbed, as you can imagine. She's even had to start dressing herself without assistance."

Arthur coughed to hide a laugh. "And what may we do for you, Lady?"

"You need to figure out who the human side of it is. If it was another immortal, I would have been able to find them, but there are too many of you. I need to know who is taking our ladies and how they're doing it. And also, if any of us, the Twelve, are in danger or if Persephone's disappearance was accidental."

"That's a tall order, Milady," Damien said, "but I would like to know who was behind Audrey's kidnapping, although the creatures that held her didn't look human."

"Audrey who?" Arthur rubbed his temples.

"Audrey Aurora Sonoma. She's a writer."

Arthur put his mocha cup down hard, his hands trembling. "Is she all right?"

"She's in the same hospital you are, likely with a broken collarbone, but she'll recover."

Hera dragged Damien's attention away from the strangely perturbed Arthur when she touched his hand with one slender finger. "That's the other reason you need to help me, young officer. The erosion of the boundaries between our worlds will also allow vampires, werewolves, and gods know what else to cross through. Those of you in law enforcement will be the first to know, and you will soon be overwhelmed."

"Point taken."

"Now I must be away. I need to keep an eye on my husband."

Arthur and Damien stood and bowed, and she made descending from the chair into a graceful action even though her feet had dangled from it.

"Thank you, gentlemen. I'm glad to know that manners haven't completely vanished."

When she reached the door, she turned and blew them a kiss. It hit Damien like a cold wind and jolted him awake.

12

Damien woke to the clamor of nurses and doctors rushing into the room in response to the alarm bells on Arthur's machines. The older man watched them with shrewd eyes while they checked everything and determined that something must have triggered an alarm when he'd jolted awake.

"How are you feeling, Arthur?" asked a large, gray-haired man in purple scrubs.

"I've been better."

One of the nurses pointed to Damien. "This young man was talking to him. I think he helped him come back."

"I wouldn't argue with that," Arthur replied. "Now, I know you all are excited, but please leave me alone with him for a few minutes."

After some grumbling, they filed out, and Arthur motioned for Damien to lean closer.

"What do you remember about what you were dreaming?"

"I dreamed we were at the Java Lemur having coffee with the Greek goddess Hera." His other questions—what the hell was Arthur, and how did he know Audrey?—wanted to tumble out, but Arthur held up a hand.

"Good, and that was no dream. You need to take what she told us to the friends who dragged you into this. They'll know what to do with it."

"But I don't want to leave you." Damien studied his friend, whose vigor of a few moments ago had deserted him and left him looking like a frail old man.

"Ah, but you must. You have to watch over Audrey since I cannot."

"How do you know her?"

"No time for that now, boy. Every moment I'm here will make it harder for me to find my true path again. But there is one more thing."

"Anything."

"Everything in my office is yours. My will is in the bottom left-hand drawer of the desk."

"Why are you talking like that?"

"There are certain risks in what I am doing, and I am not certain I can return to this form, especially since my work here is almost done."

"But you're better now." Tears pricked Damien's eyes. "You don't have to return to that place."

"But I do. It's important. Don't be scared by what will happen next. Remember, this is only a shell."

"What are you talking about?"

"Go look at some of my books. You'll find the answers. Don't worry—this old bird still has some tricks in him. Go report Hera's message to your friends."

Damien squeezed the old man's hand and backed out of the room. At the entrance of the I.C.U. he turned to see a white owl perched on the end of Arthur's bed. Tears still stung the corners of his eyes but wouldn't emerge to blur the room, which erupted in alarms, and a code was called.

The owl, unperturbed, looked at him as if to say, "Go!" and disappeared.

Damien turned and stumbled right into Charlie.

"Dude, there you are."

Charlie looked blurry through the tears that finally fell. Damien searched his brain. *What am I supposed to tell him?*

"Uh oh, that code is Rizzo, isn't it?"

Charlie's strong hand guided him down the hall to the elevator and then somewhere that seemed familiar. No matter how many times he blinked, he couldn't clear his eyes. He wondered if there was something wrong with him, if he had some sort of brain damage from having traveled to the Collective Unconscious again. The weight on his chest made it difficult to take a full breath.

He turned to go back, to tell Arthur not to be a fool, but Charlie sat him down in the large leather chair behind Arthur Rizzo's desk, and his legs wouldn't obey his command to stand. He looked around to get his bearings. The office had been cleaned, the chaos organized, and all the books returned to their shelves.

"Your girl is doing fine," Charlie was saying. "Luckily it was only a nasty bruise. She'll have her arm in a sling for a while as it heals, but she'll get better. They sedated her so she wouldn't feel it while they examined it, so she's asleep now."

Damien could only nod. The words he tried to say felt thick in his throat. Something held him to the chair, and he couldn't move, like in a nightmare where something chased him, but he was rooted to the spot.

"And Maggie is on her way here. She sent Persephone back to the C.U. in Demeter's care."

"Okay." The word crawled out of his mouth.

"So now we're back to square one, trying to find out who did this and why. The were-bats were no use, of course. My aim was too good, but I couldn't have them biting anyone. Their bodies disintegrated as soon as the sun came up. They're practically unintelligible anyway."

Damien shrugged. He didn't care about were-things, he just wanted Charlie to stop talking so he could figure out what he needed to tell him, why his brain had become paralyzed like his body. Then he could get home, into his bed, and away from the hospital.

Something told him Arthur could have been saved, but after seeing the owl at the foot of the bed, he wasn't sure.

And if his body is still alive, is he brain dead? Will he ever be the same? How does he know Audrey, and what did he mean, protect her? What is he, really?

"So you've gotten, what? Two hours of sleep, three tops for the past couple of nights, huh?" Charlie plopped in one of the armchairs on the other side of the desk. "No wonder you look like hell. At least your eyes aren't leaking anymore."

"For gods' sake, Charlie, give the man a break." Maggie strode into the room. "He's had a rough past few hours."

Maggie! I'm supposed to tell her something to do with Arthur.

"Can't you see he's overwhelmed and grieving? Even I'm not sure if Rizzo's going to make it. That was a big risk he took, and for Hera to bump him out like that..." She balled her hands into fists. "Those meddling bitches. The lives of others mean nothing to them. Nothing!"

Damien stared at her, open-mouthed. So did Charlie, who stood and cupped her shoulders with his hands. He tilted her chin up so he could look into her eyes, and the tight muscles in her jaw relaxed.

"I know you're upset," he told her, "but we have work to do, darlin'."

"Right." She took a deep breath and relaxed her fists. She also stepped back from Charlie, who wasn't quick enough to hide the disappointment that flashed over his face.

She didn't seem to notice, or if she did, ignored him. "I wish

I had known she wanted to meet with the two of you. I'm sorry, Damien, I could have stopped her."

Damien almost felt sorry for Charlie, but he couldn't allow whatever was going on between the two of them to distract him. "From doing what?"

"From almost killing him, and the *almost* isn't a guarantee right now. But you have a message, don't you?" She brushed the hair back from his forehead and looked into his eyes. She had taken her lenses off, and her eyes shone gold. They drew him into their comfort and warmth.

"I have a message," he repeated. His mind floated on a warm pool of honey, his thoughts going out from his head like threads on the surface.

"Something from a goddess?"

"A goddess. Beautiful diamonds." And a big spider, but that's not what she wanted to know.

"What did she say?"

"That Zeus is up to something. A mortal is helping. Boundaries erode. We're all in danger. More girls are missing, and she fears for the Twelve."

"As we suspected," Maggie murmured. She blinked, and the spell was broken. She returned her purple glasses to her nose.

"All right, then, sweetie," she whispered. "Go check on your girl. She can comfort you and probably needs it herself." She combed her fingers through his hair—*oh, that feels good*—and his eyelids grew heavy, although he still sat in Rizzo's office chair.

This time when he slept, he dreamed of a secluded spot by a rushing river where glowing yellow eyes watched him from the mist.

~

THE PAIN in Audrey's back and shoulder finally subsided to a dull ache. The dim light in the room where they'd taken her for x-rays had soothed her into closing her eyes, for just a moment. *Ah, blessed medications*, she thought. She floated in a gentle mist, and she heard music, some sort of classical, but the instruments didn't sound familiar. A breeze caressed her face.

"If this is some sort of dream journey, I'm not interested," she murmured. "See? I'm not opening my eyes."

"Well, darlin', if you don't open your eyes, you can't see fabulous me again."

Audrey peeked, hoping she wouldn't be on Olympus again. Nope. Candles sparkled on a thousand amethyst crystals in Zinfandel's cave. She floated a foot off the ground on what looked like a pillow of mist, but which felt like she'd always imagined a cloud would: infinitely softer and fluffier than any human-made pillows, but still substantive enough to support her. She maneuvered herself so that her feet touched the ground, and the mist gently dissipated to allow her to sit on the grassy floor, her back against the wall.

"What was that?"

"An air elemental who owed me a favor," Zin said. "I told him you'd been hurt in your waking world and that you'd need a little Zin-style T.L.C." He snorted. "And he said he'd rather support your frame than my fat ass any day."

She hid a smile. "Yeah, I definitely need something. It's been quite a day."

"Mmm, I'm sure. You've seen and heard more in a day than most of your kind will experience in their wildest dreams in a lifetime."

"I could've done without most of it, to be honest." She looked down at her hands and blinked back tears. The helplessness rushed back, and she focused on where she sat. She hadn't felt like that since the night when...

No, she couldn't think about that right now. One trauma was enough for the day.

Zinfandel handed her a cup of steaming liquid. "Like what? The vampires and were-bats?"

She breathed in the fragrant steam with a shuddering breath. Green tea chai, her favorite. "Would you believe I'm more bothered by the fact that Damien had to come and rescue me? I don't need a knight in shining armor."

"Ooh, that handsome policeman? Why in the world would that bother you, darlin'?"

Why wouldn't it? But she decided not to be snippy with her host. "It's hard to explain. I prefer to take care of myself."

"Well, honey, I'm afraid you're in his debt now. He's better for you than that med student you're dating, as cute as he is. Just like a little surfer boy."

"Kyle? Yeah. I know I need to do something about him, as boring as he seems." She looked at her tea, not wanting to meet Zin's eyes.

The dragon snorted, and twin plumes of smoke came out of his nostrils. "Let's just say there's been more than your sand in his trunks lately."

"What's that supposed to mean?" But she knew. She'd called him from the E.R. and got his voicemail. Then she'd texted him, but he hadn't responded in spite of her putting a 911 in it. And it was supposedly a day off.

"Just that he's not as boring as you'd suppose. But that's a conversation for a different time and place."

"Is there something going on I should know about?" *Just go ahead and confirm it for me.*

Zinfandel put a paw on her shoulder, and she met his coaster-sized golden eyes. "I'm just saying that you must've suspected something. Why did you call for Damien instead of him when you were kidnapped?"

"Because Kyle's not involved in all this crazy supernatural stuff, and he wouldn't have followed a dream."

The dragon crossed his arms and fixed her with a skeptical look. "I bet he didn't even cross your mind."

Audrey's cheeks heated, and she had to look away. "Fine, you're right. I didn't think of him or my stepbrother, who might've been able to handle the weirdness, but who's been M.I.A. since yesterday morning. He would've just said 'I told you so,' anyway."

"He's not available, honey. He's stuck somewhere, but it's not my place to tell you where."

Audrey's breath caught. "Is he okay? He's the only family I have left."

"He's tougher than you think, darling, but it may be a while before you see him again. As for Kyle..."

"Look, Zin, I've been independent since my mother died five years ago. I make my own living, I make my own schedule, and I make my own decisions. If Kyle had rescued me—if he had the balls, which I doubt—I would owe him something."

"And now you owe the handsome Officer Lewis."

"I know." She put her head on her knees. "That's exactly the problem. I grant you, he's got potential, but..."

"Butt? A nice one at that."

"No, silly." She scowled at the dragon. "But I need to go into a relationship as an equal, not a debtor, and I never date cops. My father was one, and one night he didn't come home. My mother died of a broken heart after suffering for a decade. So it's safer to just keep him at a distance. Even if he is a good kisser."

"Oh. My. Gods." The voice was a woman's, and it seemed to come from the air itself. "What drama! I swear, why do I let my son waste his arrows on you idiots?"

The owner of the voice materialized. First, autumn blue eyes blinked at Audrey from the middle of the cave, then long, flowing blonde hair appeared and framed a face that most cosmetics models would die for. Her flawless body, rather than being super-thin, displayed womanly curves while still trim and toned. Her breasts peaked in perfect, ripe mounds over the bodice of her diaphanous gown made of mist and rainbows. It swirled around her and provided enticing glimpses here and there but never gave away the entire show. Audrey couldn't stop staring, and something made her scramble to her feet. She felt drab and frumpy next to the goddess, even though she wore a gown of green and white satin.

"Milady," she said and curtseyed.

"Human." The goddess inclined her head. "I felt the potential for heartbreak in the air and decided to investigate. I'd normally send one of my girls, but they appear to have run off. That's why I'm wearing this old thing." She gestured to her gown.

"All of them?" asked Audrey. Hadn't Nimue been one of Aphrodite's nymphs?

"Ahem," Zinfandel broke in. "Your Radiance, may I introduce Audrey Aurora Sonoma? She's one of the humans working with Margaret of Cornwall, the Truth Seeker who is trying to locate the missing nymphs. Audrey, this is Her Radiance, the Goddess Aphrodite."

Audrey curtseyed again. Even annoyed, Aphrodite lit up the cave like a sparkling diamond, and Audrey couldn't tear her eyes away from her.

"Ah, and have you seen any of my girls, um, Annie?"

"It's Audrey, and yes, I've met Nimue."

"In fact, Audrey was instrumental in securing Nimue's release from the vampires and were-bats who kidnapped them," Zin put in.

Aphrodite arched an eyebrow and looked around the cave. "And where is the silly girl? Cupid—I swear, one of these days I'm going to slap that boy—confessed to me he's been using my maids for target practice, and Nimue fell for some sailor, slipped away, and ran off down the beach."

Audrey tried to hide her smile. "She's still in the waking world."

"Well, bring her back."

"'Tis not that easy, I'm afraid, Your Radiance," Zinfandel said and proffered white wine in a crystal glass with pearls at the bottom.

"No diamonds?" she asked with a pout.

"Fresh out. But as I was saying, it's not easy to just zap them back once they've fallen through. It requires the direct intervention of a god or goddess. Even Demeter had to bring Persephone back herself."

"She's a silly girl anyway. Never was able to handle being away from Mummy's side." Aphrodite dismissed her fellow goddess with a wave of her hand. "So what you're saying is that I'll have to go there myself and gather them up?" Her cupid's bow lips frowned, but she schooled them into a neutral position. Audrey wondered if the perfect goddess was afraid of getting wrinkles.

"You, Amy, can you take me to her?"

"Um, Audrey. And my body is confined to a hospital bed right now, Your Radiance. I'm sure that when I wake up, there will be someone there who can help you find her."

"Hmmm." Aphrodite put a French-manicured nail to her lips, leaned down, and looked deep into Audrey's eyes. "Yes, I'm seeing some intriguing possibilities there. The dark-haired, gray-eyed one especially."

Audrey clenched her teeth and attempted to clear her mind, but of course it didn't work.

"Oh, not to worry, you can have him when I'm done with him."

Audrey's stomach flipped, and her face flushed as the words tripped off her tongue. "I don't want you to come with me."

"What? Afraid you'll lose him?" Aphrodite laughed, but it was not the delightful sound that should have come from such a physically flawless being. "Don't worry, little girl, once I'm done with him, he'll be schooled in ways that most women only dream about. Of course, there's the small problem of him always pining away for me after I leave him, but I'm sure you can overlook that."

"I would never *overlook* that. Tell your son to stay away from him, and you do the same, and I'll let you come with me." Audrey put as much conviction behind her words as she could.

"Very well then, Addie, I'll stay away from your policeman. But you're not so noble in your intentions, either. I see a lot of Artemis in you—you have the potential for breaking hearts as well. Once a man starts stepping on your precious independence, you're out of there emotionally, if not physically. What do you think happened with your poor Kyle?"

"I don't know. Why don't *you* tell me what happened to Kyle?"

"Oops, you don't know?" The goddess held a hand over her mouth in mock horror.

"Your Radiance," Zin broke in, "it is not for her to learn in this world." Even though he'd been hinting at it.

Audrey made a mental note to dump Kyle's cheating ass as soon as she woke up.

"Then she'll learn soon enough. And your precious Damien will tell you. But I can assure you of this, Allie. You're the one who drove him away."

Audrey said nothing, but she trembled inside. *Could that be true? Am I chasing away my lovers because I don't want to depend on them?*

"Your Radiance? Audrey?" Zinfandel headed off the questions Audrey wanted to ask. "If you're going, you should go now. Audrey, the drugs are about to wear off, and you're probably going to wake up."

"I can feel it." Indeed, her eyelids felt heavy, and everything turned foggy around the edges.

"I'll follow you there," Aphrodite told her. "Now, Zinfandel, what should I wear?"

"Oh, Your Radiance, I have just the thing..."

13

———

Damien sat on the rock by the river and pondered the rushing water. And the glowing eyes peering at him through the fog. In spite of the eeriness of the situation, he felt no threat. Arthur would say to allow things to happen in their own time. *Arthur...*

What the hell had happened? Voices murmured around him, but they sounded like they came from the other side of a wall, and he couldn't make out what they said. He didn't care. To his back was a long street that disappeared into the mist about ten feet behind him. The fog's cold wetness pressed in on him and swirled over the river, but a shimmering barrier prevented it from spreading to the landscape on the other shore. He looked over a meadow, beyond which small, rolling hills crested like waves into snow-capped mountains. The tall grasses of the meadow undulated in a breeze he couldn't feel.

He looked up and down the path that paralleled the opposite riverbank and hoped he would see a familiar figure in a long wool robe appear, but no one came. He yearned to know whether Arthur would make it and whether they had any chance in hell of figuring this thing out. He knew he couldn't do it on his own and wished for Charlie's easy confidence. He'd never seen his friend get down, not even in the face of hopeless odds. Maybe that's why Charlie had been so much more successful than he had—he had a better attitude.

"Or luck," he said out loud, and the sound of his own voice startled him. Even the river hushed like it waited to hear what he would say next.

"Okay, fine." He took a deep breath. "This sucks. I don't want to be in the middle of this, and I want Arthur to be well. I want Audrey to be okay and to know that she's not going to be *touched* or crazy or changed permanently by all this."

"But haven't you been changed?"

The voice—more in his head than in his ears—startled him, and he nearly fell off the rock and into the water. He looked behind the boulder and saw the eyes had grown a face and large body covered in fur—a large black dog. *No,* he corrected himself, *that's a wolf.*

"Congratulations, genius. That's animal naming 101."

Anger at the creature's insolence flared in Damien's chest, but then he realized this must be his spirit guide. If it was truly a part of him, he shouldn't be surprised it had a penchant for sarcasm.

"Are you my spirit guide?" he asked.

"Correct again. No wonder you were picked for this journey."

This time, Damien couldn't tell whether the animal was being serious or facetious. He went for serious.

"What do you mean, picked for the journey?"

"Surely you don't think that you and the others are here by acci-dent, do you? Everyone has a road they must walk, or several. Some are touched by the divine, others are stuck in the mundane."

"Wait a second, I'm not touched."

"Oh, aren't you? The wolf cocked its head, a doggy smile on its face. *"If you're not now, then you will be soon."*

"What do you mean?" He choked on the words.

The wolf's ears twitched. *"The girl is waking. You should go to her before it's too late. She is playing with fire."*

"Right. Like I need any advice from you on how to handle women. I'm good at getting myself into trouble with them on my own."

This time the wolf said nothing. Damien grew heavy like he would melt through the rock he sat on, and the scenery swirled together and solidified into a wooden door.

"Go to her..."

AUDREY WOKE IN A BED, but it wasn't a hospital room. The sheets under her fingertips had a soft, slippery feel, and they caressed her naked breasts and whispered around her.

"What in the world?" She struggled to her elbows before remembering she needed to be careful with her left arm, but it didn't hurt. "Oh, a regular dream, thank goodness. The drugs must still be working."

She looked around and found she lay in a bed with satin purple sheets—classy!—and velvet drapes edged with gold fringe.

"Lovely. I've dreamed myself into the boudoir of Henry the Eighth," she mumbled. She covered herself with as much of the top sheet as she could gather since it didn't want to become untucked from the bed and peeked out from between the bed curtains. A fire sent flickering light and shadow over the stone walls, and a bright moon shone in fragments through a diamond-pane window. A small table held a tray with a decanter of red wine and two glasses.

A red velvet robe appeared beside her, so she got out of bed, put it on, and stepped into thick burgundy-colored slippers.

The fire beckoned her, and she moved toward it, holding out her hands for warmth.

"Now this is my kind of dream. Am I weaving this?"

As if in response, candles flickered to life on the mantelpiece, which was of rough-hewn wood, and in sconces on the walls. She got the sense this was someone's romantic hideaway, particularly when her ears picked up the sounds of the woods at night around her. An owl hooted in the distance, and a stream flowed nearby.

"The question is, who am I waiting for?"

A door opened on the opposite side of the bed from where she stood, and she turned and hugged the robe around her tightly.

Please don't be a fat king, please don't be a fat king...

Damien walked around the bed. His face showed the same emotions she was sure hers reflected: wonder, curiosity, and caution. He wore tan breeches and a flowing white shirt straight off a romance novel cover. It stood open to reveal his drool-worthy physique and a sprinkling of soft hair over hard pectoral and ab muscles. She recalled what Aphrodite had said, how she would always drive men away due to her independence.

Well, this is a dream. I might as well enjoy it while it lasts since we can never have anything in waking life. As handsome as he is, he's still too big a risk.

"Welcome," she said with a smile she hoped didn't appear nervous. Why would she be nervous? It wasn't really him. "Would you like a glass of wine?"

Damien shook his head like he was in a trance and then smiled at her.

"I would love one," he told her. She poured from the decanter, and the cut crystal goblet in her hand felt heavier than she would have expected. Typically dream objects were light.

"To us and our dreams," she said, raising her glass.

His eyes dropped to her chest. Her robe had opened more to reveal the edge of one areola, and she resisted the instinctive urge to close it.

"Perhaps we should take our wine to bed," he said, his voice low. It vibrated through her, making her want him to keep talking as they followed his suggestion.

"Why not?" she asked. "None of this is real, so there's no threat."

"And no chance of me passing along my flawed genes," he said and exhaled like he was getting a big secret off his chest.

She placed a warm hand on his cheek. "What flawed genes? If they gave you those stunning eyes, I can't complain about them." Her hand dropped from his face to his chest, and she tangled her fingers in his chest hair.

"They're my grandmother's eyes. I'm afraid that's not all I inherited from her."

"Don't worry about it. It doesn't matter here." She pressed herself to him, and he undid her sash. The fabric fell open, and she allowed her breasts to pillow against his chest. He slid a hand under the robe and cupped her bottom. The wine glass disappeared from his hand, and he ran his fingers through her hair and finally grasped her head so he could bring her mouth to his.

His kiss was even sweeter than it had been in the patrol car, all spice and wine, and the smell of the smoke of the fire on his skin gave him an otherworldly and manly scent. She ran her other hand—her wine glass had vanished, too—over his back and under his shirt. When they came up for air, they both panted.

"Bed," Damien growled. His erection pressed against the front of his pants.

"Yes," she replied and took him by the hand. He didn't resist as she led him.

Audrey tied the curtains back so the little room within a room would be lit by the fire. She wanted to be able to see Damien fully with every expression and every ripple of his muscles.

Damn, girl, you do know how to build a dream guy. He was definitely in much better shape than that other guy she'd been seeing—her mind tripped over his name like it didn't matter, and really, here it didn't—with harder, better defined muscles.

They tumbled on to the bed and kissed again. His kisses made her think of dark chocolate and coffee and port wine, all rich and indulgent. She ran her hands over his arms, his biceps defined beneath the soft material of his shirt. Meanwhile, her robe lay open, fully exposing her except her arms. He pulled away from her and knelt with his knees straddling hers and pinning the long tails of her sleeves to the bed. She tried but couldn't pull away, and fear flickered through her chest.

It must have shown on her face because his eyes widened, and he moved so she could free her arms.

"Is that better?" he asked.

"Yes." She smiled with her relief. *Dumbass—he's not that kind of guy.*

"I'll never trap you or force you to do something you're not comfortable with," he said. "Tell me what you want."

"More wine." She sat up against the headboard with a pillow behind her. The expression on his face when he looked at her was more open than she'd ever seen on him and showed his raw hunger for her. She caught her own desire reflected in his eyes, and the firelight flickered over both of them.

He held out a hand, and a goblet of wine appeared in it. He held it to her lips to drink, and then rather than sip it himself after she drank, he dipped his index finger in it and traced a line down her right breast and around her nipple. He followed it with his tongue, and she gasped and arched against him as the pleasure bolted through her to her core.

"More wine?" he asked.

"Yes, please," she gasped.

He did the same to her other breast, and she found herself with her fingers tangled in his hair holding his head to her chest.

"Now your turn." She rolled him over and tore his shirt open. He lifted his hips so she could remove his pants, which she did easily. Gods, he was beautiful from his tousled dark hair to his bedroom gaze to his long, lean muscles and his erection, which of course was dream-sized. She wanted to lick wine off every inch of him but didn't know when her dream would end, so she settled for dribbling a trail from the hollow at the base of his throat through the valley between his pecs and the line between his abs and ending at his cock.

"I like dream clothing, too," he told her in a husky voice and snapped his fingers. Her robe disappeared, as did the garments strewn over the bed. His hands roamed over her as she kissed the wine she'd dribbled away, and then he clutched her shoulders when she found that last little drop beaded at his head.

"I don't want to wake before this ends for either of us," he said and pulled her off him.

She smiled at the thought she was dreaming of him dreaming of her—how meta!—and said, "Me, neither." She leaned over him and kissed him with the salty-sweetness of him and the wine as she lowered herself on to him. The roar of the fire increased as they moved together, every time he thrust deep, pleasure moved through her. Each wave grew in intensity until they pushed her over the edge, and he moaned with the throbbing of his own release.

Exhaustion spread through her, and she collapsed on top of him. He pulled the sheets over them and cuddled her in his arms.

"This is perfect," he said, and she wondered for the first time whose dream this really was, but the thought barely pierced her post-orgasmic haze.

The light changed and brightened behind her eyelids, she held on to Damien as tight as she could until he faded from her arms.

"I wish you weren't a cop," she whispered.

14

---

udrey woke in a hospital room, which was dark except for the soft glow that came from the instruments at the side of her bed and the dim light that snuck through the window blinds. She felt tied down and had to quell the wave of panic that washed over her by reminding herself that it was her bandage and sling. She was hurt, and freaking out would only make it worse. At least her head pounded less than it had, and the medication had given her very sweet dreams. She smiled and tried to hold on to the golden wisps of comfort from the sex dream about Damien.

A shimmering light made her wonder if her dream had followed her, but then the luminous golden form resolved into the shape of Aphrodite, who had tucked a pair of designer jeans into black leather stiletto boots. A white T-shirt with "Goddess" spelled out across the front in blue and red rhinestones stopped just short of her navel, which had its own ruby stud. Over it all, she wore a knee-length red leather jacket. Her hair hung in a cascade of blonde curls to her mid-back. She chewed on one manicured nail and looked around the hospital room.

"So this is what healthcare looks like in your world. How does anyone survive in such a sterile environment?" She pointed at the counter that stood across the room, and a profusion of red roses, white lilies, and purple and yellow irises immediately covered it.

"Thanks." The fragrance of the lilies reached Audrey's nose and made it twitch.

"Oh, those weren't for you, hon. I couldn't take being in here for one more minute without something natural."

"Right." Audrey sneezed and tried not to move her head too much. "Um, would you mind getting rid of the lilies? I'm allergic to them."

"Fine." The goddess snapped her fingers, and they disappeared to be replaced by white carnations and roses. She walked over to the window and twisted the rod on the blinds so she could peer out. "Ugh, look at that rain. Why did I come here, again?"

"To retrieve Nimue and your other nymphs."

"Right." Aphrodite plopped into the chair by the window. "Where are they? And when are the men coming along? I'm bored."

Audrey sighed and fervently wished for Maggie to come take the spoiled goddess off her hands. "I'm not sure. I don't even know what time it is."

"Time for you to wake up, sleepyhead." Damien walked through the door and smiled at her. Heat flooded Audrey's cheeks as the image of the last time she'd "seen" him came to mind. It felt both like a few minutes and days ago.

Aphrodite stood and gave him a dazzling smile. "This must be the handsome, heroic policeman you were telling me about." Her sideways glance made Audrey wonder just where her dream had come from.

"I guess." Audrey didn't feel like competing with anyone for Damien's affections, especially not the goddess of love, who had let her down in the past. After a night with no shower and no opportunity to get her makeup off or wash her hair, she must be more frightful than the creatures who had abducted her from the restaurant.

Even so, Damien only gave Aphrodite a cursory nod and turned his full attention to Audrey. The intensity of his gaze, appropriate for a new lover, filled her mind with more questions.

Oh gods, that had *been a dream, right?*

"How do you feel?" he asked, his voice low. It thrummed through her again, although in a way that was more comforting than sensual.

"Beat up. You?"

He came to stand beside the bed, and his fingers twitched. Audrey wanted him to brush her hair out of her eyes again.

"Fine after a quick nap." The look he gave her made her wonder again what he'd been dreaming about. "Don't worry, you look beautiful."

She squirmed. "You're being too kind."

"A-hem," Aphrodite coughed.

"Oh, I'm sorry," Audrey said. "Aphrodite, this is Officer Damien Lewis. Damien, this is the goddess Aphrodite, who has come to fetch her retinue back to the dreamlands."

"Oh, nice to meet you." He gave the immortal's hand a hearty handshake, and Audrey hid a smile at Aphrodite's shock. "Audrey helped to rescue your water nymph."

"Yes," Aphrodite said, her jaw slack with amazement. Audrey silently cheered Damien for resisting the goddess' feminine wiles, but anxiety snuffed the satisfaction she had no business experiencing when Aphrodite's perfect features resolved into stone-cold anger. She'd read about the goddesses' wrath when snubbed.

"Um, Damien?" Audrey asked.

"Yes?" He brushed a strand of hair back from her face, and her cheeks heated again from the tenderness in his touch.

"Would you mind going to the vending machine and getting me a bottled water? The stuff in the pitcher tastes like crap."

"Anything you like." He rushed out.

The rage on Aphrodite's face made Audrey wince. "Look, he means no disrespect," she said after he left the room. "I don't know why he's being so attentive."

I hope.

The goddess smirked. "I'll give you one thing—he certainly is devoted to you."

"I guess." Audrey sighed. "Please don't do anything bad to him."

Aphrodite crossed her arms, a shrewd expression on her lovely face. "I don't have to. You'll break his heart in a week."

Audrey winced. "That's not fair."

"Life's not fair, sweetie. And he'll find that out soon enough if he sticks with you."

Damien returned with the water, and Aphrodite resumed her sulking by the window. He took the top off and put the open bottle in Audrey's hand.

"Is everything okay?" he asked.

Audrey couldn't help a nervous glance in the direction of the window. "Do you know where Maggie is?"

"I don't know. She and Charlie left me asleep in Rizzo's office. She did something to me, I think."

"Like what?" Audrey hadn't considered Maggie as a possible enemy. She'd automatically trusted her.

"I don't know. She did it once before. She looked into my eyes and asked me questions, and I had to answer them."

"That's truth-spelling," Aphrodite said without turning around. "It's their interrogation method."

"What did she want to know?" Audrey asked.

"What happened in a dream this morning. I was with

Arthur Rizzo—he's one of the E.R. docs and was shot by a patient yesterday—and we talked to one of them." He inclined his head toward Aphrodite. The corners of his mouth turned down, and his chin trembled.

"Are you okay?" asked Audrey.

"It's Arthur. He's a friend. I really looked up to him. And now I think he's dying. He coded after our dreaming together."

"Oh, Damien, I'm so sorry." She wanted to put her hand on his, but she still held the water in her right hand, and she couldn't move her left arm to reach over.

"So now I have to finish the task he accepted for us." He looked at the goddess again, then back at Audrey.

Supportive. She could be supportive. "He wouldn't have accepted it if he didn't think you could do it. He sounds like a smart guy."

Damien smiled, but without humor. "I don't think he would have agreed to it if he'd known what would happen to him."

"There's no way to know that for sure."

"Now who's arguing with air?" His teasing smile quickly faded. "Um, Madame Aphrodite?"

"Yes?"

"Would you excuse us for a moment? I need to talk to Audrey alone."

"Why not? I'm no good in this room anyway. That's painfully obvious." She stalked out and slammed the door.

"Check out the goddess temper tantrum," Audrey muttered. She tried to get comfortable, but there was something different about the atmosphere in the room even beyond the residual affection she now stupidly felt for Damien since she'd dreamed of making love to him, especially since he seemed to feel it, too.

But that was only a regular dream. She thought she'd feel better when Aphrodite left; the goddess' sulking irritated her, and she wished again that Maggie would appear to fetch her.

But now it felt like she was being watched by something she couldn't see.

"Please be careful and don't end up on the wrong end of her anger," she said.

"Don't worry. Rizzo gave me a book of Greek mythology to read, and I loved the subject when I was a kid, so I know to be extra careful. Would you believe she hasn't done a day of work since Athena caught her at a loom and got possessive?"

"I can believe that."

Damien's expression remained serious. "I need to talk to you about something. Charlie and I interviewed your friend Kyle last night. How well do you know him?"

THE PHONE RANG, and Lyle knew someone from the Other Side called. Whenever that happened, the poor machine took on a tinny quality, like it couldn't handle that much supernatural energy.

"She's here."

He didn't have to ask who had arrived, or even who called. Even if he hadn't recognized Zeus' voice, the crackling on the line would have clued him in. "Where?"

"Sources say the hospital, at Dekalb."

"Someone will be right over."

"No." Had he heard a clap of thunder in the background? "It'll be too obvious. Just have them watch her, then grab her and the nymph when they're apart from the rest of them. Trust me, she will get bored and wander off."

"Right. I'll send a couple of my men to keep an eye on things."

The phone went dead with a sigh, and even the digital display winked out. Lyle hung up the receiver and waited for a count of ten to calm his anger at being spoken to like one of

Zeus' servants. When he got to seven, the door flew open, and he opened his mouth to yell at his secretary.

"Don't you even think to fuss at Lonnie," said the tall blonde woman, who was dressed in a black pantsuit and had a huge diamond ring on her left hand.

"Amelia, what a pleasant surprise." He got up from his desk and gently kissed his wife on the cheek. "I'll be with you in just a moment. I have an important phone call to make. Why don't you go keep Lonnie company?"

"Don't do this, Lyle." She didn't budge. "I haven't seen you but one night this week, and you were too exhausted to even eat dinner with me."

He took her by the elbow and tried to gently steer her to the door, but her feet could have been planted in concrete.

"I've been busy working on this new project," he said. "Trust me, it's going to be huge, and then you'll be able to have that summer home in the North Carolina mountains you've been eying. I saw the brochures on the kitchen table."

"The summer home at the beach suits me just fine. And when did you see the brochures? You haven't been home in days."

He flinched from the anger in her eyes and the steel in her tone. He'd seen her in this mood before. *Keep a civil tongue,* he reminded himself.

"And when am I going to meet this Mr. Zeus you're working with? How do I know he's trustworthy? Does he have a wife? Has *she* seen much of him recently?"

"Look, Amelia, he's a very busy man. And yes, I think he has a wife. I don't know anything more about their relationship than that."

"And what is she doing for the gala? Am I to handle this all by myself?"

"If you want her to help, I can ask him to get her in contact with you." From what he'd heard and read of Hera, that would be an interesting meeting. They'd be well-matched.

"It's not just that." She sighed with the force of someone who had the weight of many responsibilities. "I just have one question for you, Lyle. Then I'll leave you alone since I'm obviously not welcome here."

"What is it?" He glanced over to the phone. He suspected Zeus would know if he didn't get his men right on the goddess thing.

"Have you been faithful to me?"

"What?" This got his full attention.

"Is there another woman?"

"No, there is not another woman." It wasn't technically a lie. He pressed his lips together to keep from saying any more.

"Then what are you doing? You never leave your office." Her eyes widened. She realized she'd said too much. The presence of the private investigator hung unacknowledged between them.

"Then you know I'm working." He gestured to the piles of paper and files on his desk. "I don't know what else I can tell you."

"Things weren't always like this," she said. He tried to keep her from going further into the office, but she brushed past him and stood by the window. A tear trickled down her cheek and fell on to the shoulder of her jacket, where it sat like a diamond on the black fabric. His fingers itched to brush it off. He hated for her to be unhappy, but he couldn't deny she smothered him.

"Look, sweetie." He walked up behind her and put his hands on her shoulders. She rested her wet cheek on his left hand. "I'll come home tonight, I promise. Have Marin make a nice dinner for us."

"What time?"

"I'll be home by eight."

"That's late." Her lips quivered, and he feared she would start crying again.

"I want to be sure to wrap things up here so you can have my undivided attention."

She turned her eyes, which sparkled with the tears she wouldn't let herself shed, toward him. He loved that about her, that she wouldn't drop the mask of perfection, at least not until she got home. She had been the ideal choice when it had come time for him to get married. Now she'd be the perfect wife, if only she would be a good girl and keep the house, plan parties, serve on charity boards, and whatever else rich housewives did without demanding so much of him.

"Hey." He tilted her chin up with his left index finger and kissed her lips. They softened and opened for him, and he suspected why she might be so upset at his inattention when her body fitted itself to his. *Is she ovulating?* Hanging out in the C.U. had heightened his senses in surprising ways. He should be flattered by the fact she wanted to bear his children, but he suspected she'd want him more involved than he was ready to be.

"You'll be home tonight? You promise?"

"I promise."

"Fine." She swept out as dramatically as she'd come in, and he admired again how gracefully she moved and her flawless beauty. Well, almost flawless. He stopped himself from making comparisons that wouldn't help either of them.

Damien sat on the edge of the bed and took Audrey's available hand in his. She would have enjoyed the gesture more had it occurred in the context of a different conversation.

"Look, I know Kyle's not being faithful," she said and toyed with his fingers. "Otherwise, I would never have let you kiss me. I'm not that kind of girl."

"How did you know?"

How did I miss it for so long? "The way any woman knows when her guy is up to something. It just took me longer to catch on because he has late nights with his residency. And then Zin told me something's up, but he wouldn't tell me what."

Damien frowned. "Who told you?"

"Zinfandel." Her lips twitched. Nothing brought absurdity to a situation like a purple dragon combined with relief that her suspicions had been confirmed.

"The wine?"

"Nope, the vegetarian dragon." Her smile escaped, and she giggled.

"Are you still high on painkillers?"

"No, well, maybe, but I'm not kidding. I know I'm creative, but I couldn't make him up if I'd tried."

"A vegetarian dragon." His expression remained skeptical.

She tried to stifle her laughter. "Yes. So far you've met goddesses, the supernatural police, and a couple of nymph-dryad thingies, so why should this be such a stretch?"

He cocked his head. "You have a point."

"Right." She took a deep breath. "So will you please tell me what happened with Kyle?"

He looked away. "When we went there last night, there was another woman."

His direct statement hit her in the gut. There was the evidence she'd been lacking, the confirmation that she'd been right, and it blasted away the remains of her doubt and denial. Audrey wasn't prepared for the succession of emotions that danced through her chest—heartbreak to vindication to a little bit of relief, but still hurt and rejection. It all weighed on her heart. "Who was she?"

"I can't tell you more. I probably shouldn't have even told you as much as I did, but I felt like I should."

"I bet it was Chastity." She searched his face, but he was good at hiding his emotions. "Great." She turned her head so he wouldn't see the tears that came to her eyes. She didn't want to cry. "Just great." She sniffled. "You know, I had wondered if there was something going on between them." She felt like she had to keep talking, the words building up behind her tongue. "For a month, it's been 'Chastity this' and 'Chastity that.' 'Chastity and I had lunch, and she laughed so hard milk came out her nose...'"

Damien coughed. "I'm so sorry you had to find out like this, but it sounds like you suspected it already."

"Right." She glanced toward the door, afraid that Aphrodite would burst back in, gleeful to have been right.

"So what did that one"—he inclined his head toward the hallway—"have to say about Zinfandel's suspicions?"

Audrey figured she'd just lay it out there. "She thinks it's in my personality to drive men away."

"Oh, I doubt that. Ow!" Damien rubbed the back of his neck and looked around. "What the hell was that?"

15

———————

"**A**re you okay?" Audrey asked and tried to get out of the bed, but she couldn't even sit up all the way.

"More than okay." He smiled at her again, but this time it was a goofy, lopsided smile. "Much much more than okay." He stroked her hair. "I'm going to make sure that you're not ever hurt again."

"Uh, all right." Audrey said. A suspicion about what had just happened materialized in her mind. The sensation of her heart dropping followed. "We should call Aphrodite back in before she feels ignored for too long."

"I'll fetch her." He walked off like a gallant knight.

"Oh, gods," Audrey moaned and would have put her face in her hands if she could have. What had the goddess done? Could things get any more awkward?

Aphrodite strutted into the room, but instead of pissed off at having been dismissed, she wore a smug smile that seemed almost cat-like. Damien trotted along behind her.

"Doesn't she look beautiful?" he asked. "I just can't get enough of looking at her."

"Oh, indeed," Aphrodite said. "Lovely enough to be a goddess."

"Damien, would you excuse us for a moment?" Audrey braced herself for him to argue, but he only smiled.

"I'll be right outside the door, my princess."

"Look, dammit," Audrey said once he was safely in the hallway, door closed. "I told you not to do anything to him."

"And since when does a goddess listen to a mortal? I'm just helping you out, honey, and *I* didn't do anything."

Now it made sense. The gods liked their loopholes. "That was Cupid, wasn't it?"

"Aren't you clever? Cupid, Eros, that Damn Chubby Archer... My son has many names. Since you're such a smart little girl, you tell me why I had him shoot your handsome policeman."

Audrey clenched her one fist like she could punch Aphrodite's condescension out of the air. "I'm guessing it's not to help me heal from Kyle's betrayal faster. You think that having Damien fall in love with me will punish him for ignoring you."

"Maybe."

Audrey wanted to ask about the dream, but she didn't want to reveal too much in case Aphrodite hadn't been behind it. And she still held out hope it had only been a dream. One problem at a time. "And you want to drive me crazy."

"Definitely."

Audrey put her hand to her face and pressed the heel of her palms into her eyeball until she saw stars on one side. How was she going to figure this out?

"Look," she said. "You're going to have to go back once you find your nymphs or whatever. I can't take much more of this."

"But you're such a brave, strong woman, Audrey. You can handle anything. Except for love, that is."

"I'm not amused."

"You're not supposed to be, dear. Now how about you bring your policeman back into the room so I can watch the fun?"

AFTER DAMIEN FLUFFED Audrey's pillows, bought her another water, and insisted on helping her eat lunch, he finally left her alone to sleep, but he remained seated in a chair at the other side of the room, his eyes fixed on her.

"Stop that," she told him.

"Stop what?"

"Stop watching me. I can't sleep with someone watching me."

He got a magazine and flipped through the pages, and she closed her eyes. But soon the rustle of paper stopped. She opened one eye. Yep, he gazed at her again.

"If you keep that up, I'm sending you out of the room." She spoke slowly, hoping he'd hear the threat in her voice.

"I won't go."

"Look." She sighed. "I need a nap. You need to stop bugging me. Go take a walk or something. Or go home and change. You're still wearing last night's clothes, for gods' sake."

He looked down at his rumpled attire, then up again with a big grin. "I can't change out of these, my princess. They're the clothes I rescued you in."

"Argh!" Audrey screamed into her pillow, which brought him immediately to her side. "I'm fine. Just go home and do *something*, then, and leave me alone for a while."

He finally left the room looking like a puppy that had been kicked. Audrey tried to ignore the guilt that blossomed in her gut—he'd thank her later once he recovered from Cupid's dart. Just as Audrey drifted off to sleep, she heard Aphrodite's voice.

"Is the absolute devotion getting on your nerves yet, Miss Independent?"

Audrey startled awake, and her eyes flew open. She wondered what Aphrodite would do to her if she threw a pillow at her. Probably not give it back.

"It's a little annoying, yes. Actually, it's very annoying because I don't know what his real feelings are and what can be attributed to that stupid arrow your brat shot him with."

And I can't stand the thought of hurting him.

"I find it all quite entertaining."

"Well, good for you. Don't you have somewhere else to be? Where's your water nymph?"

"I sense her coming to me." Aphrodite cocked her head. "Ah, there she is now."

With a knock, the door opened, and Nimue walked in, her jeans stained to the knees with red Georgia clay.

Where in the world has she been?

When Nimue saw Aphrodite, she slumped to the floor, her face down and her hands out in front of her.

"Your Radiance," she said.

"There you are." The goddess knelt and stroked the girl's hair. Nimue shook, and Audrey couldn't tell if she trembled or cried.

"Don't worry," Aphrodite murmured to her nymph, "it wasn't your fault. Someone convinced Cupid that he was getting rusty and that you girls would make good practice targets. You were hit by one of his arrows."

Audrey's mouth fell open. *Is this the same spoiled goddess I've been enduring all day? Where is the compassion for me? For Damien?*

"She needs her nymphs." Maggie said, and Audrey jumped, which sent an electric bolt of pain down her left arm. She hadn't seen Maggie come in. The Truth Seeker looked stylish as ever, but tired.

"She had Cupid shoot Damien. Now he's like an annoying

puppy dog." The words tumbled from Audrey's mouth, and she felt like a four-year-old tattling on the playground.

Maggie frowned, but the corner of her mouth twitched. "I'll see what I can do. Usually Cupid's arrows wear off in a few days in this world, but him being totally focused on you could impact our investigation. What did he do to piss her off?"

"I know he's having a hard time with all the supernatural stuff, but how does a straight man ignore Aphrodite?"

"I'm hearing all this, you know." The goddess looked over her shoulder from her customary position by the window, where she sat with Nimue standing at her side. The nymph's tears had dried, and with a touch, Aphrodite caused the mud to disappear and her clothes to un-wrinkle and become more stylish. Now Nimue stood perfect, pristine, and ready to serve her mistress.

"Audrey was just catching me up on things." The glance Maggie shot Audrey told her not to say anything else.

The goddess pouted prettily. "I was only trying to help. He was being so sweet to her, I wanted to make it last."

At that moment, a doctor knocked at the door. A middle-aged man whose gray hair seemed determined to escape from the top of his head and gather around his ears, his eyes went immediately to Aphrodite before he turned to look at his patient.

"Miss Sonoma?"

"Yes, that's me."

"I'm Doctor Shaffer. I think we can let you go this afternoon, but I wanted to ask you some questions to make sure our files are complete. I also need to give you a quick exam to see how that collarbone is doing. It's likely a bruise, but there could be a small fracture. Do you mind if your friends stay in the room?"

The last thing Audrey wanted was for Aphrodite to see her weak and in pain. Maggie seemed to sense this, so she motioned for the goddess and nymph to wait in the hallway.

"Do you mind if I stay?" Maggie asked.

Audrey thought back to her earlier suspicions about the Truth Seeker, but they seemed to have evaporated.

"No, I may need your help with some of his questions. My brain doesn't feel like it's working quite right. And maybe then you can figure out how to fix things with me and Damien."

DAMIEN HUMMED to himself while he drove to the station after having gone home to change. He almost went back to the hospital, but he had enough sense to know Audrey needed sleep to heal. And then they'd go out somewhere fun, just the two of them. And maybe he'd kiss her again.

He was glad that Charlie had told him to wear street clothes today because it had forced him to look in the back of his closet and come up with a good outfit. He wore a plum-colored, long-sleeved shirt that his mother had given him. Normally he hated whatever she picked out, but it accentuated his dark features and gave his eyes a hint of purple. He paired it with black pants and a long, black raincoat because the forecast predicted more nasty weather.

"Why do I care how my eyes look?" he asked out loud. "It's not like I'm going to allow myself to get married and have kids to pass them on." His brain had been doing that to him all morning—interrupting his internal chatter with these annoying but logical interjections.

Audrey's dismissal had hurt, but no one was nice when they weren't feeling well, and he'd heard collarbone breaks hurt. Even bruised collarbones could be uncomfortable. He had been feeling more alive than ever from the successful rescue even before that mysterious pain had shot through his neck. Then she had been surrounded by a golden glow, and just gazing upon her made him blissfully happy. He vowed to be there for her when she called, and in the meanwhile, he would get to the bottom of her abduction and its surrounding mystery.

Damien's heart twisted when he remembered Rizzo and the danger he was in, but it was time to celebrate life, and maybe doing that would send some positive energy to his friend and mentor.

Positive energy? Oh, great, I'm starting to sound like a New Age hippie.

Arthur's book still rode in the back seat. He hadn't cracked it but had every intention of reading it as soon as possible. When he did, he promised to raise a beer to Arthur, who had worked so selflessly to extend this glorious life for others.

He still hummed when he walked to Charlie's office and ignored the catcalls of his fellow officers, who hadn't seen him so nicely dressed in civilian clothes, well, ever. Charlie sat slumped at his computer, his eyes bleary, and Damien remembered that he hadn't slept in a day. Not that Damien's sleep deprivation was doing anything to him—energy coursed through his body from the crown of his head to his toes.

"Are you okay, Charlie?"

Charlie startled and rubbed his eyes. "You look sharp. I'm as okay as one can be when running on coffee and adrenaline. What's your secret? You look fantastic."

Damien shrugged and couldn't help but grin.

"And what were you humming?"

Damien hummed a few more bars. "I'm not sure. I just remember hearing it somewhere."

"Dude, that's 'I Could Have Danced All Night' from *My Fair Lady*."

"Oh." Damien's cheeks grew hot. Where had that come from? "So, uh, what are you working on?"

"I've pulled up the tax records for that warehouse where you found Audrey and Nimue. Man, what is with you?"

Damien's cheeks hurt from grinning so widely. He dialed his smile back. "Nothing. Go on."

"Right. So this is interesting. The building was bought a couple of months ago from its original owners, who built it in the sixties."

"By whom?"

"Avondale Industrial Corporation, who, in turn, had just been bought a couple of months before that."

"Okay. What are you getting at?"

"That in the past year, a number of companies somehow connected to this property have changed hands, all of them construction or construction supply."

"Who's buying them?" Damien peered over Charlie's shoulder at the tax records and sales contracts he'd pulled up on the screen.

"Jupiter, Inc." Charlie looked up at Damien, who saw the dark circles under his friend's eyes were even more pronounced than he'd originally noticed.

"Are you kidding me?" He recognized Jupiter as the name Zeus used in the pantheon of ancient Rome, which had stolen the gods from Greece and renamed them.

"Nope. It looks like this literally goes all the way to the top."

"How do we investigate that?" Damien raked his fingers through his hair and sat down on the couch, which still held a faint imprint from his nap the previous night. Then he said something he never would have imagined saying in a million years. "The king of the gods has to be even more scary and powerful than vampires and were—uh, what were those?"

"Bats. Were-bats. It seems that we'll have to find the human contact Zeus is using and go from there. Unfortunately, the secretary of state's website crashes when I try to look up the corporation's officers, and all my other electronic avenues are similarly blocked."

"Do we have another way to know who it is?" Damien clenched his fists. "We have to find them."

Charlie shuffled through his notes. "We have a description of his voice from Nimue—male, not too old, not too young. She overheard him on the phone with her captors, presumably in their human forms."

"That could describe any of a number of Atlanta businessmen."

"In that case, we'll have to go with good, old-fashioned foot work. Let's talk to the former owners of Avondale Industrial. They're almost at the end of the grace period for vacating their office space."

THE OFFICES of Avondale Industrial Corporation were located in a squat office building in Avondale Estates, a strange little town just east of Decatur. High hedges lined one side of the main thoroughfare and protected the upper middle-class neighborhood from prying eyes and through traffic. On the other side, stores varying from upper-end interior design to bakeries to consignment shops nestled on the bottom floors of faux German buildings. Damien and Charlie parked the squad car in one of the lots behind the main façade.

Bells tinkled when they opened the glass door to reveal a dusty reception desk. In spite of the front of the office being all glass, the light faded into gloom a few feet from the windows. Damien reached for his weapon, but Charlie placed a hand on his arm. The unnatural shadows made him nervous.

"Hello?" Charlie rang the bell on the counter. "We're here to talk to someone about a job?"

A rustling sound came from the back room, and the hairs on the back of Damien's neck stood so straight they pricked him. This time, Charlie didn't stop him when he removed the gun from its holster. They crouched low and walked around the desk.

The back room of the small office sprang into garish relief when Charlie flicked the light switch. White papers in various states of destruction littered every surface and a couple of suspicious lumps on the floor. The back door slammed open, and Damien chased the dark figure that disappeared through it, but it seemed to vanish in the shadows of the scraggly trees that lined the back of the parking lot of broken asphalt. He didn't dare shoot at it for fear he might accidentally hit a human on the other side of the fence.

"Did you get it?" asked Charlie.

"No, it was too fast."

"I'm thinking it wasn't human."

"I'm thinking you're probably right." Damien's heart pounded in his ears. He didn't want to look under the piles of paper, but he had to, just in case they were still alive.

Charlie called for medical assistance, his forensic team, and then for Maggie. Damien went to the first lump, which was curled behind a drafting desk and bench, and found a woman, alive but unconscious. He left her in the fetal position and went to the second one. This gentleman wasn't so lucky. His throat had been torn out, and his eyes stared blankly at the ceiling, his final horror etched on his face. The pieces of paper under his head were stained bright red.

"Poor devil," Damien said. He wanted to close the man's eyes out of respect but would probably catch hell from the forensics guys if he touched the corpse. The man's name tag had been torn off his brown shirt, and Damien didn't see anything else to identify him—at least nothing in plain sight that wouldn't require disturbing the scene. They'd have to wait for the woman to wake up.

She stirred with a groan, and Damien went to her side.

"John?" she asked before opening her eyes. She caught her breath when she saw Damien. "Who are you? Where's John?"

He remembered he wasn't wearing his uniform and showed her his badge.

"Oh, thank God." She closed her eyes, and tears leaked out of them. "I was so scared. John said they'd be back, but I didn't want to believe him."

"Who?" asked Charlie.

"I can't tell. They said if I did, horrible things would happen."

She looked around, and Damien moved back, ostensibly to give her more breathing room but also to block her view of the corpse.

Charlie put his hand on her shoulder, and she seemed to calm down. "And your name is?"

"Miriam. Miriam Spinks. I'm the office manager and receptionist here."

"And who is John?"

"He's the accountant. He was organizing all this stuff for storage since we got bought out." Her lip trembled.

The crunch of gravel alerted them to the arrival of the paramedics and the forensics team. Maggie came in with them and sniffed the air, then coughed.

"Not human," she said so only Damien and Charlie could hear, and Charlie looked pointedly at Damien.

"Told you."

"Right." They straightened and moved out of the way so the paramedics could attend to the woman. Miriam rolled to her other side and closed her eyes. "It's too much. Where's John?"

Damien couldn't disagree with her. He looked around at the mess. The paper drifts seemed to grow every time he looked at them.

"Remind you of anything, Officer Lewis?" Maggie asked.

"Yeah, Rizzo's office after he was attacked."

"So do you think there's anything in here worth looking at?" asked Charlie.

"Why were you here?" Maggie nudged one of the piles with the toe of her boot. Damien cringed.

"Let's discuss this in the other room," he suggested.

Once there and out of earshot of the other humans, Charlie filled Maggie in. "We want to know who bought this place out. They own the warehouse where we found Audrey and Nimue. The parent company is Jupiter, Inc."

Maggie arched an eyebrow. "So you're looking for the human partner in that enterprise, assuming there is one?"

"Bingo," said Damien.

"C'mon, Maggie, there's got to be someone. It takes time to establish a corporation, and if you haven't heard of anything suspicious 'til now, then he's got to be getting help from somewhere to keep things legit."

"Good point." Maggie glanced through the door into the inner office, where the paramedics lifted the woman to a stretcher. "I'll go back to the hospital with that one and see what I can find out. You boys look through the papers and see if you can find any connection with other companies."

"You got it, boss." Charlie mock-saluted.

"Maggie?" Damien touched the sleeve of her jacket to get her attention. "Is Audrey okay?" His feelings for Audrey had maintained a constant warm presence in his chest, and it seemed danger lurked on every corner. Maybe he shouldn't have left her.

"The doctor thinks she'll be able to leave this afternoon. She's sleeping right now. You boys had better get to work in here—there's no telling when whatever it was will be back with reinforcements."

16

———

They had managed to stay out of the way of the forensics team and had been through all the papers but hadn't found anything. Damien's stomach growled, and he kept having to remind himself not to call Audrey no matter how badly he wanted to. She needed her rest.

"I don't get it," he said and sat back on his heels. "We don't even know what we're looking for."

Charlie blinked. "Whatever the thing wanted to take or destroy. We know it wasn't done because we interrupted it."

"Right." Damien couldn't imagine the same creature going through the files strategically and ripping out John the accountant's throat. Somehow it was easier to picture a madman doing it. "But how do we know when we've found it?"

"Well, think about it. If that John guy was able to save the secretary from certain doom, maybe he left us something. If you were in a panic, where would you leave something important?"

"Certain doom, huh? You're getting dramatic." Damien tried to look around the office with new eyes. "I'd put it in with something they wouldn't think to look at."

"Good idea. So we're looking for something that doesn't belong with the rest of the stuff in that file or pile."

Damien shook his head. "I need to get a glass of water."

"There's a cooler in the lobby."

Damien walked out there and saw the box Ms. Spinks had been packing. Those files, unlike the others, hadn't been disturbed. Or had they, but by human hands? He grabbed a glass of water, pulled the papers out of the box, and sat cross-legged on the ground, aware his feet would be asleep in no time. If they did, he would welcome the sensation as something mundane amid all the weirdness.

He leafed through the papers and found a pink invoice tucked in amongst a bunch of tax records. When he saw the name on the invoice, he let out a low whistle at the listed amount. He didn't know anything about construction, but something seemed off.

"Hey, Charlie, come look at this."

"What?" A shuffling noise indicated Charlie must be extracting himself from the pile of papers he'd been working on.

"I mean, it could've been mis-filed, but it didn't go with the rest of the stuff in that folder." He handed the invoice to Charlie. "And that woman didn't seem the type to file things in the wrong place."

"Ames Construction," Charlie read. "You know, Lyle Ames fits the description that Nimue gave of the guy in the warehouse, and he's certainly got diverse enough interests."

"Yeah, his name's on everything. Ames Construction, Ames Regional Bank, Ames Family Restaurant... If it is him, I don't know how we're going to catch him."

"I'll give Maggie a call and get her to bring Nimue to the station again to get a positive I.D. That'll at least give us reason to question him."

"Right." Damien wished he could feel as confident as

Charlie projected. He'd never been comfortable cornering big fish like that.

"Actually, this is good enough reason. What say we drop in for a little lunchtime chat?"

"Mr. Ames is very busy today, gentlemen." The secretary, a slender young man with horn-rimmed glasses and a sweater vest, squinted at the computer screen. "He's booked from now 'til eight p.m."

Charlie and Damien had shown their badges, but they hadn't been ushered in immediately like they'd hoped. Just another way television wasn't like the real world. They'd have better luck with a warrant, but they needed more information to get one.

"If you want to come back tomorrow, he has three minutes at eight a.m. and two and a half minutes at noon, but that's when he eats lunch." The admin sat with his hands poised over the screen and blinked like an oversized meerkat.

"We'll be here at eight, then," Charlie said.

With a flurry of keystrokes, the appointment was confirmed. "You're squeezed in at eight, then, gentlemen. Please be on time. Normally I would make you wait the months it takes to get an appointment with Mr. Ames, but since you're law enforcement, I can bend the rules just a little. Of course, if you were to have a warrant, I could direct you to his lawyers."

"Hopefully that won't be necessary. Thanks for getting us in." Charlie put a hand on Damien's shoulder, then paused. "Would you happen to know a good place for lunch around here?"

"A lot of the guys from the office like a little diner on the corner. It's called 'Dream' something or other. Bye-bye, now."

"Well, that was futile," Damien grumbled. So much for figuring out who had kidnapped Audrey and running in there with a warrant, handcuffs, and... He sighed.

They walked down Peachtree Street, shoulders slumped against the wind that howled between the glass and stone buildings. Even the small trees, now devoid of all but a few pitiful leaves, sulked between gusts that bent them in half.

Charlie didn't seem perturbed, and Damien wondered again where his calm came from. "I guess the busiest businessman in Atlanta has a packed schedule. I didn't really think we'd be able to get in to see him today. Aha. There it is. You hungry?"

Damien surprised himself by saying, "Starving." So much for his daydreams of a romantic lunch.

The Dream-and-Dash Diner was crowded, but they found seats at the counter. The waitress brought them two steaming cups of coffee and menus, and Damien checked his watch: one o'clock. He wondered if he'd done enough detective work for the day and could get off early to visit Audrey. *Maybe I'll bring her some flowers.*

"Excuse me, gentlemen." The voice came from a tall, blonde, and impeccably dressed woman. Her black cashmere sweater hugged and accentuated all of her good curves and hid the bad—not that she likely had any—and her soft gray wool skirt hung in stylish folds to her black stiletto boots. For a moment, Damien thought it was Aphrodite, but the woman's eyes lacked the goddess' haughtiness, and her face, although beautiful, had stronger features. Aphrodite demanded attention and worship; this woman evoked respect and wariness.

"You are with the police?" she asked in a low voice. Damien and Charlie nodded and flipped out their badges. She examined each one closely. "I thought so. Come."

She tilted her head, and with a shrug, Charlie followed her

to a newly empty booth, Damien close behind. They sat at the back of the restaurant, where she could watch the door, but where they would not be casually observed from outside. Damien noticed a man pass the front window and thought he looked familiar.

"What can we do for you, ma'am?" asked Charlie. "First, can we know your name?"

"I thought two clever detectives such as you would have figured that out by now."

Damien looked at her again. He'd seen her face somewhere —maybe he'd glanced at it in passing on his way to the comics in the Atlanta Journal-Constitution. Yes, just that morning, there had been an article about some sort of gala.

"You're Amelia Ames." He kept his voice down, although his heart pounded. This was one of the most powerful women in Atlanta, and not only because of who she married.

Charlie nodded approvingly. "My friend here is a quick study. Loves the society pages."

Damien's cheeks warmed.

"But if you'll forgive me, this doesn't seem like the kind of place I'd expected to encounter you." Charlie flashed his charming smile.

She twisted her engagement ring around her finger, and the large stone winked at Damien even in the dim light. "I'm not sure I know exactly what to tell you, why I'm even talking to you. But there's something fishy going on with my husband." A tear escaped her right eye and slid down her cheek, but she seemed not to notice.

The waitress came and took their lunch orders. Amelia surprised Damien by ordering a fried chicken sandwich with fries.

"I eat when I'm stressed," she confessed.

"And why do you think we may be interested in the source of your stress?" asked Charlie.

"You were just in his office. Lonnie called me and said you'd been there and that you would come here."

"What do you mean by 'something fishy'?" Damien ignored the growl his stomach gave and tried not to think about how long it would take for his corned beef sandwich to arrive.

"What I am going to tell you will sound strange, I'm afraid." Her eyes filled again, but she held the tears back. "About a year ago, we were at the Corporate Broadcasting Halloween party. A man dressed in a toga approached Lyle, and they wandered off and started talking. I had a strange feeling about him, but I couldn't put my finger on it."

"What did he look like?"

"Dark-skinned, like he spent a lot of time in the sun. Dark hair, graying at the temples. Very regal-looking, kind of like some Greek or Italian prince. He had a very strong nose and dark, piercing eyes." She squinted for emphasis. "Even though his face seemed middle-aged, the body under the toga was very muscular."

Charlie took notes in his little pad. "Did he have anyone with him?"

"Not that I could tell."

"So what was so fishy about this?" Damien asked. "Don't other businessmen approach your husband all the time with propositions?"

She turned her intense gaze to Damien like she expected him to understand. "You know how sometimes you have a feeling, and every little thing that happens, that should be innocent, has a darker interpretation that is just as plausible?"

Should he tell her how strange his life had become? "I know the exact feeling."

"Lyle came home from the office the following Monday, and even though he said nothing to me, I heard him on the phone talking to one of his vice presidents. He said he was going to explore a new area of business, but it would take some groundwork first. It would be worth it because it would make a lot of peoples' fantasies come true."

"Did he say anything else about the fantasies?" asked Damien. He'd seen some nightmares, which may be some people's fantasies. Sick people, but he knew they were out there.

"No, just that people would pay a lot for them. I thought he meant an amusement park or something like that, but nothing ever came of it as far as I could tell."

The food arrived, and she gestured for them to eat. She picked the breading off the chicken and nibbled on her fries.

Damien dug into his corned beef on rye. He couldn't believe how good it tasted. It was like every little thing had a certain extra spark since he'd realized without a doubt that he was mad about Audrey. His brain tripped over the l-word, but his heart told him it was true. Of course his rational side piped up—*I'm in deep trouble.* He was so surprised by his internal dialogue he almost missed what Amelia said next.

"But then this past summer, I thought he was having an affair. Every few nights, he would come home very late, and he wouldn't want anything to do with me. I hired a private detective, but he said Lyle was at the downtown office, alone. He gave me pictures to prove it. Lyle would just take his evening medicine, go to sleep in his office, wake up, and come home. So then I worried about his health—he's in his forties now—but he just put me off."

"Is he on medication?" asked Charlie.

"He takes something for his blood pressure. Hypertension runs in his family."

"Do you know if that was it?"

"No, I thought he took that one in the morning. What could it be?"

"Did the pictures show a bottle or anything?" Charlie persisted.

"They were taken from a neighboring building and didn't have that much detail." Her words spilled out with the speed of desperation to be believed. "Does all of this sound crazy to you?"

Damien attempted a reassuring grin and hoped he didn't have anything in his teeth. "Not at all. Is there anything else?"

"No, just please don't mention this little meeting to Lyle."

"You have our utmost discretion." Charlie gave her a business card. "If you think of anything else, please give me a call."

She rewarded Charlie with a dazzling smile. "I will. Thank you, gentlemen. I knew the two of you could be trusted—I had a good feeling about you." With that, she got to her feet, and with a nod to the waitress behind the counter, disappeared through the swinging doors into the kitchen.

"Where's she going?" Damien followed her with his eyes until the door swung shut.

"I'm guessing that her car and driver are parked back in the alley." Charlie put his notebook away and picked up his burger.

"What do you think about all that?"

Charlie took his time chewing. "We really need to get an I.D. on Ames from Nimue now, but I don't think I want to get a warrant until we know what he's up to."

"Kidnapping isn't enough?" Damien asked. "Remember, Audrey was hurt." And he still wished he could kill the bastard who had done it.

"We need to go back to the office and discuss it."

Damien's cell phone rang, and he couldn't keep from grinning at the caller I.D. Audrey.

"They're letting me out today," she said after he answered. "Can you pick me up?"

"I'll be right there." He had swung his legs to the side and had half-stood before he realized it.

"Hang on, there, Romeo," Charlie told him. "The lovely Mrs.

Ames stuck us with the bill, and this place doesn't take cards. Got any cash?"

~

AUDREY LOOKED PALE, but just as beautiful as Damien remembered. He hugged her gently and planted a kiss on her forehead. Maggie had helped her to bathe and wash her hair, and she wore fresh clothes.

Man, she smells good, like roses and lavender.

"Okay, okay, it's good to see you, too." She nudged him to let go.

He let her pull away, but he put his raincoat around her and helped her into the car since her left arm was in a sling and made her off-balance. Charlie, with proper deference, held his umbrella over Aphrodite's head.

"Maggie?" asked Charlie. She frowned at the crowded car, with Audrey, Nimue, and Aphrodite all squished into the back seat.

"I've got my car. I'll meet you there." With that, she vanished back inside the hospital.

Once they arrived at the office, Aphrodite immediately lounged upon the couch without leaving room for anyone else, and Damien had to bring in extra chairs from the education room. He was happy to see Charlie let Audrey use his desk chair, which would be more comfortable. He kept glancing at her, wondering if she needed anything or if she wanted to go home. Maggie appeared shortly after the rest of them.

"All right, Truth Seeker," challenged the goddess, "what are you doing to find my nymphs? I thought you had a lead to chase this morning."

"The guys are still working on that, Your Radiance. Working in two worlds tends to slow things down a bit."

Aphrodite exhaled through her nose. "Well, if none of you

need my assistance, Nimue and I are going to go downstairs and watch the cute policemen go in and out. No, no, don't get up." She spoke over Maggie's attempts to stop her.

"Perhaps it would be wiser for you to stay here," Maggie finally got out. "At least until we can figure out how your nymphs fit into everything."

"It's warm, stuffy, and way too crowded, not to mention the ratio of men to women is much too small. If you need me, just say my name, and I'll return."

She and Nimue vanished.

"I hope no one saw that," Charlie said and closed his door.

"Don't you always make beautiful women disappear?" teased Maggie.

"Not the ones I want to stick around."

Damien sat beside Audrey, his arm draped loosely across the back of her chair, and he smiled at Maggie's blush and the answering flush in his friend's cheeks. Had Charlie fallen that hard for the Truth Seeker? Not that it would surprise Damien. Charlie was good at trying to attain the unattainable, particularly when it came to romance.

"Okay," Maggie said. With a sigh, she stood and paced the length of the small office. "Let's put together everything we know. Charlie?"

He tossed her a dry-erase marker, and she went to the white board, which normally hung half-hidden behind the open door. Everyone turned their chairs to face it.

"Our suspicious persons are...?"

"Shouldn't we call them persons of interest?" asked Audrey.

Charlie groaned. "I'm so sick of that term."

"I suspect Zeus," Damien said.

"And Lyle Ames," added Charlie.

Maggie wrote the two names at the top of the board, one on each side, and connected them with a double arrow.

"And how do we know they're interesting?"

"Their wives told us." Damien shuddered at the memory of Hera and what she'd done to Rizzo. He'd checked on his friend when he went back to the hospital, but there was no change in his condition. He wouldn't let anything like that happen to Audrey.

"It may be significant that Damien was privy to both those conversations," Audrey observed. He thrilled at hearing her say his name.

"Right, that may be important." Maggie wrote *Damien* in the middle of the board. "These things tend not to be coincidences in my experience."

"What?" Damien gave Audrey's good shoulder a gentle squeeze. "Are you jealous?"

She smiled but only said, "Nope. I'm a journalist, remember? I make observations."

"What else?" asked Maggie.

"Well," replied Charlie, "they're kidnapping goddesses, nymphs, and presumably other female mythological beings from the Collective Unconscious."

Maggie made a note on the board. "Right. So we need to know what they're going to use these women for. Hmmm. Do we have any knowledge as to who, exactly, is missing and to whom they're connected?"

Damien sat up straighter, a suspicion tickling the base of his skull. "More of Aphrodite's servants are missing than anyone else's. Hera told us."

Maggie dropped the dry erase marker. "And she's out there with only Nimue. What if she's the ultimate target? I'm such an idiot!"

Maggie vanished, and Damien and Charlie both leapt to their feet. Damien hated to leave Audrey, but he knew she would be safe in Charlie's office. They ran through the center of the hallway, past startled policemen and staff, and took the stairs two at a time.

"Do we know where she went?" Charlie panted.

"No. She just said she was going to watch the policemen come and go."

"So she should be out by the front door."

They burst out of the stairwell by the ground floor entrance and startled the front desk personnel, but there was no sign of the goddess or of the nymph, either inside or out. Damien caught sight of light-colored tresses and thought it was Aphrodite, but it was only Maggie.

"I've been around the block, and there's no sign of them."

"Wait a second." Charlie bent over and put his hands on his knees. "How do you kidnap a goddess? Wouldn't she be able to defend herself?"

"You'd think so," said Maggie, "but her powers are attenuated here, and it may have been possible to trap her by using one of her other nymphs."

"So if someone lured her off the main drag and an accomplice snuck up behind her and knocked her out...?"

"She'd be helpless," Maggie finished for him. "And Nimue wouldn't know what to do with her mistress rendered unconscious. She'd stay with her."

Damien continued to scan the sidewalks. "Do we really know that's what happened to them? Could they have just wandered off?"

"I tried calling her but she didn't appear. She said we'd only have to say her name." Maggie balled her hands into fists like she wanted to hit something. "I can't believe I let this happen. I should've seen that Nimue being stuck here was the bait for a trap."

Charlie put an arm around her shoulders. "There's nothing we can do about it now. Let's go back up to my office and see what else we can figure out. It's our only chance of finding them."

"Crap," Damien said when they were all in the elevator. "We

never got Nimue to I.D. Lyle Ames as the guy who came into the warehouse."

"That's going to make this investigation more complicated," Maggie replied with a sigh. "Now that they have Aphrodite, they're going to be extra careful when it comes to covering their tracks."

17

———

"Any luck?" asked Audrey, but the looks on their faces answered her. Damien gave her a tired smile and resumed his place on the chair beside her.

"No, they're gone," Maggie said.

"Who do you think took them?"

Maggie retrieved the marker from the floor and gestured to the dry erase board. "It's got to involve those two. But what does one want with a goddess? Zeus has a very jealous wife."

"So does Lyle, according to the service world gossip." Audrey felt Damien's arm around her again.

"But this isn't just any goddess," said Charlie. "This is the Goddess of Love, Her Radiance herself. What if all of this, starting with Persephone and all the others who fell through, was a ruse to get Aphrodite to come to this plane of reality?"

"But what do you do with the Goddess of Love?" asked Audrey. She looked at Damien, and an idea flashed through her brain. "What if there's some sort of unrequited love going on?"

Maggie tapped her lips with the pen. "With Zeus, there's always unrequited love, or at least lust."

"But what if someone wanted to market a solution to that?

Just think, a love potion that works, but which is so expensive that it's only available to those who can pay top dollar? It's the ultimate luxury item." Audrey thought back to some of her exposé articles. "For example, what if you're in love with your best friend's husband, but he only has eyes for his wife, and any attempt to seduce him—other than being damn risky—would surely be met with failure, frustration, and humiliation? You'd be desperate for a solution."

"You're cut-throat." But the look Charlie gave her was admiring. And Damien... He scowled at Charlie.

Audrey stifled a sigh, more frustrated with herself. Wasn't this what she'd told herself she wanted with Kyle?

"She's thinking like a god, or a businessman." Maggie looked back at the diagram on the board. "Let's go at this in a new way. What do Zeus and Lyle Ames have in common?"

"Power." Audrey shivered and shoved away the memory of being helpless, first in the warehouse and then on Olympus. It wouldn't hurt to remember just how vulnerable she'd been so she'd be more careful, but she didn't know how she could.

"Powerful wives," added Damien. His arm around her didn't seem as much of an imposition.

"Virtually unlimited resources," Charlie added.

"Entrepreneurial spirits." Maggie wrote everything they said on the board.

Audrey thought back to the gossip column that had been her first freelance assignment. "Sketchy reputations when it comes to women. If you think about it, they're in the same good ol' boys' club, but some of the boys are older than others."

"And what happens in the clubhouse stays in the clubhouse," Maggie finished. "Remember, they weren't just kidnapping goddesses, they were going after nymphs and other female creatures. What would you do with a whole stable full of women?"

Charlie and Damien looked at each other and then away quickly.

"No, what?" asked Audrey. "We need to think like men to figure this one out."

Charlie looked at the ceiling, and Damien at the floor.

"One of us is going to have to say it," Damien said.

"Well, ah, what do you do with a stable full of horses?" asked Charlie. For once he wasn't smiling.

"You take them riding." Damien wrinkled his nose in disgust. "And that sounds like something Zeus would love."

"They might be on to something," Audrey said.

Maggie shook her head. "And here I was thinking that Charlie was such a nice, straight-laced kind of guy."

"Yeah, but I'm a *guy*."

The look he gave Maggie made Audrey wonder if he laced himself less straight than he let on.

Wait, that doesn't make sense. Back to the problem at hand... "So what if, instead of an unrequited love potion, they're planning on opening an upscale sort of fantasy fulfillment center?" Audrey asked.

"You know, Amelia did say something along those lines." Charlie flipped back through his notebook. "Right. That it was a new line of business, and that people would pay a lot for it."

"What did Lyle's wife say he was doing that was so suspicious?" Maggie asked.

"Staying late at the office, but the P.I. only saw him sleeping at his desk."

Audrey remembered how it felt to be in the Collective Unconscious, to have the freedom to act out her fantasies without consequences. "So what if he wasn't really sleeping, but rather going to the C.U. and experiencing the demo version of the product?" She became very aware of the heat between her and Damien's bodies where they touched and slid a look at him. He gazed at her as well, and she broke the eye contact first.

"But it takes talent to get to the C.U.," said Maggie. "It can't be done by just everyone. We'd be overrun."

"Which is why they're bringing the girls here. And Aphrodite to head the whole thing, because who knows more about pleasuring a man? And how to keep him coming back? She said that any man who had been with her would spend the rest of his life pining for her."

"So this isn't just a pleasure palace." Charlie leaned back with a frown. "It's a threat to all of the men in Atlanta with flexible morals."

LYLE AMES LOOKED at the two women sprawled out on the plush black suede sofas in his private penthouse suite. Decorated in black and white with purple and gray accents, it was the image of modern chic, or it had been until they brought Aphrodite in. The goddess gathered all the light in the room—and the men's attention—and made the expensive surroundings look shabby. His men, especially Leland, couldn't take their eyes off her careless beauty. If she was that stunning in repose, he couldn't wait for her to awaken.

That's why he didn't scold the men who'd captured her and who were supposed to attend to other things while waiting for the drugs they'd given her to wear off. They just sat and stared like their boss, who enjoyed the effect she had on them. If she could melt their jaded, hardened hearts, who knew what she would do to his colleagues, all of whom had a taste for the finer things in life and would pay top dollar for the chance for better?

She laid on her side, her hands beneath her cheeks, and her golden hair half-covering her to the waist like a spun silk blanket. Her little T-shirt offered a tempting glimpse of her stomach and pierced belly button over the low waist of her designer jeans. Although he considered himself to be satisfied in his marriage to a beautiful woman, Lyle wanted to kiss every inch of exposed skin and to uncover the bits that didn't show. The other girl wasn't bad, either, with her dark hair and delicate features, but she was like the moon—beautiful in her own right, but practically invisible in the presence of the sun.

Aphrodite's eyelashes fluttered, and she opened her eyes. He respected how she immediately snapped into calculating mode, eying each of them briefly, then returning to him. Good, she recognized his power. She stretched long and full, which gave him even more enticing hints of what she looked like underneath her attire. His mouth went dry when she sat up and fixed her steady autumn blue gaze on him.

Zeus had warned him about this—that she would immediately try to capture the advantage. He wondered what would happen if he let her.

"Good afternoon, gentlemen." Her voice, soft and husky, reminded him of the old films of Marilyn Monroe. It was a bedroom voice, and he pictured satin sheets, silk robes, coffee in white and gold ceramic cups on the balcony overlooking the skyline at sunrise...

He shook his head to clear the image. "Good afternoon, Your Radiance."

The other girl woke up and immediately scrambled to a sitting position. She opened her mouth to scream, but to her credit, shut it again when her mistress raised one perfect hand.

Lyle snuck a glance at his men. Leland's pierced tongue practically hung out, but Rufus continued to stare straight ahead like he stood guard outside the door. *Good for Rufus*, thought Lyle. *He gets to guard her.*

Aphrodite caught his attention when she rose and strolled to the window, where she stood in the watery light, her back to the men. She stretched and arched her back, her adorable back-side perfectly in view, her butt enticingly round in those dark wash designer jeans. She stood with her hands in her back pockets, her back slightly arched.

"So you want something from me?" she asked, her voice again taking Lyle back to his amorous younger days. He wanted to tangle the sheets with her, to fix her Eggs Benedict and spoon-feed them to her...

He stopped that train of thought by an act of sheer will.

"I'm afraid we need something from you, Your Radiance." Zeus had said that the goddess was most susceptible to flattery. Money wouldn't impress her, and anyone who dared use force while she was awake would likely die trying, or at least end up horribly disfigured, so he needed to tread cautiously. Zeus could keep her in this room, but Lyle needed to charm her to cooperate.

"You *need* something." She looked over her shoulder at him, her lips pursed, and fixed him with a cat-like stare. "You obviously *need* something so badly you've decided to kidnap me and my nymph and hold us hostage."

"I was afraid a woman like you would never listen to a man like me."

Her half smile and heavy-lidded eyes nearly did him in. "And what kind of man is that?"

"A humble man with wealth and power but who lacks one thing."

She arched an eyebrow. "And that is...?"

"The expertise that you have, Radiance. I am just one kind of man, but I need someone to tell me how to attract all of them."

She laughed, but the sound that should have delighted him sent shivers up his spine.

"Nimue, he's calling me a slut."

"No, Radiance, I swear I'm not." He tried to think of something to turn the conversation around. "Look, as a token of faith, I promise to return your nymphs to you if you'll help me."

"And you'll let me out?"

"Ah." He licked his lips. "Not for the time being. You see, it's going to be a process."

"What is?"

"I want to build a modern temple to you, Your Radiance. I want to bring the worship of Love and Light back into this dark, drab modern world."

She crossed her arms and turned away, but said, "Go on."

"I want to bring back the old rituals, the sex-rites, the dancing and the sacrifices. I want to free the world from the puritanical tyranny that has come with modern religion and to liberate the mockery of your virtues from modern hedonism."

She walked back across the room and sat on a stool at the black marble bar, her legs crossed. She leaned on one elbow.

"And what's in it for you? Besides a goddess and a bunch of nymphs in a gilded cage."

Lyle decided honesty would be the best policy. "I know men who would pay handsomely for the chance to participate in your worship, Goddess."

"Ah, money. Is that all you humans think about other than sex? And what's in it for me?"

"Besides having your worship reinstated?"

"Right. I got over that a long time ago." She waved a hand. "While I may require it for my strength in this reality, it means nothing once I return to my seaside bower in the Collective Unconscious, where I still hold power over men in their dreams."

"I promise on my life that I will return you to the outside world and access to the C.U. once I finish the temple and have everything up and running to my satisfaction."

"Your satisfaction." She snorted. "I can guess how that will go. And if I don't cooperate?"

This time it was Lyle's turn to cross his arms and try to look threatening. "I can keep you trapped here forever. If you don't have your worship, you won't have the strength to break free."

She examined her nails, but he could tell she was thinking. She would never let on, but he had her at a disadvantage, thanks to Zeus and the invisible chain Toady had wrapped around her while she slept. To Lyle's relief, the little man had left once he accomplished his task because Zeus didn't want Aphrodite to know about his involvement yet.

"Very well, but I shall require a few things to make my stay more comfortable."

"Anything you ask, as long as you swear that you will help me make this as authentic as possible."

"It's a deal."

Lyle hid a smile. This was better than he'd hoped. Having to keep her drugged the whole time would have made the ordeal impossible. He gave a nod to Rufus, who spoke something into his radio, which transmitted the signal to the basement, where the huddled, frightened nymphs waited to rejoin their mistress.

As for Aphrodite's bower in the C.U., when his plan was over, the pathways would be so eroded it would no longer be there, and she would have to stay with him and rule men's hearts from her temple in Atlanta. If she still didn't agree, well, he had another ace up his sleeve.

"Here's a list of Ames' properties." Charlie looked at the website he'd pulled up. "We can assume they've been taken to one of them."

The others gathered around him at the computer screen, and Audrey's heart fell when it scrolled and scrolled.

"And those are only the ones under his name." Damien looked at Audrey, and the expression in his gray eyes echoed her own sense of futility.

"Do you think she's in one of them?" asked Audrey. "Wouldn't that be too obvious?"

Maggie bit her lip. "At this point, we can't rule anything out. But he wouldn't dare put her in a shabby place. Not if he wants her cooperation."

Audrey shivered. "But won't he be able to make her cooperate?"

"Not necessarily," Maggie said. "Even though they're attenuated, her powers are very real. Look at, ah..." She glanced at Damien.

"Look at how she was able to charm the doctor at the hospital," Audrey finished for her before she said something awkward. She didn't want Damien to be embarrassed by his behavior, and although she could never date him, she wouldn't mind having him as a friend someday. After that little twerp's arrow wore off and the memory of the dream faded.

"So, anyway," Maggie continued, "she won't be impressed by money, and any coercion or violence will probably only backfire on the one who tries it. The only leverage they have is that they can keep her here with Zeus' help, and they'll likely try to make her cooperate through flattery and false promises."

"What about her son?" Audrey asked.

Maggie shook her head. "He does what he wants, but he avoids Zeus. He's caused too much trouble for him in the past and wouldn't risk his own hide, not even to save his mother. At least not unless she were in grave danger, which is highly unlikely. Remember, to immortals, a few years or even a few decades of entrapment is an inconvenience, not the horrible thing it is for humans."

"Is there some way you can see where Zeus is holding her?" asked Charlie.

"I wish I could." Maggie sighed. "It just not that easy to see that kind of energy or to distinguish it from a thousand other spells and protections."

"How much is out there?" Damien looked out the window with a frown as though concerned that a hail of magic was going to come through at him. Audrey stifled a laugh.

"A lot, but most people don't have the talent or sensitivity to recognize it."

"What can we do, then?" Damien asked. The frustration in his tone echoed that which had settled just above Audrey's diaphragm.

"We try using other means." Maggie straightened. "Damien and Charlie, why don't you talk to Mrs. Ames again? She should be familiar with her husband's nicer properties and may be able to give you some direction."

"We can try," Charlie said.

"And what about me?" asked Audrey. She gestured with her good arm to her injury. "I'm not up for much, at least not with pain killers on board."

"You can go home and rest," Damien said.

Audrey tried to cross her arms. "Oh, like you can tell me what to do?"

Maggie put a hand on Audrey's uninjured shoulder and gave it a squeeze. "You and I will venture into the C.U. and see what we can find out there."

"Will it be dangerous?" Damien put a hand on Audrey's other shoulder. She braced herself—would they play tug-of-war with her?

"We'll go to places that might not be very safe," Maggie admitted, "but I don't know how we can avoid it, especially since we need information fast. I can feel the boundaries between the C.U. and the waking world eroding as we speak."

Damien tightened his grip, and she squeaked in pain. He let go. "I'm sorry, I didn't mean to squeeze that hard. I just don't want to let you go." He looked into her eyes, and his concern nearly broke her heart. "Are you okay with all this? You don't have to if you don't want to."

"I'm fine, Damien." Audrey smiled up at him. "This is something I can do even with a hurt collarbone. Go ahead with Charlie. Maggie will take care of me."

"Where will you sleep?" asked Charlie. "You have to make sure no one can sneak up on you while you're away."

"We can use my place," said Maggie. "There are guards and protections set up so that no one, either human or supernatural, will bother us."

"Will I get to see Zinfandel again?" Audrey asked.

Maggie laughed at Charlie's confused look. "Zin is a dragon, a very interesting representative of his species."

"He?" Charlie arched an eyebrow.

"Don't worry, he'd be way more interested in capturing you than me," Maggie assured him.

"Then let's go." Charlie checked his watch. "We should be able to catch the lovely Mrs. Ames at home."

18

———————

Audrey stood at the window of Maggie's top-floor penthouse suite and looked out over the surrounding buildings and trees. When they had gotten off the elevator in the hall, the outside noise had faded, and now all she could hear was the whispering of the wind. It rattled the empty branches and made shadows play on the ground below.

Maggie brought pillows out of the bedroom and tried to make the two couches that faced the windows in an L-formation as comfortable as possible. Audrey couldn't help but look forward to being back in the Collective Unconscious, where, she hoped, her injury wouldn't be present. A dull, throbbing ache told her the pain medicine she'd been given at the hospital was wearing off, and she hadn't yet filled the prescription they gave her. She couldn't afford to be incapacitated by painkillers, but how bad would the pain be? Not that it mattered—she'd survived worse emotionally.

After they stretched out, Audrey couldn't close her eyes. Having someone else there made her nervous. Her mind flicked back to Kyle's pulmonary/sleep rotation and thought about how the patients would be hooked up for sleep studies, with electrodes glued to their heads and belts around their chests and stomachs. She couldn't imagine dropping off under those circumstances. She tried to pretend she was back at her apartment, but she missed the warm rumbling of Athena's purr and the occasional noise of passing cars.

"Are you asleep yet?" she asked and glanced at Maggie.

Maggie opened one eye. "No, you?"

"Not unless I'm talking in my sleep, but I've never been one for somniloquy."

Maggie rolled over on one elbow and stared at Audrey through her blue lenses. "You've had a rough past twenty-four hours. Do you want to talk about it?"

Audrey almost put her hands to her eyes, but her shoulder reminded her the gesture would be impossible. "Yes and no." Yes, she'd had a rough past day, and no, she didn't want to talk about it. She especially didn't want to discuss the thrill-dread roller coaster Damien's attentiveness toward her had put her on, both before and after Cupid's interference. "I'm just not all that tired, and knowing I *have* to go to sleep is making it that much harder. I think I have performance anxiety."

"Do you ever need to take anything to sleep?"

"Not usually. Kyle gives, er, gave me samples every once in a while to try, but that was only when I had a big deadline coming up. I never used them regularly."

"That's one of the ironies of the C.U.," Maggie said. A dry leaf scraped the window, and they both jumped. "People aren't getting enough sleep to keep the archetypes entertained, but they constantly seek it."

Audrey yawned. "Keep talking philosophy. I think it's working."

Maggie didn't look amused. "Do you mind if I help you? I've got an exercise I used to do with my nephew when he couldn't sleep."

"Your nephew? You mean Arthur?"

Maggie nodded, a smile on her lips and a far-away look in her eyes while she gazed into the past. "He had a horrible time sleeping, especially after the whole Lance and Guinevere thing started."

"Whose fault was that, exactly? I've always wondered."

"I'll give you three guesses."

An image of Aphrodite flashed into Audrey's mind. "You're kidding."

"Nope." This time Maggie's smile turned bitter. "The gods knew they were losing ground to the Christian religion, so Aphrodite had her nuisance son stir things up to demonstrate passion wouldn't be quelled so easily."

"That explains a lot." Audrey rolled on her back and looked at the ceiling, which was painted with clouds on a blue sky.

"Are you comfortable?"

Throb, throb, throb... "As comfortable as I'm going to be unless you've got any pain pills."

"I do, but they may interfere with your movement in the C.U. Modern pharmaceuticals wreak havoc with proper sleep and dreaming."

"Fine, I'll do without." Audrey took a deep, centering breath and tried to isolate the pain into a box in her consciousness and thus separate it from her awareness.

"Good, now try to relax. Close your eyes. Now count backwards from ten, and as you do, spell the number itself, so start with t-e-n..."

Audrey did as Maggie suggested, even picturing the numerals being written with a fine-tipped brush on parchment paper. The Truth Seeker's voice lulled her such that she lost the words themselves and only saw the pictures.

At Maggie's suggestion, Audrey found herself in a corridor. She walked past the doors, and at the thirteenth one, opened it and stepped on to the bright green grass of a field. She tilted her head back to a blue sky with wisps of clouds, and she wiggled her toes in the soft grass beneath her feet. A warm breeze caressed her skin and brushed her hair back from her face with gentle invisible fingers. She tilted her head and rested her cheek against her hand.

"Walk through the field," Maggie told her, "and ignore the caress of the West Wind. He likes to lead wanderers astray, and there are many things you could explore, but you can save those for your own dreams. These are the border-lands, what the sleep experts call alpha waves, and if you stay on the path, you will get to where you need to be."

A dirt path appeared in front of Audrey, and she followed it. The fingers disappeared, and a chill rode on the breeze. With every step, her eyes grew heavier, and soon she had to sit, then stretch out on the grass. She struggled to keep her eyes open, but within a few seconds, she fell into a true sleep.

CHARLIE AND DAMIEN pulled up to the Ames mansion on West Paces Ferry just outside of Buckhead after having been buzzed through by the gate guard. It fit with the rest of the affluent neighborhood that included the governor's mansion. The red brick house with white columns and wraparound porch had been built to look like an antebellum home, and Damien whistled with appreciation.

"Lyle could probably stash a dozen nymphs here without anyone knowing it," he said.

"Ah, but you've met Amelia. She wouldn't let him bring that kind of work home with him."

A butler let them in and told them to wait as he brought Charlie's card on a silver tray to Amelia, who was in the finished basement. Damien tried to get a peek into the rooms on either side of the spacious black-and-white tiled front hall. The house even had a large, dramatic staircase.

"So this is how the other half lives," he murmured.

"Getting decorating ideas?" asked Charlie.

Damien looked away from the painting that had drawn his eye, a landscape that could have hung in a museum. He thought for a moment that he had glimpsed a black wolf on one of the bluffs that overlooked a lake with rocky shores and mountains in the distance. Something about the scene looked familiar to him.

"Not really." He bit his tongue before he said something about letting Audrey do the decorating since all he could manage was bachelor chic. What would she think about the Ames mansion? He couldn't imagine her going for opulence over comfort. He checked his watch and hoped she was safe with whatever she and Maggie were doing.

Maggie wouldn't let anything happen to her, right?

"I take it you gentlemen aren't here to discuss art." This time Amelia Ames' voice wasn't friendly. She stood with her arms folded at the base of the staircase.

"Ah, Mrs. Ames, it's so good to see you again."

"Right, because it's only been, what? Three hours or so?"

"I apologize for bothering you like this." Charlie flipped his notebook out. "But I have a few more questions to ask you."

"Have you discovered something?"

Damien was distracted by the woman who had followed Amelia into the front hall. He couldn't help but notice how the creaminess of her skin stood in contrast to the dark brown of her hair, coiled in a braid around her head, and her dark blue eyes. She wore elegantly cut khaki pants and a light blue striped shirt.

"Do I need to leave, Amelia?" the unfamiliar woman asked.

Mrs. Ames shook her head. "No, Delilah, this should only take a moment."

The hairs at the back of Damien's neck told him trouble stood nearby. He recognized her now. Delilah Butler had been married off to some rich old man for his money the year before and had made quite a reputation for herself as a party giver, and planner since it was no longer fashionable for women to just stay at home if they didn't have children. She was also known to be a man killer—indirectly. If her husband David caught her even thinking about cheating on him, well, Atlanta's streets were known for their high accident rate, and the man who got too close to her wouldn't fare well. Damien had worked one of the scenes, a nasty T-bone crash on Scott Boulevard, and remembered searching the society blogs for the rumors afterward, but he doubted she'd recognized him.

"And you are...?" Charlie held out his hand to the newcomer.

"Delilah Butler. She's helping me with this gala I'm throwing on Saturday at Lyle's request." Amelia fixed Charlie with a hard stare. "And we have a lot more work to do."

"I'm Detective MacKenzie, and this is Detective Lewis. This will only take a couple of minutes."

"Come this way, then. Delilah can continue looking at the room plans while we talk."

She led them behind the stairs, through a gigantic kitchen, and down a set of carpeted steps to a large game room that had been turned into a work-room. Delilah bent over a large table covered with lists, charts, and a diagram of a ballroom.

"These look fine, Amelia." She looked up and smiled at Damien. "Everything should go well assuming you won't end up in jail between now and then."

"As long as Mrs. Ames is cooperative, it shouldn't be a problem." Charlie winked at her. "Mrs. Ames, I'm curious about your husband's properties."

"What kind of properties?"

"Ones that may be used to house a large number of people."

Amelia raised a perfectly plucked eyebrow. "A large number of people? Can you be more specific?"

"As in a large number of people that he doesn't want anybody to know about. Captives, shall we say?"

She sat heavily on a navy and white striped sofa. "Officer, you've lost your mind. What are you saying? Has Lyle kidnapped someone?"

"I can't really go into it right now. But does he have any properties where, say, twenty or thirty people might be stashed?"

"Well, he does own a couple of spas and hotels that have lots of rooms. And gyms, if he just wanted to keep them all in one room. But what are you getting at? Lyle isn't interested in the sex slavery trade. All of his business is above-board and legal."

Damien coughed, but Charlie continued. "Let's talk about the hotels. Now let's say he has a very important guest. Someone who would require the height of luxury but absolute privacy. Where would be the best place for someone like that?"

Amelia chewed on a pinky nail. "One of the penthouse suites, probably. There's a nice one in the Plaza Hotel with a view of the city. He also has one behind his office on Peachtree that he'll sometimes spend the night in. And one at the Hotel Tres Cher in Buckhead."

"So that gives us three possibilities." Damien wrote them down.

"I think that's a great start." Charlie looked at Amelia, who licked her lips. "Mrs. Ames, may I have your cell phone number in case I need to ask you anything further? That way I won't have to interrupt you personally."

"Sure." She wrote it on a card and gave it to him.

"Thanks for your time. I'm sorry for interrupting you ladies."

Delilah Butler smiled at both of them, which showed her dimples. "It's no problem at all. I don't know why Amelia even needs me. She has this party well under control."

The expression on Amelia's face said otherwise, or maybe she just wanted to get rid of them. "You know the way out."

Damien followed Charlie out of the house, and once in the car, asked him, "What was the point in all of that? Couldn't we have just called her?"

"No, because I doubt she would have talked to us unless we showed up."

"What would you have done if she hadn't been cooperative?"

"Oh, I have my methods."

AUDREY OPENED her eyes to a room with dirty mosaic floors, their colors faded and the tiles cracked. She lay on a pile of straw covered with some sort of homespun cloth. Her clothes, a tunic and long skirt, marked her somewhere between peasant and merchant class. The sun streamed through the windows, which had no curtains, and the air smelled of salt, spices, and roasting meat. Her stomach growled and compelled her to roll over and stand and find out where the aromas came from. Thankfully her injury had disappeared.

The door opened on to a courtyard, and street sounds spilled over the high walls. Cursing, swearing, haggling, and idle conversations in an unfamiliar language filled her ears.

"Audrey, there you are."

Maggie wore something that looked like a toga, but with a piece of blue silk cloth with a gold border over it. Her long hair was tied back in a complicated style, and jewels sparkled at her neck and fingers. She still wore her light blue sunglasses.

"Why do you always get to be the noblewoman?"

"Because I know what I'm doing in this realm and can manipulate my appearance."

"Can you conjure up Charlie and Damien to keep us

company and see us in our costumes? What are we, anyway? Romans?"

"Something like that. I'm dressed as a noblewoman, and you're my servant, and we've landed in some Mediterranean town. I would guess that this is my house, and I've just caught you napping."

"So what do we do?"

"We play along until we can figure this out. I put in a request to talk to the Oracle, but she has a strange sense of humor. Sometimes the message isn't really a message, but more of a hint that you should have been paying more attention on the journey to find it. Sometimes the place where you end up is part of the message."

"Wait a second, the Oracle? Like, the chick who breathes the poisonous vapors and gives you a message from Apollo?"

"Yes." Maggie tugged the folds of cloth more tightly around her, although the warmth of the air felt comfortable to Audrey.

"What are we going to ask her?" She followed Maggie through the courtyard, through another room, and to the front door.

"That's a good question. We each get one query. We can plan it out while we walk."

Audrey braced herself for the hustle and bustle of the street, but when Maggie opened the door, it was deserted. Dust settled in the sunlight that peeked through the buildings and cast sharp shadows on the street below. Blankets and stalls full of random jewelry and clay pots sat empty. They walked past booths full of seashells, apples, sparrows in cages, small statues of the gods and goddesses, and packets of dried herbs with strange writing on them.

"Hey, this is Greek." Audrey squinted at them and recognized the letters from her math classes of long ago. "And they're claiming to be aphrodisiacs. I didn't know I could read Greek."

"You can't. It's a function of the dream world we're in."

"So we're in Greece?" She looked around with a new appreciation for what she saw. "Ancient Greece?"

"It appears so."

"Where did everyone go?"

"That's what we need to find out."

They followed the winding street to the center of town, where white limestone municipal buildings stood around an open square. Philosophers and politicians debated each other with shrewd eyes and false smiles, and jugglers and performers entertained small knots of people.

"Excuse me," Maggie said to a young juggler. "Can you tell me what's going on here today?"

"Oh, it's very exciting, Lady. Our purpose is coming back to us."

"What do you mean, your purpose?"

"The Man from the East took it away, but the Man from the West said it's coming back."

"Can we talk to either of these men?" asked Audrey.

The boy giggled. "The Man from the East is dead, although his followers claim he's not. The Man from the West comes and goes. He promised big news for us today."

"Really? And is the Oracle open?"

"I don't know, Lady." The boy ran off before they could question him further.

"So what did that tell us?" asked Audrey. The boisterous crowd threatened to swallow her, and the sun beat down on her head.

Maggie pursed her lips. "There's something big going on here today and there's going to be a V.I.P. visit."

They walked farther and found themselves in the middle of a dense crowd that pressed toward the marble steps of one of the buildings, the one that stood at the highest point on the slope. The steps led to a deep portico with fluted columns. The dress of the people around Audrey surprised her, and she recognized modern attire like jeans and T-shirts in addition to the period tunics and toga-type garments. Some of them even had ear-buds with white wires that snaked out of their ears.

"We're not the only visitors," she told Maggie.

"You can see them, too?"

Audrey couldn't take her eyes off of them. It twisted her brain to see flannel and denim in ancient Greece. "Who are they?"

"Dream weavers who have been dropped into our dream, I think."

"How is that possible?"

"The barriers are thinning, remember?"

"I remember." A chill breeze ruffled her clothes. "But I don't have a good feeling about it."

"Nor do I."

A hush fell over the crowd when the large double wooden doors opened, and a man came out and stood at the top of the steps. Audrey recognized his patrician sneer and salt-and-pepper hair from the newspapers.

"That's Lyle Ames," she whispered to Maggie. A couple of men near them shushed her.

19

———————

There was no mistaking Lyle Ames' Roman nose, the supercilious expression, and the perfectly tailored suit. He held up his hands even though the crowd waited quietly.

"Dear friends and fellow worshipers of Her Radiance, the Goddess Aphrodite, I come with exciting news."

Audrey glanced at Maggie, who frowned but said nothing.

"The *Pandemos* herself has consented for her worship to be revived."

A cheer went up from the crowd. Music played from somewhere, and the festival began. Audrey tried to keep track of Ames, but he disappeared back into the building. Maggie, apparently, had the same thought, and they pushed through the crowd to the steps, climbed them, and ran to the door.

"What does *Pandemos* mean?" Audrey shivered when they walked from the sunlight into the shade of the wide porch.

"It's an old term for Aphrodite. It means that her worship and the practice of love and pleasure unite all cultures and races."

"Something that could unite the world? Then whoever controls the *Pandemos* could control the world."

"You know, you're right. That gives us all the more reason for us to find her and get her back."

Instead of the white and gray stone temple she'd expected, Audrey found herself in the lobby of a modern building, all metal and glass with gray floors and walls. A security guard sat behind a wide black marble counter.

"You're not supposed to be in here, ladies," he said with a yawn. "Go on outside and enjoy the festival."

"We're here on official business." Maggie pulled a card from her toga and handed it to the security guard, who frowned at it.

"And who are you here to see?" he asked.

"Mr. Ames." Audrey used her *I belong here* voice. "We have some questions about the logistics of how all this is going to be pulled off."

"Right," Maggie chimed in, "we're with the Collective Unconscious Standards Committee. If he's going to revive the cult of the Goddess Aphrodite, we need to make sure he's in compliance with the Regulations for Proper Dream States and Fantasies."

"Because you wouldn't want your fantasy to be below standard, would you?" Audrey finished with a raised eyebrow. She held the corners of her mouth tight so she wouldn't grin and give them away.

"Just a moment, ladies." The guard picked up a telephone receiver and spoke into it. "Go on up." He gestured to the stairs. "Fifth floor. Sorry, no elevators in ancient Greece."

Audrey hiked up her skirt and followed Maggie up the stairs. "But there are telephones?"

Maggie shrugged. "It's different in different parts, but the C.U. isn't known for its consistent technology."

At the fifth floor, they exited the stairwell and found themselves in a hallway. They followed it to the end of the building, where a door to a corner office read, *Lyle Ames*. It was ajar, and they saw him sitting at his desk, or rather, reclining in the chair with his feet on the desk. He had discarded his jacket in the semi-tropical heat and lay back with his eyes closed and a smile on his lips.

"You ladies almost missed me." He opened one eye and peered at them. "I was on my way back to Atlanta."

"We appreciate you seeing us on such short notice, Mr. Ames." Audrey called upon the charm and interview skills she had learned with countless reluctant interviewees for her exposé articles. "My colleague and I have a couple of questions for you."

"Wouldn't they be better suited for the Oracle?"

"I wasn't aware the Oracle was part of Ames Industries." Maggie spoke through clenched teeth.

"She's not. Yet. Please, have a seat." He turned toward the window and put his feet back on the floor. "I don't really know what to tell you ladies except that all my plans have been approved of and expedited by the highest powers, if you know what I mean."

Fluttering and squeaking noises startled Audrey, and she turned to see that the corner of the room farthest away from the windows held a large box-shaped object covered with a sheet.

"Pardon me, Mr. Ames, but do you have a bird in here?"

He smiled without showing his teeth, which reminded Audrey of a snake. "It's just a pet of mine. Pay it no heed."

"Right," said Maggie. "Do you have the requisite paperwork showing that all has been approved by the Olympian committee?"

He reached into a desk drawer and pulled out a folder, which he tossed across the desk to them. "I didn't need to go through the Committee—this had expedited approval from the Chair himself."

"I see," said Audrey. The contract was in Greek, the writing small and densely packed, and her dream sense gave her the gist of it. At the bottom, in curly script, was signed *Zeus Rex Olympus*, and she smirked at the Latin. The contract told her that Ames had Zeus' permission to pursue his business ventures as long as he agreed to pay the dream tax back to Zeus.

"Tell me about the taxes you've agreed to pay, Mr. Ames."

He cleared his throat. "It's really more of a bartering agreement, Ms...?"

"Lewis," came out of her mouth before she could stop herself. "Aurora Lewis."

"And I'm Margaret MacKenzie," said Maggie. Audrey kept a straight face with effort. They were in the dream world, after all. *Why not indulge in a little fantasy?* The last fantasy she'd indulged in had made her blush, and she hoped Ames would attribute her red face to the five flights of stairs she'd just climbed.

"So tell us about this bartering agreement." Maggie leaned forward.

Music floated up from the square, and for a moment, Audrey was caught up in the melody, which had a Far Eastern sound. Maggie nudged her foot, which brought her out of the trance.

"Mr. Ames, your dream spells won't work on us. Please answer my question."

He sat back and steepled his fingers. "Very well, ladies. Zeus has free use of my facilities, both here and in the waking world."

"And where are these facilities? They will need inspection certificates if you are to operate them. Oh, and no fabrications, please, Mr. Ames. Even though you're in the dream world, your body language gives you away." Maggie touched the side of her glasses in readiness to pull them off if needed.

"All right." He almost spat the words. "The one here is going to be in the old temple next door. This was once the center of Aphrodite's worship. The one in the waking world will be near my Plaza Hotel."

"And has Her Radiance, the Goddess Aphrodite agreed to be your consultant of her own free will?"

"She has, although I do not have her contract here."

"I see."

"Look, do you ladies need anything else? I have to get back to my waking self for an important meeting. The venture capitalists won't be amused if they find me asleep."

"I don't think so," Audrey said. "Margaret?"

"Not that I can think of. If you could please direct us to the Oracle, Mr. Ames? We need to make sure her license is still current."

He rolled his eyes and breathed an exaggerated sigh. "I swear, if I could just get away from you bureaucrats, my life would be complete. She's in Suite 3-A, third floor."

"Thank you for your time."

When they rose to leave, a commotion came from the cage in the corner.

"Shush, you fool bird," Ames said. "Unless you want to be the first sacrifice at the new temple—or for Thanksgiving."

The fool bird shushed.

Once out of earshot of the door, Audrey asked, "What do you think he's got in there?"

"I don't know, but I suspect it's something he shouldn't have. Let's not talk too much here."

Audrey felt the hairs at the back of her neck prickle, and she glanced over her shoulder at the apparently deserted hallway.

"You're right. I'll be more careful. I just got the creepiest feeling someone was watching me."

"LET'S GO CHECK ON RIZZO," Charlie suggested. They sat in his office and compared notes on the interview with Amelia Ames.

Damien looked out the window at the darkening sky. The clouds hung low and promised more rain, and although the temperature hadn't dropped significantly since lunch, the wind had picked up. It rattled the branches of the scrawny trees that lined the street.

"I wonder how things are going with Audrey and Maggie." It seemed like everything brought his thoughts back to her. Right now, he wanted to wrap her in his jacket and take her home so they could make tea, order Chinese delivery, and spend the evening cuddling. Which was odd because he didn't usually cuddle—it made women too clingy.

"I do, too." Charlie joined him at the window and put a hand on his shoulder. "But we need to give them a few more hours. Time runs differently there than it does here. Sometimes it's faster, sometimes slower. You know how dreams go."

Damien remembered his dream from earlier about being with Audrey in the cabin with the fireplace and the velvet and satin bed. That one could have lasted a little longer as far as he was concerned. "Then let's go see Arthur if they'll let us."

The I.C.U. nurse waved them right through, and they found him still unconscious, but all the instruments beeped, whirred, and blinked without alarms.

"How is he?" Damien asked the nurse who came in after them.

"He gave us a scare this morning, but he's stable now."

Her voice sounded familiar, and when he actually looked at her, he saw that it wasn't a nurse, but rather Amanda Lee, the psychiatrist. He mentally kicked himself for assuming female equaled nurse.

"Hello, Amanda," said Charlie.

"Detective MacKenzie." She nodded to him. "Officer Lewis."

"So, are you here to see Arthur, too?"

She put a hand on the older doctor's frail one. "Yes. I was just about to leave and wanted to come in and check on him. I can't help but feel responsible."

"How could you be at fault?" asked Damien.

"Daniel's been my patient for a long time, but he's never done anything like this."

"There's no way anyone could have anticipated this," Charlie told her and moved to stand beside her. Damien walked around to the other side of the bed. Arthur's skin looked gray in the fading light, and the glow from the monitor displays gave the room a weird hue.

"How is Daniel?" asked Damien. "Can he be questioned yet?"

"No, he's gone into a state of purely negative symptoms—not talking or moving—and can't or won't communicate with anyone."

Damien thought about how his encounters with the beings from the C.U. had unbalanced him, and his mind was whole and healthy, or so he thought, anyway.

Charlie seemed to have the same thought. "It was probably traumatic for him, too," he said.

"Oh, so you're the psychiatrist now?" She crossed her arms, but her lips twitched.

"What can I say? I'm a multi-talented kind of guy."

Now she grinned. "I'm sure you are."

"So did Daniel say anything before he completely withdrew?"

Now the smile disappeared. "I'm not sure if I should answer

anything without legal advice. Perhaps I should take you upstairs to talk to his parents."

"Would you mind?" asked Damien. "You said you were on your way out."

"Not at all. I've been thinking about how to approach your request to question him all day. This seems to be the easiest solution. His parents have Power of Attorney, so they can decide if they need a lawyer."

Damien touched Rizzo's arm with a silent promise to come back, then followed Charlie and Amanda out of the room.

THE STAIRS BROUGHT Maggie and Audrey to the third floor, suite 3A. They walked through the door of a dark office but stepped out to the top of a hill. The breeze picked up and ruffled their clothes, and clouds floated across the robin's egg-colored sky. A girl with pointed ears and long brown hair that served as clothing sat with a tablet on her crossed legs beside a jagged gash in the rocky hillside. She gazed down the hill toward the city.

"Are we really outside?" Audrey spun around and saw no sign of the office building. "It *feels* like we're outdoors."

Maggie put a hand on her shoulder. "Don't make yourself dizzy. The laws of space and time are looser here. I wonder if Ames built a shortcut to the Oracle from his office building for his own ease of consultation, which is illegal. Everyone should have the ordeal of climbing the rocky hill path first."

"Even though we didn't?"

"We'll go back down. I doubt we'll be able to get back into Ames' office, although I want to know what was under that sheet."

They approached the girl, who said, "Good afternoon, ladies," in a high, squeaky voice. "How may I help you?"

"We're here to see the Oracle."

"One question per person per visit. Minimum thirty days between visits. Have you determined your questions?"

"Give us a moment."

They walked to the side and paused in the shade of an olive tree. Its silvery leaves sparkled in the breeze.

Audrey looked over her shoulder at the guardian of the cave. "What are you going to ask?"

"I'm going for broke," Maggie said. "I'm going to ask her to identify the mechanism by which the barriers are being eroded. What about you?"

"I don't know." She'd thought that Maggie would tell her what her question would be. "What should I ask?"

"Each question can only come from within. Use your intuition—it will tell you what you need to know the most."

Intuition? What kind of answer was that? "But what if I ask the wrong thing? What if it's something that won't help us?"

"It won't be. You're an old hat at interviewing people. Consider this to be an interview of your inner desires."

Audrey's mind returned to the conversation she'd had with Aphrodite. Her stomach twisted, and a shot of adrenaline flooded her system. "I think I know what I want to ask, but it has nothing to do with our purpose here."

Maggie put a hand on her shoulder and looked into her eyes. Behind the blue lenses, Maggie's eyes looked green, the power behind them evident. "It may, but you just don't know it yet."

They walked to the entrance. The girl, whom Audrey surmised to be a nymph or dryad or something else mythical, although she was tempted to call her Godiva, looked at each of them carefully.

"No weapons or deceptions allowed. Truth Seeker, I'll need your glasses. They will be returned to you upon exit."

"Very well."

Audrey was surprised to see that Maggie's eyes were golden here, and that she kept them cast down to the ground. "I can't make eye contact with you without my glasses," the Truth Seeker explained. "If I do, you'll be compelled to tell me more than I need to know."

"Then why do you have to give up your glasses?"

"No deceptions are allowed, and that means no magic, either. The Oracle is immune to my powers, but without my glasses, I can't lie. It used to be that we couldn't lie at all or we'd become mortal again, but that rule was relaxed since modern police work sometimes requires deception."

"Like what we just did with Ames?"

"Exactly."

They walked into the cave, which smelled of sulfur and incense. The path sloped gently upward, and torches in iron sconces lit the way. Audrey heard lute music, and the incense smell grew stronger. Lulled by it, she allowed her eyes to grow heavy.

"Don't succumb to the spell," Maggie whispered. "Only those who are worthy may approach the Oracle. This is a test."

Audrey fought to keep her eyes open and to place one foot in front of the other. She thought back to her question, and the adrenaline hit her again. It woke her up.

"I want to know the answer to my question even though it scares me."

"Then you've passed the first test."

They continued walking upward into a fog, and the music grew louder. Soon the fog became so thick that Audrey couldn't see or hear Maggie, and she stopped, confused.

"Maggie?" she whispered.

The plaintive whisper echoed around her, and she turned when someone—or something—touched her shoulder. This disoriented her further, and she couldn't remember which way she'd been going.

"Maggie?" she called.

Again, her call echoed, and she turned in the direction in which she thought she had been walking and bumped into something. Rather than the cave wall she expected, she faced her own reflection in a mirror. Her light brown hair swirled around her head in the breeze that also stirred the fog into wisps, and her reflection smiled at her. Audrey brought a hand to her mouth in shock, and her reflection did so, too, but with a giggle.

"What is this?"

"This is your choice, Audrey Aurora Sonoma," her reflection told her in her own voice. "If you turn around now, you will come to a door. Go through it, and you will return to your own life, but all will change. You will have a story assignment that will bring you a Pulitzer Prize, and then all the doors of the world will be open to you. Even better, you will find true love with a rich, handsome man, who will be able to take you to the ends of the earth so you can work toward the causes of justice and peace on a global level, as you've always dreamed. Why stay with exposing corruption in the restaurant business when you can do it for the world?"

Audrey thought for a moment. The offer was tempting, especially the part about having access to the kinds of stories she'd always wanted to write. *And true love thrown in! Then I wouldn't have to ask the Oracle my question.*

But above all, the control she would have over her destiny... Or was it? Would she always be looking for the catch? She shook her head. "If I'm to attain those things, I want to do it on my own, not with a magical shortcut." The reflection returned its posture to her own. "Thanks, but I'll copy old Blue Eyes and do it my way. Besides, I'm needed here."

The mirror disappeared along with the fog, and she found herself standing beside Maggie.

Maggie grinned and hugged her before her more reserved persona reasserted itself.

"Congratulations. You passed the test. The Oracle only speaks to those who truly desire the answer to their question."

"Are there any more tests?"

"Only one." Maggie turned her around to face the other direction, and Audrey gasped. "Not to run screaming from the cave."

20

Harold and Mary Smith were not what Damien expected after having met their skinny, wild-eyed, long-haired son. Both were short, round, and dressed conservatively. They looked like Midwest farmers who had retired South. Damien was surprised that Daniel's mother didn't wear a gingham apron over her gray dress and that his father wore blue slacks and a checkered shirt instead of overalls.

"I was an Atlanta policeman for thirty years," was the first thing Harold Smith said to Damien and Charlie, "so I know you boys have to ask your questions, especially after what Daniel did, but I just ask that you try not to upset my wife too much. It's been hard for her."

Damien raised his eyebrows. *It's been hard for* her?

"Now, Harold," she told her husband, "let the boys do their work. It's not easy for them, either. Remember when you had to arrest that jumper after he fell off that bridge on I-85 and broke his leg?"

"Ahem, right." He gestured to the plastic-covered couch in

the office Amanda Lee had shown them into. "Why don't you guys have a seat?"

They all sat, and Charlie brought out his notebook. "We were just wondering about what your son may have said after the incident."

The older couple looked at each other, and Mary spoke first.

"He was very upset." Her eyes filled with tears. "He kept talking about how he hadn't wanted to hurt the kind doctor, but the imp made him."

"Who made him?" asked Damien. He thought back to the bed in the room where Rizzo had been shot and how the mattress looked like someone had just gotten up or like something small but invisible still sat there. Had there been something? And would he ever get used to this world of invisible assailants?

"He called it an imp," Harold said. "You know, a small creature, kind of like a little troll." He cleared his throat and looked at a spot on the floor between his feet. "I looked it up."

"I'm glad you did so I didn't have to." Charlie was laying on the deep charm, which Damien respected this time. Hopefully it would put the two of them at ease and get him and Charlie some honest answers. "Was this a normal hallucination for him?"

"No!" Mary held out her hands, begging with her eyes for them to believe her. "He'd never had any visual hallucinations. They were always auditory, and they never told him to harm anyone."

"When did this start?" Damien's mouth went dry when everyone looked at him. "This current episode, I mean."

"It's hard to say." Harold took over answering the questions. "Daniel was always real clever about hiding his medicine instead of taking it. He, ah, gets off it, you see, and we don't realize he's relapsing back into his schizophrenia until he disappears. Then he usually ends up here."

Damien could understand their frustration. He'd escorted enough mentally ill people from Decatur's square to the hospital, many of them several times. They always seemed to appear on his shift. "So he's never had anything like this before?"

"No." They denied it simultaneously and so strenuously that they were either good liars or adamant about the truth.

"Where do you think he got the gun?" asked Damien. "Do you keep one in the house?"

Mary opened her mouth to answer, but Harold interrupted her. "I've got one."

Mary's mouth was a gaping hole in her chubby face. "You promised to get rid of it when you retired. You knew Daniel could hurt himself if he found it."

"But I don't know if he found it. At least, I don't think he did. The only key to that drawer is with me all the time, and it was locked."

"Let's say the gun is still where it was. Will you check the chamber to see if a bullet is missing?" asked Charlie.

Both of the Smiths looked at him like he was crazy.

"Why would I do that?" Harold finally said. "There's no reason one would be, especially if the gun is still there. I haven't shot anyone."

"Then do you mind if I send someone over there to get it?" Charlie turned his most charming smile on them. "I don't want to get in trouble with my superiors."

"Of course," Mary told him. "There's no way my son could have killed someone with my husband's gun."

"He's actually not dead," Damien told her. "He's just in a coma. He had a few scary moments this morning but has been stable since."

"Oh, thank God!" Mary fanned herself with her hand. "I was so worried Daniel would be sent to jail for killing someone."

"Your concern is touching." Damien tried not to wince when Charlie delivered a quick, painful nudge to the side of his foot.

"Do you mind if we keep in touch?" asked Charlie. "I'd like to know if he says anything else that could help us sort out why this happened."

"I think he has enough for an insanity defense, don't you?" asked Harold. "I mean, he's clearly not in his right mind."

"That's for the law to decide," Charlie replied. "I'm just a humble detective. We'll be in touch."

AFTER THE TWO women left his crappy office in the C.U., Lyle Ames leaned back, propped his feet on the desk, and closed his eyes in preparation for the journey back to the waking world. He wouldn't admit it to anyone, least of all Amelia, but he looked forward to more verbal sparring with the beautiful Aphrodite, his *Pandemos*. She was everything he wanted in a woman: good-looking with a killer body, smart, witty, and not afraid to go after what she wanted. *And powerful, let's not forget powerful...* The drowsiness and floating feeling that signaled alpha waves descended on him, and he smiled in anticipation.

A thunderclap accompanied the dizzying crash that brought his head and back to the cold marble floor with a crack. He woke with a start, surprised to see the cracked plaster ceiling of his office in the C.U.

"What the...?"

The creature in the cage snickered. Lyle's head throbbed, and his lower back tightened with a muscle spasm. He tried to make rising from the floor look dignified, but he caught his sleeve in the smoldering ruins of the chair and had to tug at it. When it released, he tumbled backwards and landed hard on his butt. He tried not to move too stiffly when he pulled himself off the floor by holding on to the desk, brushed himself off, and looked for an alternate seat.

Zeus sat across from him in one of the chairs recently vacated by the members of the Standards Committee. The god examined the fingernails of his right hand and blew on them to dissipate the smoke from having just lobbed a thunderbolt at Lyle's chair, which was now a pile of charred ash. Zeus' pinstripe suit, perfectly pressed and fitted, showed no signs of him having traveled, although Lyle was sure he'd been on Olympus that morning.

"Good afternoon, Lyle."

Lyle gritted his teeth against the pain. "Zeus, what a nice surprise."

"Do you know who those visitors were?"

Lyle gingerly lowered himself into the new chair that appeared behind his desk. It wasn't nearly as nice as the original one had been. "Members of the Standards Committee, they said."

"Mr. Ames, in the Collective Unconscious, we don't have a Standards Committee."

"You don't?" No wonder the place was falling apart.

"If you're going to do business here, Lyle, you have to start thinking like a god, especially if you have my patronage." Zeus fixed his steel-colored eyes on Lyle and flexed his fingers, which sparked. "The red tape that your government puts you through is the subject of many a dream, especially around tax time. It takes us months to clean it up. You need to get better at discerning legitimate hassles from fabricated ones."

"Point taken." He kept an eye on Zeus' fingers. *He's itching to fry someone. He must be pissed.*

"The redhead was the Truth Seeker, Margaret of Cornwall."

"Right, you've mentioned them. What are they, again?"

"Essentially law-enforcement personnel. Their task is to

keep our affairs from interfering with those of the waking world."

"So it was a police visit?"

"Yes, but not of the kind you expected, although I did tell you they had been alerted."

"And the other young woman?"

"A human whom I interrogated recently in connection with Persephone's disappearance. I tried to have her liquidated, but she is stronger than I anticipated." He smiled as though pleased, and Lyle did not envy the girl for having caught Zeus's interest. That rarely ended well for mortals.

Lyle put his head in his hands, which he regretted when his neck throbbed, and fingers of pain reached around his head from the base of his skull. "So they now know a lot more than they did before about what we're doing."

"Yes, especially since you were so helpful and indiscreet with them."

"Crap. What do I do now?"

"Capture them. You can hold the Truth Seeker until your businesses are so entrenched in both worlds she won't be able to prove interference. As for the human girl..."

A shiver distracted Lyle from his pain. "If she's trapped here indefinitely, her mortal body will go into a coma, and she'll die."

Zeus wiggled his fingers, which still emanated wisps of smoke. "A casualty of business. But you can let me take care of her once you do have her."

"Now look here, Zeus. You promised me that this would be a clean arrangement with no violence or death involved. We've already been responsible for the wheat nymph's death in the waking world—"

"A pity, but it only brought her back here sooner."

"—but I can't betray one of my own kind like that. I run an above-board operation."

Zeus leaned forward such that his face was only inches

away from Lyle's. His slate-colored eyes bored into Lyle's black ones.

"You've gotten into it too far to back out now, Lyle. We've been working on this for a year. If the girl dies, there is no way it can be traced to you. She's got an injured collarbone, and we can arrange for internal bleeding or some other complication to be the cause of her body's death."

"What will happen to her here?"

"Oh, I'll make sure she's well-entertained." Zeus got a faraway look in his eyes, and his lips curled into a feral smile. "She's feisty, just my type. I'm sure she would give me some interesting descendants. I haven't fathered one in many centuries."

Lyle pictured her and felt a pang of regret. *She seems to be an independent spirit. How can I condemn her to eternity as a concubine?*

"I can see what you're thinking, and you humans have such a strong cohesive spirit. But if she and that Truth Seeker take what they know to the higher authorities, we are ruined, and you will know the unique torture of being in prison in both places at once. Imagine not being able to escape in your dreams. Most humans in that position die within the first two weeks of an apparent cardiac event, although I may have to put you out of that misery before it happens so it won't get traced back to me."

"Right. I understand." Lyle took a deep breath to quell the panic that rose in his chest.

Zeus sat back and steepled his fingers. "Lyle, when you deal in the trafficking of flesh for whatever purpose, whether it is capital, emotional, or practical, it is never a clean business."

"You're right, as always. How should I capture the mortal and the Truth Seeker so they can't wake up in the real world?"

"I'll set a trap for them. You said they were curious about your pet over there, right?"

Lyle looked back toward the golden cage under the sheet. The creature was quiet now, perhaps listening to their conversation.

"Yes, they wanted to know what was under there."

"Then they will most likely be back, especially since you told them you would return to the waking world shortly."

"So you can rig up a trap for me?"

Zeus looked up at the ceiling. Lyle followed his gaze and saw another cage suspended with a chain.

"It will fall when someone lifts the sheet," Zeus said. "I'll make sure they come back this way."

"Right. I should be going." *It will be his guilt, not mine. I haven't touched the thing.*

"Yes, go on. Have a safe journey. I'll alert Toady to tell you when our trap has been sprung."

AUDREY FACED a blonde woman in a white dress who sat on a raised throne of black marble. Supernatural fire glowed and flickered behind the dais and cast strange shadows around them. The Oracle's eyes were rolled into the back of her head so that only the whites showed, and her neck bore two puncture wounds like she'd been attacked by a giant serpent or a vampire. Her hands and feet, both of which were shackled to the throne, had the waxy texture and color of dead flesh. Her mouth opened, and a black snake emerged and crawled down her chest, slithering across her breasts, stomach, and lap. It grew bigger and bigger until it was at least eight feet long and the circumference of her neck. Audrey wanted to turn and run, but she willed herself to remain where she stood even when the snake drew up in front of her, hissed, and opened its mouth to reveal long fangs dripping with venom and blood.

"What do you seek?"

She heard the sibilant words in her mind and said as Maggie had instructed, "I seek true knowledge from the Oracle."

"Are you not frightened?"

Audrey didn't want to show this horrible creature any weakness, but she remembered the rule against deception of any sort. "Scared shitless," she told it.

"Then you have passed the final test," the woman on the throne said. The snake disappeared with a puff of smoke that smelled like burning matches, and the woman appeared normal, although still pale and shackled to her throne. She smiled at Audrey and Maggie.

"Whom do I have the pleasure of addressing?" Her voice sounded surprisingly normal, clipped, and businesslike.

"Madame Oracle, I am Margaret of Cornwall, and this is Audrey Aurora Sonoma, a human from the waking world."

"Welcome back, Truth Seeker. It has been a long time."

"Yes, it has."

"How did the previous answer work out for you?"

Maggie shrugged. "You were right, as always."

"I'm sorry to hear that, but I understand that you have other prospects at hand."

Maggie surprised Audrey by blushing. "I may."

The Oracle laughed. "Is that the nature of your question today?"

"No, Madame, although I admit to being tempted. I come seeking a different kind of answer."

"Then I shall enter my trance and endeavor to help you." The woman leaned back in her throne, and a roaring sound filled the cave. The glow became brighter, the shadows sharper, and steam hissed and billowed from behind the throne. The Oracle took a deep breath, and her eyes rolled back. She convulsed, and the shackles kept her from jumping off her seat.

"Ask your question," said a deep voice that didn't sound like her, although it came from her mouth.

Maggie stepped forward and curtsied. "Oracle, I come seeking the mechanism that causes the barriers between our world and the waking one to erode. I need to know how it's happening. If I don't figure it out soon, we will all be lost."

The Oracle expelled a long, whining sigh and jerked to one side. "The mechanism is well-hidden, yet right in front of you. It is tiny, but its effects are large. It is something that one of you has experienced, yet it has been used for thousands of years. You have just witnessed a journey in this world parallel to the one that this mechanism took in the waking world in order to reach those who use it but do not know its effects."

She coughed, then slumped forward. Her eyes opened, and she looked at them, herself again.

"How was that?"

Maggie shrugged. "Obscure as always, but I can't complain about the length."

"And you, Ms. Sonoma. What can I answer for you?"

Audrey had so many questions. Did it hurt when she went into her trance? Why was she shackled? "I don't really feel comfortable putting you through all that. I'm okay, actually."

The Oracle surprised Audrey by laughing. "It doesn't hurt, I promise. I'm not just saying that to be nice, as our Truth Seeker here can tell you. So few pass the tests, and I don't get to interact with many, so I'm happy to help."

"Then allow me to do something for you in return."

"All right, then. I do have one thing to ask of you, but I shall wait until after I answer your question."

She leaned back and twitched on the throne. The glowing and hissing started again. Audrey didn't want to watch, but she couldn't look away, and although she'd been prepared for the deep, resonant voice, it still startled her.

"Ask your question, mortal."

21

Audrey's heart pounded in her ears. Her knees felt like gelatin, so she didn't even attempt a curtsy. She wished Damien were here and was glad he wasn't because in truth, the question was about him. She forced the words past the lump in her throat. "Aphrodite told me that I'd never find true love and be happy because of my need for independence and my reluctance to depend on anyone. I need to know if that's true and if I should just give up now."

"That is, indeed, a human question." Mocking laughter came from all sides. "I fear that you will answer that question for yourself shortly. If you make the correct choice, it will benefit all of you." She slumped over.

"What choice?" asked Audrey.

"Just one question per visit." The Oracle raised herself with effort. Her face glistened with sweat. "Did it help?"

"N-no, not really. What in the world is speaking through you?" Audrey wanted to release the poor woman from her shackles and bring her to the light of day.

"Ah, I can't answer that question because I don't really know for sure. Some say it is the will of the gods, others, the voice of the future or the over-arching power that none have any knowledge of save the snippets it deigns to give us."

Audrey wondered if the Oracle gave similarly vague answers to questions like, What do you want for dinner? But she'd made a promise and hoped she wouldn't have to do something ridiculous. "Right. I have no clue what you're saying. What can I do for you?"

"It's a small thing, really." The Oracle wrinkled her nose. "I've had this itch at the end of my nose since yesterday. I cannot be released from my shackles until the end of my term, and the imps that throw the trance-inducing mixture from the stream of Apollo on those hot coals have claws that are too sharp and clumsy. Would you mind scratching my nose for me?"

"That's it? I can't release you?"

"I serve my purpose, young human, just as you will serve yours. Please just honor my request. You promised."

Audrey looked at Maggie, who shrugged. "We can't do anything else for her. I once wasted a question finding that out."

Audrey climbed the black marble steps, and the Oracle leaned forward. Audrey delicately scratched the end of her nose, and the Oracle sighed with satisfaction.

"Thank you. That will make my days and nights much easier."

"No problem. Thanks for the answers. I wish I could say the same."

"Any time."

With that, they turned and descended through the passage, which seemed a lot shorter than Audrey remembered.

"Did that do us any good?" Audrey asked.

"Only you will know whether your answer was helpful or not. From what she said, it sounds like we've got a lot of work to do before we find our true answers."

"Were you disappointed with my question?"

Maggie wouldn't meet her eyes, and Audrey knew it was more than Maggie protecting her from her Truth-Spelling. "I was hoping you'd ask something more relevant to our quest," Maggie admitted. "But you're human. Your intuition told you what to ask, and there's no way to know how it all ties in until it does."

Audrey's cheeks heated, and shame tightened her chest. "You were human once, too. Have you never pondered the question of love?"

Now Maggie's pause made Audrey all the more curious for her answer. Finally, she said, "All the time. But there are considerations that keep me from pursuing it."

"Like what?"

"Well, I'm over a thousand years old. I outlive my lovers, or they leave me for a mortal subject of affection who can provide more predictability. Each assignment brings me to a different place, and I get very little down-time, so it's hard to build long-term relationships."

"That's what your previous question was about, wasn't it?" Audrey couldn't resist asking even though it seemed to be a sore subject.

Maggie sighed, but she answered, "I thought I had found someone, a recruit to the Truth Seekers, but he couldn't handle it, and there were other considerations I can't talk about right now. So, it's moot."

"What about Charlie, 'Ms. Margaret 'MacKenzie'?"

Maggie shook her head, but her cheeks turned pink. "He's just like all the rest of them. He'll be attracted to the adventure and the otherworldly quality of the whole affair, but then he'll bail when he finds I can't make certain promises or when I refuse to leave my calling for him."

It wasn't unlike how Audrey felt about dating cops, but from the other side. She'd never ask anyone to leave his passion for her. "Do you ever think about quitting and living a normal life?"

"Almost every day, but I won't do it, at least not anytime soon."

They came to the entrance of the cave, where the young dryad returned Maggie's glasses to her. "See you again soon, Truth Seeker."

"Probably not that soon," Maggie muttered so that only Audrey could hear her. "Which way is the path downhill?"

The girl pointed toward the view of the city, but Audrey saw something at the corner of her vision.

"Hey, look. Isn't that the door we came in?"

Maggie squinted at the door that had appeared in the side of a boulder. "I think so."

"Shouldn't we go back the way we came, then? Ames will be gone, and you said you wanted to find out what was in the cage."

"I don't know. There's something odd about this."

"Come *on*, Maggie." Audrey didn't know why, but she felt pulled to the door. "I know this is the right way to go."

"Well, then, I'll trust your gut on this one." Maggie sounded skeptical, but she followed Audrey.

As she suspected, the door led back to the building. When they stepped from the stairwell to the fifth floor, they found it deserted and silent.

"All clear," whispered Maggie. Audrey nodded, and they tiptoed down the hall to Ames' office. The late afternoon sun slanted through the windows and made golden squares on the floor. "I'll keep watch, you look."

Audrey lifted the sheet that covered the large rectangular object and saw a child with white and pink feathered wings. He tried to squeak a message through the bandage that gagged his mouth, his brown eyes wide with urgency. His arms were bound in front of him with another rag.

"What? Wait. Hang on!" Audrey reached her arms through the bars and untied the gag.

"I said, it's a trap, you dimwitted mortal."

"Audrey, run," Maggie disappeared from the doorway, but before Audrey could follow, a large cage fell over her with a resounding clang that burned the inside of her ears.

"Maggie, help!" But she didn't hear an answer.

"Maggie's gone," said a familiar voice—Zeus. "A pity, too. She would have made a good addition to my collection."

"What is this?" Audrey shook the bars of the cage, and they rattled but didn't part.

"This, my dear, is your new home." He chuckled. "Oh, that was good. I gave you enough time to escape, but you were just too curious."

She mustered her courage and looked him straight in the eye. "I'm not one of your mythical creatures, Zeus. Let me out."

"I can't do that. The information you have is too valuable."

"But Maggie has it, too."

"And you will serve as bait to capture her as well."

Audrey opened her mouth to reply but shut it before she gave too much away. Hopefully Zeus didn't know about the guys.

"Told you," said a small, young voice behind her. "Now we're both stuck."

"Who, or what, are you, anyway?"

"Some call me Cupid, some Eros." He put a chubby hand over his heart and bowed while he hovered in mid-air. "I am the one who is responsible for love at first sight, for that flutter of the heart as you look at your lover, for—"

"All right, all right, I get it." She turned to look at Zeus, but he was gone.

"We're alone now," said Eros. "I can tell when they're invisible. I'm a god, too, you know."

Audrey didn't have time to deal with another godly ego,

especially not from a being who had caused her so much trouble. "Really. That's fascinating."

"Yep, and I could make you fall in love with him."

"Don't you dare." She glared at the impudent creature and wished she could smack him, god or no, but he'd probably just flutter out of reach. "You've caused enough trouble for me today."

"Not as much as you've caused yourself, Missy. How could you not figure out that was a trap? They put the freaking door right in front of you."

Audrey's cheeks burned. He had a point. That's what she got for jumping into something without preparing. "I don't recall asking for your opinion, Chubby."

"Nope, but you're stuck here, and you took my gag off, so you're going to get it."

"No good deed goes unpunished. Why don't we just figure out how to get out of these cages?"

Eros floated to the floor and looked up at her with sorrowful puppy-dog eyes. "I've been trying, but they're solid gold dream-metal, which means that their effects carry over to the waking world, too."

Audrey's heart dropped into her stomach. "What does that mean?"

He reached one small hand out to her. "It means that if you stay here, your body will go into a coma and die."

She ignored the hand. *This little cherub thing is emotionally manipulative like his mother.* "And then what will happen to me here?"

"You will be trapped forever, and Zeus will make you into one of his playthings. He fancies you. I heard him say so."

Audrey set her jaw and ran her fingers along the joints between bars. "Then I'm going to have to get out of this mess. How long do I have?"

"Hard to say, but probably not long enough."

THE SOUND of bars clanging shut made the muscles around Damien's heart seize. Nothing in Charlie's car could have made the noise, so he gasped, "Hurry up."

Charlie, who drove out of the hospital complex, asked, "What? Where?"

"Something's happened to Audrey. We have to get to Maggie's." Damien rattled off the address she'd given them the night they'd found Persephone.

The ride from the hospital to downtown Decatur took less than five minutes, but to Damien, the air had turned into gel, and every second was a struggle. They finally pulled up outside of Maggie's building, ran into the foyer, and rang the bell.

"Hello?" The Truth Seeker's voice trembled like she'd been crying.

"Maggie? Thank gods. Are you all right?"

Damien raised his eyebrows at the relief in Charlie's tone. "What about Audrey?"

"I'm fine," she said. "But you guys had better come up."

The elevator rose, but Damien's heart sank further with each floor. His suspicions were confirmed when a tear-stained Maggie let them in. Damien immediately focused on Audrey, who lay on the sofa farthest from the door, her breathing shallow, and her skin cold and clammy.

"What happened?" Damien lifted one of Audrey's limp hands and held it. It weighed almost nothing, like her bones were hollow. He sat beside her and smoothed her hair back from her face. She slept with a little frown line between her eyebrows.

"We got caught in a trap. Well, she did. She got led right to it —I should have stopped her." Maggie's voice caught in a sob, and Charlie put his arm around her.

"It's okay, tell us what happened."

Maggie hiccupped. "I got away. I thought she was right behind me."

"Wait, start from the beginning." Charlie gently sat her on the other couch, and she gave them a summary of their visit to the Greek city and the Oracle but not the details of Audrey's question or answer. Damien wondered if it could have been about him.

Charlie held Maggie tightly, and Damien felt the emptiness in his arms where Audrey should be. Her already thin form seemed to grow less substantial with each breath.

"She's fading fast," Damien told them. "We have to do something."

"The only thing I can think of is to return to the C.U. and try to rescue her, but they'll be on the lookout for me and try to trap me, too. But I can't put you guys in danger."

A knock on the door startled them.

"Who could that be?" Maggie got up and looked through the peephole. "Lucia?" She opened the door.

"Margaret." Lucia—Damien recognized the psychic—enveloped Maggie in her hug. "I've been meaning to visit you, and then I felt something terrible happen. What is going on?"

Lucia spotted Audrey and crossed the room in three long strides. She put her hand alongside Damien's face, tilted it up, and looked into his eyes. His cheek grew even warmer beneath her cool touch.

"You've been touched by something from the Other Side," she said.

"What?" he asked around the lump in his throat. *Touched.* That's what they'd said about his grandmother, why she'd been locked away. While he'd accepted that all the supernatural stuff was real, he still wondered what it would to do his mind. Would it affect him like it had her? DeMarco's words echoed in his mind—*No one trusts a cop who's gone off the deep end.*

"I see it in you. But some good may come of it." She looked

down at Audrey. "Ah, child, have you found your spirit guide yet?"

Maggie put her hand to her forehead. "Of course. If she has her guide to strengthen her, she may last longer. Damien, when you were in the C.U., did you see any animals?"

"I had one weird dream where I sat on a rock by the river and waited for Rizzo, and I saw a black wolf. He said he was mine."

"And what about with Rizzo?"

"An owl, which I think belonged to Arthur, and a little silver dragon about this big." He held his hands about a foot and a half apart.

"A dragon, albeit a little one, is a powerful guide." Lucia caressed Audrey's check. "This one was born for great journeys."

"The dragon told Arthur she was lost."

"She needs to be led to Audrey." Maggie stood and walked to the window, which showed the streetlights below strung out like amber beads. "The question is, who to do it?"

Damien opened his mouth to volunteer, but the grief over what had happened to Rizzo twisted his words. "I... I can't. When I went there with Arthur, something horrible happened to him. I can't risk Audrey like that." And then after his dream about her, he'd felt things he promised he'd never allow himself to, and his feelings were magnified in the hospital. He saw himself for the coward he was. He dropped Audrey's hand, which bounced softly on the sofa cushion, and buried his face in his hands, his cheeks hot with shame.

"I have seen a man who is not a man," said Lucia. "In one form, he is a little older and has a long beard and round glasses. He may be able to help us."

"Arthur?" asked Damien. Lucia's description sounded a lot like the doctor.

"That is his name?" Lucia smiled with brilliant white teeth

against her mahogany skin. "Is he the one you saw in the company of the dragon?"

"Yes." He took a deep breath. "I...can go. Try to find him." But he didn't sound certain even to himself.

"This one is not ready," Lucia said to Maggie. "He has too much fear to overcome, and with whatever spell that is on him, the Olympians would sniff him out quickly. We need to communicate with this Arthur and lead him to her."

"Is it safe?" asked Charlie.

"I have seen your spirit guides, and they are here with you. They will protect you from harm that may try to cross over."

"You can see them?" Damien looked around reflexively, the hairs on the back of his neck on end.

Lucia chuckled. "Indeed, you have the wolf at your heels. Your golden-haired friend is guided by the spirit of a hawk."

"And Maggie?"

"I'm my own. Immortal privilege."

"What about you, Lucia?" Charlie grinned. "Don't tell me yours is a black cat."

"A panther. Now, let us sit in a circle and link hands."

22

Lyle pulled his car into his garage around nine o'clock. He'd thought about sleeping at the office again, but he wanted to show someone—maybe the P.I., maybe himself—that he was capable of going home and weathering domestic storms. Plus, Zeus had told him to shore up any potential information leaks. That left Amelia, who knew a little of his plans and was organizing Saturday's gala for Aphrodite's debut, although she didn't realize that was why. He needed to make sure she didn't talk to anyone between now and then.

The smells of garlic, shallots, and a rich, meaty aroma assaulted his nose when he entered the kitchen from the garage, and his stomach clenched, then growled. When had he last eaten? Hard to say. He'd been satiated by Aphrodite's beauty and company all day.

When he walked into the dining room, he saw his dinner, a despondent pair of lamb chops sitting in cold, congealed gravy beside *haricots verts* with almonds, a dinner roll that had dried out to beyond crusty, and garlic mashed potatoes. His fork stood handle-up in the mashed potatoes, which had been shaped into a face. He didn't look closer to see if the likeness resembled him; he suspected it did. He took a sip of the Rhone blend that she'd poured for him, wondering too late if it was poisoned. He pressed his lips together.

This is childish. I'm a businessman about to launch a lucrative new project, and she can't expect me to just appear at her whim. I get enough commands from Zeus during the day—when I'm home, I'm king of this castle.

He stopped in his tracks to the living room or wherever she hid, his heart still pounding. He couldn't get the image of that young woman—what was her name?—Audrey out of his mind. Trapped forever in the C.U. to be Zeus' concubine. Guilt joined and fueled his anger.

Amelia has no idea what I'm dealing with, so she could be a bit more understanding.

She was not in the living room, nor in the TV room, the master bedroom or any of the other five, bathrooms, sauna, sun porch, or parlor. He found her downstairs in the finished basement she used as her work room. She stood behind the table with a stack of R.S.V.P. cards and marked names off a list. She used only one desk lamp, and for a moment, she reminded him of Aphrodite, how Her Radiance seemed to glow. But Amelia's blonde hair stood out in frizzy clumps from her head like she'd been running her hands through it, and mascara tracks ran down her cheeks.

Anger at her for making him feel guilty made his face grow hot, and he strode across the room.

"Lyle." She looked up at him, and her eyes glistened. "Your dinner is on the table upstairs."

"I saw it. Could you not even keep it warm for me?"

"I did. Until eight-thirty. Then Marin left, and I didn't want to leave the oven on while I was down here."

It would have been a logical reason at any other time. Now he clenched his fists. "Don't you understand that what I do is important?"

She recoiled and crossed her arms. "Of course I do." She put a hand up to her suddenly flushed cheek.

"And don't you get it that sometimes I need to work late? I can't just be at everyone's beck and call. And when I get home —with time I can't afford—I expect for my dinner to be warm and ready to eat."

She looked at him, open-mouthed. *Why doesn't she say something? Why doesn't she argue?* Oh, he was ready for an argument. His mind flashed back to an encounter with Aphrodite that afternoon, when he'd almost succumbed to her charms and ripped her clothes off. When he pulled away, she'd laughed at him and looked at his crotch with a comment that it probably wouldn't be worth it anyway. That's what he liked about her—she was a challenge. *Unlike meek little wifey here.*

He crossed his arms. "Well?"

"Well, what?" Her spark of anger encouraged him. "You're the man of the house. Obviously it's too much to ask for you to actually come home once in a while."

She stood, and he noticed for the first time that she had put on the little black dress he liked so much. She wore a blue and white work shirt over it to keep her shoulders warm. In two strides, he was beside her, looking down into her blue eyes, where there was a new emotion he'd never seen before. Fear.

Gods, that made him feel powerful.

"This is how it's going to go, Amelia." He kept his voice low, his tone firm. "You're going to go upstairs and warm my dinner. You'll undo whatever effigy you've made of me in the mashed potatoes and heat up a fresh roll for me. Then I'll eat, and we'll have a normal conversation like man and wife. I need to make sure you don't talk about Saturday's party to anyone."

Her quick intake of breath interrupted him. He put a not-too-gentle finger under her chin, his thumb on the dimple he used to find so adorable.

"Have you talked to someone about the party?"

"No, Lyle."

"Good. Because horrible things will happen to you if you do. Mr. Zeus will be most displeased, and he has some rather unsavory connections that even I can't protect you from. Do you understand?"

"Yes, Lyle."

"So be a good little wife and do what you need to do. I'll be in my office. Call me when dinner is ready."

She walked out of the room on unsteady legs, and he admired the rear view.

That's how to put her in her place.

So now that he had control of his wife and his dinner again, why this crushing weight in his chest? He sank down on the sofa and put his head in his hands. He may have regained control of his household, but everything else, including his self-respect, teetered on the brink of ruin and chaos.

DAMIEN CLOSED his eyes and held hands with Charlie and Madame Lucia. They sat in a circle in Maggie's living room, but he couldn't concentrate on what they were supposed to do. Every one of Audrey's labored breaths tightened the invisible band across his chest. He must be the worst sort of coward— and a terrible police officer—that he couldn't make himself try to save her.

"The circle has been broken." Maggie breathed into the phrase. *"Damien, picture Arthur Rizzo for us."*

Damien imagined Arthur as he wanted to remember him, standing in the E.R. the night he'd brought Persephone in. The darkness behind his eyelids resolved to a vision of the old man sitting in a clearing, his head in his hands and his shoulders slumped.

"Arthur, if that's who you are, answer us. "

Arthur looked around. He sat on a log in a beautiful grove of trees with a clear pool at his feet.

"Who's there?" he asked.

"The circle has been broken."

"What circle?" he asked and gazed into the pool. The water swirled, and rather than looking at him from above, Damien felt like they peered at him from his feet like they sat in the pool.

"The one that needs your help, " Maggie said, still telepathically, but they were all joined in her mind, so Damien flowed along with her intention. She showed Rizzo what she could, how a single candle illuminated the four people seated on the floor and a fifth on the sofa behind them. The fifth lay still and quiet, as in death. The four held hands, and with Lucia's help, Maggie amplified the concern and fear for their fallen comrade. And burning love, this from Damien.

"Who is that on the couch?" Arthur asked, his voice choked.

"Her name is Audrey Aurora Sonoma. She is gravely ill, her conscious trapped in the Collective Unconscious."

"I have failed," the doctor said and hung his head. For a moment, he looked like the young man Damien had seen with Audrey in the coffee shop, but then he returned to his normal appearance.

A small silver dragon landed on his arm. It ruffled its wings and tasted the air with its tongue.

"If that is her spirit guide, it needs to be brought to her so she will survive."

Arthur looked up. "There is still hope?"

"There is, but not for long. Find her. Bring the dragon to her."

"Do you know where she is?" He closed his eyes as if trying to focus on the message.

"Corinth Plaza, main office tower, converted government chambers. No time to lose. She fades quickly."

"Corinth?" Arthur opened his eyes and looked at the dragon.

This time the voice that spoke from the vision belonged only to Lucia, whom Maggie mentally sidestepped so as to get out of her way. *"You may go wherever you wish, Guardian. It is the city of the* Pandemos. *You must keep your focus and not delay further."*

A force that felt like spiritual whiplash broke the connection, and Maggie opened her eyes to see the others in her apartment blinking in confusion.

"What was that?" Damien asked and rubbed his neck. "Where was he? How does he know Audrey?"

"I wish I knew. All I can say is that your friend isn't human." Maggie stood.

"She is correct," Lucia agreed. "There are links binding us all together, some stronger than others, and the ones tying you to Audrey may have been forged even before you, ah, rescued her."

Maggie inclined her head toward the psychic.

"Then what is he?" Damien insisted. If Arthur wasn't human, that meant he wasn't going to die. Didn't it?

"Well," Maggie said, "you grew up Catholic, right?"

Damien sighed. "Yet another thing you know without my telling you. Don't you Truth-whatevers have any respect for privacy?"

"Sorry, caught it earlier. You've heard of guardian angels, right?"

"Yes, but I never believed in them literally." Although if anyone had been one for him, it was Arthur Rizzo.

"Well, that might have to change."

～

"C'MON, a game or something. I've been stuck in here for for*ever*."

Audrey put her hands over her ears to block the child-god's whining. "No. Leave me alone."

"We can play 'I Spy.' I spy, with my little eye—oooh!"

The door opened, and an older gentleman walked in. Audrey was sure she'd never seen him before, but he looked very familiar.

"Your Mischievousness," the man said and bowed. The creature bowed back.

"I'm glad you're here," Cupid said and clapped his hands. "She's no fun."

Although the man stood on the other side of the cage, there was something reassuring about him.

"Audrey," he said.

She looked up at him with tearstained cheeks. "Who are you?"

He put his hand through the bars, and she took it. When she touched him, his appearance changed, and she found herself looking not at an old man, but J.J. her brother.

She closed her eyes. "This place is playing tricks on me."

"No, it's me," he said and knelt on the floor. "I've not been honest with you, but this is neither the time nor place for my story. What happened?"

"I'm trapped, and if I don't get back to the waking world soon, I'll die. And then Zeus will turn me into his concubine, and I'll be condemned to an eternity of having to put up with his arrogance, and I'll never see Damien again." Her voice cracked on the last word, and she sobbed into her hands.

A little dragon zipped into the cage and crawled into her lap, warm and reassuring like Athena the cat, but less dense. "Who is this?"

"Your spirit guide. Your friends sent me to bring her to you.

She was waiting outside until I could determine it was really you."

"You found me." This time she smiled at him through her tears. "You brought her to me. Thank you."

"Lucia, Damien, and the others thought that she might help you keep your strength up here, to help you last longer."

"Are they going to rescue me?" She held the dragon in her hands, and it preened. "Can you?"

He shook his head. "I wish I could, but I'm weak in this form with my physical body still trapped in the hospital. Your friends are making plans now. I saw them."

"Who are you, really?"

"I can't tell you, I'm afraid, but I'll keep you company until they arrive if you like."

"That would be nice." A memory from before their father died surfaced. "Does this have something to do with the angel at the swimming pool?"

"The what? I don't know what you're talking about." But he wouldn't meet her eyes.

"The angel." She closed her eyes, and the memory surfaced —the smell of chlorine over the jasmine in their neighbor's yard, screaming when J.J. had dived into the shallow end of the pool and hadn't come back up. And the form of pure light that had lain over him and been absorbed into him, and he'd made a miraculous recovery even though they'd thought his neck was broken and he was gone.

"I got a second chance I never should have." He squeezed her hand. "You and Mom couldn't be left completely alone when Dad died."

She opened her eyes, her vision blurred with tears. "So what are you?"

He shrugged. "Just keep believing in guardian angels."

She recognized that tone—that's all she'd get out of him. Was it possible? Sure, he'd become extra protective of her after that summer. When he'd been home. But why hadn't he been there when she'd gone back to school and had been shunned because no one knew how to be around her? She thought he'd gone back to college, but had he really? Or was he living a different life?

"Please tell me. Are you or aren't you my brother?" She couldn't lose him twice.

He reached over and squeezed her hand through the bars again. "We'll talk about it later, I promise."

She acquiesced, but only because she needed time to sift through her memories and find the evidence that would give her the truth even if he wouldn't tell her. Meanwhile, the dragon in her lap comforted her somewhat. She sighed and looked out the window. "I've never been afraid of the dark, but I don't know what's going to come out of the shadows here."

He snorted. "I don't blame you."

His response didn't help her feel any better, especially with her new knowledge about him. "How are the others? You know, I only met them a couple of days ago. Or was it yesterday?" She squinted into the dark like the days would be illuminated there.

"Time passes differently here," J.J. said. He lowered himself to the floor with his back against the wall. The owl settled on a perch where it could see out of the windows.

"I met Maggie here. And Zinfandel, the vegetarian dragon."

"The what?" J.J. smiled at her. "Tell me, did it have something to do with your dreams? Oh, and what happened with Kyle?"

Audrey surprised herself by not wanting to cry about her ex, who, if she were to be honest, had been more of an idea than a relationship. "You were right. He was a lying, cheating jerk. But let me tell you about Damien." She glared at Eros.

J.J. grinned, and as always, his smile reassured her. "Oh, this is going to be good."

"Never mind," Audrey said. "I don't date cops. I've seen first-hand how painful loving one can be."

"But if you were to make an exception," J.J. said, "Damien would be worth it. He's a good guy, Audrey."

She didn't say anything. If he wasn't her brother, he'd lost the right to give her advice. And if he was... His approval of Damien made her too happy and made her too inclined to consider giving the relationship a shot.

23

———————

Damien woke from a sound slumber, all of his senses alert. He'd gone home and collapsed after the séance, or whatever it had been, at Maggie's. He didn't know whether to believe her theories about Arthur.

Each revelation from that woman makes my world stranger and stranger. But at least someone's there with Audrey.

He rolled to one side, but his guilt didn't sit well in his chest. He should have gone to Audrey no matter what the psychic had said. And he would now, but he didn't know how. He wasn't a—what did they call it?—dream weaver.

The glow from the streetlight outside his window projected bars on the dingy carpet in his 'cheap' Virginia Highlands apartment that would be ridiculously overpriced anywhere else. He'd wanted to be there for the night life, but he hadn't counted on never being home to enjoy it.

Not that he'd wanted to after his grandmother died. Now he had a different kind of 'night life' to deal with.

A chill breeze ruffled the dry leaves of the scrawny trees beside his first-floor patio, and he shivered. Cursing the lack of insulation and weather-stripping around his windows and door, he pulled on a sweatshirt over the T-shirt and shorts he slept in and made a quick recon around his place, gun in hand. Nothing was amiss inside, but a gust of wind whipped the poor little saplings into a frenzy, their remaining leaves struggling to hold on to the branches. Damien watched, mesmerized by the rhythm and sway. That's when he heard a small sound, like someone dropping from a height to land like a martial artist on his carpet.

He wheeled around, gun aimed at the direction the noise had come from. Quiet laughter mocked him.

"A man who has been touched by the gods should not be so quick to shoot one." A man dressed all in black, his light hair and beard coiffed and trimmed like a country-western singer on Country Music Awards night, stepped out of the shadows, and the lights in the room flickered on. The man took a seat on Damien's shabby second-hand sofa that he'd recovered himself and had felt proud of until this moment. But the stranger made all his surroundings darker like he cast a pall on them.

"Who—or what—are you?" asked Damien. "And stop saying that I've been touched. That's absurd."

The intruder gestured to the easy chair. "Have a seat. Trust me, you know who I am. You watch for me every time you go out on patrol."

"You're..." Damien sank into his armchair.

"I'm Hades, King of the Underworld, Lord of the Dead, and all that rot." The god spoke patiently, as to a child. Then he looked around, a mischievous grin lifting his mustache. "And I'm not supposed to be here."

Damien tried to wrap his mind around the fact that a god sat on his sofa and endeavored to overcome his resentment at the intrusion. *They won't even allow me a good night's sleep.*

"Okay, look, I know this is hard for you." Now the god spoke in television therapist tones. "But I have something very important to tell you, and as I said, I don't have much time."

"Why not? And why are you helping me?"

"Someone—I suspect either Zeus or Hera—has set up wards on the boundaries between here and the C.U. to monitor supernatural comings and goings. Probably Hera. She knows her husband is up to something. I got through a hole, but the longer I'm gone, the higher the risk of getting caught. As for why I am helping you, if Zeus gets away with this little fiasco, none of the rest of us Twelve are safe. We all have power that can be harnessed in the modern world, and it's only a matter of time before someone tries to trap us. Sometimes they can succeed."

Damien nodded. "That's what we've figured, too, that Zeus is involved. And he's trapped Audrey." He choked around the lump in his throat. "Have you seen her?"

Hades gave him a pitying smile. "Trust me, her coming to me would be much better than what Zeus has planned for her. But no, I haven't seen her."

"Do you know where Aphrodite is?"

"I have a suspicion. Did you read the book Arthur Rizzo gave you?"

Damien looked around and saw it on the coffee table. *How did that get there?* The last time he'd seen it was in the back seat of his car. He picked it up, and it opened to a folded piece of paper. Six lines held up a triangle. *Great, Rizzo's drawing is as bad as his handwriting.*

"What is this?"

"Your friend had a dream, and that's what he saw. He has his own talents, as you probably know. That's why the nymphs all came to him, or why you brought them to him. You have some ability, too."

"So the point of this is...?" Damien arched an eyebrow. *I'm so tired of puzzles and riddles.*

"If you find that, you know that's where Aphrodite is being kept."

"What about Audrey? Can you sneak me through the hole for a just a few minutes to talk to her?"

"You're losing sight of the bigger picture, boy." Hades sighed. "But I understand since that's how I felt when Persephone was missing. Go to the mirror in your bathroom."

Damien did as he was told, and instead of his bathroom reflected in the mirror, he saw a room with two gilded cages. In one sat a chubby little angel thing, and in the other, Audrey. The anxiety in his chest and stomach loosened a little when he saw the silver dragon in her lap. A shadowy figure sat against the wall, but all Damien could make out were slender limbs and a beard.

It must be Arthur.

"Audrey," he said.

She looked up. "Damien? Is that you? You can't be here—you'll get trapped."

"I just needed to make sure you're okay."

"I'm as okay as I can be. I have company. By the way, if I don't come back—"

"Don't say that." The despair in her eyes made Damien want to crawl through the mirror and into the cage to comfort her.

She shook her head. "I'm not giving up, don't worry. But if I don't make it back, don't let your worries about your genes make you be alone for the rest of your life."

How did she...? Could the dream have been more than a regular sex dream? He didn't have time to ask, as darkness crept over the mirror from the corners in. "I'll... I'll come for you soon."

The mirror went dark and then returned to its usual reflection.

Damien walked out into the living room, where he found Hades reading Rizzo's book.

"They never get it quite right," he grumbled. "Orpheus was a whiny little prick, but they always make me into the bad guy."

"Thank you," Damien said. "Is there anything else you can do?"

Hades' impatient sigh extinguished the lamp beside him. "No."

"But I'll die if she does."

Again, that pitying smile. "I know that's how it feels, but when the effects wear off, you won't be in such distress."

"What effects?"

Hades put a hand over his mouth. "Whoops, shouldn't have said anything. Oh, dear, look at the time. I really must be going." He stood.

Damien wanted to grab him by the upper arms and keep him there, but something blocked him from reaching the god. "Wait, what effects? What have I been touched with?"

"You'll find out in good time." Hades disappeared, and his laughter lingered for a moment after.

Damien looked again at the drawing in his hand. It looked somewhat familiar, the four columns holding up a triangular roof. Something was crudely drawn in behind them, curtains of some sort. Damien tucked it in his hoodie pocket and went to bed, but he tossed and turned for the rest of the night.

"Dude, you look rough."

Damien barely noticed the cup of coffee that Charlie pressed into his hand. He felt the drawing in his pocket, the hard corners biting into his side, to make sure it hadn't mysteriously dropped out. The coffee, strong and bitter, jolted him to reality, and he squinted against the bright sunlight that poured through Charlie's window.

"Rough night. Weird dreams."

"All right, you're verbal." Charlie grabbed the keys to

Damien's car out of his hand. "But I don't trust your driving yet. Let's go."

Their first stop was the Hotel Tres Cher. Designed to look like a southern plantation in the middle of affluent Buckhead, the old money neighborhood of downtown Atlanta. The hotel stuck out among the more modern buildings. Damien felt his heart skip a beat when he saw the columns and portico, but a quick glance told him that it wasn't the building from Rizzo's drawing. Once again, he wished he could ask the older man what, exactly, he'd seen, what he was—he was still skeptical about the whole guardian angel thing—and how it all fit together.

"Worth a stop?" asked Charlie.

Damien ran his right hand through his hair. "I don't know. I'm not feeling it."

"Right, then." Charlie turned the wheel and made a quick five-point turn on a quiet street.

"You mean, we're not even going to check it out?"

"You've got that look in your eyes, like you're haunted. It's a different expression for you."

"I haven't been myself for a couple of days." He didn't want to admit it, but his heart thudded dully in his chest, like every beat pushed Audrey further away from him. He had wanted to stop by Maggie's on the way in, but seeing Audrey lying there limp and helpless would have broken his heart more.

And then there were Hades' words. What had he meant?

"This isn't like you, to be so torn up over a girl. I mean, I know it's been a rough week and all, but still. You haven't fallen this hard for someone, well, ever."

Damien looked out the window at the trees standing like naked skeletons along Peachtree Street and tried to remember specifically when the impulse to take care of and protect Audrey had hit him. "I don't know. I was in the hospital room with Audrey and Aphrodite and Nimue, and then Aphrodite and Nimue left, and suddenly I felt like I just had to be there—like it just flooded through me that my purpose in life is to be with her and to love and protect her because she's the most wonderful person who ever existed."

Charlie nodded like Damien's rambling thoughts had made sense. "Uh huh. And did you notice anything physical?"

"Now that you mention it, there was something like a bee sting on my neck, but there isn't a bite or a zit or anything there." He glanced at Charlie to see if his friend would look at him like he was crazy, but Charlie only shook his head, a wry smile on his lips.

"Just don't try to go too quickly with that one. You'll scare her off. She's a free spirit to begin with, and remember, her last guy cheated on her. It's going to take her a while to trust again."

"What are you not telling me?"

"I can't give you any info without knowing for sure. It would stir up more trouble than it's worth if I'm wrong."

Damien understood the feeling, but he couldn't help but poke back. "And what about you and Maggie?" Damien didn't want to think he could scare Audrey away.

Charlie tried to shrug it off, but his face softened briefly. "Phew, talk about a free spirit. That one's been around too long and seen too much to tie down. I'm just a pleasant diversion while she passes the time here."

Damien raised an eyebrow. "Oh, I doubt that. I've seen how she looks at you."

"Yeah, but every time I think that she's going to say or do something to encourage me and bring me out of this hell of uncertainty, she backs off right away. It's like she's got a thing about getting involved with mortals or something."

"It's gotta be something to do with her work. Doesn't she just appear occasionally when you've got a case with supernatural elements?"

"Right."

"Maybe she doesn't want to see you get hurt. She's going to have to take off again once this is over, maybe to Timbuktu or something."

"Dude, you're not helping."

"Sorry."

They finished the drive to the Plaza in silence, but Charlie's withholding of information bugged him, especially since he knew it had to do with Hades' strange comment the night before. As much as he wanted to go to Audrey, he couldn't do it unless he knew what was wrong with him. He didn't want to put her in even more danger. But why wouldn't anyone tell him?

THE PLAZA HOTEL, one of the tallest buildings on Peachtree Street in the heart of downtown Atlanta, looked like an old hotel at street-level. Its granite façade and marble accents quickly morphed into windows and steel that rose in a graceful, tapering spire to penthouse suites at the top. Damien craned his neck to look, but the sun reflecting off the buildings kept him from seeing anything useful. Not that he could stand on the ground and see if anyone stood on the balconies. *They're too high up, suicide platforms waiting to happen.*

But something told him this was it.

"What do you think?" Charlie asked.

Damien took a deep breath to loosen the tension in the pit of his gut. "Let's take a look around."

Charlie had parked the squad car in an "Emergency Vehicles Only" spot in the alley across the street and came to join Damien. "Shall we snoop a bit before we announce our presence?"

"Sounds good to me." Damien felt intimidated at the thought of just strolling through the revolving door of the hotel where the *crème de la crème* of society stayed and gathered. Indeed, something about the hotel told his inner sense, *stay away, stay away*, but he took it as a sign that someone or something wanted them away from there and imagined his spirit guide, the black wolf, walking beside him.

No one would mess with a guy with a wolf, right?

He jumped when he felt a wagging tail brush his leg, but he couldn't see anything.

"What was that about?" Charlie held the door beside the central revolving door open.

"Nothing." *Great, now the sleep deprivation is messing with my head.*

The two-story lobby seemed to stretch on for miles toward the curving, tapered staircase that led to the second floor and galleries, an illusion helped by the white, gold, and light wood that seemed to be everywhere. A giant crystal chandelier sparkled with a million tiny rainbows and hung suspended over a round cream suede divan. A couple of tired but chatty older women sat and waited for their husbands, who stood in line at the check-in desks to the left. An army of red-coated valets swarmed around their luggage.

Acutely aware of his comparative shabbiness in spite of his efforts to dress professionally, Damien noticed how no one took notice of them, and an image flashed into his brain of his spirit guide smiling its doggie smile.

"Yeah, I can see her in a place like this."

"Shhh!" Charlie looked around. "You never know who or what may be watching to make sure she stays hidden."

"Right, I won't say anything else. Where should we start?"

"Let's head downstairs to the meeting rooms and ballrooms. Then we can probably find an elevator that will take us to the top floors without someone seeing us."

They found a staircase hidden in an alcove and followed the brightly patterned carpet, likely leftover from the hotel's older days, to the gallery below, where a heavy wooden easel with a piece of poster board announcing the day's meetings sat.

"Hmm, let's see what the consultants are forcing on Atlanta's innocent businessmen and women," said Charlie.

Damien read along with him. *Synergy and You, Leadership for Dummies and Introverts, Make Every Sale Count*, and *Administrative Secrets*.

"You know, we really should have had more of a plan than this," said Damien.

"It all looks kosher except that last one. What kind of workshop title is 'Administrative Secrets'?" Charlie glanced around, then lifted the poster board off the easel. Beneath it, printed on another poster board colored like parchment, was a sign, *Meet the Goddess, Ballrooms A-F*.

"Do you think it's her?" asked Damien. "That's a little obvious, isn't it?"

"Nah, modern folks won't believe it's literal, and Ames hopefully doesn't know we're on to him. Remember the plans on Amelia's table?"

"Right, for the party. Let's go check it out."

Charlie turned from where he was going to dash upstairs. "How do you know it's what we're looking for?"

Damien brought out the folded piece of paper with Rizzo's drawing. "Arthur dreamed this. It was in the book he loaned me."

Charlie studied the paper. "So you think this will confirm our suspicions?"

"I was told I could find Aphrodite if I found this."

"Okay, but be careful. Remember, they've been using werebats and other nasties to guard their secrets."

The doors to ballrooms B through F were locked, but Ballroom A opened with a creak. Recessed lighting along the walls shone on to a ceiling painted dark blue and studded with twinkling L.E.D. stars. Tables and chairs lay jumbled against the walls, but Damien ignored them. He found what he sought under a drop cloth on a stage at the other end of the long, large room in what would be Ballroom F if the dividers were up. Three Styrofoam columns painted to resemble marble held up a triangular piece. Together, it looked like the façade of a temple, and the lines on Rizzo's drawing resolved into a crudely drawn image of it. Burgundy curtains fluttered behind it, and the way they moved made Damien's heart thud.

The sound of claws scrabbling on the wood of the stage confirmed his fears, and he jumped off the stairs and pushed Charlie ahead of him.

"Run! There's something in here."

24

"And me without my silver bullets." Charlie didn't wait for a second look. They wove around chairs and tables and leapt over piles of tablecloths and napkins. The creature, a mix of matted fur, yellowed teeth, and red eyes snarled at his heels, its leathery wings beating the air behind him. Thankfully the light fixtures kept it from being able to fully take wing. They crashed out into the hallway and shut the doors, holding the handles so that whatever had chased them couldn't follow. The doors vibrated against their shoulders, and then all was silent.

"So the locked doors..."

"...were to keep those things in," Damien finished. "As for how we got in..." The door handle tingled under his palms, and he caught a flash of how it would only open for human hands. "This one has a spell on it."

"How do you...? Oh, that's right." Charlie looked down at his own hands.

Damien clenched his hands into fists so they wouldn't shake. He didn't know how he knew, either, but he had a suspicion. "C'mon, dude, what are you not telling me?"

"You've been influenced in some way. I'm not sure how."

Hearing Charlie, who probably knew him better than anyone, say it finally drove it home. Damien's heart dropped into his knees and weakened them so he sank to the floor. He spoke around the knot in his throat. "You mean, I've been touched." A memory shoved its way into his brain, of his grandmother stirring a pot on the old stove in her yellow kitchen.

"Your cousin Lee," she said with a tap of her gnarled index finger on her forehead, "he was touched, and he wasn't never the same again. He had to go live in the hospital with the crazy people."

And she followed him a few years later. Something licked his hand, and he looked down expecting to see his grandmother's golden lab. Instead, the black wolf looked at him.

"Damien, yoo hoo. Come back, Dame."

"I'm here." He opened his eyes—when had he shut them?—and felt like he woke from a dream.

"I've called Maggie. Did you nod off down there?"

"No." But when he got to his feet, his limbs felt leaden, and he didn't remember Charlie calling anyone. *Where did I go?* "I don't think so."

"Good. Look, I know all this magic and fantastic creature stuff takes some getting used to, but you'll get there."

That's not what I'm worried about anymore. He didn't voice his concern about his own sanity to his friend, but rather asked, "Did she say how Audrey is?"

"About the same. Lucia is staying with her."

In spite of the plethora of workshop offerings on the white board, Charlie and Damien didn't see anyone in the hallway until Maggie arrived about thirty minutes later. No hotel employees appeared, either. Damien guessed the rest of the humans felt the "stay away" vibe.

"It's strangely deserted down here," Maggie said. "Were-bats can do that to people, drive them off." She wrinkled her nose.

"Ugh, I smell them. Cat pee and sulfur. It's worse when they're not allowed in sunlight and can't change into human forms."

"Can you get rid of them?" asked Damien. Just the thought of facing one of those creatures again gave him chill bumps.

"I'm more interested in finding out why they're here. Unfortunately, they're quite stupid, so if we captured one, it wouldn't give us anything useful. No, we're going to have to figure out what, exactly, this gala is about."

"That means we're going to have to talk to the lovely Amelia Ames," said Charlie. He flipped out his cell phone, and Damien remembered that he had put her number in there the day before. They waited, and Charlie grimaced.

"Number disconnected. Damn! I knew I should have checked it when she gave it to me."

"You'll have to go and talk to her, then," said Maggie. "I can stay here and see who goes in and out."

"How will you do that?" asked Damien. "Can you make yourself invisible?"

"I wish. No, there are other ways not to be noticed. I'll be right back." She stepped into an alcove, and when she emerged, she wore a hotel uniform. "Now I'm just part of the scenery."

Damien couldn't help but grin at the look on Charlie's face.

"Wow." Usually when Charlie got that expression, it was followed by a smack across the cheek. "What else do those magical clothes do?"

No slap. Maggie winked. "Wouldn't you like to know?"

Damien cleared his throat to distract them from their flirting. "While you're blending in, can you go upstairs and check the hotel computer and see if there is a Ms. Aphrodite staying here?"

"Dame, that's brilliant." Charlie clapped him on the shoulder. "Maggie, can you handle the computers?"

"I'll see."

She returned after about ten minutes. "No one under the

name you suggested," she said, and Damien blushed. He'd screwed up and said it out loud again. "But," she continued, "there is a Mrs. Diteroaph staying in the penthouse suite. Room occupancy listed at four-plus."

"That's got to be her. With her attendants."

"Right, so now what?" asked Damien. "It's not like we can just go up there and rescue her."

"No, but Maggie can bring her room service."

"Too obvious." She tapped her upper lip with a manicured index finger. "You guys go on and talk to Amelia. I'll stay here and make sure the beasties don't get out to the rest of the hotel. I doubt Ames knows the extent of the nastiness he's dealing with."

AUDREY LOOKED OUT THE WINDOW, or at least what she could see of it. The dingy glass panes with the blooms of mold between them reminded her of the gym at her high school. *Did the windows look that decrepit yesterday?* The room reeked of mildewed decay, and cracks in the plaster grew like leafless kudzu. Was this the effects of the barriers between the C.U. and the waking world eroding?

None of them said anything. J.J. stood by the door and kept watch. Eros had soon tired of their company and sat in a despondent heap on the floor. His half-unfurled wings covered his shoulders against the damp chill. Even the little silver dragon shivered in her lap, and she stroked its head, not sure how else to soothe it. She wondered what happened with her body, what Damien was doing. And why her mind kept straying toward him.

Ah, Damien. Will he rescue me this time? Do I want him to? Saving my life twice would put me under quite an obligation to him.

"How do you know Damien?" she asked J.J., whom she'd

determined knew Damien in another capacity. "I can't believe you didn't say anything when you saw who my coffee shop cop was. Or did you set that up?"

J.J. grinned. "I can't tell you that. As for Damien, he's a good guy," he said again and sat by the cage. "Did he tell you he was seriously hurt in a gun fight?"

"What happened?" Audrey's heart skipped a beat. "Wait, I don't want to know." She sighed. "Wait, I do."

"Yes, and you need to. If you're going to get over your stubbornness and be with him, you need to know what you're getting into. He dragged his friend Charlie out of the way, and he got shot near his groin area, right side. Bled like crazy. It's amazing he survived to get to the emergency room."

"At Dekalb?"

"Right. Didn't have time to get him to Grady."

Audrey sat back and pictured the tall, dark officer. The image that came to mind was of him in her dream, and she quelled the heat that blossomed in her core when she thought of them joined and the passion on his face. "I can't imagine him being weak and helpless."

"He's not as uncomfortable with it as some guys." J.J. chuckled. "But still, he gave the nurses and physical therapists a hard time, kept asking for exercises that would get him better faster. How'd you finally meet and talk to him? I thought you'd never get the guts to say hi."

Audrey ran her finger over the bars of her cage. "We exchanged a few words at Java Lemur but didn't really talk until he found me wandering an empty lot near where he had found Nimue and the others. Both of us were relieved that the other was mortal." She smiled at the memory. It seemed so long ago now.

"I bet. He told me he had a grandmother who would tell him all sorts of crazy stories. She was fundamentalist, but something not mainstream. He said he used to have nightmares of demons being after him."

"I wonder how he would feel about..." She looked at Eros, who pouted back at her.

"About what?"

"Someone's mom got pissed and told her son to shoot Damien in the neck while he looked at me."

"Hey, don't blame the archer," said Eros. "He ignored her."

"He passed by Aphrodite for you?" asked J.J., his eyebrows raised. "Don't get me wrong, you're a beautiful girl, but he must've already had it bad for you."

"Makes for the most potent spells," the mischievous archer told them. "If there are already feelings, my extra special potion just jacks 'em up a bit. Especially if someone's been having naughty dreams."

"You don't talk like an archetype," said Audrey, who definitely didn't want to discuss her dream interlude with her stepbrother or whatever J.J. was. No matter how many different ways she asked, he wouldn't tell her.

"I watch reality television," Eros told her. "There's lots for me to do on those, but I always feel like I need a shower after."

J.J. hung his head and put his hands on top of it. "No, this is not good. Damien wants to be in control of his surroundings, and especially of his emotions, at all times."

"I can understand that," Audrey said and ran a finger over one of the gold bars, which refused to decay like the rest of the office. "I'm starting to think there are worse things than the uncertainty of dating a police officer. What do you think he'd do if he found out?"

"Whatever it was, he would chew his own arm off before allowing someone else's will to dictate his emotions. If you want him to stay interested in you, you need to keep that a secret. Just let the spell run its course and see what happens."

DAMIEN AND CHARLIE walked into the Dream-N-Dash diner, where they found Lonnie, the secretary from Ames, Incorporated, at the counter with a cup of coffee.

"Lonnie, old pal." Charlie and Damien sat on the empty stools to either side of him.

"What do you want?" Lonnie scowled at them through his horn-rimmed glasses.

"We want to speak with the lovely Amelia Ames." Charlie signaled for coffees. Damien took a deep breath to anchor himself in mundane reality.

"I'm on my lunch break."

"Like that matters. We know you have her cell phone number, the real one."

"Like I could give that to you. If you're the cops, why don't you just look it up?"

"Because we want her to answer the phone, genius," Charlie said. "So why don't you give her a call? We know she'll pick up for you."

A pink flush crept up Lonnie's neck and turned his ears red. "And how do you know that?"

"Because we know you've got a thing for her, and she lets you get away with a lot because she likes the attention. Right under her husband's nose, too, you dog. Playing the gay secretary is pure genius if you ask me."

Lonnie looked frantically from one to the other. "I can't confirm or deny anything." His voice squeaked.

"It was a lucky guess." Charlie patted his shoulder. "You just told us."

"So do we need to tip off our gossip blog buddies or are you gonna help us?" asked Damien, leaning in close so that Lonnie got a good feel for his bulk. "I'm sure it would make good internet fodder."

"All right, all right, I'll call her." He picked up the phone with trembling fingers. "But I can't promise she'll talk to you."

"Oh, we don't want to talk to her. We want to meet up."

"Like that's gonna happen. She'll be busy all day with gala preparations."

"Do you know what that's about?" Damien emptied a packet of sugar into the coffee that had appeared in front of him. "The gala? Sounds like a big deal."

"All I know is that many of Lyle's closest friends will be there," said Lonnie. "It's all been very hush-hush."

"I'm sure. Now, the phone call?" Charlie nudged the phone. "Tell her it's in reference to what we discussed earlier."

They stepped aside and watched Lonnie lift the phone to his ear. "How did you know?" asked Damien.

"In that social class, affairs are often symmetrical, although sometimes it's emotional rather than physical on one side. And if we could prove that he was messing around on her without her indiscretions coming to light, she gets a bigger check if there's a divorce. Even the rumor of infidelity on her part could royally screw things up for her."

"So we played into her plan?"

"Until now, yes."

Lonnie waved them over. "She'll see you. I hope you know what you've done."

"You didn't need any help messing up what didn't exist to begin with," said Damien, "Where do we meet her?"

"Walk back through the kitchen, and a car will be waiting for you."

"Nope, we're not falling for that one," said Charlie. "Call her back and tell her that my friend and I will meet her at the Greek Orthodox Church near the country club. And no funny stuff."

"You won't get away with this." Lonnie's pout wasn't pretty.

"The Greek Orthodox Church?" asked Damien once they were outside the door.

"The second floor security office, specifically. It should be empty this time of day. The secretary knows me and keeps the lunch hour free. Once you get to be a detective, you have to have a discreet place to meet your snitches. No one suspects a church."

"Do you meet in the confessionals? Do Greek Orthodox Churches do that?"

Charlie chuckled. "No idea. And even if they did, it would be too obvious."

"So the priests let you use their building?"

Charlie started the car and eased into the traffic on Peachtree. "They're pretty cool about it. My friend, the secretary, would lose her job if anything bad happened, so I have a reason to be careful. By the way," he said, his expression serious, "I hope you're not afraid of ghosts."

25

____

Damien glimpsed a sliver of blue sky between the buildings, and soon it was behind them. The Greek Orthodox Church stood gray in the waning light under thunder heads. A black car with tinted windows pulled alongside them.

"Officers, you can't expect me to play along with this." Amelia Ames rolled down her window, her eyes covered with dark glasses, her blonde hair hidden by a dark blue silk scarf.

"Sure we can, Mrs. Ames. And you won't have your goons try anything funny since we have reinforcements here in the building."

"What reinforcements?" She looked around the deserted parking lot. "There's not a soul here."

"There are several. They're just quiet. Now, please, Mrs. Ames." Charlie held out an arm, and she emerged from the car, careful not to lose her footing on the slick pavement. She put her hand on the crook of Charlie's arm, and they entered through a side door.

Once inside, they skirted the sanctuary and the reception hall and climbed the stairs. The building smelled of incense, mint, and garlic. Their footsteps echoed through the empty halls, but Damien heard rustling sounds in the classrooms they passed.

"What is that?"

"Just some of the resident ghosts. You're not afraid of ghosts, are you, Mrs. Ames?"

She looked more like she was afraid of him. "What are you, a mad man?"

"One can always hope." Charlie showed her into the security office, where three chairs and a sofa flanked a coffee table. A desk had been pushed against the wall and supported a bank of monitors, almost all of them black. The ones that were on had spots that moved in erratic patterns across the grainy, grayscale screens.

"Please, have a seat where you're comfortable." But Charlie guided her to where she could see the screens.

Damien couldn't help but look over his shoulder. Either he'd given Charlie way too little credit for creating a good atmosphere to interrogate a witness by making her feel off balance, or his friend really was a mad man. *It's always the ones you least suspect.*

"Now, Mrs. Ames," Charlie said after she'd settled herself in one of the chairs and crossed her legs, "Officer Lewis and I have a few questions for you. And don't worry, they're not about your ambiguously gay secretarial lover wannabe. Although I imagine that's one way to find a man who will listen to you—have him write down everything you say. Does he know shorthand?"

She didn't laugh at his joke or seem to react much aside from tired annoyance. "It's not that easy to intimidate me, Officer. I'm not admitting to anything."

"Right, actually, I'm curious about your husband's affair tomorrow night. Or maybe I should use a different word. I'm referring to the gala."

"What about it? I'm planning the basic components of it, but I don't know anything else."

The rustling noise resumed, and Damien looked over his shoulder, as did Amelia. It seemed closer this time. Charlie, unruffled, continued his questioning.

"Did your husband tell you what the purpose of this party is? The theme?"

Amelia raised a perfectly plucked eyebrow. "He is unveiling his new venture, whatever that is."

"And does this have anything to do with his absences?"

She shook her head, and tears sparkled in her eyes. "I promise, I don't know anything else. Please." She looked over her shoulder at the doorway. "I don't like it here."

Tingles danced along the back of Damien's neck like ghostly fingers tickling his hair. "Charlie, maybe we should continue this somewhere else."

"No, really, it's fine. Did he have you hire extra help for the party?"

She shook her head and bit her lip before replying in a rush. "He said not to worry about it."

"So it's a major gala, but he's not having you hire any extra personnel? Is the hotel providing staff?"

"No. They offered, but he said it was taken care of."

"What kind of food did he request?"

"Greek finger foods. Stuffed grape leaves. Spanakopita."

Damien took notes and watched Amelia's reactions. She seemed genuinely frightened, but he had the sense it wasn't necessarily due to whatever lurked in the hallways. *What is she afraid of, then?*

"And how is your relationship with your husband these days?" Charlie asked. He studied his nails while she considered her answer.

"If you're asking if he would confide in me, the answer is that we're not that close right now."

"Do you think he's seeking comfort elsewhere?"

"I've already told you my suspicions, Detective."

"Right, then. I think that's a great start."

Amelia looked over her shoulder again and licked her lips. "May I go now?"

"If I can have your cell phone number. Your real one."

She sighed, and with a flourish, dug her card out of her purse and handed it to him. He flipped his phone out.

"Just making sure it works this time." He pressed the call button, but nothing happened. Now they heard a scratching noise followed by a sigh.

"What's out there?" Amelia asked, wide-eyed.

"Nothing that will bother you unless you continue to lie to me. Now, your real cell phone number, please."

"It's 404..."

He put the number in the phone while she gave it to him, and this time, when he called, her purse started playing the Black Eyed Peas' "Let's Get It Started."

"Not bad," Charlie said. "I consider myself to be more of a Marvin Gaye man."

Amelia stood, and Damien and Charlie did likewise. "Please, can I go now?" she asked with a tragic Southern-belle expression on her face. Damien couldn't tell whether bolting or fainting appealed to her more.

"I think you've had enough," said Charlie. "Just remember one thing."

"What?"

"If you're scared or frightened or need help dealing with whatever your husband has dragged you into, you now have my cell phone number. Store it when you get to the car." He walked to the door and looked down the hall in both directions. "All clear. Just stay close."

She stumbled, and Damien caught her before she collapsed. They got her to the first floor, and she regained full consciousness before they reached the side door again. Damien helped her to walk on wobbly legs to her car. When the driver turned around with a query, she just shook her head and nearly slammed the door on Damien's hand. Not that he blamed her —the rustling and sighing sounds had followed them out of the building.

Damien watched the black sedan pull out of the parking lot. "Okay, what the hell was that?"

"What?" Charlie had his cell phone to his ear. "We're out now. Thanks again, Cass."

"All the noises. You couldn't have planned those."

"Come on. Let's see how Maggie's doing."

Damien jumped into the front seat of the squad car and looked back up at the classroom floor of the church. A child with very pale skin and big brown eyes looked back at him. He blinked, and she vanished.

"Charlie, did you see that? There's a kid up there."

Charlie shrugged and waited for a gap in traffic to turn back on to Ponce. "There are several. There was a big fire at the church in the sixties, likely set by some racist, anti-anything not WASP group. It killed a bunch of parishioners there and some kids, who were trapped in the classrooms. They died from smoke inhalation before anyone could get them out. The place is haunted as anything."

"So the kid who was looking at me while we drove out...?"

"Probably little Marina. She's a doll. I leave her lollipops, and she and her buddies make noise when I bring guests up there. They think it's great fun."

"You bribe ghosts with candy?"

"They can't really eat it, but c'mon, they're kids. They like it anyway."

Damien looked out the window. "I'm finding out way more about you than I ever wanted to know."

"Maggie turned me on to the idea. It's a nonviolent way to

get answers. Witnesses who are freaked out give you what you want to know so they can leave. It's called negative reinforcement. Plus, the panic limits their cognitive resources for lying, so if they do try to deceive you, it's easy to tell."

Damien watched the passing trees to erase the image of that little girl, fifty years dead. "That's twisted."

"Hey, it also gives you an idea of who has a sensitivity to supernatural stuff. Or who might have been exposed to the C.U. You and Amelia both showed interesting responses."

"So she's a sensitive?" Damien pulled the term from somewhere, likely too much late-night television.

Charlie drummed his fingers on the steering wheel. "No. I'm thinking she's been exposed to the C.U. beyond regular dreaming."

"When would she have been there?"

"If Lyle's been mucking around, she likely dreamed about some of it. Those suspicions don't come from thin air, nor are they entirely the result of her projecting her own guilt on him. I'll ask her about it the next time we see her."

Damien snorted. "Like she's going to let you anywhere near her."

"It all depends. What did you think about how she acted?"

"I wouldn't pick her for the fainting type. She seemed more scared than unsettled by everything. It makes me wonder if something else has her nervous, even beyond the suspected affair with Lonnie the ambiguously gay secretary and its detrimental effects on her hypothetical alimony."

"Bravo. Good observations there. I had the same idea. That's why I gave her my cell. I'll text her yours as well. She'll probably be more likely to talk to you after all that anyway."

"Yeah, as long as you don't come along."

After they left the church, Charlie's cell phone rang, but it wasn't Amelia.

"Maggie, what do you have for us?" Charlie asked. "I'm driving, so I'll put you on speaker."

Maggie's voice came through with an extra echo like she stood in a small space. "I hung out around the ballroom after you left, and a toad and a couple of nymphs came down to feed the were-bats."

"A toad?" asked Damien.

"Yes, half troll, half demon, and all nasty. I overheard them talking about a transfer. I'll continue to look into it, but the toad smelled you, so you better stay away for now."

"Roger that," Charlie told her. "Doesn't sound like something I'd want to meet, anyway. You be careful."

"Will do."

Damien and Charlie spent the afternoon catching up on paperwork. Apparently the procedure went a little differently for cases of a "particularly delicate nature," as Charlie put it. The one surprise was a visit from a sheepish Harold Smith, the father of Daniel Smith, who had shot Rizzo. The front desk clerk showed him in to Charlie's office.

"Detective," he said to Charlie, and to Damien, "Officer."

"What can we do for you?" asked Charlie after shaking the man's hand and waving for him to take a seat.

"I have to apologize to you, but first, how's your friend, that doctor?"

"Still in a coma." Damien cringed inside when he remembered that he hadn't called to see how Rizzo was doing although he knew his friend was somewhere in the C.U. hopefully with Audrey, who was never far from his thoughts.

Touched, the little voice inside his head told him, *you've been touched.*

"Right. If there's anything we, my wife and I, can do to help, just let me know."

"That's very kind of you, Mr. Smith," said Charlie, "but I'm curious to know why you're here."

"The gun is gone."

"Excuse me?" asked Damien. "Which gun?"

"The gun that I kept in the house, that I knew Daniel couldn't have taken. It's gone."

"But you said you checked on it."

Harold Smith looked at Charlie. "It's the craziest thing, Detective. We got home from talking to you yesterday, and it was gone. I looked everywhere, tore the house apart."

"I appreciate you coming down to tell us this," said Charlie. "A phone call would've worked just as well."

"I thought you might want me to come and identify the weapon that Daniel used on Doctor Rizzo. Just in case. I wouldn't want to stand in the way of your investigation." He swallowed, his face gray but resolute.

Damien felt like putting a hand on the man's shoulder to steady him. It took a lot of guts for him to come down and be willing to incriminate his only son. The guy must have an honest streak the size of Lake Lanier after a rainy spring.

"We appreciate the offer, Mr. Smith," said Charlie. "But why don't you give us the gun specs and serial number, and we'll compare it?"

He nodded and pulled a folded piece of paper from his pocket. "This is my registration. It's kind of beat up. I kept it in the tool box so the wife wouldn't see it."

"I understand," said Charlie. "Thanks for coming down. We'll let you know if anything turns up."

"So?" asked Damien once Mr. Smith had gone.

"So what?"

"Are we going to look at the gun and see if it's the same one?"

Charlie's expression dropped from affable to resigned. "Yeah, that would be nice, except for one thing."

"What?"

"It's gone."

"Gone? Where?"

"Who knows? I suspect the same imp that whispered in Daniel Smith's ear and erased all the paperwork we did on the Jane Doe's."

"Can't you call Maggie and get her to stop it?" He ran a hand through his hair. "I can't believe I just asked that."

"She's working on that now, but she has to have certain contacts that are harder to reach when she's in corporeal form."

"You don't seem very upset." Damien couldn't believe it—this was the main piece of evidence they had to convict the man who tried to murder Rizzo. How was Charlie not livid?

Charlie surprised and dismayed him by laughing. "Trust me, Dame, when you've been handling these cases for a while, the impossible becomes ordinary." His face turned serious. Damien couldn't help but think it was like watching a puddle on a partly cloudy day: bright, dull, bright. "I just hope this thing doesn't pop up where we least expect or need it to."

26

When he arrived at Maggie's condo, Damien went straight to the bedroom. Audrey lay on the bed in Maggie's spare bedroom and breathed steadily but shallowly. He wanted to do something, anything, to make her open her eyes and talk to him. He kissed her on the lips and smoothed her hair back. "I'll come for you, I promise."

When he walked into the living room, Maggie looked at him, then bit her lip and turned away, her fists clenched. His jaw tightened with the same helplessness and frustration, but mostly fear that they would be too late to help her.

Charlie arrived with pizza. The four of them—Maggie, Charlie, Damien, and Lucia—sat around the coffee table and ate in silence for a few minutes. It felt like a deathbed scene where everyone was afraid to talk too loudly, if at all.

Damien finally spoke. "So what now?" He took a deep breath to announce his decision, but Maggie beat him to talking.

"We have two tasks," she said. "First, we have to save Audrey." They all listened to make sure the girl still breathed in the other room. Satisfied, Maggie continued, "And we have to rescue Aphrodite and send her back to the C.U. before Lyle Ames and Zeus can cause any more trouble." She told them about the conversation she had overheard.

"What kind of transfer did they mean?" asked Charlie.

"I don't know. I was focused on not getting caught. A battle with a toad could destroy the whole hotel. But I know one thing." She looked at Charlie, and she smiled. "I need to go to that party."

"You kids go on, then," said Lucia. "I can stay here with Audrey again tomorrow."

"Aren't you losing business right now?" asked Damien. "Someone's got to man the psychic shop."

"This is more important." Lucia emphatically waved a pizza crust in his direction. "And like it or not, you're going have to rescue Audrey."

"I know," he said, her words confirming his resolve. "I have to do something. But I've been told by several people, both human and supernatural, that something's happened to me." He clasped his hands so tight his knuckles went white. "It makes me fear for my own mind and my own life..."

"You'll get through it," Charlie said, but stopped when Maggie put a hand on his arm.

"Let him finish," she said.

"But whatever's going on, it's something that isn't going to be stopped unless someone goes to the C.U. and we all know that's the only way Audrey has a chance." He swallowed the lump in his throat. "I'll go. I can't stand the thought of losing her, and as for what happens to me, that's not important anymore. I've been touched."

"There are different kinds of magic, both positive and negative," Lucia said. "Even if you've been touched, as you say, it's not necessarily a bad thing. Stop fighting it. Let it help you and guide you."

He nodded at the psychic with a shaky smile. "Thanks, I'll try to keep that in mind. When do I leave?"

DAMIEN OPENED his eyes to see a carpet of emerald green grass, a curved roof lined with amethyst crystals, and after his vision focused, a purple and gold dragon watching him with big green eyes.

"Mmmhmm, aren't you the manly one?" the dragon asked in a tenor voice.

Damien struggled to his feet and reached for his gun, only to find that it wasn't on his belt.

"You've got a sword here, sweetie. And a nice sword it is." The dragon wasn't looking at the place where the sword should be.

Damien's cheeks heated, and he reached across to his left hip and found the weapon. "Who are you?"

"I promise, I'm no threat. I'm Zinfandel. Maybe you've heard of me?" The dragon ducked his head coyly.

A memory flickered through Damien's mind. "Audrey mentioned something about you."

"Yep, I know the girl. Sweet thing, too, but not much of a dresser. Now that Maggie, she knows how to put on a gown."

"Do you know where I can find her? Audrey?"

"Well, honey, you can look for her, but without the key to that golden cage, you won't have much luck rescuing her."

"Okay, so where's the key?"

"You'll go outside the cave and find a path, where your spirit guide's a-waiting for you. The path will lead you where you need to go."

"That's all you're going to tell me?" Damien thought for a moment about threatening the dragon with the sword, but he had no idea how to use the thing, and he didn't know whether the skill would be automatic.

"Time grows short, honey. You've got to rescue that chick. No time to chitchat here. Every step leads to a new one."

Bright sunlight spilled through the entrance of the cave, and Damien squinted, squared his shoulders, and walked out. It took a moment for his eyes to adjust, and before they could, he was bowled over by something large, furry, and panting.

"Hey, what...?" Something licked his face, and he opened his eyes to a black wolf looking down at him.

"Damien." He heard the voice in his head.

"Hey again." He caressed the large head, then stood, brushed himself off, and looked down the path, which wound through the hills to a familiar skyline.

"Is that Atlanta?"

"The road to the key is there." The sun reflected off the glossiness of the wolf's coat.

"Atlanta's a big place. I just hope the traffic isn't as bad here." He set off at a brisk pace, and the wolf matched his stride. "Audrey is in a golden cage in Lyle Ames' office in Corinth. It would make sense for Lyle to keep the key with him, so maybe it's in his office in Atlanta." The wolf snuffed, which Damien interpreted as assent. "So that's where we're going. This is going to take forever." He stopped and looked at the far-off buildings.

"This is the dream world. There is always a quicker way."

When Damien rounded the next curve, he saw a sleek, black horse.

"It's lovely, but I had pictured a motorcycle." He held a hand out for the horse to sniff. "I guess we'll just have to deal with each other, won't we?"

The horse bent its front legs for Damien to mount, and the three of them moved quickly toward the city.

Lyle's loins felt like they would burst if they didn't get relief soon. He had entered Aphrodite's suite to her "come in!" and found her stretched out on the bed naked except for a towel wrapped around her golden hair. She lay on her stomach and leafed through a fashion magazine, her bottom still pink from her bath, and her breasts fluffed from being pressed into the rumpled silk sheets.

"Forgive me," she said without sounding like she meant it or looking up at him. "I just got out of the shower and wanted to wait for the steam to clear from the mirror before I could do my hair."

"I sent you a silk robe, Your Radiance."

"And it's lovely. But sometimes I need to feel the caress of the air on my skin."

Indeed, the door to the balcony stood open. The thought crossed Lyle's mind that if he couldn't have her right then, he would have to jump to his death.

Zeus' words came back to him.

Remember, Lyle, her art is seduction, and it's a powerful weapon. When you deal with Aphrodite, you have to think with the big head no matter how hard the little one is screaming at you. She's driven men to their deaths before.

Lyle told the little head to knock it off and closed the balcony doors. Aphrodite rolled over and looked at him with a pout. He ignored the lushness of her breasts and the fact that she had gotten a Brazilian wax since the last time she'd tried to drive him mad. With the door closed, the perfume from the lilies he'd had delivered filled the air. Lyle sniffled; he'd always been allergic to the things.

"It's cold, Your Radiance. I don't want you to become ill. Your debut is tonight, after all."

"Right, right, whatever." She waved her hand like she swatted a gnat.

Those irritating dismissive gestures would be his salvation.

He gritted his teeth. "I just wanted to make sure all is to your liking and that you have everything you need for tonight."

"You know, Lyle, I don't know if I'm up for a party tonight. It's been such a long week, and I haven't really spent any quality time with my attendants." She studied her nails. "And I'm desperately in need of a mani-pedi."

"I've arranged for that already, and a massage."

"Everything for your little captive, hmm?"

He hoped she didn't see the guilt he felt over that human being stuck in his C.U. office. That reminded him of what else he held there.

Apparently Aphrodite had the same thought. "I've been wondering, Lyle, about my son."

He loved the way she said his name, like she actually licked the "y" in the middle. *No, no, can't follow that train of thought.* "What about him?"

"I haven't seen him lately. I thought you needed his help for some of your business?"

"That I do, but I've got him tied up doing other things."

She narrowed her eyes. "I'm not stupid, you know. And if you harm him, a long walk off a short balcony will be the worst of your problems." A gust of wind blew the door open for emphasis.

With a sigh, Lyle closed it and locked it. "I assure you, he's being well-taken care of. I even brought him a friend."

"Oh, good, he gets lonely sometimes." She walked slowly and seductively to the bathroom door and looked back at him over the perfect curve of her left shoulder. "What time is my spa treatment?"

"At eleven, Your Radiance."

"Perfect, you may send the girls back in now."

~

DAMIEN'S HORSE trotted toward the familiar skyline of the city. Images and scenes played out around him but made no more sense than those early sleep period dreams where a knife becomes a fish or a kite becomes a snake. Voices hummed, mumbled, and whispered without him being able to make out the words. Finally, the horse's hooves struck brick and cobbles instead of dirt. Although the familiar modern structures towered above Damien, the buildings looked like wood and clay at street level, and the people could have walked straight out of the Middle Ages. Shops and houses crowded close together, and chickens, pigs, and other livestock wallowed and pecked in front of them. They scattered at the sight of the black horse and wolf. Damien looked down and saw he wore a metal breastplate with chain mail underneath.

"This is weird," he told the wolf.

"*Such is the Dream World. You create some of the reality. The other is already here.*"

"Then I need to create a sighting of Lyle Ames soon so I can find the key. Or at least some direction."

They came to a building that looked better kept than most. The sign out front read, "Buckhead Boarding House and Ale Room."

"I'm obviously not figuring this out myself, so I'm going to stop for directions." He dismounted and gave the horse's reins to the wolf, which simultaneously held them in his mouth and growled at onlookers. With a shake of his head at the continued randomness of it all, Damien entered the pub.

The gloom seemed to swallow him, and once his eyes adjusted, he found himself face-to-face with several dirty but curious people.

A woman with tangled hair and missing teeth sashayed over to him. "Would ye be liking a pint o' ale, Milord?"

Perhaps this hadn't been such a good idea. "Ah, no thanks. I'm looking for the Ames castle. His offices, actually."

The room grew quiet, and the curious whispers subsided.

"Ye'll no find him here, Milord, if that's what you're askin'. He's too high and mighty for us folk."

"I'm actually just looking for where he works. Can someone give me directions?"

"What's this, 'ere?" The largest man Damien had ever seen came out of the kitchen in the back. The black bristles atop the man's head brushed the top of the ten-foot ceilings, and he had to duck to avoid hitting his forehead on the rafters. His eyes bulged, and he maneuvered in a startlingly graceful manner for the width of his shoulders and waistline.

"I'm looking for the location of Lyle Ames' office," Damien explained again. *Are all these people stupid?*

"They're but bits and pieces of the scenery," the giant explained to Damien while he put a hand the size of a ham on his shoulder, wheeled him about, and steered him out of the place like he was a toy. "I hide here because they amuse me."

Damien looked up at him and nearly strained his neck. "And wh-who are you?"

"Name's Craig. A voyager like you." He smiled, and Damien noted that he had all his teeth, although the chips on them said they had been used for some non-toothy activities. "My world's one of the ones that intersects yours at the corners, in the dark places, so to speak. That's where you get the legends about giants."

"These days they're called NBA players."

Craig laughed, and the sound made the walls shake, to the consternation of the people inside the building. "Sorry," he called through the door, and the shrieks and cries subsided.

"I forget how flimsy these constructions are," he confided in a stage whisper.

Damien took the reins out of his spirit-guide's mouth, and the wolf sniffed Craig's hand.

"I don't know what to make of this," the spirit guide said. *"He smells not of good or evil, just different."*

Damien didn't have time for philosophical quandaries. "Can you help me?"

"I'm here to keep an eye on things myself. If the C.U. boundaries erode between here and your world, it could spell havoc for mine, too."

"I see." Damien mounted his horse, which shied away from the large man. "Then you know where his office is?"

"Aye, but why are you so interested in finding it?"

"He's keeping something locked up there. I need the key."

"There's only one key to the golden cages, if that's what you mean. You're going to have to find the man himself and take it from him."

Damien pictured Craig holding Lyle by the ankles and shaking him until what he needed fell out of his pockets.

Craig laughed again, this time a quiet chuckle. "Your mental images are crystal clear, but you need to keep them to yourself. And no, I can't do that. You see, the Truth Seekers would be all over me in a heartbeat, and I can't let them know I'm here."

"Why not?" Damien trotted alongside the man and found he could almost see eye-to-eye with him from atop the horse.

"Rules and regs and all due to the trouble my kind has caused in the past. A few bad eggs ruined everything for the whole carton, so to speak. I didn't have time to wait for a visa, so I snuck in."

"So you're a spy?"

"Not quite, but that's probably the closest you'll get. And what about you? What has Lyle got locked up that you want so badly?"

Damien looked at the road ahead between the horse's ears and tried to erase the thought of Audrey lying limp and fragile on Maggie's bed.

"Ah, it's a girl."

"Not just any girl. This is the woman I want to spend the rest of my life with." Here in the C.U., he could be honest like he'd been with her in his dream and indulge his fantasy.

Craig looked at him with his prominent brown eyes. "You should see how she takes to being rescued before you make up your mind. Some women don't go for that at all, no matter how stuck they are."

"Thanks for the helpful advice."

"Well, first off, Lyle's dealing with the Greeks, so you're in the wrong part of the C.U. Is that more helpful?"

"That depends on where you're taking me."

He didn't have to ask further because the grimy buildings gave way to a slope covered in bright green grass. On the top lay white marble ruins. Two pillars held up a chipped triangular plinth.

"That's your gateway," said Craig, pointing to it. "Leave your conceptions behind and just take it as it comes, and you'll find what you're looking for. Knights in shining armor are good for some things, but when you deal with the gods, you need your brains, not brawn."

"Thanks. Is there something I can do for you?"

The giant put a finger over his lips. "Just keep our meeting between the two of us. And remember, keep your wits about you. Zeus doesn't like human men messing with his collection."

27

———

The light outside the windows of the office faded from white to yellow to pink to orange, and then finally to the velvety blue that meant night had come to the C.U. Audrey sighed and would have checked her watch if one had come with her peasant ensemble. J.J. had gone out to find food at lunch time and hadn't returned, so her stomach growled with anxiety and hunger. She thought about sending the silver dragon out to look for him, but she knew it was the source of her strength, which waned as the connection to her body grew ever weaker.

"So it's night time," she told Eros, who sat cross-legged in his cage. He had barely moved all day, and she worried about him, too. Was Zeus's plan to starve them all?

"Another one." He sighed.

"Yep. How long did you say you've been in here?"

"Since two days ago, when they captured my mum. I tried to rescue her and got caught, too."

"At least you tried to rescue her." Maggie's abandonment, justified as it was, still hurt. "But he hasn't killed you, so he must have some purpose in mind."

"I don't know. I guess."

Audrey looked at the despondent Eros with concern. "Are you feeling okay?"

"I was never meant to be caged up like this. I haven't had any affection in days."

"Affection?" Audrey hadn't thought about the god needing something other than food.

"I'm the god of desire. I need cuddles."

"I'm not going to ask."

"You'd probably benefit from some." He folded his wings over his head.

Audrey wished she had something to lob at the impudent creature. "I'm just fine, thank you very much."

"Uh huh. Just fine until they get too close. I heard what Mum told you. That's why I shot the nice policeman, so you'd have a fighting chance for a normal relationship."

"Like you'd know what that is."

"I bet right now he's on his way here to rescue you."

"Right." She stretched out on the floor and put her head on her arms. She couldn't sleep here; she could only achieve a doze, so she was constantly tired. *Will Damien rescue me? What the heck is taking him so long?*

And, most disturbingly, the idea of cuddles sounded pretty darn good, especially if they involved a certain silver-eyed policeman. She swatted the thought away, but she couldn't help it. She wanted to see Damien again. And she would have felt the same even if she hadn't been Zeus' captive.

~

Damien trudged up and down another hill. The horse had vanished along with his armor when he and the wolf went through the doorway in the ruins, and now he wore a simple tunic and breeches like the peasants he'd seen. No matter how hard he tried, he couldn't make anything faster appear.

"Why can't I conjure another horse?" he asked his spirit guide.

"Magic in this part of the C.U. is strictly governed by the Twelve. It can be used by permission only. They hoard the energy and only give it out to a select few."

"Isn't there some way to get where we're going faster?" He thought he could see the shimmer of water in the distance, but the rolling hills and pastureland seemed to go on forever.

"If you have a clear idea of where you want to go, the path will take you there."

"But I don't know where I want to go. Other than to Lyle Ames' office here." He thought about what they had discovered. Ames had Aphrodite. He was trying to bring her cult back. "That means I need to find the site of her worship."

"We need to head to the city of Corinth," the wolf told him. *"It is and was the center of Her Radiance's cult."*

"How did you know that?"

The wolf only grinned up at him, its tongue lolling out.

"Oh, right, that's where we sent Rizzo. It's hard to think in two worlds." Something Lucia said occurred to him. "Am I very obvious with whatever it is has happened to me?"

The wolf looked at him quizzically.

"Lucia said that whatever I've been touched with would make me stand out to the Twelve."

The wolf sniffed him. *"Whatever it is, it's very faint at this point."*

Salt tinged the air, and soon they rounded a bend. Damien squinted against the low, setting sun and saw a city of white and yellow marble and limestone. They entered the gates without challenge, and he followed the path that appeared before him. It led him to a square, which he estimated to be about the size of Atlanta's Olympic Park, but instead of fountains, the square was crowded with people. Wine flowed from a large stone structure with stairs leading to the top. Men in rough garb poured skins of wine into the stone tower, and the ruby liquid trickled out of spigots around the base and into waiting glasses.

The temple façade was as he remembered from Rizzo's drawing and the miniature version in the Plaza ballroom. It looked like the pictures of Greek temples he'd seen in school, but whole and not crumbling into ruins. Steps led up to a wide landing, which supported the columns. Pink and yellow flowering vines and ribbons twined around them.

"Damien, my boy." A rather intoxicated Arthur Rizzo appeared and put a sinewy arm around him.

"Doctor Rizzo, what are you doing here?"

"I think I was going out to get some lunch or something for that girl." Rizzo put a trembling hand on Damien's arm. "She's the one you like so much. I stopped for a glass of wine and forgot what I was doing." Rizzo squinted at Damien through his round lenses, then at the sunset. "Oh... Shit."

"Right, where's Audrey?"

"Who?"

"Audrey. The girl." He had never seen Rizzo so distracted.

"She's in there." Rizzo pointed to a building attached to the temple. "Office on the fifth floor. Place is a dump."

"Great, thanks."

"Careful, there are guards. That's why I can't get back in—they just appeared today." He shook his head. "Some guardian I turned out to be."

Damien looked at the temple and saw that, indeed, large-shouldered men with black and blue belts across their broad chests stood with scimitars at the ready. They glared at the crowds and twitched their heavy black mustaches.

"What are those?"

"Arabian guards. Very tough to get past."

"We need a plan."

"So do you ever take your clothes off?" asked Charlie.

Maggie smiled and twirled for him in her gown. She wore a floor-length black dress cut snug in the back and low in the front, her signature style: simple, elegant, and the best she could do with what she had at hand. She'd had to concentrate hard to get the look she wanted. "I do to take showers, but having magical clothes lets me pack light so I can move on to my next assignment quickly if needed."

"Do you already have another one?"

Was that dismay in his voice? "Not yet. This one isn't complete enough."

"But will you have to go soon?"

"Probably." She looked up into his blue eyes. "Why do you ask?"

"If you can't figure that one out, spirit-girl..."

Maggie breathed an inaudible sigh of relief when they had to separate so she could go through the revolving doors first. She knew what he was asking, but there was the curse. And her next assignment could take her to Scotland, Greece, China... Or to places no mortal human had ever been or could go. She'd learned that the hard way with her last partner. No, she would have to stay unattached for his safety.

Without speaking, they snuck down the side stairwell and into chaos.

Atlanta's elite lined up to enter the ballroom, and wait staff passed wine, cocktails, and hors d'oeuvres to the queue. A young woman with black hair, striking blue eyes, and a headset met them with a suspicious look that cleared into a radiant smile when she saw Charlie, and Maggie's heart thudded with jealousy.

"Who's that?"

"Her name's Delilah Butler. Trophy wife and party planner extraordinaire. She's helping Amelia Ames with the gala."

"So she's married?" Maggie cursed her relief. Like she had any right to be jealous.

"To a man with a reputation for ruthless jealousy. Not even Atlanta's dirtiest old man would dare to get close to her."

Delilah approached them. "Detective MacKenzie, how good to see you again. And this is...?"

"Margaret Cornwall. She's helping me on the case."

"And where's that handsome Officer Lewis?" She winked at Maggie. "Too many good-looking men in one place?"

Maggie coughed to stifle a chuckle. *Charlie's turning red.* "I'm a specialist they called in."

"Nifty accent. British?"

"Somewhat."

"Well, this is my specialty." With a broad wave, she indicated all the flurry.

"Do you know what, exactly, is going to happen?" asked Maggie. "We got a tip that we needed to check things out."

"Oooh, I don't know if I can talk to you about that. I'll have to call Amelia and ask."

"No, don't do that." Charlie stopped her from dialing her cell phone. "Can we just see the party timeline?"

"Sure, there's no secret. I've got it on my phone." After rearranging a few things on the screen, she handed the smart phone to Charlie. Maggie stood close to his elbow and read along with him. It was all when to put this and that out with guest arrival times, bar re-stocking schedules, and simply, "Event" at nine o'clock.

"What's the Event?" asked Maggie.

"Amelia couldn't tell me. Probably her husband getting up on the stage with that temple-looking thingy and talking about some stuff. She said he has some actors and actresses to give it the feel of an ancient Greek temple celebration." She winked again, this time at Charlie. "Hopefully not an orgy. That would ruin my reputation."

"Right," said Maggie, and an idea tickled the back of her mind. She looked at her watch. "Do you mind if I come in and keep an eye on things? I wouldn't want to make you uncomfortable, but with all the V.I.P.'s coming, you can consider it free extra security."

"There's plenty of security here already." But Delilah's face registered the doubt Maggie had planted. "All right, just stay undercover."

"Will do."

"And let me know if anything is amiss." For a moment, she looked like a scared college student instead of a premier party planner. "If this goes off well," she told them in a low voice, "I can count on my career being made. This is what I've always wanted to do."

"Has anything odd happened so far?" asked Charlie.

"No." A radiant smile broke through the concern on her face. "Actually, everything has been strangely smooth to this point. It's like the gods are smiling."

"We can only hope," said Maggie. The word "orgy" kept fluttering through her mind. *Would Zeus dare to bring the entire party to the C.U.? How in the world are they keeping Aphrodite cooperative? Surely she must feel the energy gathering here, and she's an astute enough goddess to be able to use it. No, there has to be something else.*

They ducked out of line when they got too near the front and found two brawny men in ill-fitting tuxedos checking invitations, their heavy black mustaches twitching.

"Oh, no," Maggie said. "Arabian guards. They'll sniff me out in half a second if I have to interact with them."

Charlie led her into the hallway he and Damien had found earlier. Empty meeting rooms stood open and dark.

"I just had an idea," Charlie told her. "Do your clothes do formal hotel uniforms?"

"Turn around. They won't perform if someone's looking."

He complied. She focused on the look she wanted to achieve, and the fibers of the dress stretched and pulled across her as they rearranged themselves and changed color. It felt like being rubbed down with a cotton towel.

"Okay, turn back around." She wore black tuxedo pants, a white shirt, and a black tie. She picked up a tray.

"Nice. I didn't know you could do trays."

"I don't. It was lying here. Now, I'll get into the party from the rear of the ball rooms, and you go back the way you came. Can you play the drunken party guest who's wandered to the bathroom and can't find his way back in?"

Charlie pretended to stumble. "'Scuse me, can you tell me where the bar is?"

"Perfect. I'll meet you inside in ten minutes."

As soon as Maggie left Charlie's side, Delilah Butler arrived to take her place. Maggie considered how good they looked together, like they had stepped out of *People Magazine*, a young James Bond and his beautiful mistress. Delilah gazed up at Charlie with her striking blue eyes, and he grinned back at her. Maggie watched them until they disappeared from view past the bouncers.

Waiting guests placed empty glasses on her tray, and she walked by the bouncers with a smile. One of them even held the door wider for her. She gathered more empties on the way back to the kitchen, the door of which was hidden to the left of the stage.

"Can you believe she's making us do this?" asked one young woman who leaned against a metal prep station and fanned herself with a tray. She, too, wore a hotel serving uniform like Maggie.

"I've never worked this hard, not even when I was a temple acolyte," complained another while she poured champagne.

Maggie cleared her throat, and both girls jumped.

"You're not one of us." The nymph's tone conveyed curiosity, not hostility.

Maggie put a finger to her lips. "I'm here to help you, but you've got to keep it a secret for now."

"We'll do anything to get out of this Hades-hole," the first girl, who had pretty curly red hair, said. "I thought we would be serving our mistress in her temple again, and here we are being put to actual work."

The other one threw the champagne bottle into a bin with other empties with a smash. "I just want to go back home to my nice tree by a stream. I'm afraid it will die without me. And the way the men here are looking at us..." She shuddered.

"Don't worry, we'll get out of here," Maggie assured them. She was arranging glasses on her tray when one of the security guys, thankfully not an Arabian guard, came in. He took a long look at her before turning to the other two.

"Hey, girls, less chatting, more serving. We've got thirsty people out there."

"Would you like some?" Maggie asked sweetly.

"Naw," the man said, "that stuff is drugged. I don't want to be hit by that *and* Cupid's arrow tonight. I've got enough trouble with my old lady as it is."

He continued to chuckle and walked out of the kitchen. Maggie put the tray down before she dropped it.

Drugged? And what did he mean by Cupid's arrows? I have to warn Charlie.

The tingling wave of magic that hit her when she walked into the room nearly knocked her over. She had to lean against a column entwined with pink and yellow ribbons and fake greenery. Sweat trickled down her chest and tickled the undersides of her breasts. The number of people in the room seemed to have doubled, and mist from the fog machines hung in the stuffy air. The lights dimmed by a few lumens every second, a gradual shift that the humans probably wouldn't notice, but which caught her attention. In the semi-darkness, the champagne glowed with a golden hue.

She picked up a glass and sniffed. The earthy, vinegar aroma gave it away—transportation spell. But to where? Not here, this was only the magnetic pole; the blood, or goal, pole would be somewhere else.

What had Delilah said? *"I hope it doesn't turn into an orgy."*

Oh, gods!

"Margaret."

Maggie jumped and almost dropped the tray of glasses she carried. She turned to meet the sea-green eyes of Nimue, who wore a seashell bra and skirt designed to look like a fish tail. Her dark hair curled in damp ringlets around her face, and her skin glistened with sweat. The poor girl looked like she would melt into the water that was her natural element. All the supernaturals must feel the pressure building. Maggie's ears popped.

"Nimue, where's Aphrodite?"

"She's backstage. Follow me." Nimue turned, and Maggie followed her.

"What is going on here?" Maggie whispered.

"It's going to be some sort of show."

"We have to get you out of here."

Nimue looked back at Maggie with narrowed eyes. "I'm not going without her."

"You won't have to."

Maggie excused herself to the Satyr she'd almost tripped over.

"Watch your feet, Truth Seeker," he sneered, "or you'll find your cover blown."

"Shut your mouth, goat-boy," she hissed back, and he giggled. She just couldn't get the woodland sense of humor.

But what is he doing here? No one reported any of them missing. Oh, gods...

Nimue brought Maggie to the other side of the stage, and they slipped behind it into a narrow passageway, the entrance of which was hidden by a strategically placed pillar. Maggie wrinkled her nose; this was where the were-bats had slept.

"Did anyone see you?"

"No, Mistress."

"Margaret." Aphrodite spun away from the mirror. She wore a low-cut white dress with a flowing skirt and golden sandals with stiletto heels.

"Your Radiance." Maggie bowed. "I'm glad to see you safe."

Aphrodite snorted, and a cloud of powder rose from the puff in her hand. "It took you long enough to find me."

"It's not been easy to get close to you. Have they treated you well?"

"As well as can be expected, but I'm ready to go home."

"What are the conditions of your release?" Maggie tipped her glasses down and saw the golden chain that was invisible to the goddess and her helpers. It twined around Aphrodite's waist and over one shoulder.

"I'm to help Lyle set up a temple here and in the C.U. Once it's running to his satisfaction—and to mine—he will release me."

"I see."

"No, you don't." Aphrodite looked at Maggie with all the force of her sapphire eyes. "Let's be honest, Margaret. Zeus has trapped me here, and you and I both know they want something more."

"I agree with you." Maggie put her tray on a stool and flexed her stiff fingers. "What do you know about this show tonight?"

"I'm to climb on the stage behind the curtain and wait on the throne in the temple while Lyle makes his announcement."

She rubbed her arms like she felt a chill. "Then he's going to introduce me."

"And then what?"

"He didn't say. I guess they'll applaud, and I'll leave the stage on his arm."

Maggie weighed the possibilities. There was definitely magic in the air, which could cause Aphrodite's goose bumps, but there had to be something else. "What do you think the enchanted champagne is for?"

"Lyle said he wanted a crowd. That he would join the population of the dream world to the one in the waking world."

"Wow, what a nice guy."

"He's not really all that bad. He's really sweet, actually."

Was that a note of sarcasm in the lovely goddess' voice? "You haven't, ah...?"

"Goodness, no." Aphrodite fluttered her eyelashes, the picture of innocence. "He's got a wife. I don't steal husbands anymore, at least not unless they're young and handsome enough, which he certainly is *not*."

"And where is the good Mr. Ames right now?"

"He's in the temple. He said he had to fetch something."

Maggie smacked her forehead as the pieces of Zeus' plan fell into place. "Of course. The rustling thing in the office."

"What are you talking about?"

"Eros. He's in danger. I can't explain now, but I've got to go."

28

Damien pushed his way through the crowd, and someone put a pewter goblet of wine into his hand. Before he could thank them, the person disappeared. He sniffed it and wrinkled his nose at the fruity and floral aromas. It smelled like it had been spiced or mulled. He lifted it to his lips to take a drink, but the wolf butted against him. He stumbled and spilled the wine.

"What was that for?" he asked.

"You didn't create that. This is more than a celebration." The wolf sniffed at the spilled wine and growled.

"What do you mean?"

"It has something to do with all this. And your ladylove."

Damien continued to make his way toward the temple, and the crowd thickened around him. Newcomers dressed in evening gowns and tuxedos, all heedless of the mess that the dirt and spilled wine made on their hems and shiny shoes, rubbed shoulders with fantastic creatures. They looked less substantial, almost transparent, in contrast to the rest of the crowd.

"Do you see that?"

"It's a transfer of energy." The wolf raised its nose to the air. *"Powerful magic is happening here."*

"And I bet Ames is in the middle of it." The crowd grew tighter the closer they got to the temple, and Damien found himself practically standing on top of his spirit guide.

"Can you do something about this?" he asked.

The wolf let forth a menacing growl, and the two people in front of Damien cast worried glances at it and moved out of the way. They repeated this process until Damien felt the bottom step of the temple jab his ankle.

Damien had watched the Arabian guards, who directed their gazes over the crowd in a precision pattern. He waited until he knew that they would be looking elsewhere, and he and the wolf sprinted up the steps and darted behind a column.

"Think we're clear?" he asked.

"Look there." Two heavily muscled guards, naked to the waist and brandishing scimitars, came up the stairs on the other side of the landing. Damien and the wolf crouched low and ran inside, curling into balls in the corner to the left of the door.

The cool darkness of the temple enveloped them, and the smoky, bitter odor of incense filled Damien's nose. He pinched it so he wouldn't sneeze. Once his eyes adjusted to the lack of sunlight, he saw smaller columns stretching in front of him to the altar, where two men stood, Lyle Ames and a taller man with a mane of salt and pepper hair and a strong nose, definitely Greek in heritage. He focused on a book on the altar, his eagle-like eyes narrowed. Ames stood to the side and looked around the temple.

"Did you hear that?" he asked.

"I heard nothing." The voice of the taller man reminded Damien of the rumbling of distant thunder.

"It sounded like something snuck in."

"The Arabian guards are keeping the crowd at bay."

"I'm concerned about our captives."

The Greek man rubbed his temples. "We'll be taking care of one of them shortly. The other will take care of herself."

"I've never killed anyone before."

"Oh, stop whining, Lyle. That's the nice thing about being a Greek god, my friend. If you make a mistake, you just fetch them back from Hades."

"At what price?"

"It depends on whether Persephone is down there or not. The girl's diabolically clever. Sometimes more than any mortal can pay."

"Aphrodite's not going to be happy with what you want to do to her son."

"Yes, but we hold all the cards. She won't have a choice but to cooperate even afterward."

Damien's heart beat in his throat. He crawled on his hands and knees toward the altar, pausing behind columns to catch his breath and make sure he hadn't been spotted. Once he got closer, he saw that Ames had keys on a golden ring on his belt. He looked at the wolf, who nodded.

When they reached the last column, they watched while Zeus continued to read and mumble to himself. Finally, he looked at Ames and said, "Fetch the Eros so that his sacrifice may bind all those here to our will and the worship of the *Pandemos*."

Ames bowed and walked past Damien's hiding spot. He went through a side door, and Damien slipped through before it shut. The wolf walked through the door.

They followed Ames through a courtyard, into another white marble building behind the temple, the one Rizzo had pointed out, and into a stairwell. At that point, Ames looked behind him, and Damien had to duck back through a doorway to avoid being spotted, which nearly sent him sprawling over the wolf.

"How can you go through a door but trip me up?" Damien asked after he rose and rubbed his rear end.

"I can only bend the rules so far."

"Let's go before he can get away." But they had already lost sight of Ames. The wolf put his nose to the floor and stopped them at the fifth landing.

Damien pushed the door open a crack and looked both ways. He saw Ames pause in front of an office, and Damien caught his own reflection in the window beside the office door. He realized too late that Ames had seen it as well.

"You can come out, my friend," Ames said and pointed a gun at Damien's head. "I heard you behind me the whole time."

A NOISE at the door woke Audrey from her lethargic state. How long had she been sitting there? Had another day gone by? She sighed and leaned her head back against the cage behind her. Would she never escape? And would she be stuck with regret in her afterlife that she'd never given a relationship with Damien a chance, as briefly as they'd been together? She could have at least been nicer to him.

Eros also woke, his wings rustling.

"What's that sound?" she asked after she heard it again.

"Our doom, I'm afraid." The dire words sounded ridiculous coming from him.

"Oh, quit being so melodramatic. Is it Zeus?"

Eros shook his head. "It's Ames, but he's come for me."

"What about me?"

"I told you, he's leaving you here to die."

Audrey opened her mouth, but Eros held up a hand.

"There's someone else out there."

"Can you tell who?"

"Someone tall and dark. Accompanied by a wolf. Oh, this could get interesting."

"Damien?" A jolt of adrenaline and hope woke her fully. Was she getting her second chance after all?

"That's the one, the cute policeman I helped you out with." He dodged a swat and looked at Audrey, his brown eyes wide. "He's going to be trapped like you. Unless..."

"Unless what?"

"It's a secret loophole that only I can activate," he said in a whisper. "The Collective Unconscious, being a reflection of the human psyche, has things in place to increase drama, including some special protections for lovers. As long as one is trapped, the other one can't be, as long as you're not in Hades. Have you, ah...?" He made an obscene motion with his hands.

"No, we only met a couple of days ago." But had they? "Maybe in the C.U.?"

"Oh, no, it had to happen in your world. I thought my arrows were more potent than that. Okay, then you have to let me shoot you while you're looking at him."

Audrey's heart twisted. She was willing to try a relationship, not completely surrender her feelings. "What? Are you nuts?"

"No, in spite of being stuck here with you for too long. It's the only way to make sure he doesn't get trapped and left here to die, too."

"What will happen to me?" She asked the question more of herself, but he answered anyway.

"You'll fall madly in love with him. Well, at first, but I don't know for how long. After that, the arrow wears off gradually until it's your connection that keeps you together and motivated to work on the relationship."

"You sound like a television psychologist."

He puffed out his chest. "Just call me Doctor Eros."

Audrey put her face in her hands. "I can't do that. I can't give up control of my emotions. Not yet."

"Do you want him to die here?"

What had the Oracle said? She would make a choice that would allow her to be worthy of love. Saving Damien's life fit. She looked up and said, "No." No, she didn't want Damien to die. She didn't want to die, either. And she now knew with certainty she wanted to see where this relationship could go when this nightmare was over.

Besides, if she was going to trust her emotions to anyone, she knew Damien was the most trustworthy one to take care of them.

"Okay, you can do it. But how? Your bow and arrows are over there."

Cupid grinned and brought out a tiny golden arrow from his loincloth. "I keep this one close in case of emergencies."

"Right." She took a deep breath of the stale air, straightened her shoulders, and clasped her hands. "I'm going to skip the obvious joke. Just be careful and don't make me fall for Ames instead."

"Just tell me when you have a good view of the cop. Here they come."

Audrey scooted back against the bars of the cage that separated her from Eros to shield him. The door burst open, and Damien tumbled through. Ames followed, gun aimed at Damien. Audrey resisted the urge to look at the weapon or at the large black wolf that ran into the room and instead looked at her lover-to-be.

"Now," she said. Eros jabbed her in her right butt cheek.

"Did you have to do that so hard?" It stung, and then warmth flowed through her.

Why haven't I noticed how Damien's hair curls in the damp of the evening or that he has a dimple in his right cheek? Or how nice his rear end looks in those black pants? Okay, I had noticed his ass before, but wow.

"Damien," she called, and he rushed to her cage. Heedless

of the arrow still sticking out of her butt, she went to meet him, and they clasped hands through the bars. She heard a click when another cage released from the ceiling, but it hovered over Damien's head, unwilling to trap the second half of a pair of lovers.

Ames looked, up, then at the couple, but before they could pull away from each other, he took the key ring off his belt and unlocked Eros' door.

"Hey, stop!" Cupid struggled, but Ames dragged him from his cage. The silver dragon scratched the businessman's cheek, neck and back through his shirt. Ames ignored it and held the gun to Eros' head.

"Don't make me use this."

Audrey held her breath, and the wolf whined in helplessness. Ames looked from Eros to the gun to the keys, which dangled from the lock.

"You," he told Damien. "Get the keys and put them on my belt."

The corner of Damien's mouth turned up. "You do it," he said. "They're your keys."

"Damien, please. He'll kill him." She closed her eyes, not willing to watch the carnage.

Ames cursed and darted out of the room.

She peeked. "Or not. How did you know?"

"They need the cupid for something in the temple. Undamaged, since that's the best kind of sacrifice." He unlocked her cage, and she fell into his arms. His lips closed on hers, and she felt happy for the first time that week.

"We don't have time for this," the spirit guides chorused.

"Right." Damien pulled away. "Are you okay? Can you walk?"

"My strength is returning now I'm free from the cage." She pulled the arrow out of her rear end and stuck it in her back pocket before he could see it.

Together they ran down the stairs and into the deserted courtyard. They darted outside and found the plaza deserted.

"Where did everyone go?" Audrey spun around to look at the temple, which had vanished, another square government building in its place.

"Ames must've told Zeus you were free." Damien ran his hands through his hair. "They took the party somewhere else. Or they sent us away."

The wolf huffed and lay down, and the dragon flew in ever wider circles above their heads. *"And you left the horse in the other city. Where he won't do any good."*

"Can you take us?" Damien asked the wolf.

Audrey grinned—of course he would have a strong, powerful beast for a spirit guide.

"I can go swiftly, but not with a human. I am not meant to be ridden."

"Then go and keep an eye on things," Damien told him. "We'll figure something out. All paths here lead to where you want to go."

Audrey shaded her eyes and squinted at the sunset. "Right, unless someone wants you to be really lost."

"All we can do is start walking." He held out his hand.

She took it and couldn't help but smile at him. "Let's go."

Audrey held Damien's hand and tried to concentrate on making the curve around the next hill the one that would bring the city with the right temple into view. The only things that greeted them were a sheep-path with more hills and the sound of the wind whistling around them.

"What now?" asked Audrey. She sat on a rock that marked yet another mile gone and wondered if the happiness she felt at being with him somehow blocked her ability to manifest what she needed. She was a dream weaver, for goodness' sake! But she could recognize when she was up against something more powerful.

"We need to find someone to show us the way." He looked at Audrey's spirit-guide, who only circled them for the hundredth time.

"It's nice to see you finally out and about, honey," a familiar voice called to them.

"Zinfandel." Audrey turned to see the dragon sitting on the slope above them. "Where have you been?"

Her spirit guide left her shoulder and circled Zinfandel's head.

"Unfortunately, I'm not allowed to interfere with these quest things, which is really a shame because I could pull them off with way more style than most of these shmucks."

Audrey bit back a giggle at his rueful expression. "I'm sure you could, but Damien and I are stuck."

"Together? That's so romantic." He held out a paw, and the smaller dragon landed there. The two beasts, large and small, gazed into each other's eyes. After a few seconds, the silver spirit guide nodded.

The black wolf bounded out of the shadows and licked Damien's face. Damien put a hand on his head and said, "He says Maggie and Charlie are at the temple, and Maggie has a plan, but they need our help."

"But we still can't get there."

"I can help you," said the silver dragon. It flew back to Audrey.

"What?" She looked into its emerald eyes.

"I can show you the way. Zin can't, but I can."

"But why didn't you before now?" She looked at Zinfandel, who studied his claws with an innocent air. "Oh."

"Size doesn't always matter, honey, as long as you can follow directions. But don't tell her that." With a wink, Zinfandel disappeared.

The little dragon took wing and led them off the path and up the hill. At the top, they found the ruins of a small temple, likely to some god of the country. They joined hands and were about to walk through the door formed by two columns and a straight piece of marble that had been chewed by the elements when Maggie and Charlie stumbled out. Charlie looked especially handsome in a tuxedo, but not half so much as Damien.

"Nice tux, dude," Damien said.

"I am *so* glad to see you safe," Maggie said to Audrey and moved to hug her. "I'm sorry I had to leave you there."

Audrey held up a hand. She wasn't in the mood for excuses. "How did you get here?"

"All the temples are linked, whether they're in the C.U. or in the waking world. If you know how, you can travel between them."

"Which is how Zeus gets around so fast."

"Exactly. And the magic is older than the Greeks, so they cannot block the spell."

"So what's your plan?" asked Damien.

"First, Audrey, do you have the arrow Eros used on you?"

She reached in her pocket and pulled it out. "How did you know about that?"

"There's a certain glow." Maggie clapped a hand over her mouth and looked at Damien.

"What? Wait a second..." Damien sat with a thud on the crumbling steps. "The way you've been acting here—that kiss—is that why? It was Cupid's arrow?"

Audrey's blush suffused her with warmth from head to toe. "Yes, there's a romantic loophole. That way you wouldn't be trapped."

He ran his hands through his hair. "And what about me, Maggie? Do I have that certain glow? Is that what happened to me at the hospital? These feelings, this overwhelming emotion, are they real?"

"Eros can't create something out of nothing," Maggie assured him. "There has to be something there for it to stick for more than a couple of hours. He just enhances it."

"It all makes sense now. I was touched by Cupid's stupid arrow." Damien looked at Audrey like she was a snake he'd almost stepped on, his contempt a stake to her heart. "Yeah, whatever. We'll talk about this later."

"Damien, I do care about you," Audrey said. She reached for his hand, but he folded his arms.

"Do you? And do I feel the same for you?" He shook his head. "I can't deal with this right now."

Audrey opened her mouth, but no words came out. She couldn't think clearly, Damien's rejection piling on top of past ones.

"That's enough." Charlie's authoritative voice cut through the haze of Audrey's heartbreak. "We've got work to do."

"Audrey," Maggie said, "this is going to put you in greater danger than being trapped in the golden cage, but we need a female to distract Zeus. He's already attracted to you, and he'll incinerate me on sight."

Audrey's heart beat in her throat. She'd thought she could trust her feelings to Damien, but... Then again, she was coming to realize there was no happiness without risk, and she was willing to risk everything to keep Zeus from unleashing awful dream creatures on the waking world. "I'll do whatever it takes to stop them and make my world safe again."

"Then we'll all have to work together." Maggie pointed at Damien. "No matter what you're feeling. Time is of the essence. Here's what we'll do."

29

Damien crouched behind the altar and looked around the temple. He couldn't see any of them, but he could feel Audrey through the connection he had to her thanks to those stupid arrows. He wanted to catch a glimpse of her, to make sure she was okay, but he stuffed his emotions. There was no point in pursuing anything with her, not now, and possibly there never had been. Although he knew now that his grandmother hadn't been hallucinating, he wished he could know whether her contact with the supernatural world had eventually caused her downward spiral and death. Maybe he should thank Eros for screwing things up for them before he'd allowed himself to change his mind.

Meanwhile, the tableau played out on the altar longer than anyone had expected. In spite of his weakened state, Eros had put up quite a struggle, and the two men at the altar couldn't hold him down enough to kill him, much less draw blood. Finally, after about ten minutes of what looked similar to cartoons of cat fights with limbs going every direction, Ames got a lucky jab with a syringe full of something, and Eros went limp. Damien nodded, and Maggie gave the signal from behind a column.

Now assured of Zeus' full attention, Audrey stepped into the torchlight. She wore a simple white acolyte dress that gathered at her shoulders and left a tempting amount of cleavage exposed. A wreath of white flowers sat on her head, and her spirit guide whizzed around her to give her a white glow. Damien swallowed the pride he felt in how good she looked after her ordeal—who knew if those were his true feelings?

"Zeus?" she asked in a meek voice. "Your Excellency?"

Both Zeus and Ames looked up from their grisly work. Zeus paused, knife poised to deal the death blow to the cupid, and narrowed his eyes. "What do you want, human? How did you get in here?"

"You—" Ames tried to say more, but Charlie, who had used the distraction Audrey provided to creep close enough, clamped a strong hand over Ames' mouth and dragged him into the darkness.

"We have your business partner, Zeus," Maggie called from behind her column. "Give it up."

Zeus laughed, and the building shook. "You think I need that puny human to get what I want? He has set up the paths and whetted the mortals' appetites. Once I harvest the energy from Aphrodite's worship through the golden chain, the humans shall flock to my worship, and I will once again live amongst them and have my pick of women and wealth."

"I don't think that's possible." Audrey's voice, low and quiet, got his attention. "There are powers greater than yours."

"Such as...?"

Audrey chanted to herself and danced, her movements slow and sensual, and her arms above her. Zeus' gaze locked on Audrey, but Damien wasn't prepared for the wave of rage and protectiveness that rushed through him. He almost forgot what he was supposed to do, but his wolf nipped at his rear end, snapping him back to attention. Blocked from Zeus' view by the shadows and the altar itself, Damien crept forward. He slithered under the stone table and jabbed the arrow into Zeus' foot.

Zeus yelled in rage and pain. Damien shimmied backwards and ducked to the side of the raised altar as lightning sizzled across the vaulted ceiling and thunder filled the space. He looked around for the others, but the only one he saw was Maggie, who had to dodge an errant thunderbolt.

Damien peeked at Zeus, who held on to the altar with both hands, his chest heaving. He held his breath. Although Maggie had told them what should happen, Damien knew all too well how unpredictable the gods could be. Again, he resisted the urge to throw himself in front of Audrey. He trusted that she could handle herself.

Zeus' angry gaze fell on Audrey, who stood seemingly unperturbed by the wind and light show raging around her. And when it all fell quiet, the sudden silence pressing on his ears, Damien tensed, ready to do something. He just didn't know what.

The god's words echoed through the temple although he didn't raise his voice. "I recognize you now. You are a marvel, human girl. So brave, so fascinating. I would have you bound and trussed on my temple floor as you were the first time I saw you." He licked his lips.

Damien clenched a fist.

Audrey held up a hand. "I have only one wish, Excellency."

Zeus' eyes bugged out, and he sounded like he struggled with the words. "Anything for you." He panted and clutched the sides of the altar. "Damn Eros' magic. No—yes—I will grant what you desire."

"For you to close the pathways that have opened the waking world to the dark creatures that live in this one. The human race needs to be left in peace."

Thunder shook the building again when Zeus realized the extent to which he had been tricked. But he had to keep his word.

"Very well, human." He crossed his arms. "This shall not be the last you hear of me." He looked at her intently, and she fell to the ground, clutching her stomach. With a low rumble of laughter, he disappeared.

Maggie ran to Audrey and reached her just before Damien did. "Are you okay?"

"I think so." Her dragon curled around her waist like a belt. "It felt like he punched me."

Damien helped her to a sitting position and let her lean against him. He tried to block awareness of the pleasure of having her in his arms, but memories of that damn dream kept returning. And that had been before Eros shot him. Could his feelings be genuine? He looked down at her. She'd certainly been brave to face Zeus like she had.

"I need to check on Eros." Maggie darted behind the altar, and she lifted Eros' limp form. "He's still breathing, just knocked out. Hopefully he only remembers the party." She smoothed the little god's hair back from his face.

"Can we just leave him like that?" Damien asked.

"I can stand now." Audrey's voice shook, and she accepted Damien's help, her cheeks pale. "I feel off-balance."

"Likely because your body is in a weakened state," Maggie told her. "You need to get back to it soon. But we need to do one more thing."

"What's that?"

"Keep any more paths from opening."

Lucia and Rizzo burst into the temple and led a band of merrymakers in a conga line that threaded through the pillars and up to the altar itself. Damien had to smile. Eros slumbered peacefully on the white marble table amidst the implements that would have killed him. Maggie gestured to Audrey,

Damien, and Charlie to follow her, and they crept out of the temple for the last time.

The revelers still danced outside. Aphrodite appeared beside them, finally free from her golden chain and aware that her son was also not captive anymore.

"Where's Lyle?" Her eyes blazed with anger.

"Still in the temple where Charlie and Damien left him tied up and knocked out," Maggie said. "Your son is in there, too."

"Is Eros okay?"

"His ego is probably bruised, and he's sleeping off the sedative that Lyle gave him, but yes, he's fine."

Damien watched Aphrodite's hurried but graceful progress into the temple. "Should we be supporting the release of that little menace?"

The hurt in Audrey's eyes said more about her broken heart than even she, as a writer, possibly could, and Damien looked away. He didn't need to be an ass.

"Okay, so back to the puzzle at hand," Charlie said. They found a table where they could watch the party without being dragged into it. Soon Aphrodite emerged from the temple, Eros drunkenly fluttering around her. She raised her hands, and a cheer went up from the crowd.

"What do you think she'll do now?" asked Damien.

"Probably enjoy the worship," Maggie told him. "A true goddess never retires. Just look at Cher."

"Back to the problem," said Audrey, her tone back to neutral journalistic. "What did the Oracle tell you? That it's well hidden, yet right in front of you, tiny with large effects, has been used for millennia but recently by one of us, and that there was a parallel journey it took to reach those who are using it."

"I've got lots of experience dream weaving, but my abilities come with my job and my training as a former priestess of Avalon," Maggie told her. "But you hadn't done it until recently."

"Nope. The first time was earlier this week, when I heard Demeter's cries."

"What did you do differently that night?"

"I took a shower, got ready for bed..." Her eyes grew wide. "That's the night Kyle gave me the new sleeping pill to try. I told him I'd been stressed about deadlines, especially for the Bistro Moderne review. He's on a sleep rotation right now—I guess they gave him some samples."

"Which sleeping pill? There are several."

"The new one. It's supposedly a mix of natural and synthetic ingredients, and it's available over the counter."

Charlie leaned forward and filled the cups that had appeared in front of them with non-magical wine. "And what do you want to bet that those natural substances have been used before, say by shamans and other holy men, to reach the dream realms?"

"And the parallel journey?"

"How did the drug get to market?" asked Damien. "Did the FDA expedite its approval?"

"Kyle did say something to that effect, that since it's natural plus over-the-counter stuff, it was considered safer and partially beyond FDA jurisdiction. But what did we witness?"

Maggie set her cup down so hard the wine almost spilled out of it. "Lyle Ames' approval for his business venture, expedited by Zeus himself. How could I have been so dense?"

"So the sleeping pill fit the Oracle's description." Audrey swirled the wine in her golden cup. "But how do we make sure?"

"And more importantly," said Maggie, "how do we get it pulled from the market?"

"Oh, I think we may be able to get a little extra help." Charlie cocked his head toward Aphrodite, who sat on a golden throne in the middle of the square and accepted flowers and gifts from her followers. She looked at their group and gave a little wave.

"She'll be more creative in revenge than any of us ever could," Audrey said. "Believe me, I know."

LYLE AMES WOKE and squinted at the bright rays of sun that snuck through the cracks between the thick curtains in his private suite at the Plaza. He wore his tuxedo shirt from the night before, unbuttoned, and his cheeks stuck to his teeth like he'd drunk too much wine. In fact, there was a rather strange taste at the back of his tongue and a draft on his bare ass. His face and neck burned like he was covered with scratches, but his fingers didn't find any, and the back of his head throbbed.

He eased himself up on his elbows and willed the pounding in his temples and the rushing noise in his ears to stop. A royal blue dress lay on the floor in a crumpled heap atop a pair of silver heels. Someone was in the shower—that explained the rushing noise.

He rolled to his back and put his hands over his eyes, the darkness a temporary relief. *What the hell happened to me?* The last thing he remembered was standing beside Zeus on the altar in Aphrodite's temple. He had been trying to drug that infernal cupid so they could sacrifice him to keep the pathways open, and he thought he'd succeeded, but that's where the memory stopped.

"Good morning, darling."

Ames rubbed his eyes. "Oh, shit."

Delilah Butler frowned, her hands on her hips. The terrycloth bathrobe she wore peeked open at her chest, but she was otherwise covered. "Now that's not a very nice thing to say. You were much happier to see me last night, so grateful that I'd helped to make the party a success."

He rose too quickly and had to sit to keep the room from tilting and throwing him against the wall. "Did we...?"

"Oh, yes, and you were magnificent. You know, I've been thinking about leaving my bore of a husband for a while now, and you'd be a good replacement. I know there's no love anymore between you and Amelia."

"A good what?" He jumped up and swallowed the acid that rose in his throat. He imagined the headline the following day —*Prominent Businessman Dies in Fiery Crash.*

"A good replacement. You're rich, not that bad looking, and you're good in the sack."

He pulled the sheets over his lap to cover his nakedness. "Delilah, I have a wife. This was a mistake, a horrible mistake. Look, I'll do anything to make it up to you."

"You're breaking my heart, Lyle, especially after all those sweet things you said to me." She sat on the bed, her long legs crossed.

He got up and gingerly bent down to retrieve his boxers. He hopped on one foot to put them on without sitting beside her on the bed. His stomach gurgled, and he swallowed against the sour taste in his throat.

"You told me I was your goddess—that I was prettier than Aphrodite, even though that actress you got to play her was a real knockout."

"Whatever I said, I didn't mean it. Please, Delilah, ask anything. You can have money, cars, houses, jewelry, whatever."

She leaned back so that the robe opened a little in front and revealed the plump, ripe top of one of her breasts. "Anything?"

"Anything."

She narrowed her eyes, and he felt like a rat that's just been spotted by a snake. "Pull the new sleeping pill from the market. I know your corporation is behind it."

He stopped putting on his tuxedo pants and looked at her. "What?"

"That new sleeping pill. It's got to go, Lyle. It gave me the weirdest dreams, and I'm still afraid to go to sleep sometimes because of what it did."

He tried to shake his head but discounted that as a bad idea and simply frowned. "I can't."

"Then I'll be sure to call Amelia when I get home. And my lawyer." She got up and walked toward the bathroom.

"Wait." He sat back on the bed and willed the nausea to subside. "Okay, okay, I'll call the head of that division today to have it pulled."

"Good. If it's not pulled out of stores by the end of the week, you'll be hearing from me."

He made sure he was out of sight when she came out of the bathroom.

AUDREY WOKE to the smell of fresh coffee. She blinked at the unfamiliar ceiling, and her stomach growled. She tried to sit up, but the pain in her shoulder kept her pinned to the bed. A whimper escaped her lips before she could bite her tongue over it.

"Nice try, but I heard that." Maggie came in the bedroom and gently helped Audrey to a sitting position. "You need some food in your stomach so you can take your pain meds."

"You got the script filled?" It felt like such a long time ago that she'd been in the hospital. "Where's Damien?"

"He was here, but he's already up and gone. Hold on, I'll be right back."

Maggie returned with a bed tray laden with coffee, orange juice, and a chocolate croissant.

Audrey wolfed down the croissant and savored the coffee under Maggie's watchful eye. Once her stomach settled, she took a pain pill and leaned back to wait for it to take effect. The throbbing in her collarbone matched the sick thud of her heart.

"So, what happened in Lyle's office?" Maggie asked. "Did Eros get you when you weren't looking?"

Audrey recounted Eros' strategy to keep Damien from being trapped. "It worked, too. The cage started to fall but hovered over his head." She blinked, and a tear plopped into her coffee. "I'm afraid he'll never want to talk to me again."

"And you want him to?"

"Yes." She shifted so she wouldn't sit on the tender spot where Eros' arrow had jabbed her. "But is that the spell talking?"

"Not necessarily. What happens in the dream world tends to fade quickly. Whatever you're feeling today is probably all you. Maybe it's what would have happened had Damien not come on too strong to begin with."

"Great."

The doorbell rang, and Maggie ran to get it. "Hello, Charlie."

"I thought you ladies could use some pastries."

Audrey heard Maggie's laugh and their low conversation. It sounded like they had some sort of understanding. She sighed and blew on her coffee, which had magically refilled.

It's not like I need to get involved with someone so soon after Kyle's betrayal anyway. Now there's someone who could use an inconvenient arrow in the ass. I need someone I can trust, someone I can count on to go to the ends of the Earth and beyond for me. Someone like Damien.

Another tear splashed into the coffee.

Maggie came in with a plate of chocolate croissants, cheese Danishes, and cherry turnovers. "Want some more?"

"Yes, I'm still hungry. I can't mend a broken heart, but I sure can feed it." She tried to smile and selected a cherry turnover, but she had to bite her lip.

"Hey, now, there's no reason to cry," Charlie said and brushed her hair back from her face. The gesture made her sniffle louder because it reminded her again of Damien and the way he'd looked at her when he did it.

"Charlie, you know Damien better than any of us. Is there any hope for him and me?"

He sat on the end of the bed, careful not to jostle her or the tray. "Yes and no. Yes because he was definitely interested in you before he got pricked by Eros, no because he doesn't like losing control of his emotions. I bet he's thinking about the past few days and squirming over his behavior."

"Even if I had nothing to do with it?"

"Damien's a deep guy. Just give him time. Remember, he's been dealing with the whole Rizzo thing, too."

Audrey shook her head. "We all have. Rizzo, J.J.—whoever he is has a lot to explain."

Maggie selected a bear claw. "He does, but his kind likes to keep their secrets, so it might be a while." She frowned. "And the fact that one of them has been involved in both your and Damien's lives means there's more trouble to come."

"What about the sleeping aid?" Audrey asked. She couldn't deal with J.J. and his secrets until she knew the current situation had at least somewhat resolved.

"I can't say too much since she technically bent the rules," Maggie said. "But Aphrodite took care of it. She posed as someone Lyle Ames wouldn't be able to refuse and convinced him to pull it."

Charlie raised his coffee cup in salute. "She must have done a hell of a job. I heard it on the news on the way over, so he acted fast."

Maggie touched her cup to his. "Never underestimate a determined goddess. Or mortal, for that matter. All of you were amazing."

Audrey looked down at her food. She didn't feel amazing. She just wanted to be home in her bed and to know what to expect.

30

When Damien walked into Arthur's hospital room, Lucia handed him a sausage biscuit. "Here, darlin', I knew you'd be coming without having eaten breakfast."

He took a small bite. It was perfect. "I don't normally do this."

"What? Eat breakfast in the hospital?"

"Well, that. And I don't normally talk to psychics. But you seem to have a handle on all of this weird stuff."

"I only see patterns and point them out to others." She put a hand on Rizzo's arm, careful not to disturb the I.V. that stuck out of his wrist.

"What about him? Do you see that he'll make it...in this form?"

Instead of answering, she asked, "What happened with you and Audrey in the C.U.? It looked like you two would make a good couple."

He gave her a quick summary of what had happened. "And I finally found out what no one would tell me. Maggie and

Charlie had figured it out, but they also knew how I'd feel about it."

Instead of offering him sympathy, she said, "What matters is how you feel about Audrey."

"My heart yearns for her, but my mind thinks that it's all because of the poison arrow. What if I figure out I'm not interested in her at all after a while? It would be too painful for both of us."

"You know, Damien," said a hoarse voice, "that's not an unusual risk even for those who fall in love the normal way."

"Arthur!"

"Doctor Rizzo."

Damien had just enough time to rush to his side and squeeze his hand before a nurse came in and alerted the attending physician. He and Lucia stood against the back wall as vitals were checked and re-checked, and Rizzo's status was downgraded from "critical" to "serious." When all that was done and the nurse admonished them not to stay too long because he needed his strength, Damien and Lucia returned to their positions on either side of the bed.

"Like I want to go back to sleep right now," Rizzo scoffed. "I've been asleep for the past three days. Damien, my boy, you did magnificently. You found the sketch?"

"With a little help."

"And the imp?"

"Charlie and Maggie are going on critter cleanup today with Charlie's team. I wanted to go, too, but he insisted I take a day off."

"Good, good. Now about you and that young lady..."

"I just wish that what I feel was all me."

"Why wouldn't it be?"

"Because she's perfect for me. I've never met anyone like her." The words felt true to him even in spite of Cupid's arrow.

But hadn't Maggie said the greatest effects were for the first twelve hours?

"That sounds like you, not the spell," Rizzo told him. "Remember, you went to see her at her job."

"Yeah, but that was professionally motivated. I wanted to give her an update." Damien's face heated in response to Rizzo and Lucia's skeptical expressions. "Fine, a lot of it was me."

"And there's something else," said Rizzo. "Go on, spit it out. We won't judge."

The words tumbled out—did Rizzo have truth-spelling ability, too? "I don't want to be manipulated. If I'm going to be in a relationship, I want to have all my rationality available."

Lucia and Arthur exchanged an amused look, then Lucia asked, "And how will you know you have that?"

"I don't know." He ran his thumb over the top of a pink rose in the bouquet on the table beside Rizzo's bed. "But I won't feel so out of control."

"Look, Damien, when you were going into the temple to rescue her, were you focused on her or on the task at hand?" Rizzo asked.

"The mission, of course, and not getting caught. Even if it did end up being a trap, which I should have known."

"And then what?"

"I've already told you."

"But you knew exactly what to do?"

"Yes." Damien licked his lips, where he thought he could still taste her kiss. "It was standard procedure with some creative stuff."

"Then I think you answered your own question," Arthur said with a yawn. "I think Ms. Sonoma brings out the best in you, and you're scared to lose it."

Damien knew they were right. Working with Charlie had made him nervous because he might prove himself worthy to be promoted to detective, and now getting involved with

Audrey would push him to grow in a different way. Hell, it had already propelled him past his fear of the supernatural and into the C.U. three times, and two of those had been before he'd been shot by Eros. He'd faced things he could have never dreamed up on his own. And he was still sane. If his mind was going to crack, wouldn't it have already?

"You'll have your chance to talk to her soon," Lucia told him.

"Is it something you sense?"

"No, Maggie and Charlie are going to take her home once she's awake and has eaten something. We should go, too. Arthur is tired, although he doesn't want us to know."

"That's what I get for getting involved with a psychic," Rizzo grumbled, but he didn't protest. "What do you see happening to me next?"

Lucia grinned for a moment, but then her brows came together in a frown. "Retirement, but only partial. Your kind never fully rests."

"You know me too well."

THE DESERTED BALLROOM had the despondent look of a party the morning after with tumbled chairs, decorations, and glasses strewn about the floor. Stray bits of magic sparked and fizzled, and Maggie avoided them when she rolled to the side and shot the last of the were-bats with a silver bullet from the pistol she rarely carried. The creature screamed, then disappeared in a puff of smoke. The toad had already been bagged by the DCU—Demon Containment Unit—so she only had one more thing to do before the decontamination squad arrived.

"Maggie, did you get them?" asked Charlie when she called him.

"Yep. How's the imp?"

"Struggling and squeaking in the bag you gave me for it.

The chocolate croissant was genius. I would've never guessed the things have a sweet tooth."

"Great. I'll be there to pick it up in a few."

She arrived at his office half an hour later. The leather sack on Charlie's office desk moved and squealed beside the revolver in a plastic evidence bag, but Maggie ignored it. Charlie stood by the window, his cell phone to his ear, and he waved her to have a seat. He continued his conversation while he closed the blinds between his office and the rest of the floor.

"Yes, Mr. Smith, we got what was responsible. Yes, Doctor Rizzo is awake and is expected to make a full recovery. No, thank you very much for your help. It was very noble of you to come to us with such honesty. I hope Daniel gets stabilized soon."

With that, he closed his phone with an emphatic click.

"Are all the loose ends tied up?" asked Maggie.

"As tied as they're going to be." He took a couple of plastic cups and a miniature bottle of red wine out of his drawer. "I'm not supposed to have these here, but I wanted to celebrate. This was a tough case."

She accepted the glass he handed her. "I'm technically not supposed to be drinking on the job, either, but what the hell?"

"Right." He sat beside her on the sofa and put an arm around her.

"Are you trying to make a move on me, Detective MacKenzie?"

He leaned closer, his blue eyes twinkling. "What if I am?"

She looked into her wine and saw dark shapes and visions on its surface. "You're putting yourself in danger."

"What?" He laughed, but it sounded nervous. "Are you a black widow in disguise?"

"No, Charlie, I'm cursed." She looked at him through lenses blurred by her tears and then closed her eyes. She could see the Oracle, the taut muscles of the girl's neck when she forced the words out and recited them. *"If you are to love or to be loved, to share possession of heart and soul, then woe to he to whom this gift is given, for he will be destroyed."* She opened her eyes and looked outside at the lacework of bare tree branches against the icy blue sky. "I saw it happen with my sisters. Igraine, Arthur's mother, lost her husband to battle and her lover to politics. Morgause was the smart one—she married for money—but she suffered much because her husband didn't love her. I'm afraid that if we were to come to an understanding, it would spell your doom."

"Oh." Charlie stood and walked to the window. "You know, Maggie, I sometimes forget who and what you are. You seem like such a normal woman to me."

"And that's why I like you so much, Charlie. You see the real me, the girl that played knights and outlaws with the boys so long ago. You're a good friend, but that's all I can ever let you be. I care about you too much to put you in danger."

"Any chance of breaking the curse?"

"I should have some down time. I haven't gotten my next assignment yet—it feels like there's something big brewing, but it may take a while to manifest—so I'll research it. Lucia reminded me that every curse has a key."

"You haven't looked into it before?"

"I have, but not recently. And when I did, work interrupted my search."

He turned away from the window, regret on his face. "Just try to make it quick. Some of us don't have forever."

The lump in her throat would only allow her to nod in response.

❧

Audrey dug her keys out of her purse to unlock the front door. Everything was harder with just one hand, and in her efforts to isolate the front door key from the rest of the mass, she dropped them. She reached for them and didn't even look up when Lucia's door opened. The pain meds helped, but they made her feel slightly off-balance, and she didn't want to move her head too much.

"Wow, Lucia, wait 'til I tell you..." She looked up into Damien's silver eyes. He bent over and retrieved the keys for her.

"Need help?"

"You're just all about rescuing me lately." She tried not to sound bitter.

He didn't say anything or laugh while he unlocked her door and stood back so she could go in. Athena went into a sniffing frenzy, and Audrey nudged her out of the way, grateful that Lucia had taken care of the cat while she was away.

"Would you like to come in?" she asked. "We have some things to talk about."

"I agree."

Her heart pounded, and she pointed him to the loveseat. She sat in her recliner and didn't object when he put a pillow behind her before sitting down himself.

"Do you want to go first, or shall I?"

He leaned forward and put his head in his hands. "Look, Audrey, I'm confused right now. I feel like I've been trapped in several ways in the past few days, and I don't know what to do about it."

"You don't have to do anything about it," she said. "You can wait and see how you feel."

"But that's the thing. Part of me wants to wait..."

"And the rest?" She held her breath, hardly daring to hope.

He raised his head and looked at her, the confusion evident in his gray eyes. "And the rest of me is ready to rush in, and that scares me."

Audrey shifted a little, her shoulder throbbing again. At

least she told herself the tightness in her chest was caused by her collarbone. "I'm afraid I'm not really in any place for a relationship, Damien. I just found out that Kyle cheated on me, and we haven't even officially broken up yet. I've got my own stuff to work through."

"Right. I'm sorry, I forgot."

"We need to just give it some time. Just call me. You have my number and know where I live."

Damien stood and came to stand beside her. He looked at her for a few seconds, and she felt like he looked straight into her heart. She swallowed but didn't say anything. If he was going to argue for what was between them, fine, but she was conscious of what Charlie had said, that pushing Damien into something would only drive him away.

"Is that what you really want?" He spoke quietly.

"I don't know what I want."

"Then that's all I need to know. You know where to find me."

She closed her eyes so she wouldn't see him leave, but she heard the door open and close, and he was gone. Then the door opened again.

"What in Hades do you think you're doing?" Aphrodite stood in the doorway, her arms crossed. She wore her designer jeans and "Goddess" T-shirt ensemble.

Audrey wanted to get up, but she couldn't. "Oh, gods, can't you just leave me alone? It's your fault I'm in this mess."

"Look, he's perfect for you." The goddess sat on the edge of the loveseat. "He's also very independent, so you'll be good for each other."

"This from the goddess who likes to make things more complicated."

"Right. I should turn you into a toad for that. But since you've done me a great favor in rescuing my son, and since I am sworn to uphold the cause of true love, I'll overlook it. Eros might be a pain in the neck, ass, or wherever his arrows land, but his magic won't work unless there's something there to magnify. It's not like in the old days, when he could make the most unlikely of matches happen. Now he's like a microscope—he calls what's already there to attention, but he can't create it."

Audrey mulled over her words. "I apologize, Your Radiance, I think I may have underestimated you."

"And I, you. You have enough troubles yet to come. Why pass up the chance to have a good man with you?"

A wisp of fear uncurled in Audrey's stomach. "What do you mean?"

"I can't say. But trust me. No one comes away from a romantic encounter with Zeus unscathed."

And with that, she was gone.

Audrey looked at the phone. A number with the words, *Damien cell—don't screw it up.* was printed in calligraphy on her message pad.

"Who am I to argue?" she asked Athena.

"Meow."

"Right." She picked up the phone, left a short message for Kyle telling him it was over—in case there was any doubt—and dialed the number Aphrodite had left for her.

DAMIEN HAD JUST TURNED on to Ponce when his cell phone rang.

"Lewis," he said without looking at the number. He guessed it was Charlie calling with an update about the imp.

"You said I'd know where to find you," said the voice he had given up hope of hearing again anytime soon. "Can you come back?"

When Damien reached Audrey's front porch, he found a dozen red roses in a vase on the steps. The note tucked among the flowers read, *To make amends for all the trouble Eros caused. You're perfect for each other. She needs you.* He put the note in his pocket, picked up the vase, and knocked on the door.

"Come in."

He opened the door and saw that Audrey still sat in her recliner, phone in hand.

"Um, these are for you."

"Wow. That was a quick florist trip."

"I had some help."

He set the flowers on the coffee table and sat on the loveseat, which felt warm like someone had just been sitting there.

"You wanted me to come back?" he asked. He didn't say anything else.

"Did you want to come back?"

He nodded.

Her smile melted the protective resolve he'd started to build around his heart again. "I made a mistake. I think we'd be quite good for each other, and I'm ready to try."

"I see. What changed your mind?"

"A visit from Aphrodite." She smiled and looked at the flowers. "I'm guessing your help was of divine origin?"

"I'm still getting used to the idea, you know."

"Me, too." She gave him the same grin she'd given him in the empty lot, which he'd interpreted as relief that there was another human as overwhelmed as she was. "And she said something strange. I have a feeling this story isn't over yet."

"Really?" He hoped she didn't see the fear that blossomed in his chest. Just because he'd accepted the supernatural and didn't seem to be affected by it like his grandmother, it didn't mean he liked it.

"Yes, and if the rest of it's going to be challenging like the first part, I need someone to help me through it."

"I thought you didn't want me to rescue you anymore." Not that he minded. She'd rescued him, after all.

"I'd prefer to work as a team. As equals. I'm just not a good damsel in distress."

"I see."

"What do you think?"

Five minutes ago, Damien had been ready to put all this god and goddess crap behind him and move on with his goals. Life shouldn't be that complicated. But when he looked at Audrey, he felt like he could handle anything. And he was willing to try.

"I might need to be rescued," he said.

"Oh?"

"Yes, from this horrible idea that I don't need a woman in my life."

She grinned. "I can handle that. But there's just one more question."

"What?"

"The morning I was in the hospital, did you dream about me? In a stone cabin with a fireplace?"

He couldn't help the wide grin that erupted when he remembered the dream. "And wine?"

"Yes. I don't think that was really a dream."

He got up and stood beside her chair so he could lean in and whisper, "Or maybe it was the best kind—a shared one." He put his lips over hers, and it was better than in the dream. She tangled her fingers in his hair, but he pulled away.

"I don't want to hurt you," he said.

"And I don't think I can do more than cuddle with my shoulder feeling like it is."

"That I can definitely handle." He picked her up, brought her into her bedroom, and laid her on the bed. The cat followed them and curled up by her feet. "Hi, Athena," he said and scratched her behind the ears. "What if she really is the goddess herself? She might smite me."

"She's certainly bossy enough, but I doubt it. Besides, she always hid when Kyle came over. She didn't like him but seems to have accepted you right away."

"Just to make sure, you're officially broken up, right?"

She nodded. "Very."

He stretched out beside her on the bed and studied her. She still looked fragile, but strength shone in her steady gaze, and certain parts of him stirred to attention in response to the hunger in her eyes.

"What?" she asked. "Do I look different?"

He caressed her face and kissed her again. "You look beautiful and taste like chocolate and coffee."

Her green eyes met his, and she blushed. "I'm a mess," she said.

"Yes, but you're a lovely one."

"Wait here." She went into the bathroom and came out wearing a long T-shirt. "Do you have something you can change into to sleep?"

"I'll just wear my T-shirt and boxers, if that's okay."

"Very."

He took his turn in the bathroom, and when he came out, he found her watching for him. When he lay beside her, he put a finger under her chin and tilted her face toward his for one more kiss. She snuggled into him and was soon asleep, but his eyes wouldn't close, at least not right away. The strange events of the past few days played through his mind. Was it possible that his grandmother's mistake had been to not seek out like-minded people who would have believed and supported her? Like Audrey.

My grandmother would have been proud, he thought and drifted into a dreamless sleep.

· · ·

THANK you so much for reading Tangled Dreams! It would be super helpful if you were to leave a review at the site where you bought it, and/or on Goodreads if you're reading it in paper. Reviews help out with sales rank and let other potential readers know that this is a group of characters that are worth spending time with.

Thanks again!

- Cecilia

WEB OF TRUTH

"This is such an amazing series, and this installment is no exception!"

The final bounty was supposed to be the easiest. So why is she the one being hunted?

Morgan le Fay, once the most promising priestess on Avalon, lost her powers due to her unwitting role in the fall of Camelot. She's survived by becoming a bounty hunter for Faerie Queen Maeve. After she completes her tenth, and final job, she will be free to live her own life and regain her powers.

The problem – the situation isn't as simple as it seems. Her final target, the fledgling vampire Philippe, turns out to have ties to her family, and her handler isn't telling her everything.

Nightmare creatures, faerie plots, and murder follow Morgan as she navigates past hurts and attempts to unravel the truth. Will she be able keep her friends safe and find forgiveness in time to figure out what the faerie queen wants with Philippe? And will Morgan deal with her old wounds and risk her powers – and her heart - to secure her future?

Web of Truth is the second full-length book (but can be read on its own) in the Dream Weavers and Truth Seekers series, which is being hailed as a unique addition to the urban fantasy land-scape. If you like tales featuring strong heroines, tricky Fae, and hidden worlds that exist beside our own, then you'll love Cecilia Dominic's new series.

Buy or read Web of Truth to start or continue this intriguing and addictive series today!

Please enjoy this preview of *Web of Truth*, the next story in the Dream Weavers and Truth-Seekers series...

One more week.

Morgan crossed October 31 off her calendar. Sure, it was only noon, but the revelry in her normally quiet - if there was such a thing - neighborhood just outside New Orleans said people were already partying like night-time, so she may as well count it. She hoped she wouldn't have to hose too much vomit off the sidewalk in front of her magic store the next morning. But it was Halloween, one of her busiest days, so she didn't dare close.

She'd need a source of income once she retired from being the Fey queen's bounty hunter in, oh, a week. While calendars may have changed and shifted, she always remembered the day ten centuries ago a week after Samhain when she'd made her bargain. Not with the devil, although the Fey queen was close enough, and her messenger handsome as sin.

Just one more week, and she'd be free. Ten jobs or ten centuries, whichever came first. Then she'd have her powers and her retirement, and she could finally live life without always looking over her shoulder.

The bell over the door tinkled, and a dark-haired young man walked in. Morgan's heart joined her stomach in a free fall of despair, and she barely kept herself from letting out a disappointed moan. Of course she wouldn't get off that easily.

Ten centuries or ten jobs? Ten jobs it is.

She leaned on her elbows on the glass case that displayed the objects that were either nicer or small enough for easy shoplifting, typically crystals, fossils, and wands. Their magic auras wafted up to her through the glass, steadying her.

"Decided to skip the drama today, Elric?" As much as she hated what his appearance meant, she fought a sly smile. Fine, she liked the adventure, both of the chase and of him in bed, and it had been a long time. "Since when do you come in the door like a normal person?"

He grinned, his teeth perfectly straight, and the thoughts of what he did with his lips made her cross her legs where she stood. He always dressed congruent to the century he appeared in. Today he wore skinny tan corduroy pants, pointed toe boots, and a dark green cashmere sweater under a brown faux leather jacket. Although he appeared neat, he'd allowed his hair to grow long enough to cover the pointed tips of his ears, which made it shaggy and gave him a bohemian air. Or rebellious.

She liked, and she licked her lips at the thought of getting him out of the outfit and raking her fingers through his hair.

His intense expression - was he as hungry for her as she was for him? - gave his words a delicious double *entendre*. "I have a job for you."

"From you or the queen?" There was always the possibility he'd missed her, after all. Maybe he wasn't here for official business. Maybe they could finally be -

"From the queen." He nodded, but his gaze flicked up and left before he returned it to her, his smile more dazzling than before. Yep, he was walking sex, and her mind clouded with both memories and hopes for what would happen when she got those pants off him--

She waved away the glamour. The power to see through Fey spells had come back after job number six, much to Elric's irritation and her relief. But she'd always been able to sense when he was lying. "And this will help me fulfill my deal with her."

"This will count toward your ten."

"As my tenth." She stood so she could look him in the eye. She'd made it through nine jobs so far by ensuring there was no Fey trickery.

"As your tenth," he agreed through clenched teeth. He didn't look nearly as pretty now that she'd irritated him. She almost sighed as the ache between her legs eased. Good.

"And after this, my obligation will be finished, and I'll get the rest of my powers back," she pressed.

He gave her a curt nod.

"No, say it." She leaned forward and pressed her palms to the counter, heedless of the hand-prints she'd have to clean from the glass. Otherwise she'd grab his shirt and shake him. "I need your word that this is it, Elric."

He sighed, and she almost applauded the drama of it.

"Fine.When you deliver this bounty to the queen, you will fulfill your obligation to Queen Maeve, and you will get your powers back."

"Once I deliver it. Say it again."

"Yes, once *you* deliver the bounty to her, he repeated." He rolled his eyes. "Do we have to go through this every time?"

"Yes." She rubbed her hands together, already pondering what she would need to do with the store while she chased down whoever or whatever had caught Maeve's interest this time. Sometimes there were insults to avenge. Sometimes it was simply a matter of the queen seeing in someone a pretty, shiny thing she wanted. At the beginning, Morgan hadn't understood the queen's whims or how she could treat living thinking beings as objects, and in truth, she still couldn't. Morgan made it a point of pride that she hadn't let her almost-immortality make her unsympathetic to those whose lives were but a blink. Well, assuming they didn't get in her way.

"Who are we after this time?" She looked up at him through her lashes. "And when do we leave? I want to get this over with as soon as possible, although I need a day to get things settled here." She waved her hand. "One does not simply abandon one's magic shop on Samhain."

But her mind already sorted through details. She could call Lacey, her assistant and a talented magic-wielder who had figured out Morgan was more than she let on. Killing people had gotten too messy in the twentieth century - damn forensics - so she'd decided to make the girl an ally rather than eliminate her as a threat. Lacey would be happy to help and to watch things while she was away.

"Understood, although I don't see why you bother. Silly mortals, thinking that trinkets can make them into powerful magic-makers." After the seventeenth century, they both instinctively avoided the word witch, although it had lost some of its negative connotations since. He walked around. "What kind of wards do you have on this place? You've gotten better at them."

Heat came to Morgan's cheeks and frustration to her chest that she still preened under his praise. Was that why he'd used the door rather than just appearing as he usually liked to do? Discretely, of course. He wouldn't just appear in the middle of a store or someplace else where humans would see him.

Or was he complimenting her? Morgan sensed Elric wanted to be away quickly. That, the fact he'd apparently done some Earth-crossing before arriving rather than using the connections between the Faerie realm and human ones to expedite his trip, and the sense of something being off, like milk just on the cusp of souring, made her delay. If there was a loophole that would allow her to not take the job and wait out her time, she aimed to find it.

"And who are we after?" she asked his back, as he stood and studied the bookshelves to the right of the door.

"Some vampire." His shoulders lifted and dropped in what she assumed was another sigh. "The queen wants a new pet."

Morgan pulled the glass cleaner and a roll of paper towels from the shelves under the register to rid herself of the handprints on the formerly clean case. "What the heck does she want with a vampire? She doesn't typically bother with the nightmare creatures."

"Indeed." He bent to examine a book more closely.

"Let me know if you have any questions," she said automatically. Her mind worked as she cleaned the top of the case. Then the front, since no matter how much she tried, she couldn't keep fingerprints from gathering on it. She'd put away the glass cleaner and found the duster for the shelves inside when a weight on her shoulder brought her back to the present.

"It's fine," Elric said. The impatience and irritation had gone from his tone, and now he looked at her tenderly. "I thought you'd gotten treatment for that."

She put away the duster and clenched and unclenched her fists to distract herself from the gritty feeling on her fingers. "I did, but it's an ongoing thing, especially when I'm stressed. Maybe I'll go back for a booster course once we're done with this. Where are we going, anyway?"

He put his arms around her, and she snuggled into his chest. Anything more than an ongoing fling was impossible, but she'd take what she could get. Even his smell contradicted itself - the odor of plants in a rainstorm over sun-warmed rock.

"There's an island in the Caribbean owned by a man you may have heard of - Merlin. The vampire is being held there."

"Merlin?" Morgan pulled back and looked up to study Elric's face. "We're going up against the Truth Seekers?"

Elric traced a finger over her cheek. "Not necessarily. This vampire poses some sort of threat to them. That's why the queen wants him."

Morgan shivered, both from the journey of Elric's hand, which traced down her cheek and along the line of her jaw, and the thought of what she'd be getting into. No one wanted to be in the middle of the ages-old conflict between the Truth Seekers, the self-styled supernatural law enforcement agency that more than a few paranormal creatures considered to be a band of well-organized vigilantes, and the Fey. She should've known her final job wouldn't be that easy.

"Good, now make the cloud bigger."

Audrey frowned as she focused on the cloud that hung above them in an impossibly blue sky. The grass she laid on tickled the backs of her arms and legs, and she had to keep from being distracted by the waving leaves on the nearby trees. Her spirit guide, a small silver dragon, made for a comforting weight on her belly. Maggie had explained that this part of the

Collective Unconscious remained in a state of eternal summer, hence the green. But it was also a good place to practice a variation of what Audrey had done as a child, only this time she made the shapes in the clouds. Or tried to.

The vaguely cat-shaped white and gray puffball above them suddenly expanded, then dissipated. Audrey sighed, and the dragon squeaked in protest.

"I'm not very good at this." She turned her head to Maggie, who lay next to her.

Maggie smiled and patted Audrey on the hand. "You're doing fine. You can't be good at everything on your first try."

"But this isn't my first try." Audrey turned her face back to the sky. "We've been at this for a week, and I can barely manipulate the clouds. How am I supposed to be of any use?"

"A week is nothing. It took much longer for some of us to master even the most basic magic on Avalon." Maggie snorted. "At least if you make something blow up here, it won't hurt anything."

"True." Audrey turned back to her. "Tell me about Avalon."

Maggie shook her head, but behind her, an island shaped cloud appeared. It looked like a semicircle with rectangular things sticking up at the top - standing stones? "It's gone into the mists, although there is likely a reflection here."

Wispy gray clouds covered the island-shaped one, and it all blew away.

"Do you ever try to go to the reflection, to see what happened to the people there?"

"No." Her tone had gone flat, and Audrey drew back, stung. "I'm sorry." Maggie patted Audrey's hand again but didn't look at her. "I made one of my biggest mistakes there, and it changed the course of history."

"I'm sorry for asking. By the way, nice cloud work."

"What?" Maggie looked to where Audrey indicated. "I wasn't doing it." She sat, and Audrey did as well. "What did you see?"

"An island with standing stones on the top, and then gray clouds covered it and took it away."

Maggie grinned. "Avalon didn't have standing stones. That must have been your version of it."

"Oh!" Audrey clapped. "But I wasn't trying."

"That means you've been trying too hard." Maggie stood. "And you need a break." She helped Audrey to her feet, and the dragon made lazy circles around them.

Audrey sighed. She'd never get used to this topsy-turvy world, which Maggie had told her was like a dimension. No one had figured out why humans could reach it in their sleep but no one else could. Or why they could stash their collective cultural memories here in the forms of gods, goddesses, and other mythological beings. Audrey wondered if she'd meet Thor someday, but she wouldn't rush it. She hadn't felt quite right since her encounter with Zeus, but she couldn't describe how except that she often had the sense of someone peering over her shoulder and waiting. For what, she didn't know.

She followed Maggie to the edge of the woods, where the reflection of the sky filmed the surface of a small pool of water about three feet in diameter. The sky darkened, and Audrey looked up to see that dark gray clouds had rolled in. A cold breeze teased the hair at the back of her neck, and she remembered she wasn't the only one engaged in supernatural pursuit. Or, in Damien and Charlie's case, pursuit of something supernatural and nasty.

"Time to check in on the boys?" Audrey asked. Maggie would never admit it, but they were both nervous about the guys hunting a rogue were-bat that day.

"Yep." Maggie pulled her hair back and secured it with an elastic. "I wish I knew how the nightmare creatures keep getting through like they are. The barriers between the CU and the waking world should be mostly healed by now."

Audrey had pictured the barriers as stone walls, but in

reality - or what passed for it - they were more like sheets of elastic that could heal like skin. Or that's what she pictured after Maggie had explained their nature. "Is there another way?"

Maggie shook her head. "Not unless a neighboring realm is letting them through, but the rulers like the nightmares as much as we do, which is to say, not at all."

"Oh." She had to prove she wasn't a total failure. "Can I try to summon the vision?"

Maggie smirked. "Feeling confident after your accidental cloud-work?"

"Yes. Plus it's easier for me to do this because I truly want to see Damien."

"Go ahead then." Maggie stepped back.

Audrey took a deep breath even though she didn't need to breathe here and looked at the pool, allowing her eyes to blur their focus. "Show me Damien," she whispered, the desire to see him and make sure he was safe thick in her chest. The surface of the pool shimmered although no breeze stirred the leaves of the plants around its edge, and it cleared to show late fall woods, the trees almost bare. She could make out a couple of dark-clad figures crawling along, but a gray film covered the scene.

"I think I have a bad connection." She huffed. "Is nothing going to work right for me today?"

"There's no such thing here." Maggie stood beside Audrey and looked at the vision. "That's a cloud of obfuscation. Something doesn't want us to see them."

Panic crawled up Audrey's throat. "They're in danger?"

Maggie squeezed her hand one more time and disappeared.

Thank you for reading! If you'd like more information on Web of Truth, please go to the book's page on my website (http://www.ceciliadominic.com/web-of-truth-td) or you can order it from any paperback retailer using the following ISBN: 978-1-945074-43-1.

For more information about me and my books, or to be alerted when new books are released, please sign up for my author newsletter. You'll also receive a free short story when you sign up (see below).

ABOUT THE AUTHOR

Cecilia Dominic wrote her first story when she was two years old and has always had a much more interesting life inside her head than outside of it. She became a clinical psychologist because she's fascinated by people and their stories, but she couldn't stop writing fiction. The first draft of her dissertation, while not fiction, was still criticized by her major professor for being written in too entertaining a style. She made it through graduate school and got her PhD, started her own practice, and by day, she helps people cure their insomnia without using medication. By night, she blogs about wine and writes fiction she hopes will keep her readers turning the pages all night. Yes, she recognizes the conflict of interest between her two careers, so she writes and blogs under a pen name. She lives in Atlanta, Georgia with one husband and two cats, which, she's been told, is a good number of each. She also enjoys putting her psychological expertise to good use helping other authors through her Characters on the Couch blog post series.

Find Cecilia Online

Mailing List - https://www.ceciliadominic.com/PTDbooknewsletter

Website - ceciliadominic.com

Facebook name - CeciliaDominicAuthor

Twitter name - @ceciliadominic

Instagram name - @randomoenophile

Also, please look for Cecilia on Goodreads and Pinterest.

Cecilia's books available everywhere e-books are sold. Look for paperbacks in select brick-and-mortar stores, which should be able to order them for you through Ingram Spark.

PERCHANCE TO DREAM

Please enjoy this preview of *Perchance to Dream*, the first story in the Dream Weavers and Truth-Seekers series...

Emma stood in the doorway and squinted into the peach-colored light that had appeared without warning to disrupt her sleep. She put a hand out to steady herself and snatched it back when she touched the rough-hewn wooden door frame. The walls of the room seemed to have just been put up, the beige dry wall barely set. Sawdust and wooden curls littered the plywood floor. The sounds of others murmuring and moving about reached her ears. She backed up until her back touched the wall and...

Emma woke, her hands still clenched. She lay in bed, awakened by her husband bumping into her. He rolled away when she gently shoved him back. She snuggled into the flannel sheets, twitched her shoulder blades until they were comfortable, and closed her eyes. With a sigh, she slept...

...and found herself back in the room, standing in the door. What kind of hella-vivid dream was this? The sweet-sharp smell of the wood filled her nose, but at least the sawdust on the rough plywood floor didn't make her sneeze. Normally in her dreams she had difficulty moving, but this was no different than her waking life. She walked through the room and found a door on the other side, also unfinished, and a hallway. More rooms lined the hall, some with only wooden framing, others further along but not complete.

Voices carried down the hall, lively conversations and laughter. This comforted and frightened her simultaneously. Where were these people? She heard footsteps behind her and turned around...

...and woke again to the sound of a car alarm going off outside the window.

"Just effing steal it already," Greg mumbled into a snore. Emma nudged him.

"Turn over," she said. He did. She didn't want to go back to sleep, but drowsiness overtook her...

She found herself in the same doorframe in the same room off the same hall. *What the hell?* She knew that in the past, she had continued a dream upon awakening once, but twice was unheard of.

"Oh, there you are."

She spun around and found herself face to face with a person, mid-twenties, who seemed to be simultaneously gender-less and dual gendered. Slender and with dark hair, they wore a simple tunic and pants outfit of navy blue. The person's large brown eyes captivated her, as they seemed to belong to someone far older than the chronological age of the rest of the being.

"Who are you?"

"Adrian." The person's voice gave no clue as to gender, as it could be a low-pitched female's or tenor male's.

"I'm Emma."

"I know. Lucy told me about you."

"Lucy?"

"The Madam Lucia? The psychic you spoke with today? Yesterday, actually."

Emma shook her head. She knew that had been a bad idea, but, really, what could she have done?

She'd gone to Target for packing supplies and was headed back on Highway 29 when her cell phone rang. Lightning overhead had made the reception poor, but she could hear the voice of Grace, her mother-in-law.

"Hello, Emma," Grace snapped. "Is this a bad time?"

The corners of Emma's mouth tightened. "Yes, actually."

"Well, I won't keep you but a second. Is my son there?"

"I'm driving right now. In the rain." *And Greg's at work, as you well know.*

"I just wanted to ask him if this would be a good weekend for us to come see the house. We're so excited for you."

Of course she'd called to ask him, not them. "We're excited, too, but we need to see how the move goes before we can make any plans. As it stands now, we're planning on having a house-warming party at the end of the month."

Emma swerved to miss a puddle and earned a honk from a driver whose lane she'd invaded.

"Sure, but don't you want us to come up before that? To help out?"

Not really. "I really appreciate the offer, but I'm sure we'll be fine."

"Well, I'll just talk to Greg and see what he says. Go on with your errands, and we'll see you soon."

Emma sighed and tossed the telephone into the passenger

seat. She knew how it would all play out. Grace would call Greg and guilt trip him for not inviting them up before the house-warming—*"But honey, don't you want to spend time with us?"*—and then they would come and pick and nag—*"I don't mean to tell you how to set up your kitchen, but I've had my glasses in the cabinet by the sink, and it's just worked out so well for me for twenty years"*—and do it so sweetly that protesting would make her, Emma, look like the bitchy, ungrateful daughter-in-law.

She hadn't seen the glass bottle until she rolled over it and heard the pop under the right rear tire. The car groaned and pulled to the right. She drove into the first parking lot, put her forehead on the steering wheel, and cried in frustration.

A tap on her window startled her, and she looked up to see a tall, dark-skinned woman dressed in blue jeans and a black linen top embroidered with flowers in red metallic thread. The woman wore her hair long and in braids, and it faded from copper-colored at her crown to blonde at the bottom. She looked at Emma with friendly black eyes.

"You are having a rough day, yes?" she asked in a lilting accent.

Emma looked up and saw that her car was one of two parked in front of a small whitewashed frame house with purple curtains in the windows. The sign over the door said, "Madame Lucia, Palm Reading $5."

"Yes," she sniffled.

"Come inside, and you can call a tow truck from there."

Emma straightened. Did everyone think she was completely helpless? "Thanks, but I can change a tire."

"Then let me help you." Madame Lucia, Emma presumed, held a large red and white golf umbrella. She helped Emma change the tire—an unwieldy process since it involved unloading and reloading the trunk. By the end of it, Emma felt doubly grateful she'd had someone to hold an umbrella over her.

"Um, thanks," Emma said once they'd completed the task. The woman inclined her head. "Do you have anywhere I could wash my hands?" Emma held up her grease- and dirt-stained fingers.

"Of course. I have a bathroom inside. You may clean up there."

When Emma emerged from the bathroom, Madame Lucia had an old-fashioned tea set on the small coffee table in the living room. Emma thought of excuses she could make to leave, but her growling stomach gave her away.

"This is all really very nice," she said, "but..."

"But nothing. It is a slow afternoon, and I had the kettle on for tea anyway."

Emma sat on the couch. "Thank you."

She sipped her tea in awkward silence and nibbled at a scone. "These are very good," she finally said.

"Thank you. I made them myself."

"Do you usually serve them to, ah, clients?"

Lucia shook her head. "Oh, no. Only to, how shall I say it? Equals? Colleagues?"

Emma put the scone back on the delicate china plate. "What do you mean?"

"Your palm, when you showed me, said that you have some sort of perception beyond that of normal people."

"No, nothing out of the ordinary here." At least nothing helpful.

"Then please forgive me. I can make mistakes sometimes."

Tea ended amiably enough when an actual customer drove into the parking lot. Emma hoped it wasn't anyone she knew as she ducked out, got in her car, and drove home.

"I didn't really consult her," Emma said to Adrian. "It just happened that I ended up in her parking lot. I had a blowout."

Adrian shrugged. "Regardless of what brought you to her, it was meant to be that you saw her."

Emma wasn't going to argue. "What is this place?"

"A new extension of the dream world, the CU."

"CU?"

"Collective Unconscious."

"Oh." She'd heard something about that in her intro to psychology course. "So the repository of dreams?"

"Yes, the archetypes that visit people's dreams." Adrian walked down the hall, so Emma followed. "This is a new phase to allow those with talent to have easy access to the place." They lowered their voice. "They're trying to improve customer service."

Emma peeked in rooms. Some were completely finished and decorated in widely ranging styles from a seventeenth-century boudoir to a twentieth-century New York penthouse. Some lacked even drywall.

"I don't have any talent."

Another shrug. "You must have some if you were able to get here."

Emma decided this was a very interesting dream and that she might as well play along. "Like what?"

"Clairvoyance, psychic, ESP, whatever you want to call it. Strong intuition beyond that of 'normal' human beings."

"I tried to tell Lucia—there's nothing special about me. I must have gotten let in by accident."

Adrian gave her a patient *you must be a dolt* smile. "You were invited, and you accepted. You may not realize that you accepted, but you did. And now you have a room."

Obviously arguing wouldn't make a difference. "Why are they all the same size and shape?"

"It's how they're doing all the new developments these days. There are also some lovely amenities, like free access to most of the Manor parties."

"Manor parties?"

"The dwelling places of those who live here."

Emma shook her head. "This is all very confusing. Where are we going?"

Adrian didn't reply but continued to walk, so Emma followed. They passed down one long, straight hallway that seemed to have no end in sight.

"Where are the windows?" Emma finally asked to break the silence.

"Oh, they'll be put in last," Adrian replied with a wave of one hand. "That way they won't interfere with ideal object placement."

"The windows will be cut out after the rooms are done? That will be a mess."

"No." Adrian gave Emma a quizzical look. "They'll be hung."

"I don't get it. How can you look out a hung window?"

Adrian turned to her with the same infuriatingly patient expression. "The same way you look out any other kind."

"But won't there be a wall behind them? What will they overlook?"

"Whatever the resident wishes."

"Oh, so they're more like screens?"

"They'll have screens if you like. Especially if you decide to look over scenery where things may fly in."

A faint beeping floated through the air and grew louder. Adrian halted, cocked their head, and looked at Emma with gray eyes. Before Emma could ask why they had changed color, Adrian said, "That will be your alarm, I think. Bother, I had wanted to take you to the manor. Ah, well, another night, then."

"Right."

Adrian and the scene melted away, and Emma rolled over to turn off the alarm and turn on the bedside lamp. She sat up and swung her feet over the side of the bed. For a moment, the light caught something that fell from her foot to the floor. She picked it up—a curl of wood.

"What's that, hon?" Greg asked.

"I'm not entirely sure." Emma crushed it in her palm, then threw it in the small wastebasket by her side of the bed. "I had a very interesting dream this morning..."

Wait, what's happening to Emma? Is the Collective Unconscious a real place? Can dreams really come true, and if so, would you want them to?

*If you'd like to read the rest of **Perchance to Dream** and get updates on when new Cecilia Dominic novels will be released, please go to https://www.subscribepage.com/CDbackofbook to sign up for my newsletter. I hate spam and promise to keep your information safe!*